ISBN -13: 978-1719356220

COMEBACK

BY

Jim Mullaney

Stories Never End

<u>Contents</u>

THE PROLOGUE

Excerpt from Comeback, an unpublished novel by Sam Parker.

THE PROLOGUE

The woodland is dark, save for isolated beams of moonlight that break through the summer canopy and fall like spotlights on a stage. Moments ago there was only the noise of the bugs and the creatures that feed on them, but now the night is full of human sounds.

Foul curses punctuate laboured breathing. Shoulders snap obstructing branches, and thorns tear at sleeves and cuffs as three men struggle with their burden, stamping the undergrowth flat under shoes caked with drying blood. Between them they carry a body, like pallbearers who have no coffin.

The body is male, naked, and terribly wounded, and although it appears to be dead, they know that it is not. Together they have poisoned the body, beaten and blinded it. They have shot it and stabbed it, and the black plastic bag they used to suffocate it is still taped over its head. Yet even in this incapacitated state they can feel the raw, elemental power thrumming through its limbs.

They know that if they hesitate now, if their resolve weakens, the body will rise.

When the woodland ends, they break out of the tree line and enter a wide field of heather. At the other side of the field is a wide millpond, its gently eddying surface like milk in the moonlight. Away to their right is the mill house with its ever-turning wheel. As the men have arranged, a single light has been left on inside.

They stop at the edge of the pond, and one of the men rips the bag from the body's head. They see its face and realise that despite their best efforts it has struggled back to a semblance of consciousness. The split lips of its mouth curl into a smile, while the punctured, weeping eyes seem to damn them.

Together they heave the body forward until its head and shoulders are submerged beneath the luminous waters of the millpond. Rosy air bubbles rise to the surface and burst, and the water around the body slowly turns pink. But after five whole minutes, the bubbles have not stopped coming.

Finally, one of the men nods towards the mill house, and the others grunt their assent.

In the mill house, they set the wheel turning, and then begin to feed the body, feet first, between the millstones. Its mouth begins to twitch, its jaw to spasm, as its feet and calves are consumed. Muscles, ligaments and cartilage are ripped to shreds and bones pulverised. Shattered teeth chew up its tongue, but it will not scream.

One of the men, perhaps out of mercy, or perhaps out of a strong desire to not hear anything the body might attempt to say, takes this chance to slit its throat with his cutthroat razor. But the three men imagine that they can hear its voice anyway. Words ring out in their minds. An incantation, a threat, a promise.

A prophecy.

I will come back...

A long wooden stave is found, so that all of the body can be forced into the grinding millstones without the men risking their hands. A can of petrol has been left for them beside the mill house's small generator, and its contents are used to saturate wooden beams and sacks of grain. They pour the last of the petrol onto the bloody, contorted face, and they start the first of the fires right there.

Moments later, they stand in the field of heather watching the mill house being consumed by fire, the destruction perfectly mirrored in the pond. Sometimes they think they can hear screaming, and sometimes laughter, and when the thick blanket of evil-smelling smoke begins to crawl across the water towards them, the men quickly turn and run...

Part I
THE BEGINNING

1

The auditorium was full and in good spirits, even though the Meet the Authors gig of this fringe Horror, Science Fiction & Fantasy Convention didn't quite live up to its name. The conventioneers didn't get to chat with their favourite writers, or see how many hairs were growing out of their noses when they laughed. They got to sit on uncomfortable moulded-plastic seating and peer across at four middle-aged men sitting behind a table set up on a rostrum. They got to sit under the cool, dispassionate gaze of a number of security men, stationed deliberately indiscreetly around the walls.

The thing was, nobody seemed to care.

Applause was still rolling for the short speech and introductions made by the Convention President, but once he reached the short flight of stairs that led down from the rostrum, it quickly faded. This audience knew what it was about. This was probably their only chance to speak to the men who once a year threw a bucket of petrol on the flames of their imaginations. It was the Q&A session organised by the writers' publishers and the audience had a mere hour to interrogate them.

The writers were, right to left, Charles Beckett, Nigel Cassidy, Nathaniel Longman, and last, but by no means least, Sam Parker.

Charles Beckett was a bear-like man who looked older than he really was, affecting the appearance of a Papa Hemingway-clone. He radiated an air of belligerent self-confidence, and this, together with a tendency for arrogant disdain, repelled most people within seconds of meeting him. He wrote massively-researched, mind-numbingly detailed science fiction novels the size of phonebooks, and had no more idea of human emotion and character than the average railway sleeper.

Acting as human buffers between Beckett and Sam Parker – between whom no love was lost, as was well-known among the fantasy fraternity – Cassidy and Longman chatted quietly as they waited for the audience to settle.

Of the guest authors, only Nigel Cassidy looked as though he belonged in the audience, in that section dominated by nerdish-looking young men who came to such conventions solely to pick holes in authors' time continuum stories. Cassidy wrote future-shock novels, full of malevolent artificial intelligences and the like, his output fuelled by a very genuine horror of modern technology. Famously, he even wrote on an old manual typewriter, refusing to share house-space with any kind of computer. With his thinning red hair, freckled, pale complexion, black-framed glasses and nervous energy, he looked like a young Woody Allen might have if he'd been really neurotic.

In complete contrast to Cassidy's uneasy quirkiness, Nathaniel Longman was the very image of smooth, sophisticated urbanity, like a black Cary Grant. He was tall and handsome and out-of-the-closet gay, with the body of a natural athlete and a

Savile Row wardrobe. Longman wrote wry and witty fantasy novels in which creatures from different dimensions saved the various worlds from destruction while talking like the characters in an Oscar Wilde play.

At the end of the row, Sam Parker, looking a little younger than his forty years, scratched at his short thatch of brown hair and waited silently for the hammer to fall. He knew full well that the bulk of the audience's questions would be directed at him alone. Already he could feel hundreds of eyes boring into his face.

Sly Jack Road, the first novel set in his fictional city of Eldritch, had been about a haunted stretch of country road on the city's outskirts. Its publication had been greeted with massive financial and critical success on both sides of the Atlantic, and he had published a further eleven since. It was a series that had encompassed every aspect of the supernatural genre, all polished off with a hard-boiled noir sheen that had drawn a large and committed following. The more fanatical fans, those who sent Sam bizarre gifts and wrote hundred page letters, sometimes scared him. They believed his fictional city, his alternate reality, actually existed. He called them the Eldritch Obsessives.

How many EOs are there here today, he wondered.

Sam poured some mineral water into a glass, and then took small, nervous sips, as the Convention President, Howard Medak, stepped into the twelve-foot wide strip of no man's land between the audience and the rostrum and asked who had a question.

Every hand in the auditorium went up immediately, including those belonging to the panel of authors, and everyone laughed. When the laughter had subsided a little, Medak pointed to someone, and the rest of the hands went down.

Here it comes, Sam thought.

A middle-aged woman, still wearing her heavy woollen coat despite the auditorium's warmth, asked, 'Mr Parker, are the rumours true that *Swinging Town* was the very last Eldritch novel?'

As one the audience went completely silent, suddenly as focussed as a predator stalking lunch.

Sam cleared his throat, leaned towards his microphone, and said, 'No, the rumours are *not* true.'

The audience seemed to explode with joy.

The ecstatic cheers and universal applause surprised everyone, even Sam, who had known what the first question for him was likely to be, and had even anticipated the response that would greet his reply. Egotistical, of course, but he'd been right. Lately, it seemed that he was *always* right, as though in some way his imagination was creating the reality. This thought worried him, and he wondered if he might be catching whatever mental disease the Eldritch Obsessives had contracted.

Nevertheless, he leant forward again and spoke to the questioner over the last echoes of applause.

'No,' he said. 'What happened was, I decided to take a holiday from Eldritch. After twelve novels, I thought I deserved one. So I've taken time out to write something else, that's all. You want to hear about it?'

The affirmation from the audience was deafening.

'Okay. It's going to be called *Deep Water*, and it's about two families holidaying together on a schooner in the Caribbean. It starts out pretty well perfect for them, but then they run into a few difficulties. There are a number of severe personality clashes between members of the families, and then their schooner's caught in a hurricane and badly damaged, and then they find some people marooned on a small island - who turn out to be rather unpleasant. Sadly, there are a large number of fatalities.'

He smiled into the audience's rumble of laughter.

'It should be published early next year, if everything goes to plan. I hope you all like it. It's not Eldritch, but it's… well, it's what you might call a home away from home.'

'Have you started the next Eldritch novel yet?' the woman in the overcoat wanted to know.

Sam shook his head. 'Not yet. I've been playing around with a few ideas, and I know what it's going to be about. I'll start soon, I think. All I'm really waiting for is some additional information to reach me from Eldritch – but you all know what the postal service there is like...'

There was another low rumble of appreciative laughter. Eldritch's postal service was notoriously dreadful. In the past, extreme sex aids had been delivered to old ladies, and body parts intended for analysis at the morgue had been sent to children in time for their birthdays.

8

'Why didn't you just ask the Listmaker to help you out?' someone called from the back of the auditorium, and the knowledgeable audience erupted into laughter once more.

The Listmaker was a fairly constant character in the Eldritch novels, and was as popular in his own way as Drunk Dave Hawkins, Sam's alcoholic, self-destructive detective. The Listmaker was a vindictive worm of a man who acted as a professional informant for anyone willing to pay his fee, and he was a shit-stirrer to his last molecule. In *Family Owned*, the fifth Eldritch novel, he'd sold DI Dave Hawkins a list of men he claimed were drug dealers, but were in fact the owners of a swanky club to which he had been refused membership. A few days after discovering the truth, Drunk Dave went to visit his informant after consuming nearly two litres of Absolut vodka, and he put the Listmaker in traction for six weeks.

On cue, the next person the Convention President pointed to said, 'I'm worried about Drunk Dave Hawkins. In *Underlined Twice* his ex-wife was murdered, in *The Torturer's Apprentice* his brother was hit by a car and killed, and in *Okra* he broke his leg and his sister had a breakdown after being raped and ended up on a psychiatric ward. Is there a curse on his family?'

'Yes, definitely.'

More laughter.

'In *Hospital Whites*, why did…'

And the questions kept on coming. Eldritch, Eldritch, Eldritch. Cassidy and Longman hardly had to open their mouths, although neither of them seemed upset by the audience's clear favouritism. But

Charles Beckett wasn't asked a *single* question. His frustration and, as he saw it, humiliation, were more than he could bear.

Eventually, he used his microphone to speak over a young woman asking Sam a question about a minor character in *Bad Blue*.

'Look, I'm contractually obliged to be here, so does anyone have a question for me?' He tried to make it sound light and amused, but it came out bitter and full of bile. Beckett's temperament was a one-trick pony.

The silence that followed his question lasted for ten full seconds, and they were the longest ten seconds of Beckett's life. Like him or hate him, no one had ever ignored him before. But not one of the hundreds of hands had gone up. Not one. The half-stifled giggles and snorts of derision that ended the silence finally tipped his anger over the edge.

'What you people see in this idiot's work mystifies me,' he growled, pointing a thick, blunt finger at Sam Parker. 'You must all be complete morons.'

'That's it, Charles,' Sam said quietly, 'Go on, win them over to your side.'

Beckett turned on him, immediately in rant mode.

'I don't need anybody on my side to know I'm right, Parker. Your infantile scribblings are garbage, offal, puerile shite without the slightest meaning or significance. Whenever anyone mentions that old chestnut about an infinite number of monkeys and typewriters, I inevitably think of your books. I wouldn't wipe my arse on any one of them, much less read them. And,' he added as a vicious afterthought, 'your film versions are shite, too.'

Initially, the audience had been shocked into silence by Beckett's outburst, but now they began to boo him, some of them rising from their seats and shaking their fists. Sam had the feeling that if they'd had tomatoes they would have thrown them.

Medak was calling for everyone to calm down but could hardly make himself heard, even with the aid of his microphone. The security men had stepped away from the walls and were watching the audience nervously.

Sam raised a hand and said, 'No, it's all right. I don't mind a little criticism.'

The audience instantly fell silent again, as he'd known they would.

He turned in his seat to face Beckett, who looked ready to froth at the mouth.

'Everyone's entitled to their own opinion of the books, of course. As for the film adaptations, it's quite well known that I had nothing to do with them. In fact, Charles, for once I actually agree with you. They are fairly terrible. But you know what? At least they were successful at the box-office... and they didn't have their world premiere on YouTube.'

Beckett's face, what little could be seen of it through his beard, turned scarlet with embarrassment. Beckett's brainchild, the movie of his first and most highly-regarded novel, had been translated to the screen from his own screenplay, and he had been both its co-producer and co-director. The result was so dire that it had been denied a theatrical release.

Beckett held Sam with his enraged glare as the audience hooted, whistled, and screamed with laughter. Then he stood up so quickly that his chair fell over backwards. At first, Sam thought he was going to be attacked, but Beckett whirled away instead. He stormed from the rostrum, mouthing obscenities that easily reached the audience without benefit of a microphone, and then stormed out of the auditorium altogether.

The applause that followed his unscheduled departure was long and loud.

And after the applause finally faded, the questions began again.

2

As it turned out, the hour long Q&A session lasted for over one and a half hours, the vast majority of that time taken up with Eldritch fans attempting to slake their thirst for insider knowledge on the city and its characters. Sam had a hard time trying to satisfy all their enquiries, and there were times when he felt the audience knew he was winging it. He muddled through somehow.

The session was finally ended by the Convention President leading the applause for the panel of authors while they made their exit, and then reminding the audience that the book and memorabilia sale was just about to begin in the hotel's main function room. Before they parted, Sam arranged to meet Nigel Cassidy and Nathaniel Longman in a local bar, then made a swift, much needed visit to the staff toilet in the service corridor behind the auditorium.

As he stood at the urinal, his eyes closed in blissful relief, he said these words aloud:

'And that, as they say, is that.'

But it wasn't.

The mistake Sam made was thinking he could slip straight back into anonymity, or naively believing that people would allow him to. He tried to leave the hotel through the lobby, where he immediately found himself caught between conventioneers still filing out of the auditorium, conventioneers who had remained in the lobby after failing to gain entrance to the auditorium, and still more conventioneers who were passing through the lobby on their way to the main function room to snap up a few bargains. But now the biggest bargain of the day was standing right there in front of them, and everyone seemed to want a piece.

All at once, Sam was hemmed in on all sides by Eldritch fans who would never get enough of their favourite city, not even if they had been able to read his mind.

He was bombarded with more questions, all the voices overlapping and weaving. He had copies of his books, convention timetables, scraps of paper, and even copies of other authors' books thrust at him for his autograph. People were trying to pass him manuscripts of their own novels, bellowing unintelligible synopses of the plots and asking for Sam's help in finding a publisher, an agent, anyone who was interested, who might care. Someone, a man whose face he didn't see, tried to slip into his jacket pocket a sheaf of A4 pages he said was an Eldritch story he had written in homage. He wanted Sam to *bless* it.

Bewildered, off-balance, and a little frightened by the aggressive clamouring for attention, Sam tried to answer as many questions as he could, not even aware of who he was speaking to half the time. He tried to sign all the autographs, even though he'd already done a long signing stint that morning. He tried to refuse all the proffered manuscripts as kindly as he could, because he still remembered what rejection felt like.

In short, he tried to make everyone happy. But he couldn't, there were too many of them.

Claustrophobia had never been one of Sam's problems, but he felt an attack coming on now. He was finding it increasingly difficult to breathe, and the air that he did manage to take in all seemed to be second-hand, composed of other people's perspiration, deodorants, perfumes, and stale breath. His flesh wanted to cringe away from the intimate, uninvited press of bodies, from the tiny droplets of other people's spit that had begun to speckle his face. It was too much. It was far too much.

In desperation, he tried to see above the crowd, looking for someone to come and help him out of this bedlam. Where the hell were the security men? Where the fuck was Medak? Probably trying to salve Beckett's ego, he imagined − Charles still owed the convention a signing session tomorrow morning. Sam now looked back on his own chaotic signing session with a kind of fond nostalgia. It had been bad, but it was nothing compared to this.

He was surrounded, harassed, crowded, jostled, held, and pressured until he wanted to scream. It went on and on, and escalated to the stage where he felt he would be unable to *prevent* himself screaming.

Which was when he had his funny turn.

He was trying to edge towards the lobby doorway, signing things without looking at them, answering questions without trying to find the faces of the questioners, and constantly peering through the tightly packed maze of people for a clear route of escape. Seconds later, a tiny gap did open, but before he could move into it, *something* moved through it ahead of him; a long, low, sleek black-furred body that sliced through the crowd as easily as a shark through water.

The body shape had been something like a panther. Another one followed it before the tiny gap closed.

Sam couldn't have moved now even if there had been space. His whole spine had gone straight and stiff, and his feet felt nailed to the floor. His neck seemed to audibly creak as he turned his head to follow the hidden passage of the two creatures he had seen, and for a moment he caught another, clearer glimpse of them.

They were panthers. At least, they had the *bodies* of panthers. But they had the heads of eagles, with plumage as black as their panthers' fur, large, piercing eyes, and cruelly hooked beaks which appeared to be made of solid gold.

Sam felt himself begin to tremble. People were still asking him questions, but he didn't hear their voices anymore. Mouths opened and closed like those of goldfish. All he could hear was the double

15

hammer-blow of his own heartbeat and the blood fizzing through his veins. The world turned grey, and he thought he might faint.

He knew these creatures. He had *invented* them. They were the Guardians of Justice, and they flanked the steps of the Eldritch Courthouse on Lower Noose Street, carved out of solid blocks of granite.

Sam also knew that the Guardians existed only in his own imagination. He was fully aware that he was 'seeing things', but that didn't stop him being afraid. In a short story he'd written for an American anthology a couple of years back, the Guardians had come to life to hunt down a suspected child-killer. They had torn the man limb from limb and left his mangled remains spread out over the Courthouse steps like a hellish jigsaw puzzle.

Sam swallowed a mouthful of coppery saliva. His ears popped suddenly, and his hearing returned to normal. Everything returned to normal. Colour leeched back into the world. There was no sign of his imaginary creatures, and it was almost a relief to find people still talking at him.

His right arm was being held by an older woman with blue hair, asking him what was going to happen to Johnny Ronnie Sudds, a small-time thief who had briefly appeared in both *Death in a Dream* and *Family Owned*. A tall man wearing sunglasses like a bad disguise held Sam's left arm tightly, asking something else − did Sam want to know where the *real* Sly Jack Road was?

Eldritch, Eldritch, Eldritch. *Ad infinitum, ad nauseam*.

So Sam was 'seeing things' now, was he? Well, who wouldn't under this kind of relentless pressure?

Suddenly he wanted to get out of the hotel more than anything else in the world. The trouble was, he couldn't see how he could achieve his escape without running the risk of being torn limb from limb himself – not by the Guardians of Justice, but by the Obsessed of Eldritch. On the other hand, Sam was now beginning to believe that staying put could well end in the same result. The people closest to him were showing distressing signs of being prepared to fight for his attention.

At that moment, at the other side of the large, crowded lobby, a woman screamed. A host of raised male voices followed, along with the sounds of colliding and falling bodies.

For a couple of seconds, Sam half-believed that the Guardians of Justice really had slipped free of his imagination and were with him in the lobby. He saw their terrible claws dragging their victim down, saw the golden beaks darting down towards an exposed throat, and the bright sprays of blood that followed.

Then he heard someone closer to the commotion say, 'It's a fight, there's a fight down there.'

Of course that's what it is, Sam heard himself think, and yet he was stunned to find sweet relief sweeping through him like a drug. Ridiculous as it seemed, maybe he had more than half-believed. But why should he feel relieved?

A small voice inside his head, his own interior voice, answered the question instantly: he would have been responsible for anything the Guardians did, because he had created them

17

A moment later, Sam felt another surge of relief, one that was entirely more understandable. Their collective attention temporarily broken, the crowd had turned away from him, leaving Sam an almost clear shot at the lobby doors.

He took the opportunity gratefully.

3

Vox Pops, collected outside the Springfield Hotel and Conference Centre, Wembley, London, by Stories Never End, the official Eldritch fan club.

"Scariest? No contest. *Okra*, without a doubt. It's all your worst nightmares rolled into one, except it's too real to be a nightmare."

Claire Mead, Cape Town, SA.

"They're like Charles Dickens by way of Castle Rock. I mean, even *Professor Wysiwyg's Cure-All* is terrifying, and that's the comedy."

Pia Daniells, Perranporth, Cornwall.

"Oh man! Read *Bad Blue*. If you had to read just one – and you wouldn't be able to, I promise – but if you had to, read that one. Just read the first page and you'll be hooked, completely. Jesus! Before the end of chapter one you'd sell your soul just for it to be over. And when it is finally over, you'll go straight back to the beginning and read it again."

Jim Gorganza, Brooklyn, New York, New York.

"They're like the gospels of the Fallen Angels."

Beverley Simmel, Sepulveda, Los Angeles.

"I sometimes visit Eldritch, in trances. You don't believe me, hardly anyone does, but it's true. I've been there, and it's a dangerous place. I expect one day I won't make it back."

Name and address withheld.

4

Corrigan's, the bar where he had agreed to meet Nigel Cassidy and Nathaniel Longman for their post-Q&A relaxer, wasn't at all like Sam had imagined it would be after Longman had made the suggestion.

It wasn't an Irish theme-pub where the staff looked ready to break into the Riverdance at the drop of a hat, nor was it the clubby sort of place that might have been capable of containing the splendour of Longman's Tommy Nutter-inspired charcoal three-piece. It was just a re-fitted, re-named pub with the sole advantage of being a long, meandering walk away from the Springfield Hotel – and, consequently, far from the massed ranks of Eldritch fans.

No, not its sole advantage. This late in the afternoon, the bar was completely deserted.

Walking hesitantly into the Lounge Bar and realising that there was no one at all reclining in the many comforting shadows was one of Sam's more pleasant recent experiences. Better still, the lone barman didn't look as if he could even read, let alone recognise authors from their dust-jacket mug shots. Sam couldn't have wished for a better venue had he chosen it himself.

Over the next twenty minutes he consumed two pints of beer with Jack Daniels chasers. If he had been a smoker, he suspected that he would have taken his drinks outside and chain-smoked his way through half a pack. His memory of the hotel lobby was holographic.

'There he is,' Longman said to Cassidy. 'You were right.'

Standing just inside the doorway with Nigel Cassidy at his shoulder like a pet elf, Nathaniel Longman smiled at Sam along the length of the Lounge Bar.

Sam raised a hand in weary salute.

In a louder voice, Longman called to Sam, 'I just bet Nigella here you wouldn't make it. I thought you'd been devoured by your adoring public.'

'I nearly bloody was.'

Longman chuckled and pointed at Sam's glass.

Sam nodded gratefully, and Longman stepped up to the bar, summoning the barman with an imperious flick of his forefinger. Sam watched Cassidy move toward the table in his awkward, almost limping gait, as though his shoes were full of hot coals.

'What took you two so long?'

'We were delayed by an unforeseen situation,' Longman said before Cassidy could reply.

'What, you mean you had to help Nigel fend off all his groupies?'

Cassidy offered him a small acidic smile.

'Well, that too, of course,' Longman grinned. 'Mostly, though, we were delayed by having to pull half a dozen punters off Charlie Beckett's head before they pulled his beard out at the roots.'

'What?' Sam exclaimed, sitting up.

'Charlie was doing his best to fight back, but he was heavily outnumbered. He should never have started it in the first place.'

The fight in the lobby, Sam thought. Jesus Christ.

Sam turned to Cassidy. 'Beckett actually attacked someone?'

'Other way around,' Cassidy replied. 'A whole bunch of them jumped him, fell on him like a pack of wolves.'

He stared at Cassidy, completely puzzled. 'But why?'

Cassidy's face twisted up into a strange little grin. 'Oh come on, Sam, why'd you think?'

Sam couldn't think why. But then, suddenly, he could.

He went cold.

'Oh no…'

'Oh *yes*,' Longman said, settling a tray of drinks on the table. 'Oh yes, my friend. That's why I said that *he* started it. Our great and respected colleague, the Good Pedant of Highgate Village, committed a heresy, didn't he? He publicly criticised and condemned Saint Samantha's Letters to the Eldritchians as infantile garbage, as offal, as puerile, meaningless, insignificant – what was that charming word old Charlie used? Ah yes, I remember now – *shite*, and so he had to be punished in accordance with the laws of said city. They had no stones, so they used their fists and feet.'

Sam couldn't believe it, but he had to, because their eyes told him they were speaking the truth.

'Jesus, I'm stunned,' he eventually said in a small voice. 'I'm just… well, stunned.'

21

'So was Beckett,' Cassidy replied blandly, but not without some satisfaction.

'Look,' Sam said a little while later. 'Is it me, or is it them?'

'What's that, dear?' Longman asked.

'Well, I knew that some of the Eldritch fans are what you might charitably call... *intense*. Either that or just out of their tiny minds. But all this today, question after question after question... and the way I was mobbed in the lobby, you saw that, didn't you?'

'We were on our way to try to help you when Beckett got pounced on,' Cassidy said.

'And that fight business,' Sam sighed. 'That's just crazy. Surely that isn't normal?'

Cassidy was silent for a moment. Then he said, 'The obsessive interest? The protectiveness? Yes, I'd say that was fairly normal, for Eldritch fans. The violence? Maybe that, too.'

Sam felt deflated. How could it be normal?

Longman put his drink down, carefully placed his elbows on the table, and measured Sam with his large, expressive eyes.

'Let me ask you a question, Sam. How long is it since you've been to one of these conventions?'

'I don't know. Maybe nine years.' Sam thought for a little while. 'No, it's more like eleven, actually. The last one was just after the publication of *An Hour of Darkness*. I didn't enjoy it, and I swore I'd never do another.'

'What made you decide to attend this one?'

Sam sighed. 'My agent badgered me into it.'

'I'd have thought he'd have pushed for the biggie, the World Horror & Fantasy Conference in the States.'

'No, I was still working on *Deep Water* back then, and Horace would never stop me working.'

'But he was hot for this one?'

'Yeah, tell me about it. In fact, now that I come to think of it, Horace has talked me into a *lot* of publicity stuff just recently. Interviews with magazines, all the things I don't normally do. But it was the convention he was most concerned about. He pestered me for weeks until I finally agreed. He kept saying it would be good exposure.' Sam drained his glass and picked up a fresh pint. 'In a way, I suppose he was right. I've never felt so exposed in my whole life.'

'Why do you think Horace was so insistent?'

'Beyond publicity?' Sam shrugged.

'But there must be something else.'

Sam frowned at Longman's sombre expression. 'I don't know, you tell me.'

'He wanted you to see,' Cassidy said.

Longman and Sam both looked at him, all pale and twitchy and black spectacle frames.

'He wanted you face to face with your readers,' Cassidy amplified. 'To see their hunger for a new Eldritch novel. Horace didn't want you extending your holiday after *Deep Water.*'

'Why should he care?' Sam asked. 'The new book's good, it'll sell.'

'I'm sure it will, but I don't think this is about money. The new book isn't *Eldritch.*'

'So what?'

Cassidy took off his glasses and painstakingly cleaned them on the hem of his sweater before speaking again. 'Sam, you published two novels before you created Eldritch, didn't you? Was Horace your agent then?'

'No. I fell out with my first agent over Eldritch. Nobody even wanted to look at the first chapter of *Sly Jack Road* after reading the synopsis. Nobody seemed to get the idea of genres I was trying to blend. Except Horace. He lapped it up and asked for more.'

'Exactly,' Cassidy said. 'That's what I'm saying. Horace may be your agent, but he's a fan too. He has the same emotional connection to Eldritch as all those people back in the hotel lobby. He didn't feel that *he* could tell you to get straight back to Eldritch, so he made sure you came to the convention. He knew that everyone here would tell you for him.'

Sam slipped into thought. There was an odd logic to Cassidy's idea, but it all sounded a little too subtle for Horace Jepson, whose grand passions in life were good food and young women. Horace could be sneaky, no doubt about that. Horace, Sam had discovered, was capable of being many things. But one thing he was not was backward at was coming forward. If he had something to say, he'd say it. Even to a best-selling client.

Sam winked at Longman, and then turned to Cassidy. 'Nigel, are you trying to make me as paranoid as you are?'

Cassidy just shrugged.

Sam leaned back in his seat and yawned hugely. 'Christ, what a day. Beckett really went for me, didn't he?'

'And they really went for him,' Longman agreed.

'God yes, if he didn't hate me before, he will now. What did I ever do to him, can you tell me that?'

'You mean aside from that bad review you gave him in The *Sunday Times*?'

Sam stared at Longman. 'You've got to be joking? That was almost five years ago. He can't still be holding that against me.'

'Small minds have long memories,' Longman smiled.

'But it was a *bad* novel.'

'Charles Beckett doesn't write bad novels, just masterpieces.'

'Also,' Cassidy said, 'you can't discount envy. You probably outsell him about twenty to one, worldwide. Maybe more these days.'

'So what? I probably outsell you two losers by the same margin, and *you* don't hate me.'

'Oh Sam, of course we do,' Longman said kindly. 'We're just clever enough not to let it show.'

'And then, of course, there's the obvious,' Cassidy said, and Longman nodded.

The obvious? Sam wondered. Cassidy and Longman were both grinning at him.

'I don't get it.'

'Obviously, he resents your mockery of him.'

Sam was puzzled. 'What mockery?'

Cassidy laughed.

'Honestly, I don't have a clue what you're talking about.'

Cassidy and Longman glanced at each other, their grins widening.

'Methinks the lady doth protest too much,' Longman intoned. 'Come on, Sam, you're among friends here. You can tell the truth.'

'Yeah,' Cassidy said. 'Either Beckett was lying about never reading your books, or someone told him.'

Sam still looked puzzled, so Longman spelled it out for him.

'The Listmaker.'

The Listmaker? Sam thought. What did that character have to do with−?

'Old Charlie Beckett's the model,' Longman added. 'Surely?'

'Pedantic, petty, egotistical...' Cassidy counted out on his fingers with the nails bitten down low. '...misanthropic, bitter, vain, reactionary… who else could it be?'

'But I never…' Sam almost whispered. 'I didn't…'

The expression of confusion on Sam's face convinced them where any amount of denial would probably have failed. He noticed that a lot of their good humour seemed to leave them once they realised that he hadn't deliberately caricatured Beckett.

'That's what everyone believes, anyway,' Cassidy said, sipping at his orange juice as though it might have been poisoned.

5

PC Peter Groves and WPC Wendy Tiller usually chatted freely in their patrol car, but today, because of their passenger, they travelled in virtual silence. They had tried more than once to strike up a friendly conversation with him during their short acquaintanceship, but when he hadn't responded to their overtures they found themselves gagged by the sour atmosphere he seemed to exude.

It had been the same during the trip from the hotel to the hospital, where he had demanded to be taken even though he didn't appear to be badly hurt, and the same in the hospital itself. He seemed to treat everyone, regardless of who they were or what they were doing for him, as though they were his servants, of too low a caste to be accepted as human beings.

Groves and Tiller weren't, in truth, very surprised by their passenger's superior attitude. It only served to prove what they already knew from past experience. Celebrities, even ones you'd never heard of, could be a pain in the arse.

As they waited in a long queue of traffic for a filter light, the police officers shared a number of meaningful glances. Later, after their shift had ended, they would discuss the precise meaning of these glances over a couple of drinks. They would say that if they hadn't been *ordered* to escort the writer safely home, they would have happily dropped him back at the hotel to face the people he'd managed to piss-off so thoroughly. They would say, with great satisfaction, that they'd never even *seen* one of his books on the shelves in WH Smiths or Waterstones. They would say that if they'd had to chaperone a writer for a few hours, why couldn't it have been a *good* one, like the bloke who wrote those seriously strange Eldritch books?

Finally, they would agree that what had happened to their passenger today would one day end up in one of his unheard-of books, because the man had spent the whole of the journey from the hospital to Highgate Village bent over a notebook, scribbling like a mad bastard.

But Charles Beckett had not spent his time in the back of the patrol car writing a fictionalised account of his day. No, he had been busily organising names and addresses and telephone numbers, and jotting down ideas of what he could do with them. Busy making lists.

Shit lists.

He had begun, naturally, with the six people who had attacked him in the lobby. Did he want to press charges, some mealy-mouthed fool of a policeman had asked him. Of course he did! And if the police wouldn't prosecute, he *would*. He'd brought private prosecutions many times before, and he'd won his share of the cases, even though the courts were against him, too.

Below these details, he made a note of the people who had agreed to act as witnesses to the assault, although it had to be said that this was a short list. Considering how many people had been in the lobby at the time, there were very few who would admit to seeing what had happened, or who had started it. He knew that there was a conspiracy at work against him, but that was nothing new. He had suffered from these kinds of crime for years, and now he expected nothing less.

Next he wrote Sam Parker's name. After all, he had probably put Beckett's attackers up to their cowardly act in the first place. Parker went on the list in block capitals, underlined twice in brutal slashes, like knife scars. So did Nathaniel Longman and Nigel Cassidy. During the Q&A, they had certainly done their part in inciting the rabble to violence upon his person, and Beckett wasn't going to forget it. Neither would they, once he had finished with them.

The Convention President went on the list, too, of course. Medak had been shamelessly brown-nosing Beckett as he started to elbow his way through the crowded lobby, grovelling in a manner Beckett had found entirely to his taste, but as soon as the shit had started to fly, so had Medak. The next time he'd seen the Convention President had been after the arrival of the police.

Beckett next added the security men to the list, those whose names he had been able to collect. Parker had probably bribed them to stay out of the way – he didn't put anything past that liar.

That accounted for the convention, but Beckett hadn't finished yet. Oh no. He turned his notebook over to a fresh page, and started in on the hospital.

First he wrote the name of the doctor who had examined him after he'd had to wait a whole *half-hour* in an A&E waiting area simply filled with coughing, groaning, bleeding nonentities from whom he could have caught anything. His cheeks were still burning with embarrassment from the encounter with the doctor; sitting in the tiny cubicle with the police officers standing just outside, where they could hear everything. Everything.

Beckett had demanded a full series of x-rays, and a full-body MRI scan, and a series of digital photographs of his injuries, and a written medical report. What he got was a cursory examination at best, followed by a contemptuous look and a weary, 'Go home and stop wasting everybody's time,' as the doctor walked away.

Next he added the name of the bitch of an admissions clerk, who, amongst her other examples of incompetence, had completely failed to recognise his name. Then he wrote the names of the two nurses he had seen giggling behind their hands after the doctor had so callously dismissed him, followed by the name of the A&E manager, supposedly some kind of consultant, who had refused to find him another doctor for a second opinion.

As an afterthought, he added the names of his police current escorts, who, he justifiably felt, had been both unprofessional and unsympathetic to his needs.

Beckett was so busy making his lists that he didn't notice when the patrol car stopped outside his house, and when WPC Tiller and PC Groves informed him that he was home, he left the car without a word. Had he looked over his shoulder and seen the identical hand gestures the two police officers spontaneously offered his back, he would have immediately gone back to his lists and underlined *their* names, too.

6

Nathaniel Longman tried to suppress a smile. Nigel Cassidy was sharing his black cab, and holding on to the edges of the seat as though the snail-like rush hour journey were a white-knuckle ride in a theme park. Cassidy mistrusted technology in general, but vehicles in particular held a special horror for him, because there was no way he could completely eliminate them from his life. His life in the hands of a machine, it didn't bear thinking about. The only time he'd ever had to take a plane, Cassidy had had to be dosed up by a doctor hired by his publisher.

Trips in taxis and private cars were usually bearable as a rule, Longman had travelled in them with him many times before, but today's journey seemed to mark a new high for Cassidy's paranoia. He looked terrified, and hadn't spoken for more than ten minutes. When Longman had started to say something about what happened to Beckett in the hotel lobby, Cassidy had jumped as though scalded.

Now that Longman was thinking about it, he realised that Cassidy had been a little withdrawn ever since that scene, even while relaxing in the bar with Sam afterward. Maybe the violence had upset him more than he'd let on.

Eventually, Longman thought of a way to bring Cassidy out of himself – and to satisfy his own curiosity at the same time, hopefully. Sam had invited them both back to his house after they left Corrigan's looking for taxis, but Longman had to cry off because he was expecting company. Like a knee-jerk reaction, Cassidy had immediately said that *he* was expecting company, too.

Knowing Cassidy as well as he did, Longman found this a very unlikely scenario.

'So who is it?' he asked.

Cassidy, lost in thought, didn't respond.

'Nigel, who is it?' Longman repeated, giving the little man a nudge.

'Huh, who's what?'

31

'Your company.'

'What company?'

Longman sighed. 'The company, your guest or guests, the ones whose imminent arrival meant you couldn't accept Sam's invitation.'

Cassidy looked blank for a moment while his brain rebooted. 'Oh. Yes. It's… Well, you know… friends…'

He shrugged and wouldn't meet Longman's eyes. He knew full well that Longman was aware of how few friends he had, and how much he disliked anyone in his home, violating his personal space. Now he realised that Sam must have been aware of it, too.

'Nigel, you are the worst liar I've ever seen,' Longman laughed. 'Why didn't you want to go to Sam's house?'

Cassidy shrugged again. 'Too tired.'

'Why didn't you just say that?'

'Didn't want to seem rude.'

'And lying isn't rude?'

Cassidy was back to looking blank, and obviously didn't want to continue the conversation. Longman wasn't giving up, though. The cab would soon pass the traffic lights that had been holding them up, and shortly would be reaching the dizzy speed of 20mph, or more. Unless he was adequately distracted, Cassidy might have a fit.

'I haven't stayed at Sam's house myself for a long while,' Longman mused.

'Why not?'

The instant sharpness of Cassidy's question surprised him.

'Well, I–'

'Is it because of his girlfriend?'

Longman grinned at Cassidy's serious face. 'Nigel, are you implying that I might be jealous?'

'No, no,' Cassidy replied, shaking his head. 'I mean, is it the girl herself? Does she make you feel… uncomfortable?'

Longman looked out of the window. 'She's certainly not the warmest person I've ever come across, I have to admit. The last time I stayed overnight, she…'

Cassidy waited. 'Yes?'

Longman made a face. 'Nothing in particular, really, it's just the atmosphere she seems to generate. She clearly prefers to have Sam to herself, but it's not just that. She made some comments when Sam was in a different part of the house that were a little odd.'

Cassidy was nodding. There was a hint of relief in his eyes. 'I think she makes the house feel haunted,' he said.

They travelled for a time in silence, watching the buildings and the pedestrians pass by. Cassidy held tighter to the seat as the cab picked up speed.

'Mind you,' he mumbled, mostly to himself. 'I think Sam's house is haunted anyway.'

Longman gave no sign that he had heard.

7

Excerpt from Sam Parker's interview with Writers Monthly to coincide with the publication of Swinging Town:

WM: First of all, let me say how thrilled we are, both for ourselves and for our readers, for this opportunity to speak to you – we know how rarely you grant interviews.

SP: You're very welcome.

WM: A lot has been written about the City of Eldritch over the years, but how did it all start?

SP: It was an accident, really. First of all, it had never entered my head to create a fictional city, let alone one that existed in an alternate reality. I had always envisaged real-life settings. You know, this one in London, this one in Miami, etc. But I had all these incredible characters and stories in my head, and I couldn't think of anywhere real that was wild enough for them to happen. Then one night, while I was writing notes for a story that would eventually become *Imaginary Families*, the second Eldritch novel, I suddenly thought, 'If they were all set in the *same* place, what kind of place would it be?' And the answer was pretty obvious. It'd be hell on earth.

WM: And so Eldritch was born?

SP: I don't know about born… Let's just say the city sort of tapped me on the shoulder, and someone said, 'I've been waiting for you.'

WM: You heard a voice? Literally?

SP: Yes. It was as though someone had whispered into my ear.

WM: Were you scared?

SP: No, not at all... Well, not at first...

8

Sam waited until the taxi that had brought him home departed, and then checked that there were no passers-by before typing in the key-code that unlocked the high wrought iron gate in front of his house. If nothing else, today had taught him two invaluable lessons, one of which was that he had to guard his privacy even more carefully. The other was to put nothing past Eldritch Obsessives, nothing at all.

He even paused outside his front door, scanning the windows of the houses opposite for the lens-gleam from a pair of binoculars, and then, realising what he was doing, shook his head forlornly.

Christ, he thought, I *am* getting as bad as Cassidy.

Sam was still upset about what had happened at the convention, but he felt a real sense of pleasure and contentment as he unlocked his front door. The house was the only thing he'd ever spent a great deal of money on, and he didn't mind if people thought he'd been extravagant. He didn't even care if anyone thought he'd been just plain greedy. Situated in one of the leafier suburbs of North London, the house had six bedrooms, four bathrooms, a games room, and a plunge pool and sauna in an outsize conservatory. It also had an entertainment room, a sitting room, a dining room, and a kitchen the size of a squash court. The garden to rear of his property was an acre and a half of landscaped perfection.

It sounded like an awful lot for a single man, living alone except for the occasional female stopover, and he supposed it was. But this was the place where he worked, ate, and slept. He ordered his groceries over the Internet and had them delivered to his door, bought most of his clothes the same way, and rarely went out socialising anymore. Sometimes a month might go by without him leaving the house at all, and if it had been any smaller he thought he might have gone mad.

Home, he thought gratefully, home at last.

But as soon as he had disabled the alarm system and closed the door, he became aware that something in his house wasn't right.

At first he sensed it only on a subliminal level, and wrote it off to tiredness. But by the time he'd hung his jacket in the hall closet, it was too in-his-face to ignore. He stood at the foot of the stairs, feeling the house's disturbed atmosphere wash over him, and he knew beyond any doubt that he was not alone.

'Hello?' he called, and then winced.

He had meant to project his voice like a Shakespearian actor, but what he'd actually managed was a little Disney chipmunk tremolo. It sounded so ridiculous it made him laugh, which also partially broke the spell that had fallen over him. If there were someone else in the house it would only be Jo, his current girlfriend. They'd been seeing each other for eight months now, and she'd had the keys and the alarm codes for the last three. Jo liked to call herself a free spirit, and her visits were appropriately spontaneous. Sam set out through the house to find her.

Jo Branagh was a girl he'd met at one of his extremely rare social events, a noisy, boisterous house party thrown by an academic friend with whom he shared his agent. There were a few people there from the publishing world, but not many, and certainly no one Sam knew well. Not even Horace was there, and noisy, boisterous parties were definitely his kind of thing – they were where he found his young female companions. Sam and Jo, both usually wallflowers at large parties, had met on the deck overlooking a sunken garden and begun a conversation that was well under way before they even thought of introducing themselves. There was an instant and remarkably strong mutual attraction.

But for Sam, the introductions, when they eventually came, were when he seriously became interested in Jo.

She'd told him her name, and that she was a mature student working for a mathematics degree. Reluctantly, he'd told her his name, and then waited for her eyes to pop out on stalks. They didn't. Instead, she actually asked him what he did for a living.

Hardly able to believe his luck, Sam told her he wrote the Eldritch books, and the embarrassed, ignorant shrug she offered him by way of reply was one of the most seductive things Sam had seen in a long while. He took her home with him from the party that night, and they didn't get out of bed for three days.

Sam walked into the sitting room, smiling at the memory, and aroused by it, too. But his smile quickly faded. The sitting room was empty, no sign of Jo. No sign either in the kitchen, or in the attached utility room, where she would usually dump a bin-liner full of dirty laundry when she arrived for a visit. He checked the whole of the ground floor, including the gardens, before heading upstairs.

His earlier sense of unease had not only returned, it had intensified.

He wanted to believe that he would find Jo upstairs, lying on a bed, sleeping or just reading, but it was becoming increasingly unlikely. She usually left her keys on the table in the hallway and her overnight bag underneath it when she arrived, and they weren't there. No washing in the utility room. No wet footprints weaving around the plunge pool or to the sauna. No TV or radio blaring out anywhere in the house. No shower running, no blasting hairdryer.

See how it all adds up, he thought.

By now Sam was not just uneasy again, he was actually beginning to be scared. Jo didn't come here to sleep, or to read or study, anyway. She came to enjoy herself with a man who interested her, and who wrote books that didn't.

But if Jo wasn't the person he could feel sharing his house, who was?

At the top of the stairs, Sam paused at the start of the first floor's central corridor, wide and lined with doors to all the bedrooms. At the end of the corridor he could see the first three or four steps leading up to the attic rooms, which Sam had converted into a single huge workplace for himself, a distance of approximately seventy feet from where he stood. Somehow, today, it seemed to be much longer. All the doors he could see were shut. He could feel his heart racing.

This is so stupid, he told himself angrily.

Sam forced himself on. He checked all the spare bedrooms carefully and methodically, only to find that they were still spare. His own bedroom was empty, too, and the en-suite bathroom dry as a bone.

He should have been relieved, and in a way he was. But there was still the attic to contend with, and for some reason he couldn't explain to himself, his office suddenly seemed a much more dangerous proposition than anywhere else in the house.

On impulse, he slipped back into his bedroom on tiptoe for a moment and then came back out carrying his only home-protection weapon, an old wooden baseball bat he called his Inflexible Friend. Then he started on the flight of stairs that led up into the corner of his attic office. He had never really noticed before, but the stairs, suspended between floors and windows, were a haven of gloom and shadows. Hardly any daylight reached them at all, and he felt as though he were climbing up through a subterranean shaft. Halfway up, he could hardly see his feet.

Sam held his breath as he poked his head above the attic's floor level and into daylight once more, scanning his office in a wide arc. He let his breath out again noisily when he saw no one ransacking the place. His arms, suddenly weary, dropped, but the death-grip in which he had been holding his Inflexible Friend stayed. He couldn't relax his hands. He walked up the remaining steps, dropped onto the old battered leather couch he sometimes slept on when deeply involved in a novel, and closed his eyes.

Stress, he assured himself, that's all it is. Like imagining you saw the Guardians of Justice back at the hotel. A reaction to the stress of the convention, of finding that your fans are lunatics, one and all.

My fans? Sam wondered. No, they're not *my* fans, they've never been *mine*. They belong to *Eldritch*.

He opened his eyes again, and paranoia flooded back into his mind. The office was exactly the way he had left it this morning, but now it seemed *too* exact. He imagined a number of shadowy figures searching his office, turning it upside down, and then replacing everything the way it had been. On the coffee table by the couch, the galley proofs for *Deep Water* he had tossed there so casually now seemed to have been artfully arranged into careless disarray.

Clever hands, they had. So clever.

'That's it!' he said aloud, disgusted with himself. 'Paranoid episode over and done with, everybody back to bed, thank you and goodnight!'

He rose to his feet, turned back to the stairs, and took a step down. Then his breath became locked in his chest and his calming heartbeat seemed to stop altogether.

From the gloom of the staircase, a bone-white face that seemed completely devoid of life stared up at him. Dangling below it were a pair of hands, curled up in mid-air like claws. Sam reared back, a sound that was half-moan and half-scream escaping from his lips, and he raised the baseball bat high over his head and prepared to launch it down the stairs.

'Nice welcome,' the face said, its lipless mouth opening and closing in mean little movements. Then it turned about and seemed to disappear like a ghost. But Sam heard footsteps trudging down the steps, and despite its unfamiliar tone, he *had* recognised the voice.

It was Jo's.

9

He found her in the kitchen, leaning back against a worktop and hugging herself as if she had a stomach ache. A bad one.

Jo, he thought. My God.

Even in the kitchen's good light, Sam would have had trouble identifying her if he hadn't heard her voice first. The vibrant young woman he knew had been extinguished from this person like a flame from a lamp. Her shoulder-length chestnut hair had been brutally scraped back from her face and fixed at the back of her head with pins. Her face, without make-up, was almost entirely colourless, and her usually lively dark eyes were as dead as stone. She was dressed from head to foot in black, including a baggy wool sweater that swamped her torso into shapelessness.

As he began to move towards her, Jo coldly eyed the baseball bat he still held. Sam immediately laid it down on the butcher's block.

'Sorry about that,' he said. 'I'm a little bit jumpy today.'

Jo just stared at him. When he tried to approach her, she withdrew, her back sliding along the edge of the worktop.

'Jo, what's wrong?' he asked.

'As if you care,' she replied, in what was almost a growl. He had never noticed how thin and colourless her lips were without lipstick. But then, she had never curled them up like a dog and snarled at him before.

'Look, I'm sorry about the bat. You wouldn't believe the shitty day I've had, it's been a nightmare.

I'd tell you about it, but it'd bore you stupid. Let's just say that it's the last convention *I* ever go to.'

No reaction. Sam tried again.

'Jo, if you've got a problem, I wish you'd share it with me. I do care. You know I care.'

Jo stared at the floor. 'Just down,' she mumbled.

'Well, I think I can remedy that,' Sam said. This time when he went towards her, she didn't flinch away. She kept her arms wrapped around herself, but allowed him to embrace her.

'Shall I tell you what I have in mind?'

Her head nodded against his chest.

'We'll send out for food, anything you like, and we'll open a couple of bottles of champagne and settle down together. We'll watch one of your favourite films while we eat, then we'll have a long bath and listen to music. And after our long bath, I'll give you an even longer massage. And after that, I'll take you to bed and make passionate love to you. How does that sound?'

Sam hadn't noticed the way Jo had tensed up while he'd been speaking, but as soon as he'd finished, she uncoiled like a spring, and he found himself thrust backwards, dancing on his heels until his lower back collided painfully with the butcher's block. The baseball bat rolled towards the edge, fell, and twanged around on the kitchen's tiled floor.

'That's your idea of making things better, is it?' she screamed at him. 'Take me to bed! Is that all we are, is that all we're about, sex?'

Sam stared at her in shock. Who was this woman? He didn't know her.

Without another word, Jo ran out of the kitchen. He could hear her footsteps thudding as she stormed through the house. The front door slammed with the finality of a gunshot, and he was reminded of Charles Beckett, storming away from the Q&A.

Sam, rubbing his tender lower back, wondered how he had got so good at making people storm out on him.

Time passed slowly after Jo's departure. Sam wandered aimlessly around his house, walking faster and faster as his confusion over her behaviour steadily changed to anger. He walked around and about until he realised that the night had come, and then had to retrace his steps, turning on lamps.

Is that all we are, is that all we're about, sex?

Well, he thought, now that you mention it, lady – yeah, that's exactly what we're about. *Were* about, maybe.

To try and occupy his mind he went to the kitchen and looked in the fridge, but found nothing that he wanted to eat. The idea of ordering food in seemed like too much trouble, so he poured himself a large glass of wine instead. He tried to watch TV, but was quickly bored, and then started to watch a DVD someone had sent him of Charles Beckett's atrocious film. After only five minutes he heard his frontal lobe screaming for mercy and he switched it off.

In the games room he played a few frames of pool, but every shot he took sounded like the start of an avalanche and made him feel nervous. He tried to listen to music, but every track he selected sounded discordant, jangling irritatingly, even Miles Davis's sublime recording of *Nature Boy*. On impulse, he jumped into the plunge pool with all his clothes on, but climbed out only moments later feeling completely unrefreshed.

Sam was listless, filled with negative energy and incapable of concentrating on everyday things. This was a feeling he knew very well, and had deliberately courted it many times in the past. It was a writer's call to arms. Now it was all over him, like a spirit manifesting itself without the aid of a séance.

Far sooner than he had ever expected, Sam found himself in his attic office with the night pressing at the windows like a giant moth. He was a little chilly even though he'd exchanged his wet clothes for dry ones, but like everything else the chill didn't register in his mind, because his mind was already full to bursting.

Sam blinked and he was sitting before his computer, which had been fired up. He had no memory of moving there, or of turning on the power.

He opened a new file with the format he always used for his novels. It was time to be honest, he thought. When you were looking at a blank screen that was the only thing to be if you wanted to write something worthwhile. He had told the audience at the convention that he'd just taken a holiday from Eldritch. That's what he'd told everyone, including his agent and his friends.

But really, it was more like he'd run away from the city.

For some reason he didn't understand, the idea of writing the thirteenth Eldritch novel had begun to fill

Sam with absolute dread the very moment he had finished the twelfth. The more so because he knew exactly what it would be about, what it *had* to be about. It had a pre-ordained quality he didn't like, but couldn't trust himself to resist.

Hence the distraction of *Deep Water*. By looking at unfamiliar skies he had felt that he was striking a blow for self-preservation, and it had worked for a while. But all holidays end, and someday everyone has to come home. As Sam was home now. He was wary of his fear and apprehension, but he still wanted to write the book. He wasn't sure he even had a choice.

One of his office walls was dominated by a large, framed Eldritch promotional poster. In heavy Gothic type against a blood-red background, it featured the three-word epigram that prefaced every Eldritch novel, and which had given the Eldritch fan club its name.

Stories Never End.

Sam had always believed that. He believed it now.

Unconsciously, he had allowed his hands to creep into the home position on his keyboard, and now he consciously pulled them back. Intellectually, he knew that he couldn't start this book. He hadn't planned anything. He had no synopsis, no outline, no notes. But tonight his intellect was asleep and his gut feeling was in control, and this told him that the story would write itself.

Even the title was a foregone conclusion, referring as it did not only to the ultimate ambition of the book's protagonist, a former Eldritch crime-boss who was dead and didn't want to be, but also to Sam's own return to the city.

No plan, no synopsis, no outline, but Sam knew exactly how it would begin, and where. Still filled with that strange combination of fear and excitement, he let his hands go back where they wanted to be. The keyboard, like his house, felt like home.

It was time to tell the world what really haunted Sly Jack Road.

10

COMEBACK
Part One
THE BEGINNING

CHAPTER ONE

Smooth Harry Flanagan, talented seducer of Eldritch's young women, had parked under the trees less than ten minutes ago with a seventeen-year-old called Rena White. Rena was a bright girl who knew her own mind, or thought she did. "Take me somewhere spooky, Harry," she'd demanded, so he'd driven her to the spookiest place he knew, Sly Jack Road.

Smooth Harry had opened the windows and lit Rena a cigarette even though he didn't smoke himself, because he was smooth enough to realise how sophisticated the cigarette made Rena feel. She was bright but she was still young enough to deceive herself that easily.

Perhaps it was thinking of her as a child that encouraged Smooth Harry, more than twenty years her senior, to tell Rena a few stories about dirty old Sly Jack Road. About the number of bodies reputed to have been buried here over the years, in shallow graves, and about the unquiet spirits that walked here after dark.

Tonight the night was dark indeed, and at this hour very few cars passed along the country lane. Even if there had been a traffic jam, however, the cars' occupants would not have seen Smooth Harry's ride. The old Honda Accord was black, and Smooth Harry had parked it deep under cover of the trees on the eastern side of the road. It was a good spot for intimacies, explorations, and fledgling understandings. He had used it before.

The ghost stories were going down very well, which was precisely what Smooth Harry was hoping young Rena would do after he'd loosened her up a little. Rena had lovely white skin, and when aroused or excited her face and arms turned bright pink, as though she'd just stepped out of a hot bath. Smooth Harry was desperate to see if the rest of her body reacted the same way.

Rena was staring at him with those big, big eyes as he spoke and the cool night air slipped into the car through the open windows. Without interrupting the flow of the story he was telling her – and making up as he went along, as it happened – Smooth Harry casually leaned across to take off Rena's safety belt. As he eased the belt across her chest, he let the back of his hand graze over her breasts and felt that her nipples were already hard, like little knuckles under her thin blouse. Her colour rose and her eyes seemed to shimmer and dilate at his touch, but Smooth Harry never let on that he had noticed, because that wouldn't have been smooth.

He wanted to be so careful, so very gentle with this one. He was gentle with most of his conquests, those who needed it to be gentle, but this one was special. He didn't understand why, but this one was very special indeed.

Smooth Harry's mouth, spinning tales, seemed to be working independently of his brain, which was making up its own rather different story. He imagined Rena's mini-skirt rucked up high around her waist, little black panties twisted into a glistening cord dividing her labia, her white thighs spread wide and burning like radiators. So gentle. Her sweet succulence oiling his fingers. The provocation of her nipples to bite, bite, bite. But so gently. He saw the image of his large tanned hands roving over her white body, roving everywhere, before they settled on her throat, her white throat.

Her throat.

Wind soughed in the dark, giant trees, and the night that entered the car also entered Harry. There were whispers, snaking through and around the girl's heartbeat, skipping like stones over the incoming tide of his own pumping blood, and he reached for her. He wanted to be gentle, and he thought that he was being gentle. Even after it was all over, he still believed that he'd been gentle.

It was only when Sly Jack Road stopped speaking to him that he realised its voice had ever been there at all. But by then, of course, it was too late. The evil had been set in motion, and it had attained its first claw-hold in the long struggle.

To come back.

The next thing Smooth Harry knew, his car was moving again, cruising through the neon wasteland of Eldritch's strip. Then he saw a blue light flashing in the Honda Accord's rear-view mirror…

Sam's fingers lifted from the keyboard and he felt the flow of power halted, as though an electrical circuit had been broken. He frowned at the screen, now filled with words, and wondered what had broken his concentration. Then he heard Jo softly calling his name. Before he had begun to write, the unexpected voice would probably have made him jump like a kangaroo. Now, simply because he had written something, all his fear and nervousness had evaporated, and it evinced nothing but mild surprise.

He swivelled around in his captain's chair. Jo was on the stairs, her head barely appearing above floor-level, and he realised that this was as far as she had ever intruded into his workplace – this far and no farther, as if he had actually forbidden her to enter, which he hadn't. It was some kind of innate respect for his creative privacy, he thought, a small gesture he had always appreciated. He took a closer look at her now and saw that there were a few tears in her eyes, and she was trying to smile. She looked human again. Sheepish, but entirely human.

'I've come to apologise.'

Sam nodded. She wouldn't have come back otherwise. 'Why don't you come up?'

She glanced at the monitor behind him. 'Are you working?'

'Yes. It's Eldritch time again.' Sam was amazed that he could announce this so calmly.

'Then I won't come up. But I'd like it if you came down. I mean, if you can, if you're not too busy.'

To show Jo there were no hard feelings, Sam put on a brief pantomime of frantically saving his work and backing it up. He heard her laugh a little, and thought that everything between them would be all right.

She waited for him on the stairs until he came, and then took him by the hand to lead him down to the first floor and into the bedroom where she had lit two aromatic candles, one either side of the bed. She swung the door shut behind them and grabbed Sam in a fierce embrace, which he responded to passionately. Her hand snaked around to the front of his jeans. They kissed almost hard enough to bruise.

'We could have been doing this all night,' Sam breathed into her mouth.

'Yes, but then you wouldn't have started the new book.'

Eventually, Jo sat him down on the end of the bed. 'We can't make love,' she said.

'No?'

'No. It's my time. That's why I've been in such a terrible mood, I suppose.'

'I would have been happy if we were just together,' Sam said. 'All that stuff earlier was just−'

'I know, I know. But shush now.'

Jo let down her hair, which seemed to have regained its life, and it cascaded over her shoulders in rich, glossy waves. She knelt between Sam's thighs and gently pushed him onto his back.

'Just lie down.'

Sam closed his eyes as she began to fondle and stroke him through his jeans. After a few moments of divine pressure, she unbuckled his belt one-handed and then pulled down his pants. Her soft hand continued to stroke and roll, pull and tug, but then withdrew.

Sam opened his eyes to see what she was doing.

'Shush,' she said again. She lifted her sweater over her head and dropped it to the floor. Underneath, she was naked, her body magnificently heated. 'I'm going to take care of you.'

Jo leaned forward between Sam's thighs, her heavy breasts mashing against his balls, and then bent her head to take him between her lips.

Sam gasped. He reached out to hold her hair away from her face so that he could see her mouth working on him and feel her eyes on his, and then he abandoned himself to image locked to pure sensation, to a world where words didn't matter.

11

Nigel Cassidy was still awake at midnight. Very tired, but very awake. His flat was little more than a studio apartment, with a narrow single bed tucked into an alcove, and the main area dominated by a huge wooden kitchen table which functioned as Cassidy's desk. There were two doorways, one leading to a small kitchen, the other to the bathroom and the front door. The only other pieces of furniture were a sofa covered with a blanket and a second-hand coffee table with a clockwork radio on it. Books were stacked against the walls in tall columns that always looked in danger of toppling. The wallpaper was peeling in places, and the floor covered by what may once have been a carpet.

'Congratulations, my dear old lad,' Longman had enthused with a broad smile on the occasion of his only visit. 'It's an absolute shit-hole.'

It didn't matter. The only entertaining Cassidy did was on paper.

Right now the large table was covered with library books, a jumble of photocopied magazine articles, and a mess of other research materials – no Internet searches and Wikipedia misinformation for Cassidy. Notebooks filled with his untidy scribbles formed a second layer. A plate with the drying remains of his evening meal sat atop his manual typewriter. Light was provided by a low wattage overhead bulb that had no shade.

Although he had been sitting at his desk for hours trying to work, Cassidy had no more than glanced at the notes for his new novel. His mind kept going back to his conversation with Longman in the black cab, when they had talked about Jo, Sam's girlfriend. Cassidy thought that this girl was one of Sam's problems. He probably couldn't see it, but she was playing a role. On the few occasions he'd seen them together, Jo had been fine around Sam. Warm, affectionate, intelligent, and sensitive. But whenever Sam had left the room, it seemed as though a part of her went with him, leaving Cassidy with a kind of human husk.

You could almost see her turning off, powering down, emptying out. Once, in that very situation, Cassidy had tried to talk to Jo, but the words had died on his lips when she'd looked at him. That was when he had felt that she was a ghost, that there was nobody alive behind the eyes. A cold wind seemed to blow through her as though she were a broken window.

After that night, Cassidy had only stayed once more, because the whole of Sam's house had begun to feel like Jo's empty stare. He had started to feel that chill wind in every room, even when she was absent. Every time Sam had invited him since, he'd found an excuse not to accept.

His reluctance to stay at Sam's house wasn't just down to Jo, either. It was a dozen other things, other ideas, suspicions that had been coming together in Cassidy's head over the last couple of years. He had tried his best to ignore them, all too aware of the ability of his mind to create large-scale paranoia out of simple observations. That and the ingrained habit of fantasising about anything within reach common to all writers of fiction. But Jo was just one more thing to add to what was becoming a very long, very disturbing list.

And now he could add something else to that list – what he had seen in the lobby of the Springfield Hotel.

He recalled stepping out into the lobby with Longman and pausing at the top of three plushly carpeted stairs, looking out over the milling crowd. He'd spotted Charles Beckett barging his way though, the fawning Convention President dancing around his feet like an anxious spaniel. Longman had directed his attention to the tight knot of people at the other side of the lobby, who were hemming Sam in.

'Let's go pull him out,' Longman had mouthed above the noise.

But then Cassidy had seen two long, low shadows twisting their way through the crowd around Sam as though circling prey, and he couldn't move an inch. They were hardly there at all, almost smudges in the air, but he definitely saw them. They were… beasts of some kind.

Longman had been looking at Cassidy questioningly, wondering why he was hanging back, and why he looked so shocked. Cassidy wished now that he had pointed at those dangerous looking smudges, he wished that he had *made* Longman see them. Then Cassidy wouldn't have been so alone in this. Someone else would know what he knew. What he suspected, at any rate.

Then the screams had begun, the shouting, the fighting, and Beckett going down in a huddle of Eldritch fans, the obsessives, which Sam called the EOs. The atmosphere Cassidy had sensed in Sam's house was very strong in the lobby at that time, as though Sam, however inadvertently, had brought it with him.

At the last moment before Longman had dragged him down the stairs to help Beckett, Cassidy had seen Sam running for the exit. He remembered thinking that if his suspicions had any truth to them at all, running away wouldn't do any good. In fact, if he was right, he wasn't sure what would.

Cassidy looked up from his thoughts, shivering. He closed all his notebooks, finally accepting that he was going to get nothing done tonight. Exhausted though he was, he doubted if he would even sleep.

12

It was a quarter past two in the morning, and PCs Chris Waverley and Don Starr had been following the erratically driven Honda Accord for five minutes as it passed through Potters Bar. During that short space of time, the old black Honda had been weaving from lane to lane, flirting with the curb and parked cars, and, just now, had passed through a red light without even attempting to stop.

Don Starr, driving tonight by virtue of winning the toss, had just opened his mouth to say what he usually said in such situations, 'Okay, we've got enough', but before he could speak his partner leaned across him and switched off the on-board CCD camera that would have provided the bedrock of their evidence if the case ever went to court. He glanced across at Waverley in open surprise. Waverley was known to detest drunk drivers.

'We aren't going to stop him, then?' Starr asked.

'Yes, we *are* going to stop him, but I don't think we'll be making an arrest this time.'

Waverley tut-tutted and shook his head at the Honda, which had dallied at a junction, started to turn right, then changed its mind and gone left. There had been no use of the indicators for either direction. The driver obviously still had no idea that a police car was only yards behind.

'Why aren't we going to arrest him?' Starr asked. 'He's obviously pissed as a fart.'

'Because I think I recognise that car.'

Understanding came to Starr. There were many times in a policeman's day when the urge to be idealistic came off second best to having to be realistic, and this was one of those times. Someone once said that everything is politics. Starr didn't know who it was, but he agreed with the sentiment completely.

'Oh,' he said. 'It's a copper.'

Waverley nodded. Starr could see his muted disgust.

'I think it's a CID bloke. DS Allison.'

'Oh shit.' Starr nervously tapped his fingers on the steering wheel. 'Shall I pull him over, then?' he asked, hoping the answer would be no.

His reply was another curt nod.

Starr flashed his lights and siren briefly, and then his mouth fell open. Instead of pulling over, the Honda suddenly accelerated away from them.

'Silly bastard,' Waverley muttered. 'Get after him, Don.'

Don did, but it wasn't much of a chase. The Honda driver's rush of blood only lasted a matter of seconds, and then the brake-lights came on. Starr brought the patrol car to a halt behind the Honda, which had stopped with its front on-side wheel up on the curb, the wing narrowly missing a post-box. The driver had also turned off his engine, which was a good sign.

Waverley turned to Starr. 'Let me talk to him, okay?'

'Sure, no problem,' he replied, thinking, rather you than me. He knew that some of those CID men had tongues like rasp files when crossed, and ideas of vengeance that wouldn't have looked out of place in the Old Testament. Starr didn't want to get on the wrong side of this one.

The two officers got out of their car, Waverley leading the way to the Honda and Starr hanging back a little. Waverley rapped on the driver's window, and when it came down a few seconds later, he bent down and looked in.

The driver *was* Detective Sergeant Allison, and he had either got himself outside a massive skinful or just received the most terrible shock of his life. The sodium streetlights didn't help his appearance, but even allowing for the light's sickly colour, Allison's face had an awful, sallow gauntness to it. He looked like a skull, with bloodshot eyes.

Waverley couldn't smell alcohol, but there was a strong odour of cheap perfume in the car, which he may have used to try and hide it. Allison was staring through the windscreen, refusing to face Waverley directly. Waverley thought there was a chance he may have been crying.

'You all right, sir?'

Allison didn't respond, but his red, fugitive eyes flicked from side to side.

'Sergeant Allison, it's Chris Waverley. Are you all right?'

This time, Allison turned his head fractionally towards Waverley. He cleared his throat. 'Oh…hello, Chris…what's wrong…?'

'Sir, you've been driving…erratically.'

'Have I?' Allison chuckled unconvincingly. 'I'll be more careful, then. Thanks, Chris. Thank you for your concern.'

Waverley turned his head and glanced up at Starr, standing a few feet away. Starr shrugged – your call, the shrug said – and Waverley turned back.

'Why don't you let me drive you home, sir. You're looking a bit under the weather tonight.'

For the first time, Allison's skull-like face became animated with an honest emotion. 'No!' he said in alarm. 'No, I'll be all right, I'll drive more carefully from now on, I'll take it nice and slow.'

'Sir…'

'I haven't been *drinking*,' Allison blustered. 'I haven't had a drink all night. You'd smell it on me, wouldn't you, but you can't, because I haven't had a drink.'

'No, of course not, sir, but all the same–'

'Thanks, but I'd rather just…'

Waverley's hand clamped over Allison's as it settled on the ignition key and stopped it turning.

Despite his well-known dislike of drunk-drivers, Waverley was fully prepared to let Allison off – only this once, because no damage appeared to have been done, and because he was widely regarded as a good copper – but there was no way on earth he was going to let the man drive away.

He'd had to lean a little way into the car to stop the CID man starting the engine, and Allison had immediately jerked his head away, averting the left side of his face. Waverley suddenly realised that he'd been doing this all along.

Allison hadn't been ashamed to look him in the eye. He was hiding something.

Waverley removed the keys from the ignition, ignoring Allison's clutching fingers, and dropped them into his pocket.

'Sir, would you look at me, please.' The concern he had earlier forced into his voice to hide his disgust had gone. It may not have been drink, after all, but he knew when a man was behaving guiltily.

Allison had stiffened in his seat, the gleam in his eyes now pure panic. His hands, resting on the steering wheel, were shaking.

'Sir, please turn to face me,' Waverley commanded.

Slowly, as though he were fighting against restraints, Allison turned his face towards Waverley's, and Waverley saw.

There were four deep scratches on Allison's left cheek, each only several millimetres apart, the highest uncomfortably close to the corner of his eye. The scratches were still weeping blood. Allison's deep-set eyes, meeting Waverley's at last, looked haunted.

Waverley felt the hairs rising on the back of his neck, and the usually clear frequency of his thoughts dissolving into a numbing white noise. This was not what he had expected. This was not what he had expected at all. Then, as if from a great distance, he heard Starr calling his name.

'Chris, look!' Starr's face was slack with shock. He had been peering into the Honda's backseat, and now he was pointing.

Waverley looked in, too, and his stomach seemed to plummet towards the ground. A huddled mound lay under a tartan travel-rug spread out over the backseat. An arm hung down from one of the folds, and the hand at the end of it rested lifelessly in the foot-well. The hand was small, delicate, and feminine. The broken fingernails had blood on them.

Waverley swung back to Allison, and met his haunted eyes once more.

'I tried to be gentle, Chris,' Allison said quietly, beginning to cry. 'I tried to be so gentle...'

13

At 3.00am, Sam awoke to darkness and Jo's left leg lying over his thighs as heavily as a sandbag. The bedroom smelled of scented wax. Jo had put out the candles before they had settled down to sleep, and now the only light in the room came from a streetlight, filtering through the curtains. Everything looked flat and grey, like a still life in monotone.

Sam's head was instantly, unusually, clear, and he had an erection like a stallion. Unfortunately, he had the need to piss like one too, which, he thought, just went to show that every silver lining had its cloud.

He gently began to move Jo's leg, but she was a dead weight and he ended up almost heaving her off. Her sleep must have been very deep, for she didn't roll over onto her other side with a grumbling moan, as she usually did when disturbed in the night. She just lay there in a heap, not moving, not even audibly breathing. As his eyes became more accustomed to the grey light, he saw that her face in repose resembled a slab of clay, and wished he hadn't looked. She looked like a corpse.

After spending a few minutes in the en-suite bathroom trying to convince his penis to melt a little so that he could urinate, Sam began to return to bed, even though he no longer felt the slightest bit sleepy. He was thinking that he could always try waking Jo up, and see if she could suggest a way to relieve his stiffness.

But just as he prepared to slip under the duvet, he heard something that killed all his lustful thoughts instantly – soft footsteps whispering over the carpet in the corridor outside his bedroom.

For a couple of seconds he experienced a rush of thoughts and emotions identical to those he had suffered earlier that evening. Identical except for one detail – this time, Sam knew that it couldn't possibly be Jo. This was the real thing, an intruder. Someone clever enough to make it past the high-security locks, someone confident enough to wander around the house while he was still here.

Someone dangerous.

He knelt down and began to fumble under the bed before realising that his Inflexible Friend wasn't there anymore. He had left it down in the kitchen, after Jo had walked out on him. From somewhere in the otherwise quiet house, downstairs he assumed, he heard a series of cupboard doors opening and closing. Whoever his intruder was, they were searching for something. Whatever that something was, they hadn't found it upstairs.

Sam sat down on the edge of the bed, astonished to find himself trembling violently. His erection had faded so completely that he barely seemed to have a penis at all. He looked across at the phone on the nightstand, but was curiously reluctant to call the police. He was also reluctant to wake Jo, and he was as confused by these reluctances as he was by the intensity of his fear.

He heard another cupboard door being opened.

Okay, he thought finally. This is something, for whatever insane reason, you seem to want to deal with yourself. So go ahead, do it, get up off the bed and deal with it.

His body, however, made no attempt to stand.

Okay, so wake Jo, so call the police. Lock the bedroom door and wait for the sirens. Let somebody else take care of it.

His body immediately stood up.

Oh shit, Sam thought. Here we go.

He had pulled on jogging pants and a sweatshirt, and collected a heavy brass candlestick from one of the spare bedrooms on his way to the staircase. Now he was carefully descending into the shadowy bowl of the hallway, agonisingly slowly, to avoid making any noise. It occurred to him that this was the way the intruder should be conducting himself, not barging around like he owned the place. He could feel large drops of perspiration crawling down his back like teasing fingers.

From below the level of his feet he began to hear a soft rustling sound, and when he looked over the banister rail into the darkness, he actually saw the intruder.

He was just a shadow among many shadows, visible only because he was moving and the rest were static. Sam could make out no details other than his general outline, but he could see what the intruder was doing. He had opened the closet door and was rummaging around in all the coats and jackets, apparently searching through the pockets.

Sam clutched the candlestick harder, took a deep breath, and made a stern mental vow to himself − no chipmunk squeak this time, only a full actorish roar would do.

'Are you having fun?' he suddenly yelled.

The intruder actually jumped in the air in surprise, got his feet tangled up together, and fell on his backside with a startled cry. The reaction was so comical that even under the circumstances, Sam might have laughed. Except that when the intruder had cried out, Sam had received a surprise of his own.

He'd had no idea who the intruder might be − some wildcard EO had been his best guess, some medication-dodging creep who had managed to follow him home. But he had never once suspected that it might be a woman.

While the intruder was still recovering from her fall, Sam rushed down the rest of the stairs and snapped on the lights. He intended to stand over her and ask who she was, what the hell was going on, and what did she think she was doing breaking into his home like this? He thought that the threat of the candlestick he was brandishing would be enough of an incentive for her to provide the answers with a fair degree of haste.

But when he got close enough to see her clearly, and when she looked back at him, all the conventional, natural, perfectly reasonable questions he had formulated suddenly seemed redundant. The girl he saw sitting on his hallway floor was no Eldritch Obsessive.

She was *from* Eldritch.

14

She didn't have a name, nor had she ever actually appeared in any of the books, but there was no doubting who she was. As for *what* she was, that was a different matter altogether. Sam had 'seen' her among the crowds at numerous crime-scenes he had written, and once or twice in bars and clubs his central characters had frequented. He had never written her down because it was obvious that she was more than just an Eldritch extra, to be mentioned once and forgotten forever. He had sensed that there much more to her than that, but pursuing such a strong character would have pulled his stories way off-track, so he'd let her go.

But she was here now, and she'd done it on her own.

The girl rose unsteadily to her feet. She was young, maybe twenty-one or twenty-two, with short, gamin-like brown hair and brown eyes, and about five-nine in height. She wore a long coat of some kind of dark fur that didn't look synthetic. Below this her legs were bare, as were her feet. She wore no make-up, not even a trace of foundation, but unlike Jo without her dib and dab, the absence did not detract from her appearance. Rather, make-up would have gilded the lily.

For what seemed like the longest time, Sam found himself completely unable to speak. The candlestick dangled from his fingers, forgotten, as the girl returned his stare. She was entirely real, that was the hell of it. He could see the heat in her cheeks, the tiny mole on her throat, and the glistening skin of her cleavage as she breathed. All he could think of at this moment was the Guardians of Justice he had seen in the hotel lobby. If this girl was real, so were they.

'What—'

'Shhh!' The girl glanced up the staircase sharply. 'You've made enough noise as it is, don't make any more or you'll wake her.'

Jo, Sam thought. She's talking about Jo. She knows about her.

He wondered why he was whispering when he said, 'She's a heavy sleeper.'

'You can't trust her anymore.' The girl made a little sound of disgust. 'Not that you ever could. You don't mean anything to her, she's on *his* side.'

'On whose side?'

The girl's head turned back to the stairs. She listened for a moment, her eyes half-closed, and then

65

said, 'I have to go. Turn out the lights before she sees them.'

'No,' Sam said. 'I want to know what's going on. How can you be here?'

'I can't tell you, and I can't stay. He can't find out I've been here. Don't think about this. Don't think about me.'

'You're not going anywhere until you talk to me,' Sam said as he moved towards her.

'Stay back!' she said, and such was the force of her authority, Sam halted immediately.

'This is ridiculous,' he said hopelessly. 'You're a part of my imagination, for Christ's sake.'

'I wish that were the whole truth.'

The girl glanced up above Sam's head, and her face became pinched in concentration. He heard the light bulbs in the chandelier above his head popping just before they were plunged into darkness once more. He reached out quickly, hoping to grab her coat, and found his hand caught in both of hers.

'You shouldn't try to touch me,' she said.

Her hands were long and soft and cool, but they held him in a powerful grip. Her touch made him feel dizzy, almost nauseous, and she carried an odour with her he couldn't place. It wasn't at all pleasant, but it did seem very familiar.

'Just tell yourself I haven't been here,' she said. 'Then make yourself believe it.'

Sam opened his mouth to respond, but then he felt the pressure of her hold not so much letting go as dissolving. He knew that she hadn't moved away. She'd just gone. By the time his eyes had fully adjusted to the darkness again, he was alone.

He stood there for a long time, lost in thought, troubled by everything that seemed to be happening to him. He tried to think of the girl as a very weird dream – stress-related, of course, like everything else that had happened today – and he found himself all too willing to believe it. The alternatives were almost too terrible to contemplate.

Suddenly tired again, Sam began to straighten up the coat and jackets, picking up a couple that had been knocked to the closet floor. The disorganisation they had suffered was real. Maybe he'd done it himself, sleepwalking. That idea too, he discovered, was preferable to the alternatives.

'Sam?'

This time Jo's voice did make him jump. It sounded like it had earlier, before she'd come back to make peace. It was lifeless yet demanding.

'Sam, what are you doing?'

She was getting closer. He heard a light switch upstairs clicking.

'The light doesn't work. Has there been a power cut?'

'The bulbs have blown, that's all.'

Sam could make her out now, leaning over the banister rail, naked, a slightly lighter patch in the gloom. On her large pale breasts, the wide brown circles of her areolae looked like the pupils of an enormous pair of eyes.

'What were you doing?'

'It's all right,' Sam called. 'I…I had a bad dream and came down for a cold drink. I'll be back in a minute.'

There was a long pause, as though she were considering this excuse for his absence from every angle.

'Okay.' Her shape vanished. 'Come back to bed soon.' Her voice was farther away now, as she went back along the corridor.

Sam waited for a while but heard nothing more, and then finished putting the coats away. He wondered why he had lied to Jo, but that was an easy one to answer. Because he didn't want her to know that he had either been dreaming and sleepwalking, or seeing things he had no business seeing. Because he didn't want her to know he might be crazy enough to be emptying closets in his sleep.

Or maybe that wasn't it at all.

Perhaps it was the way the Eldritch girl − figment of his overwrought imagination or not − had glanced up the stairs, instantly wary of Jo, instantly suspicious, condemning. But there was something else, too, something Sam couldn't quite get a fix on, but which niggled away at the back of his mind, like an elusive word on the tip of his tongue. It was something Jo had either said or done earlier in the night.

What was it?

He closed the closet door, leaning his forehead against the cool wood, willing it to come, but it wouldn't.

Sam stood by the open door of the refrigerator, taking the cool drink he'd told Jo he'd come down for, only it wasn't the orange juice he had originally intended, it was a can of beer. He wanted the alcohol, because

68

he now knew what Jo had said that had been so very wrong. It had come to him only seconds ago.

He'd opened the fridge door and the light inside had come on, which had reminded him of a car at night - which had immediately reminded him of the first chapter of the new Eldritch book, as Sly Jack Road added Smooth Harry Flanagan and young Rena White to its long list of victims. Smooth Harry as murderer, poor Rena as sacrifice. It was the connection his subconscious needed to dredge up the memory that had proved so elusive in the hallway.

In his mind, he heard himself mumble, 'We could have been doing this all night,' into Jo's mouth as he kissed her and her hand made firm circular movements over the crotch of his jeans.

And she'd replied, 'But then you wouldn't have started the new book.'

Which was true. If she hadn't stormed off earlier, no matter if they'd made love or not, he wouldn't have written a single word tonight. Without the feeling of emptiness her anger and desertion had created in him, he might not have felt moved to start writing for another week or so. Maybe even longer, considering the way he had been feeling about starting the thirteenth Eldritch novel.

Sam shuddered, feeling a chill that had nothing to do with the cold beer or the open fridge. Since when had Jo ever cared about his writing? Why would she care if he ever went for another tour of duty in Eldritch or not?

And then he remembered something else the Eldritch girl had said, that his girlfriend wasn't on his side anymore, and he wondered whose side Jo could possibly be on if not his.

When Sam finished his drink, he grabbed another before closing the fridge. He went back upstairs slowly and quietly, tiptoeing past his bedroom door, and he slept on the sofa in his office.

For some reason, it seemed like the safest place to be, and just before he finally dropped off to sleep, Sam worked out why that was – it was the only room in the house that Jo would not enter.

15

Neither Dwayne nor Josh saw where the man came from. One moment the street was empty and quiet, the next he was there and the harsh sound of his asthmatic breathing, carrying in the thin night air, was alarmingly loud. Of course, the street lighting in Gower Road was almost non-existent – they had seen to that themselves with Dwayne's airgun the night before – but they should still have seen the old man before they did. It was like the bastard beamed down from somewhere, or came up out of a trap door.

The two teenage boys were stationed diagonally opposite each other at either side of Gower Road, hidden in the doorways of broken-down, boarded-up shops, of which there were many in this deprived area. Their scam was an old one, but it was tried and tested, and generally profitable.

After spotting a target, one of the boys would approach him or her and pretend to beg for money. While the target was trying to figure out whether to give him the benefit of the doubt, the other boy came up from behind and whacked them.

The scam usually worked, even if the target was hip to it and tried to run away. Mostly it worked because it was always two against one, but also because Josh and Dwayne selected their targets with care. Pissed, old, high, or knackered pretty well summed up their preferences. With practise it was easy work, and the boys had become very good at it.

Their target tonight was obviously a very old man, swaddled in an overcoat that must have been new around the end of World War II, and a hat with a curling brim that may have been even older. Josh and Dwayne weren't much concerned with his clothes anyway, except that they were a pointer to his age and vulnerability. His heavy breathing was another pointer. He appeared to walk with a stoop, too, which they also liked the look of. They didn't mind that with most of the streetlights off they couldn't see his face. As they had planned, it meant that he couldn't see theirs either.

Josh stepped out as the man approached the doorway he was hiding in. The old man's eyesight must have been failing as well as the rest of him, because it didn't look as though he was going to stop until Josh spoke.

'Excuse me, sir, have you got any spare change?'

The old man swayed on the spot as he peered at the polite young man, but he didn't reply.

'Can you spare some money, to help me out,' Josh said keeping his voice pleasant and low as he held out his hand cupped into a bowl. 'Anything'll do.'

Over the old man's shoulder, he could see Dwayne's dark form like a shadow puppet, streaking towards them, his trainers silent as he crossed the deserted road.

'Money?' the old man asked, his voice slow and draggy with some kind of thick accent. Polish or Jewish or some other kind of *ish*. 'What you want my money for? Leave me alone, please!'

'Just for food,' Josh replied. 'I haven't eaten for three days. Come on, what do you say, help me out.'

The old man seemed to glance about the darkened street, really aware of his surroundings for the first time. Josh was grateful that he didn't look over his shoulder. Dwayne was on the pavement now, coming up behind the old man like an overloaded lorry.

'I don't understand this,' the old man wheezed. 'Where am I?'

Josh allowed himself to grin. 'The land of nod.'

He prepared himself. In about two seconds Dwayne was going to collide with old Wheezy. When this happened, Josh would throw his right knee forward, and wherever it caught the old man, balls, belly, chest or face, it would put him down. It would take Josh and Dwayne all of ten seconds to roll him for his wallet and watch, another ten or so seconds to get out of Gower Road, and twenty more to reach their stolen car in Sussex Avenue.

In under a minute they'd be gone. It was a beautiful scam.

Josh shot out his knee at precisely the right moment, and it took the stumbling body directly in the balls. Wheezy collapsed to the pavement with a strangled cry of agony, which was a sound Josh always found highly amusing. He glanced up to share the crack with Dwayne, but Dwayne wasn't there. The old man, however, *was* there, some four feet to the left of where he had been standing a split second ago.

The writing body at Josh's feet was struggling for speech.

'Y-y-y-yuh…' Dwayne was glaring up at him with eyes that looked ready to burst from internal pressure.

Josh looked back at Wheezy. He knew he should be running. If by some shitty miracle the scam went wrong, you ran. That was the boys' SOP. But it had happened so quickly that he didn't understand how it had gone wrong. The old geezer had somehow sidestepped Dwayne's attack, that much was obvious, but Josh was sure that he couldn't have done it deliberately.

He's just an old man, he thought. Just some feeble, wheezing old immigrant. He'd probably tripped over his own feet and stumbled out of the way by accident. Dwayne's momentum had carried him on, and then… Yeah, that's *exactly* what happened, Josh decided.

Yet the longer the moment dragged out and Josh went on staring at the black nothing of Wheezy's face, he became convinced that there was something terribly wrong with it. His face seemed in some way to be the wrong shape. His loud breathing no longer struck Josh as being asthmatic, but as the respiration of a large, aggressive animal.

'The land of nod?' the old man asked in his funny foreign voice. 'I am sure you meant this as a joke. But you know, in a way I think it is almost true.'

There was now something in the man's voice that was even more wrong than his hidden face, and it had nothing to do with his accent. Josh began to back away.

'K-kick 'is fuckin' lungs out!' Dwayne commanded as he began to recover. He had got to his knees, his hands buried between his thighs as he massaged his aching balls. When he realised that Josh had taken no notice of him, that he was still backing away, he panicked. 'Help me up, you bastard, don't leave me with him!'

Josh ignored him. Leaving Dwayne was exactly what he intended to do, because this was all wrong. He didn't like the way they hadn't seen Wheezy arriving until he was almost on top of them. He didn't like the greasy way the old man had escaped attack. Josh didn't like the look of him, the sound of him, or anything else about the whole fucked up situation. Dwayne could look after himself. At least, that's what he was always telling people, so now was his chance to prove it. Josh had the car keys, and he was out of here.

But he'd left it too late.

A fraction of a second before Josh turned to run, the old man's figure seemed to expand towards him, flowing like ink through water. A wave of utter blackness crashed into him, and he was thrown backwards. There was an instant of total, impossible pain, and then, for a while, there was nothing.

He didn't even hear Dwayne's screams, which rose through the scales until they could almost have shattered windows, but which, curiously, attracted no attention from Gower Road's few remaining residents.

Moments later, Josh opened his eyes.

He lay on his back on the pavement. He could see a few stars through the patchwork of clouds. He thought for a moment it was raining, because he could feel drops of liquid falling on his face, but then he realised that the drops were very warm. With a great effort, he refocused his eyes and saw that from somewhere on his body a thin fountain of blood was spraying. He could feel it on his face but nowhere else, and when he tried to sit up he found that he couldn't move his arms or his legs, only his neck.

The fact that he was paralysed would only occur to him later, when sense began to return to his concussed brain and he realised that movement was the only thing that might have a chance of saving his life.

There was a sound to his left, and Josh let his head roll that way.

He saw the old man crouching above a mess of rags and flesh that he guessed was Dwayne. *Had* been Dwayne, anyway, because even in the poor light Josh could see that his partner in crime was dead. He was messed up so badly it looked as though he'd fallen into a threshing machine. He'd come apart in so many places.

How did that happen? Josh wondered. Did a car hit him, or…?

His mind too numbed by shock and injury to find the sight distressing, or even believable for that matter, Josh watched Wheezy's dark outline reach into the pulp of Dwayne's abdomen and yank out a slithering clump of viscera, which he then tossed onto the pavement. The old man then appeared to closely study the glistening pattern Dwayne's innards had made, tracing the lines with his hands.

'Good,' he mumbled to himself. 'Good, yes, very good. I begin to understand this.'

Then the old man, or whatever he really was, turned his head to look at Josh.

'Retirement is not all it is cracked up to be, young man,' he said. 'Do not allow anyone to tell you any different. A man needs a job. It gives him dignity, and makes him strong, it keeps him alive and potent. I had forgotten that.'

He moved across to Josh's side, and reached out. Wheezy, Josh discovered, smelled quite strongly of shit and piss. Josh saw the stream of his own blood halted, but didn't feel the flow being blocked, just as he didn't feel any kind of pain. Slowly he began to realise exactly why he couldn't move his arms and legs. As the realisation grew, he tried to scream, but found that he couldn't − not even when the blood began to flow again as the old man started to enlarge his wound, ripping at the unfeeling flesh.

'Now my little friend, my dear little chicken,' the old man grunted. 'Let us see what there is to learn from you, eh?'

Before he eventually lost consciousness, Josh had the feeling that the old man had learned a good many things.

16

It was four-thirty, just over two hours since PCs Waverley and Starr had pulled over DS Allison's

Honda Accord, and Allison was now in a holding cell at the station. Two male constables stood leaning on the counter in the charge room, gossiping about the night's big news.

The young girl found in DS Robert Allison's car, it was rumoured, had been raped and strangled. It was further rumoured that her mouth had been packed with earth and leaf mulch and ashes, and that her breasts were covered in horrendous bite marks, her nipples dangling from tiny threads of elastic skin. It was terrible to think that one of their own could have done such a thing. Just terrible. Already, old sick jokes were being reworked to fit the situation…

One of the constables looked up as he heard sharp, precise footsteps cracking down the corridor towards the charge room. They had the regularity of a metronome. He glanced at the other constable and raised his eyebrows.

'That'll be the Count,' he said. 'Get your fucking cross out.'

'The Count?' the other replied. 'I think you've used one letter too many there.'

They both stood up straighter, pretending to be examining the information on a clipboard together. The Count took a dim view of sloppiness. The way he carried on, they reckoned, you'd have thought he was the Commissioner, not a common or garden DI.

A moment later, DI Duncan Hyams came into the charge room. Tall and dark-haired, Hyams was smartly dressed in his usual black suit, and was clean-shaven and obviously wide-awake, even at this hour of the morning. Hyams wasn't a very popular figure among his colleagues, largely because he was not one of the lads. He didn't drink, smoke, or, as far as anyone knew, fornicate. No one had known him to even eat on duty. He did everything by the book, and forced those around him to do likewise. There were those who said that DI Hyams never slept, and there were those who said that if he *did* sleep, it was probably in a coffin. There were others who just wanted to see him in a coffin.

Hyams came to a halt, glancing around the grey charge room.

'You took your time getting here, sir,' the gobbier of the two constables said, grinning. 'Anyone we know?'

'I've been to the crime-scene, Gibbons. Where's DS Morley?'

'What condition's the girl in?' the second constable asked, fishing for more juicy details.

'Still very dead. Where's Morley?'

'Already in with DS Allison, sir.'

A shadow passed over Hyams' habitually neutral expression. 'I told him to wait for me out here.'

Both constables shrugged, rejecting responsibility. 'He didn't say anything about that,' Gibbons muttered.

'He wouldn't. Which cell?'

'Err…' They consulted the clipboard they had been studying so assiduously when Hyams had arrived. 'Five.'

'How many other cells are in use?'

'Err…' The clipboard was consulted once more. 'None.'

Hyams nodded. 'Why don't you gentlemen take a break, you look rushed off your feet.'

He walked by them and down the corridor lined with cell doors. Number five was the last cell on the left hand side, and the door was closed but not locked. Hyams could hear Morley talking inside.

'…go on, son, it'll do you good…'

Hyams deliberately coughed before opening the cell door, but was still in time to see DS Morley guiltily screwing the cap back on a silver hip flask. He gave Morley the disapproving stare that frequently had his colleagues wishing for a hammer and stake.

'You've had better ideas, Ken.'

Morley winced as he slipped the hip flask back in his jacket pocket. 'He's in shock, Guv, I thought it might help.'

Bob Allison sat on the edge of the cell's bolted down cot, his head on his folded arms, his arms resting on his knees. His wounded cheek hadn't been dressed yet. His clothes hadn't been taken, bagged and tagged for forensic analysis. He still had his belt and shoelaces. Essential measures were being neglected because the suspect was a policeman.

'If he's in shock he needs a doctor, not whisky.'

'It's brandy, Guv.'

'I don't care if it's a dry martini, shaken not stirred. Go get a doctor. And evidence bags for his clothes. And Ken,' Hyams added as Morley began to leave. 'In future, when I say wait, you wait.'

'Okay, Guv.'

Hyams pushed the door closed. There was nowhere else to sit, so he sat down beside Allison. He didn't speak, just listened to the other man's uneven breathing. There was mud on Allison's shoes, leaf mulch wedged into the angle between heel and sole.

These materials were among the other foreign objects that had been found jammed in the dead girl's mouth, and also inserted into her other orifices. Hyams wondered if anyone had emptied Allison's pockets and found the girl's missing knickers.

Eventually, he said, 'I've been to see your car, Bob.'

Allison didn't respond. Hyams didn't expect him to, not yet.

'I'm going to want some answers from you soon. I'll want to know the girl's name, where you picked her up and where you took her. I'll want you to tell me what went wrong.'

Allison's breathing became more ragged. He was crying, and Hyams felt his heart contract with sorrow.

Before tonight, Hyams would have sworn that Allison was completely straight. Christ, half the local force knew him as Honest Bob. Detectives would say, 'Hey, where'd you get that shitty tip-off?' 'From Honest Bob Allison.' 'Shit, you mean it's true?' Hyams had heard them.

He looked down at the crying man's bobbing head, and wondered how long he'd be able to take this. How the hell had it happened?

In Hyams's personal experience, Bob Allison was not only a good detective, he was probably the best DS he'd ever worked with. He was also the only one of Hyams's colleagues with whom he'd had anything approaching a real friendship. The only officer he had ever confided in – Hyams had done a lot of confiding around the time his fiancée had ditched him – and Allison had kept his trap shut about it. An intensely private man, Hyams had valued this discretion above everything else. The two men had occasionally taken dinner together, and seen the odd movie. They had leant each other books.

'Bob,' Hyams said gently. 'Talk to me now. Make me understand.'

17

When Sam eventually made his way down from his office, after what had been a surprisingly good night's sleep considering his state of mind, he was dreading facing Jo.

What could he tell her? That because of his supremely stressful day at the convention he'd started having hallucinations? That he'd left her to sleep alone because of something one of the hallucinations had *told* him? That a chance remark Jo had made in a moment of passion had sparked off in him a paranoid fantasy that could easily have graced the pages of a Nigel Cassidy novel?

Could he really tell her that for the space of one nocturnal hour, he had suspected her of being an Eldritch Obsessive?

Lying there on the leather sofa in his office, his ears pricked for any sounds of movement Jo might make even as his eyes began to droop, Sam had wondered if his lover was what she had always claimed to be. After all, what better way was there for an EO to get close to the oracle of their city than by sleeping with him? And what better way to hide an obsessive heart than to pretend a complete lack of interest?

He'd wondered if her PMT-prompted walkout had merely been a strategy to kick-start his writing, and her sexual generosity afterwards a reward that was only supposed to be noticed subconsciously. He'd wondered if the 'he' whose side she was on might be his own agent, Horace Jepson. He'd wondered if Nigel Cassidy had been correct about Horace's secret agenda. His tired mind had wondered about many such things as it sank into oblivion.

Of course, after a good night's sleep and in the light of morning, all these speculations, these ugly little fantasies, seemed ludicrous. Far too ludicrous − and insulting − to offer Jo as an excuse for not sleeping with her. So the question remained, what could he tell her?

However, Sam soon discovered that he didn't have to tell her anything at all. Jo had gone. Sometime between his falling asleep and waking up, she had taken her leave of Sam and his house. There was no note.

Sam made coffee and nuked a couple of frozen bagels in the microwave. He ate at the breakfast bar, staring at the baseball bat that still lay on the kitchen floor. He wondered if Jo had taken off in anger, or just taken off, as she sometimes did. A free spirit, she called herself, but now Sam wondered about that, too.

By the time he'd finished eating, he'd decided not to chase her. He'd give her some space and time, and call her at the end of the day. If she had gone home angry, this would give her time to cool off. If she hadn't, it would just seem normal.

Sam really liked the idea of getting things back to normal.

As he showered, shaved and dressed, Sam could feel Eldritch pulling at him. It was as though there were a line connecting him to his computer, and that the city which lived inside it was trying to reel him back. Despite all his earlier misgivings about writing the thirteenth novel, it was the best feeling in the world.

But before he could start writing today, there was something Sam had to do first. Something he wanted to do. He was going to beard his agent in his den. He was going to walk into Horace Jepson's offices totally unannounced, and he was going to give him merry hell about the convention.

Yesterday, Sam knew he'd have been bitter and angry. Today, he knew he was going to have fun.

He trotted downstairs, smiling to himself. He would tell Horace that rather than sending him scurrying back to Eldritch, the madness of the convention had forced him further away. *Much* further away. His next project would be a clog-and-shawl trilogy, a two-thousand-page epic following the fortunes of his heroine, one Eliza Coggletontwist, an orphan who overcomes crushing poverty and a childhood case of rickets to become one of the best fish-gutters in the whole of Grimsby. Then Sam would sit back and watch Horace sweat like a pig in a slaughterhouse.

Out of the closet in the hallway, Sam chose the same jacket he had worn to the convention because it still had his keys and wallet in the pockets. It was also his current favourite, a dark suede three-quarter length that looked ancient and lived in but wasn't. When he pulled it on, he discovered that it contained something else besides the keys and wallet: a folded slip of paper, tucked into one of the pockets.

He remembered all those straying hands in the hotel lobby, and groaned. He hadn't been vigilant enough.

He unfolded the paper, expecting some cack-handed story idea or something of that kind, but he found instead an address of sorts, written in black ink. It said:

Blue Door, Sheridan Row, Camden Town

And it said nothing else.

Sam was still trying to guess what kind of invitation this might be when the doorbell went off. He went across to the front door and pressed the intercom button.

'Hello?'

'Sam Parker?'

'Yes.'

'Police.'

Sam peered through the door viewer and saw a tall, well-dressed man in his thirties standing patiently at the gate. A policeman. Sam thought he knew what this was about, and the knowledge made him angry and weary at the same time. Charles Beckett had made a complaint, obviously, and had probably blamed Sam for the way he had been attacked in the hotel lobby. He'd probably also blamed Sam for the low sales of his backlist, the poor state of his marriage, and the depreciation of his portfolio of stocks and shares.

Typical, Sam caught himself thinking. Just typical.

But then he realised that the 'person' this kind of stunt would have been most typical of was the Listmaker.

18

Sam examined DI Hyams's warrant card closely, then examined the man. Hyams was just as smartly turned-out as Sam's first sight of him through the door viewer had suggested. Moreover, he was extremely polite, and trailed a discreet odour of good aftershave. He was a long-faced man with kind brown eyes, and he had smiled when he said hello. Sam ushered him into the sitting room, feeling unexpectedly guilty about Eldritch's detective stereotypes, which were the precise opposite of the man before him.

After putting away his warrant card, DI Hyams declined an offer of coffee but accepted a seat. He gave the sitting room a brief once over, and then had eyes only for Sam, who despite the detective's pleasant manner began to feel uncomfortable under his unshifting gaze. His anger at Charles Beckett became anger at the policeman.

'All right, what am I supposed to have done?' Sam snapped.

'I beg your pardon?'

'You must think I've committed some kind of crime, you're staring at me like something you just trod in.'

Hyams seemed genuinely surprised. 'I'm sorry, I didn't mean to.'

'Come on, let's have it,' Sam demanded. 'What has Beckett told you?'

'Beckett?'

'Charles Beckett.'

'The writer?'

'That's what he claims to be, yes.'

Hyams cleared his throat. 'I think we're talking at cross-purposes, Mr Parker. Are you referring to the scuffle at the hotel in Wembley yesterday afternoon?'

Sam nodded, and thought that Beckett would probably have a fit if he'd heard his great drama being described as a 'scuffle'.

Hyams said, 'I saw the report they had on the local news, and that's all I know about it.'

'Oh.' Sam's anger began to filter away, and he felt vaguely embarrassed.

'I was already on my way home from the hotel before the fight started,' Hyams continued. 'And Wembley's not my patch anyway.'

'Excuse me,' Sam said in surprise. 'You were at the convention?'

'Yes, at the Q&A,' Hyams smiled, 'but I never got to ask my question.'

'I see.' He paused. 'What was it?'

'What is the new Eldritch novel going to be about.'

'Oh,' Sam said again. 'Well, I don't normally talk about my stuff when I'm in the middle of writing it… Is that why you came, for the answer?'

'No, I'm afraid not.'

Sam frowned. 'Okay, I'll answer your question if you answer mine. Deal? The new book is about the return of the most evil man Eldritch has ever known. Now, why don't you tell me why you're here?'

Hyams looked slightly embarrassed himself for a moment. Then he said, 'I've come to ask you about *Sly Jack Road*.'

'*Sly Jack Road*?' Sam asked. 'What about it?' He wondered why he had begun to feel defensive again.

'I was wondering, did you base any of it on reality.'

Reality? Sam thought. A haunted country lane? Bodies in shallow graves, ghosties and ghoulies, and all the rest of the hocus-pocus? He experienced a brief moment of vertigo, and dearly wished that he could have another look at Hyams' warrant card, to make sure that it was for real. Then he realised that it could be perfectly real, and Hyams could still be a high-functioning EO. They came from all walks of life.

'I'm not sure what you mean.'

'Not the events in the book, as such,' Hyams said quickly. 'Just the place. When you first wrote about Sly Jack Road itself, did you have a specific location in mind – one that someone familiar with your work might recognise, say, if they came across it by accident, or actually lived nearby?'

Sam thought for a while, then slowly shook his head.

'Not as far as I'm aware. Obviously, there may be a few details, observations, which I didn't make up, but they could have come from any one of a hundred country lanes in the greenbelt. Anything specifically identifiable came straight out of here,' Sam said, pointing at his head.

'In the book there are the ruins of an old burnt-out windmill...?'

Sam pointed at his head again.

Hyams nodded and looked away, as if even though this was exactly the answer he had expected, it still disappointed him. Sam realised that beneath his pleasant demeanour, Hyams was miserable.

'What's this about?' he asked.

Hyams was silent for a long while, and then he shrugged. There was no harm in talking to Sam Parker about this. It would be in the newspapers' later editions, anyway. Certain officers had large mouths and expensive tastes.

'I suppose the reason I was staring at you so intently earlier is that I'm an admirer of your work. I mean, *obviously* I am, otherwise I wouldn't have been at the convention. I've been a fan for a long time. I'm not fanatical, like some,' he carefully assured Sam. 'But I've got all the books, and I reread them from time to time. Over the last few years, I got a friend of mine interested in them, too. In the end, he got to be an even bigger fan than I was.'

Here, Hyams's voice faltered a little.

'Last night my friend was driving around, and he got stopped by a patrol car. They found a dead girl on his backseat, and it looks like he may have raped and strangled her. There's some evidence to support the idea that the crime may have been committed in or near woodland, and we have to find out where that was. When I interviewed him earlier, all he could tell me – the only thing he'd say – was that Sly Jack Road *made* him do it.'

Sam had turned into a statue, and he knew that the policeman had noticed.

Hyams leaned forward, and Sam suddenly caught an odour from him. It came from his mouth and nose and steamed out of the pores of his skin and the vents of his good clothes, and there was no mistaking what it was. Seventy proof vodka. Just for a second, it was as though Hyams had bathed in it.

Vertigo again. Sam felt as though he were falling down a very deep hole, and in the diminishing circle of light at the top, he saw Hyams's face change. The policeman's cheeks and nose seemed to swell up and become ruddy, full of burst blood vessels, and above them his soft brown eyes became compressed into cold nuggets of coal. Sam was looking at the face of Drunk Dave Hawkins, the one he saw in his mind when he wrote. Even the initials were the same. DH. Dave Hawkins, Duncan Hyams.

Sam came back to himself with a snap. Hyams was himself again, still leaning forward, still faintly smelling of expensive aftershave. He looked concerned.

'You okay? You went a bit funny on me just then.'

Sam swiped at his forehead. It was soaked with sweat. His clothes seemed to cling and bind, and his underpants were making a determined effort to locate his prostate. 'I'm fine. It's just…'

He *couldn't* tell the truth. He couldn't tell Hyams what he'd written last night, about Smooth Harry Flanagan, seduced into killing a girl by the evil spirit of Sly Jack Road. The policeman wouldn't see a connection between that fictional crime and a real murder. It wouldn't make any sense to him. It didn't make any sense to *Sam*. Either that or it made too much sense.

Sam remembered thinking at the convention that recently his imagination seemed to be shaping reality. He thought of the Guardians of Justice, and the girl from Eldritch last night. Were they really something as innocent and harmless as stress-induced hallucinations, or could they possibly be more substantial phantoms, conjured from his mind?

'I suppose it's hearing something like that,' he told the policeman finally. 'Even if you don't know any of the people involved, it's still a shock.'

'I'm sorry, I didn't think,' Hyams replied. 'I just assumed, with some of the things that happen in Eldritch…'

'That's only fiction,' Sam said sharply.

'Yes,' Hyams said. He didn't sound as convinced as he might. 'Of course it is.'

19

Resplendent in a royal blue silk dressing gown, Nathaniel Longman answered the front door of his Chelsea townhouse, dabbing at the corners of his mouth with a white linen napkin.

He was clearly surprised by the identity of his caller this morning, and for a moment seemed unsure of how to greet him. Nigel Cassidy had never called on him uninvited in all the years they had known each other. Usually, he had to be bullied into accepting invitations, picked up and dropped off like a child going to a birthday party. Longman had often wondered if Cassidy was afraid that he might get propositioned.

This morning the little man looked even more worried than usual, scrunched up into himself like something that dearly wished to hibernate, his face a watch-movement of ticks.

Something wrong, not a social call, Longman thought. Problem big or problem small, he wondered. Cassidy had them all, both real and imagined.

'Nigel, what an unexpected pleasure. Please, come in.'

Cassidy edged past him in time to see someone wearing a matching dressing gown disappearing up the staircase with a steaming cup and a side-plate piled with toast. He turned back to Longman, momentarily distracted and definitely confused.

'That,' Cassidy said with a frown, 'was a woman.'

'Yes, my sister's staying with me for a while,' Longman replied as he closed the front door.

'She was white.'

'Well spotted. Have you never heard the word mulatto? It means−'

'You don't *have* a sister,' Cassidy said stubbornly. 'You don't have *any* sibs.'

Caught in a lie, Longman smiled and shrugged easily. 'As I think I read somewhere, man cannot live by beefcake alone.'

Cassidy, who had no discernible sexuality, looked blank.

'Don't worry about it, Nigel. Come through the kitchen and I'll explain it to you, all about the birds and the bees, and the love that can't make up its mind about its name.'

91

The kitchen was small and cosy and Cassidy didn't see it. He sat facing his host across the table. As he sipped decaf' with many a suspicious sniff, as though expecting it to be poisoned, he was typically silent, but Longman could sense the agitation that had brought him here. Cassidy hadn't shaved, and his cheeks were alight with peach fuzz. Behind the thick glass of his spectacles, there were dark patches under his eyes. He looked like an ancient child.

'Problems?' Longman asked.

'Maybe.' Cassidy tried a moment of direct eye contact, but didn't like it any better than usual. 'I want you to know in advance, everything I'm going to tell you is going to sound weird.'

'I hate to tell you this, Nigel, but everything you say usually does.'

Cassidy fidgeted on his comfortable chair. 'Do you read Sam's books?'

'I've been known to.'

'No, I mean do you *read* them. Not scan them to be polite, because he's a friend. Do you read them for pleasure? Do you reread them?'

Longman had begun to look less easy. He would have been far happier discussing his emerging bisexuality, and his deeper fears that he may, in fact, be a latent heterosexual. He could draw a line between where their conversation in the taxi last night had ended and where this morning's conversation had begun, and he could see where Cassidy wanted to take them. It was a place he had been before, but always alone.

'Yes, sometimes I do.'

'Whenever you see Sam, do you have to stop yourself talking about Eldritch, asking him questions about this book and that book, what this character said, what this other one did?'

Longman just stared at him.

'I do, you see,' Cassidy admitted. 'I have to concentrate hard so I don't slip up. At first I thought it was my ego, as though I wasn't prepared to let him know how highly I thought of his work, sort of a professional jealousy. Then I thought it was about our friendship, that I didn't want to lose it – Sam doesn't really like the people who love his books, you know. I honestly don't think he likes *himself* when he writes them.'

Longman said nothing.

'That's what I thought before I realised the truth,' Cassidy continued. 'And the truth is that Eldritch scares me.'

Longman went to refresh his cup of Earl Grey, wondering how he could respond to this shining example of Cassidy's paranoia working at its absolute apogee. Under no circumstances did he wish to admit that he understood Cassidy's fears completely, because they were *his* fears, too. He tried to deflect the conversation.

'Nigel, let's face it, you get scared by anything that has more working parts than you do.'

'This isn't the same thing. I admit I'm paranoid, but that isn't what this's about.' Cassidy shook his head almost angrily. 'Nat, there's something wrong with Sam. Something wrong in his connection to Eldritch.'

Realising that Cassidy wouldn't be denied, Longman gave in.

'Nigel, you're talking about that place as though it were real. And please don't call me *Nat* − it makes me feel like an insect.'

'Well, isn't it real to you? I know it feels real to me, and to all those people at the convention, and to millions more.' He sniffed at the decaf' again, frowned, and put the cup on the table. 'Do you remember *Inanimate*?'

Inanimate had been Cassidy's last novel but one. In it, he had postulated the idea that all man-made objects were steadily becoming capable of intelligent thought, of self-awareness. They were achieving this in two ways. First, by volume − if enough of a certain object had been manufactured, no matter how simple, they attained a kind of collective consciousness. Secondly, other objects were making even greater strides by dint of their individual complexity, their moving parts and their components. The other idea the novel offered up for the reader's consideration was that inanimate man-made objects were inherently hostile to their creators, and would soon turn on them. Frankenstein for the mass-production age, one critic had called it.

'Yes, I remember,' Longman said. 'Let me see if I understand your reasoning. You're saying that it's more or less the same with Eldritch? Enough people believe in it and it *becomes* real? The killers and the crazies and the monsters of Eldritch walk out of the pages and they're real?'

'They don't have to believe in it, Nat, I think it's all about awareness. So many books, so many copies, so many readers, the films, the websites – all that is the volume. The complexity comes from every book being set in the same place, with lots of consistent characters, which we learn more about from book to book. Sam is the focal point for all this power, he's the conduit. I don't know if Eldritch existed before he started writing about it or it all just came out of his head, and I don't think it matters.'

'Nigel, I–'

'Eldritch is *real*. Sam knows it. On some level, at least. That's why he's been trying to write around it. Ask to read the manuscript of *Deep Water* if you don't believe me. It's exciting, it's fast and it's thrilling, but that's only because it reads like a man running for his life.'

Longman wasn't looking at Cassidy, but he was listening. He had already read the first draft of *Deep Water*, and he knew exactly what Cassidy meant. Sometimes, because of his indiscriminate paranoia, Longman tended to forget just how bright and perceptive his friend really was.

'Nigel, don't you think you might be overdoing the–'

'I saw something in the hotel lobby yesterday,' Cassidy said suddenly. 'Two somethings, actually, like the shadows of animals. Of *beasts*. They were circling through the crowd around Sam.'

He closed his eyes, to hide from the expression of disbelief he was sure was growing on Longman's face.

'I've seen other things like that in Sam's house, things I couldn't explain. That's why I don't like to stay there anymore. They're what scare me. I think

95

they're from Eldritch, I think they're the ghosts in Sam's house. I think some of his creations are breaking out into the real world.' He opened his eyes again. 'There, I've said it.'

Cassidy actually looked a little better after this confession, as though he'd sicked up something that had been making him ill.

After a moment's consideration, Longman asked, 'Have you ever spoken to Sam about your fears?'

'No, of course not. You saw me yesterday, pretending everything was normal.'

'I'd keep on doing that, if I were you.'

Cassidy took off his glasses and rubbed his eyes. 'You're right, of course. I'm sorry to unload on you like this, when you have company. *Real* company, not like mine yesterday,' he added with a feeble grin. 'I'm sorry. I'm crazy, I must be.'

'No, you're not crazy.'

'Yeah, right. I'm perfectly sane, of course. Did *you* see two shadow creatures in the lobby? I don't think so.'

Longman was silent for an unusually long time. Cassidy put his glasses back on and looked at him. This time he held Longman's eyes, and in them he could see a reflection of his own anxiety. It was amazing.

'You *did* see them?'

Reluctantly, very, very reluctantly, Longman nodded. He kept nodding until Cassidy suddenly realised that he was acknowledging not just the sighting of the shadow creatures, but everything.

'You feel the same way I do,' Cassidy marvelled. 'You do, don't you? You've already thought about this?'

'Wait here,' was all Longman said.

Cassidy pushed a few toast crumbs around on the table, hearing faint voices from upstairs, and he knew that Longman was asking his lover to leave so that they could talk openly. How did you politely ask a lover to leave your home? Cassidy wasn't sure, never having had a lover of his own, although he had often wondered what it would be like to share a bed with someone, to be woken by another person's voice, or to feel someone's hand on his shoulder in the middle of the night.

Rather terrifying, he suspected.

Longman came back down ten minutes later, and his girlfriend came with him. Cassidy caught a glimpse of her as Longman ushered her past the doorway, and even he recognised that she was beautiful. He tried not to listen to their affectionate goodbyes at the front door.

When Longman came back into the kitchen, he brought with him something that looked like a scrapbook, and he dropped it on the kitchen table. It was very heavy.

'The first time I met Jo was also the last time I stayed at Sam's house,' he told Cassidy in a flat monotone utterly unlike his usual urbanite drawl. 'I couldn't stop staring at her, and at first I thought this was because I'd recently started to find women sexually attractive. But later that night, around midnight, I finally figured out why I couldn't keep my eyes off her.'

He swallowed nervously.

'I realised that she had a very slight double image, as though there were two of her, one solid and real, the other… ghostlike. At first I thought I might need my eyes tested, but then I noticed it was only when I looked at Jo that this odd doubling effect happened. And the way she phrased her sentences when she spoke… it was like *dialogue*. Dialogue from an Eldritch novel. I kept glancing at Sam, to see if he was picking up on any of it, but he clearly wasn't.'

Cassidy was nodding. 'And that's when you began to suspect that something was wrong?'

'Oh no. I'd suspected long before then.' He laughed shakily. 'God, I'm such a coward. I didn't *suspect* anything. I *knew*.'

'You'd seen other things in Sam's house, like I did?'

'No. It came to me a different way.'

Longman sat down heavily opposite Cassidy and pushed the scrapbook across to him.

'I started collecting newspaper clippings when Sam was writing *The Torturer's Apprentice*,' he said.

20

After Hyams left, Sam was confused and upset, and he didn't know what to do with himself. He knew, however, that he didn't want to travel all the way across London to see his agent. He wasn't in the mood for practical jokes anymore. He did try to telephone Horace, but his secretary, Rosie, said that he was out.

Sam asked her if Horace was merely 'out', or was he 'out-out'.

'Sam,' Rosie told him, 'he's so out-out he hasn't been in-in for three days. If you want to know the truth, I think he's cheating on me.' Rosie was seventy-three, and her relationship with Horace had always been entirely professional. In the main, she treated him like the amiable idiot he gave the impression of being.

After saying goodbye to Rosie, Sam called Jo at home. He despised himself for his weakness, but he wanted to hear a comforting voice, a voice that wasn't fluent in Eldritch. He let Jo's phone ring twenty times before he replaced the receiver. She was out-out, too, had to be. In the bedsit where she lived, the ringing phone sounded like a squealing animal, and no one could have listened to it ring for that amount of time.

Where was she? Was it even Sam's business anymore?

He pottered around the house for half an hour, thinking about the policeman's visit, before realising what he would have to do, if only out of decency to the real-life murdered girl.

He had to change the start of the new book.

In his office he powered up the computer and opened the file named COMEBACK1/1. The screen filled with words. Smooth Harry Flanagan and doomed Rena White. A story of lust and murder, and of manipulation from beyond the grave. He scrolled through what he had written, reading the story but hearing it spoken inside his head by DI Hyams. He was shocked all over again. The similarities were even more pronounced than he had thought. But the biggest shock was still to come.

The sordid little scene did not end where he had left it when Jo came back to take him to bed. It did not end with Smooth Harry Flanagan about to be stopped by the police. It continued.

Once the policemen had seen what was in the back of Smooth Harry's black Honda Accord, covered by a travel rug, they'd pulled him out of the car and cuffed him. One of the policemen carefully pulled the rug from the girl's body. Her eyes were open, showing bloodshot whites, and her throat was almost black with bruising in the shape of hand-prints. Her shredded blouse was saturated with blood from the bites Smooth Harry had taken from her breasts, her mini-skirt was torn half away, and she had no underclothes. The girl's mouth was distended, packed with forest earth and leaves. A clump of similar material bulged obscenely from the centre of her scant, reddish pubic hair. Her white skin was dusted here and there with grey ashes.

Sam clamped his hand over his mouth. Who had written this, and when?

But the answers to both these questions were obvious. *He* had written it, sometime after sneaking up to his office to sleep. Maybe he'd written it in his sleep, but he had no doubt that it was definitely his work. He'd never seen it before, but as he read it, he instantly recognised it. It was in his style, his rhythm, his voice.

He wondered if the earth and leaves the girl's mouth and sex were stuffed with were what Hyams had been referring to when he said that there was evidence the murder had been committed in woodland. Sam was very sure that it was.

When the chapter ended, Sam scrolled down to the top of the next page. He wasn't entirely surprised to see that a new chapter had already been begun.

21
CHAPTER TWO

Steve Adams, a care-worker employed by the Eldritch City Council, unlocked the door of Flat 13 of the sheltered accommodation building with his passkey. He entered the corridor of the small flat in complete darkness, and this made him very angry. If the lights weren't on, it meant that the old bastard who lived here didn't have his mental lights on tonight. In turn, this meant that he wouldn't have remembered that he had to go to the toilet once in a while.

It was true that the old man wore an incontinence pad, but as Adams was at least five hours late for this visit, mostly due to an impromptu lock-in at the Stag and Cross public bar, it would now be saturated.

So would the old man.

Adams snapped on the corridor light, and then stomped the short distance to the bed-sitting room. He opened the door and turned on the overhead light. The single bed, covered with an old orange candlewick bedspread, hadn't been disturbed. For a moment, Adams was afraid the man it was his duty to care for had gone AWOL, but no. There he was, sitting in the high-backed armchair facing the dead TV. His eyes were open, seeing nothing, what was left of his mind idling in neutral, which was now his brain's most constant gear.

Alzheimer's is a terrible disease, a progressive whittling away of every mental faculty, from the long- and short-term memory to control of the bowel and bladder. This last was amply demonstrated by the odour that suffused the room, a shit-piss ammoniac stench that made Adams sick to his stomach. Adams's mates wondered why he worked as a care-worker. The hours were anti-social and the work was, to their minds, extremely unpleasant. Dribbling old people, who had to be bathed, changed and fed like babies. Sickening.

Adams always told them he found it a very rewarding occupation, and he made sure that it was.

The old man was, in fact, currently dribbling, his stubbled chin shiny with spit. Adams sighed and leant back against the wall. He found his cigarettes and lit one. It was the last in the packet. After a few inhalations, he crumpled the pack in his fist, and then tossed it in a low, lazy parabola at the old man. It struck his angled forehead, rebounded vertically, and came down in his sodden lap.

'Basket,' Adams grunted. 'Basket-case, more like.'

He glanced across at the uncovered windows. At this time of night there were no lights visible in the second wing of self-contained flats at the other side of the lawned quad, but you could never be too careful. He went over and closed the curtains, then went back to the old man and stood above him. As always, Adams was astounded afresh by the old man's incredible ugliness, which age and infirmity had only made worse. He looked like a mutant bat.

'Mr Wizeman. Mr Wizeman, you ugly old bastard. You smell like a pigsty.'

He slapped the old man's face a few times, the bald, wizened head rolling from side to side with each blow. His eyes widened a little, but that only let Adams see how empty of recognition they were.

Adams went into the small kitchenette attached to the bed-sitting room, and saw immediately that the woman he suspected was the old man's grand-daughter had visited again today. She was a fit bitch, and probably a rich bitch as well. Fur coat and no knickers, that type, he thought. She never stayed for long when she visited, but she came often and she always left Grandpa some goodies.

On the kitchen shelf was a fresh half-bottle of whisky, and tucked underneath it a crisp fifty-pound note. What she imagined Wizeman was *doing with all this money and booze Adams didn't know, and he didn't care as long as it kept on coming. He found a glass in the cupboard, filled it with whisky and exchanged the fifty-pound note for a fiver from his own pocket.*

'Cheers,' he called through to the silent bed-sitting room, and then swallowed a substantial amount of whisky. Yes, it was a very rewarding job, caring for the elderly. He opened the fridge, looking for something tasty to nibble on.

The old man Steve Adams knew as Mr Karl Wizeman was probably a nonagenarian, but no one was quite sure of his exact age. He'd had Alzheimer's for nearly a decade, and was now at the point where death was very close. His body was steadily atrophying around the still-living but largely non-functioning brain it surrounded.

Soon his mind would forget how to breathe, or keep his heart beating, then that would be it. Even in his brief moments of semi-lucidity, Wizeman did not know who he was. Which had been very lucky for Steve Adams.

Wizeman didn't remember the occupation he had pursued for the majority of his life. Nor did he recall his beloved employer, who so many years before had been one of the most notorious crime-bosses the country had ever seen. He didn't remember the hypnotic voice that would fondly say to him, 'Karl, you are my beast.'

Wizeman had been a gangland assassin whose methods had spread terror among his employer's contemporaries. He didn't remember extracting information with torture prior to killing his many victims. He did not remember extracting even more information from their cooling remains after they were dead. His boss would sometimes say to him, 'So they call you inhuman, Karl. So what? It is true, you are not entirely human.'

All these were memories so far gone it was like they had never been there. But now something extraordinary was happening to Wizeman's brain.

If Adams had chosen that moment to come out of the kitchen, he would have screamed. Wizeman's head, his wrinkled skin and the misshapen skull beneath it, were physically pulsing. His arms and legs shivered and shook as though a low current of electricity were being passed through his nervous system.

The old man's eyes rolled up into his head, and when they rolled back seconds later, they were no longer vacant. His limbs ceased to quiver.

Silently, he rose from his chair...

Sam read on and on, instantly familiar with all that was happening. He read on as the spirit of Sly Jack Road continued to repair Wizeman's mind and reconnect it to his body. To achieve this tricky task, it was utilising the power it had gained from the young girl's death. But it needed more, much more, to complete the process.

Sam knew that it would find some measure of that power in Wizeman's tiny kitchen, tucked away between Steve Adams's life force and his meagre soul.

...Adams had filched a large chunk of stale Edam from Wizeman's fridge and was gobbling it down as he heard the sound of the cutlery drawer opening behind him.

He turned around with the cartoonish carelessness of a man who believes he has nothing to fear, and scarcely had time to register surprise before the carving knife swept under his chin like a shining fan and his throat opened up like a fish gill.

Carried out in the enormous torrent of blood were two pieces of masticated cheese pulp, like yellow coagulates of animal fat...

Sam didn't want to read anymore, but he did because he had to, because he was powerless to stop.

He read on as Karl Wizeman made his escape from the sheltered accommodation building, and then wandered the dark streets of night-time Eldritch. The old man's mind slowly grew foggy again, but help of a sort was at hand. Two young muggers attacked him, and his murderous, inhuman instinct took over. The boys died horrible, violent deaths, and Wizeman, a necromancer, used their guts like the entrails of chickens to help divine his purpose in the plan.

There the chapter finally ended, and it was all Sam could do not to start writing again immediately. The pull was very strong. In the end he had to physically push himself away from the computer. He was shaking badly.

The process was clear to him.

Yesterday evening he'd had Smooth Harry Flanagan murder Rena White on Sly Jack Road, and now in the real world a girl was dead. Her murderer was blaming the murderous influence of Sly Jack Road on his actions. Then, sometime during the night, he had sleep-written about Karl Wizeman. Did that mean three more real people had died? And if so, what about the others, the ones still to come? Sam knew that there would be more murders, even if as yet he didn't know the precise details.

Except for one. The very next.

Among the steaming coils of the muggers' intestines, Wizeman had discovered the identity of the next person he would kill. A young prostitute, whose street-name was Fee.

Sam saw every detail of her brutal, lonely death in his mind's eye – and then uttered a harsh cry of alarm. Unconsciously, his whole body had been creeping back to the computer, his hands reaching out for the keyboard, to put into words what his mind was seeing.

Through sheer force of will he curled his fingers in until his hands were fists, his knuckles bloodless and white. Sweat poured off him. Slowly, very slowly, he allowed one finger, the right index, to spring free. Feeling as though he were lifting an immense weight, he moved that finger towards the keyboard, towards the backward delete key.

He didn't know if this made any sense or not. He didn't know if it might help in any way, somehow make time flow backwards. Death into life. He didn't know anything. He simply knew that he had to try.

His finger landed on the key with a thump and he pressed down hard.

Delete, delete, delete, delete.

The cursor blinked but did not move. Not one letter was deleted.

22

Shocked as he was by the contents of the scrapbook, Cassidy had to admit that Longman had done his homework. He may have started his collection of newspaper clippings with *The Torturer's Apprentice*, the sixth Eldritch novel, but he had carried out his research assiduously, and now also had Xerox copies of all the news items he thought were related to the plots of the earlier books.

All the clippings were about murders, or about bizarre accidents claiming one or more lives that may not have been accidents at all. There were a minimum of five clippings per book, and two of the later ones, *Okra* and *Hospital Whites*, had eleven apiece.

'While I was reading *Death in a Dream*, I started to get odd memory flashes about some of the things that were happening in the story. It was almost as though I'd read parts of the book before,' Longman explained. 'At the time I was in the process of moving into this house, and I was unpacking boxes that I'd had stored for months. I was taking glasses out of the newspapers I'd wrapped them in, and one of the reports just leapt out at me.'

Longman leaned over the table to flick through the scrapbook.

'There, that one.'

The clipping pasted onto the black sugar paper was from The *Daily Mail*. The report concerned an eighty-four-year-old woman named Deborah Price, who had murdered a young couple who were her immediate neighbours. She'd used a combination of rat poison and knitting needles. The local community was shocked, not least because Price had been a pillar of respectability, a charity shop volunteer worker and an active member of the Anglican Church. She and the couple she had murdered, the Allens, had been close. Mutual friends described the young couple as "the grandchildren Deborah never had".

'I worked out that Sam had actually been in the process of writing Death in a Dream when this happened,' Longman said. 'You see the parallels?'

'Yes,' Cassidy said. 'Dottie Percival. She fell in love with the Angel of Death when she began to see the compassion in his work. She wanted to share the knowledge with her friends, and it killed them. She worked in a charity shop, too. God, even their initials are the same. Dottie Percival, Deborah Price.'

Longman nodded. 'No wonder it jumped out at me the way it did. Out of all the reports I have, that's the real event closest to what happened in the relevant books. The rest are so abstract, you have to really know what you're looking for to see the connections.'

'And you know what to look for?'

109

'After I read the completed novel, yes. I collect a lot of clippings whenever I know Sam's writing. I look for anything strange, either the circumstances, or the method, or the absence of motive. Then I lock them away until either publication day or until Sam asks me to read a draft. With the novel as a guide, I'm able to pare the clippings down.'

Cassidy almost asked how Longman could have known all this for so long, and just sat on it. He bit his tongue just in time. He'd been sitting on his own suspicions for months and months, and he knew how fear had a way of gluing you to your seat.

'So now you know how I spend the long winter nights,' Longman said.

'Beats stamp collecting, I suppose.'

'You notice that the general trend is towards more real murders per book as the series progresses?'

Cassidy nodded.

'But at the same time, the Eldritch novels haven't become any more violent, have they. They've been fairly consistent in terms of body-count.'

'What do you make of that?'

Longman shrugged. 'I don't know that anything can be made of it, and proved. But I'll tell you what I believe. I think that the power of Eldritch's influence on real life, on the real world, has steadily been growing, book by book. With the later stories, it's been able to cross over more often, and cause more damage when it did. I think you're right. Sam's getting too good at conjuring Eldritch up.'

Cassidy turned a few scrapbook pages as he thought. Beside each clipping, Longman had written notes, cross-referencing the reports with the books, including page numbers and character lists.

'Have you considered that Sam may have been fictionalising these real life stories and incorporating them into his current plotlines?'

'Considered it and rejected it,' Longman nodded. 'Sam doesn't read the papers or watch TV until he's finished a project.'

'So he says.'

'Yes, so he says. But I believe him.'

'So do I.'

'I even considered the possibility that Sam may have committed the murders himself.'

'For the purposes of research?'

'Naturally.'

Cassidy and Longman both laughed. The idea of Sam Parker causing anyone harm, let alone killing them, was quite ridiculous. It felt good to laugh about something.

'There's another reason why I rejected both those theories,' Longman said. 'In real life, all of these murders, all these maybe-accidents that are echoed in Sam's work – none of them should ever have happened, not in a million years. Every one of them is completely nonsensical. *Here*. But in terms of Eldritch, of what Sam was writing at the time, they make perfect sense.'

Longman paused.

'So what do you say, Nigel. Am I crazy, too?'

Cassidy shook his head. 'I don't think so. God help us all, but I don't think either of us is.'

The two men stared at each other.

'What are we going to do?'

'I don't know.'

23

Sam's hands were trembling as he guided the tumbler of whisky to his lips, and some of it spilled on the sitting room carpet. He paid it no heed, just got the remaining stuff down him as quickly as he could. The fact that he had been unable to delete anything he'd written had been the final straw, and he'd given up pretending that what was happening to him had a rational explanation.

Quite apart from the backward delete key, none of his word processor's other editing tools had been able to affect the completed work. And when, panicking, he'd yanked the computer's power cable out of the wall socket, the damn thing had refused to go off until it had safely shut itself down. That was when he'd run downstairs, desperately in need of a drink.

Now on his second large drink and still feeling stone-cold sober, Sam wondered why he'd never had the foresight to get into hard drugs, like some people he'd known in the past. Right now, he felt that a good hit off a crack pipe might just have brought him down to earth again.

'I've got to do something,' he said to himself. He said it again and again, but no amount of repetition could tell him *what*.

Gradually, he calmed down, and an idea came to him. If all this is real, he thought, then nothing is coincidence. It's just like a novel. Everything has meaning. Everything is significant.

He thought of the note with the handwritten address he'd found in his jacket pocket just before DI Hyams had arrived to ask about the provenance of Sly Jack Road. Sam had suspected that it had been slipped into his pocket by an EO back at the convention, in the confusion of the hotel lobby. And maybe it had.

But what if you added the Eldritch girl into the equation?

Last night she had been going through all the coats and jackets in Sam's closet. Had she been searching for the note in order to remove it, so Sam wouldn't see it? Or, in the pitch darkness of the hallway, had she been looking for exactly the right jacket to place it in, Sam's current favourite? That was an unknown.

But perhaps the girl herself wasn't quite so much of a mystery now.

Not if you thought about Karl Wizeman, and Steve Adams's recollection of the woman he thought was Wizeman's grand-daughter. "Fur coat and no knickers", that was the way Adams remembered her. Sam found that he thought of her that way, too. If the Eldritch girl was Wizeman's grand-daughter, did that mean that it was Wizeman she had referred to when she said that 'he' must not know that she'd been in Sam's house? If so, why mustn't he?

Questions. The last twenty-four hours had all been about questions.

It was all so crazy. What was real, what was unreal. Reality, fiction. It was like a cosmic see-saw, with Sam trying to balance in the middle.

113

'Come on,' he said to himself roughly. 'What else do you know?'

He knew some things about what was going to happen in the next few chapters of *Comeback*. He knew What, Where, When, How. He didn't know shit about Why. In the back pocket of his jeans, the handwritten address felt as thick as a phonebook.

'Forget it,' Sam thought aloud. 'You're not going there.'

He knew that the next person Wizeman killed and butchered would be the young prostitute, Fee.

'You're not going,' he insisted.

He knew that Fee's horrible, agonising death wouldn't be the last.

'No way.'

He knew that he would be responsible for them all, because he had created Eldritch.

'I'm not,' he whispered into his empty glass.

He knew that the Listmaker was in the process of going completely insane.

'No.'

He knew far too many things.

The morning was golden with sunlight when he left his home some fifteen minutes later, but Sam left all the lights on. He had no idea how long he'd be out, and he didn't want to come home to darkness.

24

Charles Beckett's Highgate Village home is a large, gracious stone-built property, the arbour to the rear hung with living, fruit-bearing vine. The house, and almost all that it contains, belongs to his wife. No one who knows only his public persona would believe the change that comes over him in her presence, nor the way she so easily dominates him. Beckett thinks of himself as a man among men, but in his wife's home he is a mouse. She wears the trousers, and has long ago taken his balls. Everything about him now is just show.

Beckett's private space is his study, an attic room without windows. It is the only place in the house where Beckett can be the man he considers himself to be. His wife never intrudes upon him here, not least because she knows that even a mouse will eventually turn and fight if it has nowhere to hide.

He sits in his study now, idling at his desk. The walls of the small room are lined with shelves, with two of the longer ones devoted to out-of-date NASA technical manuals, textbooks on physics and astronomy, and scientific periodicals, mostly American. The rest of the wide shelves are entirely filled with copies of his seventeen published novels, both hardback and paperback, and the translations into French, German, Spanish, Greek, Italian, Japanese…

Surrounded by himself, he can be himself.

Up on the English language shelf, the books' spines jut out a little over the shelf's lip. Concealed behind them is Beckett's secret shame. Paperback copies of every Eldritch novel, all of which he has read more times than he can remember. He has heard the gossip about himself and the Listmaker, but that is not the reason he hates Sam Parker.

He hates Sam Parker for creating a world which touches him so deeply that his own fictional worlds have died in his imagination. He cannot write anymore. He hates Parker for not recognising that the Listmaker, Eldritch's eternal fall-guy, is the city's true, perhaps its only, hero.

Parker misunderstands everything the Listmaker does. Deliberately. He refuses to give credit for the risks the Listmaker takes, ignores completely the sad chivalry of that tarnished, injured knight. He belittles the Listmaker's struggle to be accepted, respected even, by characters no better than he. Parker mocks the Listmaker's moral disabilities, conveniently ignoring the harsh environment in which they were formed.

Beckett hears laughter from the floor beneath his chair. His wife is entertaining yet another of her young men. The laughter is loud. Perhaps they are moving upstairs now, on their way to the master bedroom which Beckett hasn't seen for so many years. He tunes out the laughter, the voices, and the images they conjure, imagining that his shelves extend over the door itself, that his room is truly sealed.

Made sexually impotent by his domineering wife, Beckett is a cuckold many times over. This is terrible. But it is a greater indignity that Sam Parker has made him creatively impotent. This is unbearable.

He comes out of his bitter thoughts, dragged out of them by the sound of his phone ringing. He notices that he holds a pen in his right hand. Spread out over his desk are pages from the notebook he'd taken along to the convention, the pages filled with the lists of names he had made afterwards. A number of names have been crossed off the lists.

The phone call is from Beckett's solicitor, who has been busy considering the civil actions Beckett has instructed him to set in motion. There are more questions he needs to ask, points that need to be clarified.

Beckett looks at his lists, and at the crossed-off names. Then he begins to speak.

Mr Clive Bolton, of Garrett, James & Palmer, Regent Street, is astonished by his client's abrupt change of attitude. He listens, mute with surprise, as Beckett explains that now he has calmed down he sees everything that happened yesterday in a more rational light. He'd been as much to blame as any other party, he is sure. Pursuing the poor people he'd been unfortunate enough to butt heads with through the court system would be both petty and foolish.

'Please do not proceed any further in these matters. I apologise for having wasted your valuable time. A cheque is in the post to compensate you for this inconvenience.'

Mr Bolton, who has gone to court on his client's behalf so many times in the past and borne his unpleasant personality, is stupefied when Beckett ends the call with a cheerful goodbye. After putting the phone down, he feels that he has to lie down in his office with the blinds drawn for a little while. For the rest of the day, perhaps.

In his study, Charles Beckett resumes crossing names off his shit-lists, one by one, until only two are left. Without intending to, he has happened upon a simpler solution to his problems. Simple, but radical.

He has decided to kill his tormentors, beginning with the closest to hand.

25

By the time Sam climbed out of the taxi, unforecast clouds had raced over the horizon and blotted out the sun, and Camden Town was grey, grey, grey. Men in T-shirts and women in halter tops folded their arms and rubbed their shoulders against the sudden chill.

Sam stood at the end of Sheridan Row, a long road north of the tube station, which combined a mix of local shops and retail outlets with private residences and small hotels. The whisky he had drunk on a nearly empty stomach churned in his guts. His head and the heavens were a perfect match, full of dark turmoil and ugly presentiments.

He slowly started walking down the left-hand pavement, scanning both sides of the street for a blue door, and failing to see one. When he reached the point where Sheridan Row was intersected by Booth Road and ended, he crossed the street and walked back along the other pavement.

There was no blue door.

The proprietor of a cheap-shop, responding instantly to the grey-yellow light the street was now cast in, rushed out with two wire baskets stuffed with a variety of umbrellas, and Sam had to walk around a small crowd of people who stopped to buy. A roll of thunder passed overhead and the low clouds began to spit rain.

Sam found an unoccupied doorway to wait out the shower. His stomach echoed the thunder, rolling noisily. He should eat something, to take the burn out of the whisky. At the other side of the road, side by side, the Eager Beaver Café and a McDonalds competed for trade. Both were packed with people who were suddenly hungry and thirsty and wanted to stay dry.

Which one? Sam wondered. Heads or tails? One-potato, two-potato, three-potato, four. Eenie-meenie-miney-mo…

A sudden flash of blue between the two premises halted his deliberations.

'Wow, lightning,' someone called, hurrying by with a newspaper held over their head.

The rain began to pour. Sam kept his eyes fixed on the narrow gap between the greasy spoon and the golden arches. There seemed to be no space, no reason, for the blue door he could now see. Sam couldn't imagine how he'd missed it earlier. It was narrow and it was low, but it was there.

Yes, he thought. *Now* it is.

A couple dashed into his doorway as if he wasn't there, roughly jostling him, but Sam didn't take his eyes off the blue door. He was afraid that if he did, it would disappear. He stepped out into the rain, shouldering his way between the couple with the same lack of politeness they had shown him. They didn't seem to notice, but carried on a conversation in absurdly deep and drawn out voices. Their hand gestures were so slow they appeared to be performing a T'ai Chi exercise.

Sam walked across the road, heedless of the traffic. Cars slowly swept by him, front and back, throwing up sheets of rainwater that took many seconds to rise and fall. As he reached the other pavement, Sam caught a movement out of the corner of his eye. In the Eager Beaver, an elbow had

119

knocked a cup from a table, and it fell in slow motion to the floor.

The blue door waited for him, shimmering and flickering as though the falling rain interfered with the transmission of its image. It had no number, no letterbox, and no handle, just the hole where one had been.

Sam had never been so afraid in his life. He wanted to run away. A single large raindrop passed before his eyes, moving at the speed of a snail. In the cafe, the cup finally hit the floor, and silently exploded. Sam reached out and pushed the blue door open.

Uneven stone steps led down into utter darkness. A complex odour came out through the doorway. It was ozone, tar, exhaust fumes, grass cuttings, cough mixture, fermenting hops, decay, dog shit, cigarette smoke, cheap alcohol, sweet cloying perfume, sweat, semen, disinfectant, and blood.

It was Eldritch.

Sam took a deep breath of the atmosphere he knew so well, and then stepped in through the doorway.

Part II
THE MIDDLE

1

The instant Sam was through the doorway, every sound from the street was shut off completely. The traffic, music from the pub on the corner, the falling rain. He could look back out and watch a silent movie, *The Summer Storm*, with people dashing for shelter. He doubted that anyone in the movie could see him. He was behind the camera now.

A long way behind.

There was one panicky moment when the impulse to bolt for it threatened to overwhelm him, but it passed quickly. Sam knew that this was something he could not run away from. He felt danger here, just as he always did when writing about Eldritch, and he tried to deal with his fear in the same way. As though, ultimately, no matter how crazy it got, he was in control. He was the author, his mind split in two. One side to cause the fear, the other to experience it.

He started down the steps into the darkness, watching it creep over his shoes and up his legs, as though he were wading into tar. Behind him the door swung gently shut and then he was engulfed. He steadied himself with a hand on either wall, feeling carefully with his feet for each step. His shoes made a muted crunching noise on stone padded with layers of unbroken dust. He began to count the steps, but as the

121

atmosphere of Eldritch grew ever thicker he lost his concentration.

The steps seemed to go on forever, and the darkness he moved through reminded him of the gloom of the staircase leading up to his attic workspace. He shivered as a subterranean chill began to seep through his light summer clothes, and his mind started to play tricks on him.

He imagined great insects scuttling across the walls just ahead of his hands, armoured carapaces and twitching antenna only millimetres from his fingertips. He imagined twin points of red, feral light blinking in the dark as he passed, and the shrouded heads of ghosts leaning out of the walls to taste his breath. He imagined he heard sounds, too. Low growls, the scrape of a knife blade against a whetstone, and the filthy dirty chuckle of a madman on heat. He heard footsteps, hiding within the sound of his own, and foreign voices slyly whispering unmentionable secrets. Eldritch sounds.

Finally, he saw the beginning of weak light.

Far below the level of his feet, the darkness had developed a milky cast, and Sam began to see shapes materialising as though through fog; uneven walls laid with hand-made bricks, worn steps of sandstone, and where they ended, a passageway of flagstones that immediately cut to the left.

When he reached the bottom of the steps and hesitantly turned the corner, Sam saw that the passageway's light came from a single, low-wattage bulb dangling from a frayed brown fabric flex. At the other end of the short passageway was another blue door. As he approached it, he saw that like its predecessor, it had neither lock nor handle, and yet Sam was reluctant to simply push this one open.

He knew that someone was on the other side of this door. Or, because this was Eldritch, *something*. And, again because this was Eldritch, whatever was inside was likely to be aggressively territorial. His city was riddled with places like this, holes in the ground where things were buried or hidden, and where evil patiently waited for nourishment like a trap-door spider waiting for prey.

Sam looked back along the passageway and saw his own footsteps in the dust, as though he'd walked through snow. He noticed that the air was now almost frigid enough to *produce* snow. His hair, previously slick with nervous sweat, had ice-crystals in it.

Are you really going to do this? he asked himself. The quick answer was yes, and he gave himself no time to reconsider.

He knocked on the door, and then stepped back as far as the narrow passageway would allow. Seconds passed, slow-slow, quick-quick-slow, and he heard nothing from behind the door. No footsteps, no verbal enquiry. He was about to knock again when the door was suddenly thrown open and a flood of light hit him. Sam jumped back with a small cry of surprise.

A man stood framed in the doorway, his eyes wide. He looked at Sam once, briefly, and then carefully checked out as much of the passageway as he could without venturing through the doorway. Only after he was sure that the passageway was otherwise empty did he turn his attention back to Sam. His gaze roamed, probed, and lingered with too

123

much freedom, as one might look at a photograph, and unconsciously, Sam replied in kind.

He saw the other man's contained terror, and a terrible apprehension that perhaps mirrored his own. He was about Sam's age, but looked older. He had a beard, and was wearing an old, heavy tweed suit with a pullover underneath, and tan leather gloves against the cold.

The man found Sam's eyes, and they stared at each other. Gradually, Sam saw the fear fade away. It was replaced by relief, and something that Sam eventually recognised as scorn.

'So it's come around at last,' the man said in a cultured, educated drone.

He stepped back from the doorway, gesturing Sam to enter.

'Come on. I've been waiting for someone like you to show up for a very long time.'

Sam edged through the doorway, careful to keep a distance between himself and his host. He found himself in a vast single room apartment, wider than it was deep. There were two lacquered Chinese screens of black and gold, and around the side of the one to his right, Sam could see the curve and the lion's paw of an old cast-iron bathtub. He couldn't see what was behind the screen to his left, but he guessed it was a narrow single bed. An enormous square rug worn down to the weave covered most of the floorboards, and a selection of awkward, lumpy-looking furniture had been placed on it, like a doll-house display. Covering a large window, hideously mottled green crushed-velvet curtains hung like decaying animal hides.

A shade of deep neglect stained everything, a smell of dust and grime, and dirt of every persuasion. If anything, it was even colder inside the apartment than outside, and Sam put his hands in his jacket pockets to warm them.

The other man nudged the door shut with the toe of his shoe and turned to face him.

'My name is Lionel Hepplewhite,' he said, and watched Sam's eyes. When no sparks flew there, no hint of recognition, he nodded to himself and walked across to the other side of the room.

'Somehow, I knew that my name would not survive. Who are you? Not that it really matters.'

'I'm Sam Parker.'

Hepplewhite glanced at him speculatively, taking in his clothes. 'What year is it now?' he asked.

Sam told him.

'Two thousand and…?' Hepplewhite said, then repeated it a number of times, amused, incredulous, dismayed. 'Then I've been here for almost seventy years.'

'You're not old enough for that,' Sam said.

'I'm a lot older than I look, believe me. Time's different here in Trinity.'

'Where?' Sam asked, startled.

'Here, this city. Trinity.'

Hepplewhite peered at Sam, and then his eyes lit up.

'Ah, you probably have a different name for it. You changed a lot of other things, so why not the name.'

Trinity, Sam thought. *Bad Blue* had been set in a district of the city named Trinity. So had *An Hour of Darkness*.

'I call it Eldritch,' he said.

'Eldritch.' Hepplewhite seemed to savour the word. 'As good a name as any, I suppose. Eldritch – magical, otherworldly, nightmarish, haunted. Yes, it's a very good name. Would you like to see it?'

Without waiting for a reply, Hepplewhite went to the covered window, trapped a drawstring between his gloved hands, and pulled. The heavy curtains swung jerkily open to reveal the night-time skyline of Eldritch, and Sam felt all the breath leave his body.

Everything was there, just as he'd always imagined it.

From the landmarks Sam could make out, Hepplewhite's apartment appeared to be on the old Dock Road, which ran along the south bank of the River Leeth. Across the turgid darkness of the wide river, Sam saw the lawless, no-go area of the derelict northern docklands, like a black hole in the heart of the city, and above it the towering gothic architecture of its buildings, their shapes defined by their lighted windows. Eldritch is a place where the lights are always left on, because monsters, like cockroaches, grow bolder in the dark. In the distance beyond the immediate city, the floodlit dome of St Jude's Cathedral seemed to float in the air like a helium balloon.

Every part of Sam's body was tingling, and his eyesight was grey around the edges. He wanted to sit down before his legs gave out, but he didn't dare show any weakness now. Hepplewhite looked harmless enough, but that was precisely the same opinion Drunk Dave Hawkins' late partner, Bernie Alder, had formed of a young porter he'd found hiding in a morgue in *Hospital Whites*. And Bernie had ended up holding in his guts with both hands, Sam recalled.

Without Sam noticing, Hepplewhite had quietly come back towards him, and such was Sam's agitation that when he did notice, he recoiled dramatically. And he did a very bizarre thing. He straightened two fingers in his jacket pocket and pointed them at Hepplewhite like a pistol.

It was the sort of thing that he had seen in a dozen stupid movies, and spoofed as many times, and no one who had ever seen it done found the bluff even faintly believable. Yet he could see that Hepplewhite *did* believe it. And Sam did, too. In fact, he could *feel* the gun in his hand, a revolver, its thick rubber handgrips and the cold lethal weight of its barrel.

I thought it into being, he realised. This is Eldritch.

Hepplewhite took a couple of steps back, eyeing the protuberance in Sam's jacket pocket with wariness. But also with a glint of amusement.

'You know,' he said, 'Raymond Chandler once wrote that guns never did any good, that they were just a fast curtain to a bad second act.' He chuckled a little before he saw that Sam wasn't smiling. 'Well, *I* thought it was funny. Have you heard of Chandler? Do people still read him in the new millennium?'

'Yes,' Sam managed to say. 'His books are considered to be classics of their type.'

127

Hepplewhite nodded. 'That's the kind of immortality I wanted for myself,' he said. He glanced around at the diseased apartment. 'Not this.' He turned to the window, and Eldritch. 'And certainly not that.'

'You're a writer,' Sam said. It wasn't really a question. He knew. His fingers were just fingers again. He took his hands out of his pockets to rub away a numbness they had developed.

Hepplewhite turned back to him. 'Yes, I *was* a writer – once upon a time, you might say. I don't write anymore. It's too dangerous.'

He looked Sam up and down.

'From the look of you, I would have thought you'd learned that by now.'

Sam looked at the Chinese screen to his left. He knew what was behind there now, and it wasn't a bed. He went towards it.

Behind the screen, a single shelf graced the dingy wall. On it were five ancient hardback books, so dusty the titles on their spines could not be read, and seven manuscripts barely held together by withered rubber bands. The desk below the shelf was heavy and ornate, with many drawers. Centred on its leathered surface was an old typewriter, and to its right was a three quarter-inch pile of yellowed foolscap that probably represented about one half of a novel, facedown. Everything was covered in a layer of dust nearly as thick as that covering the flagstones in the passageway outside. It looked like grey fur.

Sam saw Hepplewhite's face appear around the other side of the screen. He didn't look at Sam, just at the unfinished manuscript, fearfully, as though it were

128

a dark idol at which it would be unwise to stare too long.

Sam reached through the layers of dust and turned the manuscript over. Dust swarmed around his head like a cloud of gnats.

The title page said:

THE HOMECOMING
by
Lionel Hepplewhite

Sweating despite the deep chill of the apartment, Sam turned over the title page. With his eyes stinging, breathing through his mouth to stop himself sneezing, he squinted at the blocks of fading type while blood rushed to his head.

Although he was in no state to read properly, Sam scanned the text closely enough to realise that the differences between this and the first chapter of *Comeback* were only cosmetic. The first four pages of *The Homecoming* concerned an older man killing a young woman in a car parked in a secluded country lane shortly after midnight.

The car was a black Model-T Ford, not a Honda Accord. The cigarette the man lit for his conquest was an unfiltered Gold Flake, not a sleek kingsize Benson & Hedges. The girl was a chorus girl, not a schoolgirl. The country lane was not named at all as far as Sam could see, but the man who would shortly become a murderer was called Sly Jack McFadden.

Sly Jack Road.

Sam turned to Hepplewhite. 'You've got to help me,' he said.

'If I could help anyone,' Hepplewhite calmly replied, 'do you think I'd still be here myself?'

2

DI Duncan Hyams bursts out through the door of the CID general office, nearly knocking a WPC off her feet, and goes tearing down the long, blue-carpeted corridor towards the stairs. His arms are pumping as he sprints. People have to be swift to avoid him, and not all of them are. Hyams does not waste breath on apologies.

Behind him, he has left the receiver of a telephone twisting in the air and knocking against the leg of his modular desk. There is no longer a voice at the other end of the line. The officer Hyams has spoken to is now calling for an ambulance on another line, and his voice is still hysterical and uneven.

Hyams hurtles down the concrete steps like a rubber ball, bouncing from wall to wall, the shoulders of his formerly impeccable black suit jacket streaked grey with concrete dust. Each floor has two flights of stairs. He descends two, four, six, eight flights, then careers out through the door at the bottom and almost slips, setting a water cooler rocking. He is running again even before he has recovered his balance.

His long stride swallows a hundred yards of empty corridor and he's through into the charge room. The same two PCs that were on duty the night of DS Allison's arrest are on duty now, and they turn to follow Hyams as he passes, their faces white, their eyes huge and frightened.

Someone, a drunk from the thickness of his voice, in one of the first two cells is screaming, demanding to be told what is happening. No one is listening to him. At the end of the corridor connecting the cells is a knot of shocked uniformed officers who cannot move away from the doorway of cell five or the spectacle of what waits for Hyams inside. One of them, possibly more than one, has vomited in the corridor, and the air is sweet and foul.

Hyams roughly pulls the knot apart, pushing the blue uniforms away, and then stands in the doorway alone. The tracksuit DS Bob Allison has worn since his clothes were finally collected for analysis is balled up on the cot. Allison himself lies on the cold concrete floor, naked and dead.

Despite the fact that he has been subjected to a full body-search that included his orifices, despite the fact that he has refused all visitors, refused even the services of a solicitor, Allison has somehow acquired a knife with a wicked four-inch blade. It rests loosely on his palm, his still, stiff fingers splayed around the handle like the bars of a cage. The blood on his hand is like a thick glove.

Allison has used the knife to slit open his belly, castrate himself, and strip away most of his face.

Hyams blinks once at the sight of crazed suicide. Some might see this as justice, he realises, considering what Allison did to the young girl. She has been identified as one Rebecca Walton, a sixth-form schoolgirl with a minor reputation for dubious relationships with older men, and Hyams knows that her parents will view Allison's terrible death as just revenge. But his own oddly calm thoughts run to cats' paws, and patsies, and tiny wheels in larger mechanisms.

Blood is still drooling from the dead body, slowly oozing to cover nearly every inch of the cell's concrete floor. As it approaches Hyams's well-polished shoes, he does not step back. He hears the wail of an ambulance siren as it approaches the station, and he wonders why they bothered to send for one. One look is enough to convince that Allison is beyond all help now.

Hyams studies the erased face, the burst look of the abdomen, and the gobbet of genitalia adrift from the body and surrounded by blood, like a bizarre delicacy framed in a raspberry coulis. The blood has completely surrounded his shoes now. The handle of Allison's knife is old yellow bone, carved in the shape of the symbol for infinity.

Yes, Hyams thinks, without knowing why.

3

A light began to grow behind the dome of St Jude's, as though the floodlights that illuminated the cathedral were being turned away to face the sky. It became a vast corona of thin, lemony light that for a moment overcame the stars and the clouds, and then shot across the sky and over the horizon in a great, soundless pulse.

Sam, watching this display from an armchair, asked, 'What the hell was that?'

In the other armchair, Hepplewhite turned back from the window to reply.

'A local phenomenon. They call it The Light of Souls. It happens, I think, whenever someone dies for Trinity. Someone from the real world, that is.' He offered Sam a small, mocking bow of his head. 'I'm sorry – when they die for *Eldritch*.'

Hepplewhite watched Sam's face as he took this in.

'You're surprised you didn't know that, aren't you? Don't be. There are lots of things you don't know, Sam Parker. You couldn't be expected to get everything right. I certainly didn't.'

Sam, who was now beginning to doubt that he had ever really known anything in his whole life, said, 'Enlighten me. Please.'

Hepplewhite looked down at his hands, sheathed in the tan leather gloves. They were stiff and unmoving, fingers slightly curved, as though Hepplewhite suffered from crippling arthritis, as well he might living in conditions like these for seventy years.

When he finally spoke, his mind seemed to have doubled back on itself and flitted to another subject altogether.

'I actually *knew* Raymond Chandler, you know,' he said. 'We were at Dulwich College together for a while, and remained friends until his mother took him back to America.'

He nodded at Sam's surprise.

'Yes, it's true. We got on well enough to realise that we had a lot in common, so it isn't so surprising that we started producing the same sort of work, even though we were on different sides of the Atlantic. Do you know what the crime writers of our time used to say? They used to say that crime doesn't pay – *enough*. That didn't matter to us, Chandler or I. Each of us wanted to finish what Dashiell Hammett had started. Each in our own way, we wanted to put the dirty truth back into crime. We wanted to take that

133

Christie cunt down a blind alley and beat the crap out of her.'

Hepplewhite suddenly laughed at himself, startling Sam. Just as suddenly, he became serious again.

'I had three fairly straight crime novels published. They were very dark, and a little strange. They didn't sell very well in Britain, but the publisher Alfred Knopf had some success with them in America. That success got me a contract for another two, which my British publishers reluctantly honoured. After that nobody wanted to publish anything of mine, not even in the United States, because the books had become far too strange for public consumption.'

'What do you mean? How were they strange?'

'They were full of monsters, and graphic, gruesome deaths. It was beyond my control. They came out as they came out. I tried to put a stop to the worst excesses, but it was as though I were possessed. And I was definitely addicted to my city. Does this sound familiar to you?'

Sam didn't respond. He was rigid.

'I completed twelve Trinity novels in all,' Hepplewhite continued. 'Seven of them unpublished manuscripts, as you've seen. By that time, my wife and I were living on favours from friends. We had no money, and my wife had threatened to leave me on more than one occasion.

'But then, having gone from one Trinity novel to the next for years, I suddenly stopped writing. It seemed that I'd finally got the place out of my system. After a while, I wrote a very light-hearted crime story, something in tone like Hammett's *The Thin Man*, and it made a lot of money. Warner Brothers bought the rights, but I can't tell you if they ever made the movie. I can't even remember the title now. The point is, my wife thought I'd turned the corner, and so did I. Everyone did. But then the urge came on me, a pulling sensation more relentless than it had ever been before. Trinity called me, and I thought I could go there again, and be safe.'

Hepplewhite shook his head at Sam. The smile on his lips looked as though it tasted rancid.

'That's what it *wanted* me to believe, of course. It let me write my little piece of escapism, because if I believed that I could stop writing about Trinity at any time, if I believed that I had some control, then I wouldn't be so afraid to start the thirteenth novel. It worked.'

Sam thought of *Deep Water*. Is that all it had been, a strategic pause? The illusion of freedom? And like Hepplewhite before him, hadn't there been a part of Sam that had thought, see, I gave the city up once, I can do it again?

'Was it the city that called you?' Sam asked. 'The *whole* city, as though it were a single, huge character?'

'No,' Hepplewhite sighed. 'In a sense, I think it was another writer – the author of all the evil in Trinity, a dark force that predated my poor chronicles. It was gathering all its strength.'

'Gathering its strength for what?' Sam asked, the hair on the back of his neck rising.

'Well, to come back, of course. To be resurrected, to walk in the flesh again. That's what

135

The Homecoming was to be about. I presume that your latest has the same subject at its heart.' Hepplewhite sighed again. 'It's a good story. But we both know, you and I, that it isn't the *whole* story. This dark force won't be content just to come back as fiction. It wants to be real.'

Sam swallowed nervously. *Comeback*. It wasn't just a matter of Eldritch infringing on the real world. It was the whole thrust of the plot. It was the crime boss coming back from the dead – for real.

'It couldn't happen,' he said.

Hepplewhite nodded at the window and its view of Eldritch. 'Don't confuse *couldn't* with *shouldn't*. That's one of the mistakes I made. I believed that I could go to Trinity, but Trinity couldn't come to me. I was wrong, and someone very dear to me paid for my mistake. For *all* my mistakes.'

His voice became very low, the tone of confession, and he would no longer meet Sam's eyes.

'I don't know about you,' he said, 'but when I was working on a book, it took over my life. I poured all my time and energy into the writing. Even when I wasn't getting it down on paper I was composing it in my mind. There was no space in my head for anything else. I didn't read the newspapers, I didn't listen to the wireless. I never left the house except for a long solitary walk first thing in the morning, and I barely spoke to my wife.'

Sam was nodding his head. Of course he understood.

'Well, my wife came to me one day a few weeks after I started *The Homecoming*, and she made me listen to her, although she eventually had to smash the

136

study window to get my full attention. She told me that I was killing people. She told me that my fiction was forcing itself on reality. Of course, I laughed in her face.

'She went away for a moment, and when she came back she had a photograph album. It was full of newspaper clippings, reports of people being killed, and horridly murdered. She'd written one of the titles of my Trinity novels at the top of each one. She made me read the clippings, and forced me to make the connections that lurked under the surface differences. Eventually, I was unable to deny the similarities between fact and fiction, although I badly wanted to.

'She'd suspected for years, she said, but there had never been quite enough of a consistent pattern to make her believe in her suspicions. *The Homecoming* changed all that. Every gruesome death in the thirteenth book had its *exact* parallel in the real world. Without taking her eyes from mine, she quoted my own work back at me, the text of *The Homecoming*, and then showed me the newest newspaper stories. They were almost one and the same.'

Hepplewhite first closed his eyes, and then shielded them from Sam with one of his stiff hands. His leather glove looked dry and ready to crack along the seam.

'A terrible anger rose up in me. I thought I was angry because my wife had read my work behind my back, sneaking into my study while I was asleep. But really it was because if she was right, I would have to stop writing. And I didn't want to do that. So I hit her. I'd never hurt her before, never once struck her, but that day I beat her until she couldn't move. Then, while she was still lying on my study floor, unable to move and sobbing in pain, I calmly sat down and carried on with my work.'

'She left you?' Sam asked quietly.

'No. I wish she had, I wish to God she had. Are you married, Mr Parker?

Sam shook his head.

'Count yourself lucky. You can never lose what you've never had. My wife, she… ah, you must never underestimate the strength and foolishness of a woman motivated by love. She made no threats over my abuse of her, saw no doctor for the injuries I'd inflicted, called in no bobbies to caution me. She just went about the business of recovering – recovering and planning.'

'Planning?'

'To save me. Exactly a week after I'd beaten her, she put her plan into operation. She drugged my food with her sleeping tablets, then dragged my unconscious body down to the cellar and locked me in. She imprisoned me, with food and water, but nothing which I could use to write. I raved at her, of course, to let me out, to let me go back to my book. I was an addict, words were my opium. She tried to burn the existing manuscript of *The Homecoming*, but she couldn't. I remember the horror in her voice when she told me she couldn't burn it, no matter how she tried. The paper *wouldn't* burn, because I didn't *want* it to. That's how far it had gone for me.'

Hepplewhite's hand dropped like a stone into his lap, and he relapsed into a deep silence. He stared at the damp plaster of the ceiling, ruminating, as though Sam wasn't there. He was in a musty cellar some

138

seventy years ago, with his wife crying at the other side of a locked door, saying, 'It won't burn, Lionel, why won't it *burn*?' Sam could see the memories passing behind his eyes like a drowning man caught in the undertow beneath a lake of ice.

'What happened?' he asked.

'The Golem came and killed her,' Hepplewhite replied simply.

He didn't see the expression on Sam's face as he made another connection between their separate works.

'He'd killed earlier in the book, of course, but he killed my wife, too. Just so that I could go on writing. He could have simply unlocked the cellar door, but no, he had to kill because that was his nature. That was the character I gave him. He isn't human.'

'His boss knew that, too,' Sam said quietly.

He saw his own version of the same character in his mind's eye, Karl Wizeman, and saw too his terrifying, bloody career, and his blind obedience to the dead master who had set him in motion. Hepplewhite's name was the right one. Sam could see Wizeman going on and on, like a robot or automaton, remorseless and remorselessly driven. He was the Golem.

Hepplewhite's eyes glittered, bitterness and anger amidst the unshed tears.

'His boss, yes, that's what it's all about.'

Yes, Sam thought, this is what I'm here for.

He had yet to reach the point in *Comeback* where details about Eldritch's worst crime boss were revealed, and consequently, he knew almost nothing about him. He didn't want to wait until he had written this human monster, quite possibly in his sleep, to find out how truly awful he had been. And, at least according to Hepplewhite, hoped to be again.

'How did he die?' he asked.

'I don't know,' Hepplewhite admitted.

He sounded tired now, and a little petulant.

'I didn't get that far in my book, thank God. But I know that he wasn't killed as much as he was *destroyed*. You can't kill what was never really alive in the first place. Apart from that I know very little about him. No one ever did. He never had a name, not even an alias. His allies, his thugs, his women, just called him 'Boss'. That's the most of what I know. Whatever destroyed him happened a long time before I came to this city. It was even before Lennie the Lush's time, and as I wrote it, he'd been here forever. Maybe that was something else I got wrong.'

'Who's Lennie the Lush?' Sam asked.

'Lennie was my detective. Leonard Brandt.' For a moment, Hepplewhite's ancient eyes shone with remembered pleasure. 'Old Lennie, he was a card. The best and the worst detective in Trinity. He never cared for the law too much. Only two things really concerned him – justice and the juice.'

He glanced up at Sam curiously.

'What's your detective called?'

'David Hawkins,' Sam said, and after a pause, added, 'Drunk Dave.'

Unwillingly, the two writers grinned at each other.

'Drunk Dave, I like that,' Hepplewhite said.

'Before he got his promotion and came to work in Eldritch, he was hooked on a brand of sherry called Monte Cristo. His colleagues in his hometown used to call him the Count.'

Hepplewhite smiled.

'Our characters are our children. No matter what they do, we can't help loving them.'

The smile soured.

'Even if they are evil.'

Sam got up and walked to the window. Hepplewhite was right, time was different here. As he'd stepped out of Sheridan Row it had been lunchtime. Here in Eldritch, dawn was just beginning, advancing even as he watched. After a minute or two, it looked as though a distant part of the city was on fire.

As Eldritch began to redeem itself from the night in shades of grey, Sam saw that the normally choppy waters of the Leeth looked completely still, like a photograph. For a moment he was puzzled, but then he realised that the river was actually *frozen*. It was deep winter. He'd started *Comeback* in the wrong season.

No wonder it's so cold here, he thought. Damn it.

But Sam's initial irritation over this mistake was short-lived. For one thing, as Hepplewhite had said, he couldn't be expected to get everything right. For another, at least it wasn't a mistake on the scale of allowing a wife to be murdered. And it didn't matter anyway. Untroubled by atmospherics, heat-wave or freeze-down, Eldritch remained itself. Its stories were timeless. Now it turned out that they were seasonless, too.

141

'I still can't believe it,' he wondered aloud. 'I created all this.'

'You didn't create it,' Hepplewhite said sharply. 'Do you think you're God? This was always here, in one form or another. You and I, we just shaped it, with our natural talent and our craft. At other times it was other things, other places, no doubt. Perhaps it was Huxley's *Brave New World*. Perhaps it was Coleridge's *Xanadu*.'

'Maybe it was Castle Rock,' Sam muttered under his breath.

'What did you say?'

'Nothing.'

Sam turned back to Hepplewhite, trying not to shiver from the cold.

'Why didn't the Golem's boss − his spirit, whatever you want to call it − why didn't he make it back? What stopped him?'

'I believe there were two reasons,' Hepplewhite said. 'The first being that it did not understand even the *concept* of love, let alone its reality. My wife's murder ended my addiction to Trinity, instantly. I wanted nothing more to do with it. But I still didn't trust myself. I had been writing in blackouts before my wife put me in the cellar, why would anything change?'

Sam uneasily thought of himself, writing in his sleep.

'The power that controlled me − or more properly put, worked *through* me − failed to understand the effect of her death on my mind. I became unhinged, although not in the way the power would most have liked.'

Sam returned to his chair. Even during the few moments he had been away the seat had grown cold again. When Hepplewhite spoke, his breath was visible.

'After I found the cellar door unlocked and discovered my wife's body in the kitchen – I knew it was my wife's body, but only because it wore her wedding ring. Her face was...'

Hepplewhite shook his head a little, as though that might dislodge the image from his memory.

'Afterwards, I went for a walk. It was my usual morning constitutional, perfectly in keeping with my habits while writing. Except that day, I walked farther than usual, and eventually found my way to a local engineering firm, telling myself that I was conducting research for a new chapter in my novel. I bribed my way into the metal shop, and looked for the ugliest, most lethal machine they had. It was a kind of automated guillotine for cutting sheet steel. When I had watched it long enough to time its mechanism, I stepped forward before anyone could stop me, and I put my hands into it.'

Sam's eyes went to Hepplewhite's leather-gloved hands. As a demonstration, Hepplewhite knocked one against the other. The sound they made was of a cricket ball rebounding from a willow bat.

'I woke up, if that is the correct term, here, and I've been here ever since. I'd come too far to get back, you see, and I was trapped in this halfway house, this limbo, suspended between two worlds and part of neither. I wouldn't write. I couldn't type anymore, even if I wanted to. So the power abandoned me here, and moved on to begin again. I can't imagine how many false starts it must have made before it found you.'

Sam was finding it difficult to take his eyes from Hepplewhite's false hands, but his brain was still working. Just.

'You said there were *two* reasons the power failed. You've given me one…'

Hepplewhite nodded. 'It's obvious, really. In a sense, the power is vampiric. You'll already have realised that, of course.'

Sam hadn't, and found the idea appalling.

'The deaths in my books, and in yours too, I suspect, are its dead dreams. When they break through into the real world, they fortify it in the pit. And the more people know of its world, expressed as fiction, the stronger it becomes, feeding off their attention and energy.'

Hepplewhite shrugged.

'As very few people read a word about Trinity after the first five books were published, the power wasn't strong enough. It's that simple. But if I had been *more* popular, if the books had been *more* successful, I don't think that anyone could have stopped it.

'Now, if the reading public of the twenty-first century have a taste for real horror, then…'

Hepplewhite looked up at Sam suddenly, and Sam's expression told him everything he needed to know about the taste of the modern reading public.

In a hollow voice, Sam told him that he had sold over forty million Eldritch novels worldwide.

Hepplewhite looked out through his window at the city, dawn light now revealing the perpetual smog in a palette of chemical colours.

'Dear God,' he said.

4

DS Morley stood at the back of the small office Duncan Hyams had commandeered, and watched his DI with real concern. He and Hyams had never gelled, and Morley had never glimpsed the warmth and camaraderie that Honest Bob Allison claimed to have discovered underneath the cool and rigid exterior. But he saw now in the naked display of anger and outrage something that simultaneously both pleased and worried him.

What pleased him was the emotion, the sheer visibility of it. What worried him was the rage, so huge, it was as though Hyams had gone through an entire personality change. For the last thirty minutes, Hyams had tyrannised the four constables who were present in the charge room when Allison's body was discovered, hammering them with question after question.

When was Allison last checked on? Who was the last to see him alive? Who conducted his body search? Was the cell searched at the same time? Had there been any visitors not listed on the log-sheet?

The knife itself was a curiosity. Strange. A four-inch blade of discoloured steel, grey except for its cutting edge which was a gleaming silver strip. It had a heavy, carved handle of what looked like bone, fashioned into the shape, Morley thought, of an elongated figure eight. Morley also suspected that the bone the handle was made of was human bone, but he kept that suspicion to himself. Hyams had placed it in an evidence bag on the desk before him. His hands wouldn't leave it alone, although Morley had seen him trying to make them.

Hyams asked the constables once again, didn't anyone hear or see anything suspicious?

No, no, no, and no.

Hyams stared at PC Tony Gibbon for a long while, until the other man could no longer meet his eyes. Then he told Gibbon to stay put and the rest to get out. Morley realised that he had been included in that order, but he stood firm, leaning back against a filing cabinet. An experienced policeman, he could feel waves of antagonism and violence radiating from his DI. Gibbon wasn't his favourite person either, being both lazy and incompetent, but if Hyams's self-control broke, Morley intended to put himself between them.

He was surprised to realise that he was prepared to do this for Hyams's sake, and not Gibbon's.

Now it was just the three of them. Hyams leant across the desk, his hands scrunching the evidence bag around the knife so tightly Morley thought that it might slice through the plastic.

'What did you see?' Hyams demanded of Gibbon. 'What did you hear?'

Eventually, after considering his boots for a time, Gibbon admitted that he thought he had heard voices coming from cell number five.

'Voices? You mean a conversation?'

'Yes.'

'When he was supposed to be alone?'

'Yes.'

'And you didn't think to investigate?'

Gibbon's face and neck were almost purple with shame and embarrassment.

'Well?' Hyams shouted.

'He was barmy, wasn't he?' Gibbon said, looking at Morley for support. 'I thought he was talking to himself. That's what barmy people do.'

Hyams thrust himself up out of his chair and started around the desk, but Morley was faster. He reached Gibbon two paces ahead of Hyams and shielded him. The DI had the plastic-wrapped knife in his hand, and Gibbon was staring at it, bug-eyed with fear. Morley, forcing himself to appear calm, waited until Hyams seemed to have a grip of himself again, then he told Gibbon to go back downstairs and make out a report. Gibbon was gone so fast he may as well have teleported.

When they were alone, Morley sat down in the chair Gibbon had just vacated, and eventually, responding to the calm, Hyams sat back down, too. He put the knife, the evidence, into his jacket pocket, and Morley let him do it.

'Gibbon isn't worth it,' Morley told Hyams.

Hyams nodded once, then a second time more definitely. He thanked Morley for stepping in when he did. Morley told him not to mention it, and Hyams said, okay, he wouldn't.

It was the first time Morley had felt close to his DI.

5

When Sam came out through the blue door and stepped back into Sheridan Row, back into the real world, the afternoon had gone. It was night, and the pavements were puddled with rainwater. The carbon monoxide spewing from the rush-hour car exhausts, the garbage piled on the streets awaiting collection in the morning, it all smelled like fresh air. He walked a few steps before he felt his legs start to give, and he had to clutch at a lamp-post for support. At the same time, his stomach and chest tightened up like a clenched fist.

This is what happens when you move too rapidly from one atmosphere to another, he thought. Like the bends.

Lionel Hepplewhite's last words to him echoed around inside his skull. As he'd hurried to the door, too spooked to stay any longer, the man had raised his false hands and said, 'Don't leave it too late, like I did – kill yourself soon, while you still can.'

Sam had run away from Hepplewhite's voice, but it seemed to have followed him, and it was many moments before he could stand unaided once more. He watched the passing cars and wondered if he had the strength of will to throw himself in front of one, to sacrifice himself the way Hepplewhite had sacrificed his hands. The justifications for not doing it instantly leapt out on him:

You don't know that your situation is as bad as his was, he thought, or even if it's the *same*. You don't know that he was telling the truth. You don't know that your death would stop it. You don't know that you couldn't live and win.

148

Sam moved closer to the curb, but only to hail a taxi.

The journey home seemed to take hours, and it drained whatever remained of Sam's strength. On more than one occasion he was jerked awake by potholes in the road, or by the cabbie, who tended to be heavy on the brakes. He felt as though he had just competed in a marathon, although he guessed that the sheer intensity of his fatigue was more mental than physical.

His mind wanted to shut off and grab some downtime, work out how to negotiate the stark impossibilities it had been forced to accept as truth and then reboot. By the time the taxi dropped him off, it was all Sam could do to stay on his feet, and he hobbled to his front door like an old man.

After letting himself into his house, extremely grateful that he had left all the lights on, he carefully locked the door behind him. He was incredibly thirsty, dehydrated, but he didn't once think of heading for the kitchen and the chilled drinks in his refrigerator. There was only one place for him now, and there was no time to delay. He was so tired he was nauseous, and he started up the stairs with the mind-set of a mountaineer focussing on the most demanding part of his ascent.

As Sam finally collapsed onto his bed, one of the very last conscious thoughts that went through his mind before sleep snatched him away was that up in his attic office his computer had registered his presence, and was powering itself up.

While he slept, the half of his mind that scared the other half would interface with his word-processing program, and the plot of *Comeback* would continue to unfold, claiming real lives and building a bridge between this world and Eldritch.

He would have dreams that he now knew were not entirely his own, dreams from a dead place where a spirit of terrible patience and cunning had waited through twelve novels and fifteen years to bring him to this point. Those dreams would become fiction, which would in turn become reality. Or some strange hybrid of the two that was infinitely worse.

Had he had time to form a real opinion of this whole idea, Sam would not have considered it a good thought to go to sleep on.

But sleep he did.

And he did dream.

6

...a quarter of a mile from Eldritch's neon strip is Queen's Point railway station, huge, dark, and haunted, like a cathedral without windows. Travellers pass in and out through the great lobby doors, peddlers squat on blankets displaying their counterfeit wares, and touts fan the ink dry on bootleg theatre tickets to the best shows in Tyburn Square.

There is no moon tonight, or if there is, both it and the stars are hidden by a leviathan cloud bank. The lights of the galaxy are nullified. If there was no electricity, there would be no city. Just a jungle full of hungry animals.

The network of streets and alleyways behind Queen's Point are just such a jungle. The streetlamps are few, the roads narrow, the pavements mean, the shadows tangible as creeping vine. When cars crawl along the curbs, the girls use the headlights to show themselves to better advantage. They even smile, although their faces are of least concern to most of the hunters.

One girl, however, does not smile. She does not pose. She only walks impatiently to and fro, and the light, such as it is, does not touch her...

Every district has a red light area. It had been quite some time since Fee had seen one, though. Close up, that is, working it. Through various contacts and a very special arrangement, she hadn't had to work the streets for a long while, and she had never believed that she could miss it. But there had to be some reason for her being here now. Some reason.

Maybe she missed the danger of being a working girl. Being hurt by clients, hit on by wannabe pimps, attacked by other girls if they felt that she'd wandered onto their patch...

No. Some other reason then?

She didn't know. The world was a fog, slipping and sliding as it had years before when she had been flirting with the needle, but she was sure she was straight. It was one of the few things she *was* sure of.

Fee walked slowly in the shadow of Kings Cross station, carefully sizing up her competition. She was still one of the best looking girls around, if no longer the youngest, and the last eight or so months of easy living had given her a lustre the others had lost. She saw one or two girls she half knew and tried to make eye-contact with them, but they froze her out. Maybe they resented the way she'd dropped out, or maybe they were envious of the polish she had regained. Whatever, they were pretending not to see her.

Punters came and went. She watched them. They picked up girls and brought them back only a short while later, handjobs for sure. They picked them up and didn't reappear, although the girls eventually did, usually chewing fresh sticks of gum. They haggled too hard on price and didn't pick anyone up at all. They were rejected by girls who valued their safety and were prepared to lose money for it. Two or more men in a car were a definite no-no. So was a man in a transit van with the windows blacked out.

Other, less definable objections raised themselves as Fee waited her turn. The empty look in a man's eyes, the shallowness of his quick insincere smile. The greedy avidity of the woman who wanted to watch. Lots of no-nos. But everyone got picked up at some point. Everyone except Fee. During the course of an hour, no one had approached her, no one had even eyed her up, and she knew she was worth that much attention, at least.

What is it, she wondered. Am I dressed too well? Have I lost the look, the expression, the walk of a woman who can be had for a price? Don't I look as though I would satisfy, as though I'm prepared to spread my legs or turn my back or open my mouth? Or…

Fee suddenly turned to the plate glass window of a closed pharmacy and found that she cast no reflection on its dark surface. She could see the buildings behind her, and the passing cars. The pavement where she stood was lit by one of the few streetlamps, but Fee was not illuminated. She was invisible.

'Fee.'

She whirled about.

He stood a dozen paces away, waiting for her. She was so pleased to be seen, to feel real again, that she didn't wonder that while he knew her name, she didn't recognise him at all. He was an old man in a hat and an overcoat. The hat brim cast a deep shadow over his face. His back was bowed.

Who cares what he looks like, she thought. Who cares how old he is? He *sees* me, he *wants* me. He probably won't be able to get it up, anyway. He'll want to squeeze me and stroke me and dip his gnarled old fingers. He'll want to watch me touch myself... Or perhaps like one old regular she'd had when she was only young and just started, he'd want to smell her, nothing more. Gently pressing his face into her hair and her breasts and her bush, inhaling.

That would be sweet right now, she thought. Almost like affection.

Fee watched him approach her, breathing heavily, and she brazenly told him her price. She was surprised to hear the figure her voice named, the extent to which she had subconsciously devalued herself out of desperation.

He nodded, and clamped a hand on her arm. His grip was harsh, but she did not struggle. She could see his face now, and in some way she *did* recognise it, like a dream from the womb. No one had a face like that, no one human, and yet she was not shocked, she was not revolted. Nor was she afraid.

153

This was, she realised, exactly what she had been expecting.

'Your work is done now,' the Golem told her kindly. 'It is time for me to send you home, little orphan.'

Fee nodded.

'It will hurt, very badly,' he said, tightening his grip on her arm even more. 'But in the end, the peace will be so very sweet.'

She nodded again.

He glanced around, at an alleyway, at the arches, anywhere it might be done in privacy. 'Where do we go?'

'There's a hotel not far from here. I've used it before.' Fee was crying, and didn't know it. 'They rent rooms by the hour.'

'It won't take an hour,' the Golem promised. 'Is it safe there? Is it quiet?'

'No,' Fee said. 'But nobody cares.'

7

Nigel Cassidy lay asleep in Longman's guest bedroom with the bedside lamp on. Cassidy never slept in complete darkness – one of his little quirks, of which there were many. He was on top of the covers, fully dressed as always when circumstances forced him to sleep anywhere other than his own home. The only things he had removed were his shoes and his glasses, both of which he had left within easy reach in the circle of light beneath the lamp. His off-white socks had numerous holes in them, and his pale face looked featureless without the heavy black-framed glasses.

He shifted in his sleep and moaned a little as the bedroom door cracked open, but he did not wake. In the build-up to confessing his fears to Longman, sleep had been scarce.

Longman, also still dressed, quietly stepped into the room and looked at his friend.

Cassidy looked vulnerable, even more so than when he was awake, and for the first time in a long while, Longman realised that he actually felt vulnerable himself. He felt as though he were stepping into the light after hiding behind a persona for so many years – a charmingly glib mask for which nothing was serious, disturbing or demanding. It wasn't that the persona was false, exactly, it just didn't cover all the things he was. He had created it like any other character, but for a far different adventure than the one which beckoned him now. Longman didn't know whether to bask in the light or run away from it.

Actually, he *did* know. It was simply a decision he knew he was going to find hard to live with.

Cassidy moaned again when Longman gently sat down beside him, and when Longman touched his arm he jumped instantly awake, rearing away like a scalded cat. Unfortunately, without his glasses he could hardly see at all, and he thrashed his fists about ineffectually until Longman spoke.

'Nigel, calm down, it's just me.'

Cassidy stopped swinging, but kept his arms defensively raised.

'What is it, what's happening?'

Longman pressed Cassidy's glasses into his hands, and Cassidy snatched them away and jammed them on his face.

'Take it easy, for Christ's sake,' Longman said. 'Nothing's wrong – and I'm not trying to grab your skinny white arse, okay?'

'Never thought you were,' Cassidy huffed. 'I think I was dreaming something bad. I'm glad you woke me up.'

Some of the tension left his shoulders and he dropped his arms. Longman waited for him to come fully awake.

'So what did you want at this time of night?'

'Time of the night? It isn't even midnight yet.'

'Oh, isn't it?' Cassidy asked, scratching his head. 'What time is it, then?'

Longman looked at Cassidy's scuffed shoes on the bedside table and realised that the clock had disappeared. Cassidy had dumped it elsewhere in the house. He didn't want it next to him while he slept, probably for the same reason he didn't wear a wristwatch. Longman knew Cassidy believed that timepieces had an adverse affect on the body's metabolism, speeding it up over the years until the wearer's life cycle became that of a mayfly. He actually believed that this was most people's real cause of death.

Cassidy's short story based on the same theme, *Bodiclok*, had won awards. In any other walk of life, Longman thought, it would have won him a reservation for a deluxe rubber room.

'It's eleven-thirty-something,' Longman said, 'and while you've been curled up asleep, I've been

156

sitting up, thinking this thing through. By the way,' he added, 'you mumble in your sleep, I heard you.'

'I know. I used to record myself, so that I could find out what I was saying.'

Longman stared at him for a long moment, but finally declined to comment.

'Look, the point is, I think I know what we can do to stop Eldritch becoming even more real than it already is.'

'Good,' Cassidy said. 'What?'

'We've got to get Sam to stop writing.'

Cassidy sighed. '*Obviously* we have to stop Sam writing.'

'Yes, I suppose it is obvious,' Longman replied tartly. 'I rather suspect that everything must be obvious to a man who records himself sleeping. But I also think that all the inroads Eldritch has made into our world will eventually fade away – if only we can get him to stop.'

Cassidy nodded dubiously.

'Well, maybe,' he said. 'But, Nat, you know the hold Eldritch has to have on him. Not to mention the pressure from his agent, his publishers and the fans, all the Eldritch Obsessives like those at the convention. Just how do you plan to stop Sam writing, are you going to cut his bloody hands off?'

'Please, Nigel,' Longman winced. 'No, what I thought we could do was try explaining the situation as we see it. We'll go to see Sam, we'll all sit down together, and we'll discuss our fears with him in a very calm and rational manner. We'll show him my clippings and notes as our evidence, we'll express our

157

doubts about Jo, and tell him everything that we've seen and felt in his house.'

Cassidy looked even more dubious.

'And when *that* doesn't work,' Longman added, 'we're going to kidnap him.'

8

...there were certain members of Eldritch's police force who enjoyed laughing at DS Keith Muggins to his face. Muggins by name and Muggins by nature, they said, as if he hadn't been hearing that one since he was a child.

The source of their mockery came from Muggins's obvious attachment to his beloved DI, Drunk Dave Hawkins, whom he idolised and revered. He longed to rise to the same level in Dave's estimation as the late DS Bernie Alder had occupied before his untimely, unpleasant death. To this end, Muggins always carried a hip-flask of Scotch in his jacket pocket, as Alder had done, even though most of the time it was his DI who ended up drinking it.

In addition, Muggins supplied nearly all Drunk Dave's other refreshments, drove him wherever he wanted to go at whatever time he wanted, and made sure that he remembered to supplement his liquid diet with the occasional solid, even if it was just a bag of salted peanuts.

He cleaned up Dave's frequent messes, handled all his paperwork, made his apologies, and strove mightily to keep his actions at least within shouting distance of the law. It wasn't an easy job, and there were never any thanks forthcoming.

Sometimes, Muggins wasn't even sure if Drunk Dave was aware of his presence, much less his devotion.

But if he wasn't, everyone else was.

In spite of his colleagues' opinion of him, Keith Muggins knew that when the elusive, mercurial DI Hawkins needed to be found, there was only one man to turn to...

DS Ken Morley stepped into The Truncheon, a drinking club exclusively for off-duty police officers, all low-level lighting and leather booths. A place where they came in an attempt to lose most of the baggage they'd picked up during the day, so they wouldn't have to take it home with them.

Most of the shadowy heads he could see turned to examine him, and a few of them nodded before turning away. Morley preferred to do his drinking in public bars and was not a regular at the club. And as he was technically still on-duty, he was not here now to drink. He had come to confirm a rumour that was nothing short of stupendous.

DI Hyams had left the station hours ago, just walked off without telling anyone where he was going. His mobile phone was turned off. The rumour was that he had been seen drinking in The Truncheon, and Morley had to know if it were true. His concern about his DI was growing. He wasn't aware that his concern was very nearly excitement.

One of the few things Honest Bob Allison had told him about Hyams had been when Morley asked why Hyams wouldn't come to the pub with the rest of the CID boys. Even if he didn't drink, couldn't he just be sociable? Did he think he was too good for them?

'No, that isn't it at all,' Allison had replied. 'It's the temptation. I think deep down he knows he's the wrong sort of person to be around alcohol. He'd only have to have one drink, and that'd be it. He'd never be able to stop. Underneath that cold mask of his, Ken, there's a really nice bloke. But underneath *that* mask, there's a wild man trying to get out. Duncan wants to keep him there.'

And there the wild man was. Sitting on a stool at the small bar, drinking mineral water from a half-pint glass. Sighing in relief, and perhaps with a little disappointment, Morley made his way over.

Hyams turned to face him as he approached. He'd probably spotted the DS in the mirror behind the ranks of optics. Hyams's face was flushed, deepening to its darkest shade in the centre, around his nose. Drunk's blush. Morley abruptly realised that the substance in the half-pint glass was not mineral water. He couldn't smell gin, so there was only one thing it could be. The barman was in the process of fitting a new Smirnoff Blue bottle into the optic.

Morley caught the barman's eyes when he turned around. A former police officer himself, the barman was usually strict when it came to not letting anyone's drinking get out of hand. He was big and tough, and had only quit the job after being knocked back to constable as punishment for use of excessive force. What Morley saw in his eyes was the look of a

160

man who had recently been intimidated and frightened. Morley also noticed a bulge in Hyams's jacket pocket. He still had the knife Allison had killed himself with.

'Hello, Ken,' Hyams said. 'Care to join me in a drink?'

Morley was surprised that Hyams's speech seemed to be unaffected by the alcohol. Usually, a man had to have a great deal of experience to speak clearly with a skinful. He glanced at the watching barman and ordered a zero alcohol pilsner.

Hyams tut-tutted him. 'Don't tell me you've taken the pledge?'

'No, Guv, I'm driving.'

Hyams glanced at his wristwatch, momentarily confused when it turned out to be on his right wrist rather than the left. 'Where the hell are you going at this time of night?' he asked.

'We got a call from Kings Cross. They've found a dead prostitute in a knocking shop. Pretty badly torn up.'

'What's that got to do with us?'

'Well, they say she used to be one of theirs, but she disappeared from the scene just under a year ago. Seems she's been living on our patch since then.'

'I repeat, what has it got to do with us?'

Morley eyed the way Hyams was getting through the vodka, gulping, swallowing without tasting, and he wondered if the barman had had to replace the bottle more than once.

Vodka in a half-pint glass, he thought. Jesus.

COMEBACK

'They were wondering if… well, as she lived in the same area, if Bob Allison might have done this one as well as the schoolgirl we caught him for.'

Hyams drained his glass. 'Any similarities in the MO?'

'They wouldn't give me many details over the phone.'

'Pricks,' Hyams said, and belched loudly enough for heads to turn. 'Did you tell them he was dead, and that we'd had him in custody for nearly thirty-six hours before then?'

'Yes, but they say there's some confusion over the time of the prossy's death. The knocking shop's night porter found the body. He claims he never saw a punter with her, but he's sure he rented her the room tonight. That's why he went up to the room in the first place – to roust them out because their hour was up. Thing is, Kings Cross's pathologist says it looks like she's been dead for two or three days. Says he'll know more when he gets her back to the morgue.'

'And they suspect Bernie Alder?'

Morley frowned. 'Who?'

Hyams shook his head. 'Bob Allison, I mean. They really suspect him?'

'They're just trying to make a connection, Guv. You know how it goes.'

'Yes.'

Hyams slammed his glass down on the bar, making the barman wince. Morley was aware of heads sharply turning in their direction again, and one or two disapproving coughs, as though to suggest that his DI ought to be kept on a shorter leash. Morley wanted to tell them he'd never imagined that Hyams would ever need one.

Instead, he showed them a palm, a silent apology on his DI's behalf.

'Well, let's go set the arseholes straight, shall we?' Hyams said loudly.

'Yes, Guv.'

'Right.'

Hyams climbed down from his stool and followed Morley to the door. Once they were out on the street, moving towards the car, Hyams suddenly grabbed Morley by the shoulders and spun him around until they were face to face. Morley could feel the DI's breath stripping the enamel from his teeth.

'If we're going to get along, Ken, there's just a couple of things you have to understand,' Hyams said. 'Bob Allison wasn't responsible for Rebecca Walton's death, and he didn't commit suicide. He was murdered.'

He patted the knife in his pocket.

'*Murdered*, you understand?'

Morley nodded as though he did.

Back inside The Truncheon, the barman drank Morley's untouched zero alcohol pilsner and promised himself that once his shift was done, he was going to have a real drink. Not even wanting to touch Hyams's empty glass, he picked it up with a bar towel and dropped them both in the bin.

9

Sam Parker, deep, deep in sleep, has dreamed many dreams. They have flashed through his mind like tube station posters seen from a moving train. The vivid, half-seen images have disturbed him, but he has passed them by and mercifully forgotten the majority of what he has seen. All he is left with is the impression of having travelled a great distance in a very short time.

Now he is slowing, and he finds himself in a place, a time, where he has no desire to be. His journey has deposited him at some kind of terminus, a place of immense importance, he feels. But where is it?

At first he cannot see at all, and there is a terrible pain pulsing out from his sightless eyes, the intensity of which seems matched by other pains spread throughout his whole body. Gradually, a list of his injuries forms in his mind, and it is substantial.

Broken bones in his arms and legs, broken nose and teeth. Puncture wounds and gunshot wounds and pieces of sensitive skin flayed open in terrible flaps. Ligaments have been cut so that his broken arms and legs are doubly useless. He feels a terrible internal burning, and he knows that he has been poisoned. Something is sticking to his face with every shallow breath that he attempts to draw. A plastic bag. It occurs to Sam that whoever he is in this dream, the man went down like Rasputin.

He is dead, but he feels everything. He knows that he is being carried, many hands clutching at him, not caring that they are grinding the edges of broken bones together, or that blood still leaks out of him like water from a sponge.

Suddenly, he is dropped to the ground. The impact increases the scale of his separate pains exponentially. They grow like towns and villages that eventually overlap and form one vast city, and the sheer size of his agony thrusts him out of his body. He is free and painless in a darkness so complete God might never have spoken.

Very well, Sam thinks. *I* will speak.

Small columns of light appear. It takes a while for Sam to realise what they are, but once he has, he knows exactly where he is and what he is seeing.

The lights are shafts of moonlight breaking through the canopy of the ancient forest that dominates the land either side of Sly Jack Road. What he is witnessing is the destruction of Eldritch's nameless crime boss by three of his contemporaries. They had arranged for the Listmaker to pass on false information to the Golem so that he was walking into a trap far away from his master's side when they mounted their attack. Their betrayal.

He is back at the beginning, Sam realises. This really is the beginning of it all, of everything. This is the prologue, he thinks. It *has* to be the prologue.

Bodiless, invisible, Sam watches the sweating, cursing men roughly gather up the body, naked save for the plastic bag taped over its head, and continue their journey through the woodland. He wills himself to follow them.

When they approach the tree line where the woodland ends, only a blankness exists, and working purely on instinct, Sam fills it. Having created the shafts of moonlight for the depths of the forest, he now makes the moon itself appear, larger and lower and brighter than it could ever be in reality. He needs to see everything. Under it, he decides to place a wide field of heather. He adds a millpond and a mill house to the scene, and then mentally snaps his fingers.

Got that wrong the first time, he thinks.

He'd written a ruined windmill for *Sly Jack Road*, when really it should have been a mill house. But like the seasonal mistake he's already made in *Comeback*, it doesn't matter. This is still Eldritch.

Sam follows the three men as they go about their grisly task.

Even without a body of his own, he feels physically sickened when they rip open the bag they have suffocated the body with and he sees the mess they have made of its face. What makes it worse is that despite the disfigurements, the crime boss's face strikes a chord with Sam, as though it belongs to someone he might once have known.

When they hold the body's head and shoulders under the milky surface of the millpond and the bloody air bubbles start to rise, Sam has to turn away.

After that, he keeps his distance.

He stays outside the mill house, hovering like one of the clouds he has created to balance his composition, while the three men feed the body between the millstones. He allows himself to drift even further away when they begin fracturing its skull in a futile attempt to make that fit between the stones, too.

He waits for the men to return to the field of heather. When they eventually come, he hovers just above their heads as they watch the mill house begin to burn. He feels their cautious optimism that they have succeeded of ridding themselves of a business acquaintance who had become both a tyrant and a monster.

But unlike the three men, poor characters who live their lives in a world of perpetual horror, Sam knows that the crime boss's beast, Wizeman, the Golem, is already on his way back from his false mission, having slaughtered his would-be killers. Before the Alzheimer fog claims him, he will avenge his master's destruction in the only way he understands. The men have the mark of death on them, an invisible stain Sam has put there himself.

He watches them run as the smoke begins to pour across the millpond, and he lets them go. He has no time to follow them to their fates. He too has heard the crime boss's final, disembodied words, his prophecy.

I will come back.

Not if I can help it, Sam thinks grimly as this dream, too, is snatched away.

10

...the Listmaker only thought about the past in terms of grievances. Of injustices visited upon him, or corners he had been painted into, of mistakes he had been forced to make. All of these came to his mind as he thought of the girl he had married in his youth, during the years he had been an outcast from Eldritch.

In the city to which he had fled, he had proposed to the daughter of one of the local villains, a man so deadly his nickname was the 'The Undertaker'. The Listmaker had hoped to be protected by the father's reputation, and his standing in his new community lifted accordingly, and for once his plans appeared to be bearing fruit. The daughter accepted, and the father approved.

But then, as always before, he had been fucked by the fickle finger of fate.

The wedding reception had still been in progress when an assassin's bullet had entered his new father-in-law's forehead and exited above and behind his right ear, spattering the bride and groom and their wedding cake with blood and gore. Seeing no further advantage to be gained from prolonging the union, the Listmaker had left his bride scraping her father's brains off the wedding dress and abandoned both her and his ruined new life.

But now, just look! the Listmaker thought angrily. Just look!

Here she was in his house, having finally tracked him down, messing with his head while he was planning, plotting, for his future. During the few days she'd been here, she had brought men into his house and made love to them. He supposed it was a woman's idea of revenge, and it shouldn't have worked, but it did. Somehow it did. He had no doubt that this was one of the reasons that men hated women.

She knew full well he could hear her through the wall – if he pressed a glass against it. Just as she knew that he would have a glass in readiness.

168

It made him so… angry. And he wouldn't have it, he wouldn't.

He smiled suddenly as he heard her waking, listened to her moving around his house as though she owned it. He put down the glass, rubbed his ear where it had made him sore.

Let her enjoy her moment, he thought. Her feeling of triumph. She wouldn't feel that way for much longer. Only a few minutes. After that, she wouldn't feel much of anything. Not even when he finally consummated their marriage…

Charles Beckett stood with his ear to his study door, listening as his wife went downstairs and began rattling around in the kitchen.

Good, he thought. One last breakfast together, for old times' sake, and then it's farewell, my lovely. No more the mouse.

He tittered a little over the idea of a killer mouse, and then something happened to him that was truly miraculous. He felt his cock get hard. For the first time in God knows how many years, he had an erection, and what had started it was the thought of killing his wife, the thought of actually starting downstairs to do it.

He pictured his wife lying dead on the quarry-tiled kitchen floor, gazing sightlessly up at the eggshell ceiling with her dressing gown splayed open. She would have been terrified in the moments immediately preceding her death − Beckett understood that he would need to see her terror − and her pubic hair would be jewelled with urine.

Beckett had spent the whole night in his study, brooding over the choice he had made even as he slept at a coma-like depth, his bearded chin resting heavily on his moobs. When he had awoken at dawn, it was to an aching back and a severe pain in his neck, but as he spent the next three hours waiting for his wife to rise, he found that he didn't mind either of them. Today he intended to rid himself of all his pains in the neck. And, as if there wasn't already enough to be cheerful about, now that he had an erection, he'd be able to give his lower back a little exercise, too.

Once his wife was dead, of course.

After that he would kill Sam Parker. He had already made arrangements to buy and collect a gun later in the day. He'd found his contact for this criminal purchase on the Internet, and followed it up as though he were researching for a novel. That's what he intended to say in the event that the police questioned him later.

Not that he intended to kill Parker with the gun. The gun was just to slow him down. He would finish the bastard off in a much slower, more personal way.

And afterwards, what then? Beckett found that he didn't care. Even if he were caught and sent to prison for the rest of his life, they would let him have a pen and a writing pad. With Parker dead he would be able to write again, and the future would once more spring from his imagination.

But first things first, he thought. Let's take care of the present before we worry about the future.

He followed the scent of brewing coffee downstairs, trying not to look as happy as he felt. He had already pulled his shirt out of his trousers. It was wrinkled to hell, but at least it covered his erection, which refused to go away and pushed out the front of his trousers like a misplaced carrot.

Stop smiling, he silently urged himself.

If his wife even *suspected* something was out of the ordinary, her back would go up. There was very little he still respected about his wife, but he was always prepared to admit that her instincts were second to none. He didn't intend to give them a chance to send up the alarm.

She was standing by the Aga as he entered the kitchen, her back to him. She had a pan on the hob, and eggs, a mixing bowl, a whisk, and smoked salmon on the work-surface beside it. She wore her favourite robe with a vine of blue flowers climbing up the back. She hadn't opened the Venetian blinds yet and was working by the tiny light in the ventilator hood.

Beckett took a step forward, but then stepped back again with a frown.

Beneath the familiar robe, his wife's body seemed to be entirely the wrong shape. And her shoulder-length blonde hair was closer to brown. And there was a large amount of dark hair on her legs. Then his wife turned around, and revealed that she was a young man.

Beckett was struck dumb. He hadn't known anyone else was in the house. He hadn't planned for this.

The young man, olive-skinned, with the kind of sculpted features his wife always went for, and sometimes paid for, gave Beckett an insolent once over, eyebrows arched.

171

'Oh, I get it, you must be *Charles*,' he said, as if even Beckett's Christian name were a joke.

Beckett nodded, too dismayed to do anything else.

'I'm Philip, a friend of Malcolm's? No? Oh well... if you'll excuse me.' He turned back to the Aga, where he was dropping slivers of smoked salmon into his half-scrambled eggs. He had set out one plate, and one coffee cup. Making breakfast only for himself, not for Beckett's wife.

Feeling shell-shocked, Beckett sat down at the kitchen table. Interestingly, even when presented with this living, breathing symbol of his own inadequacy, his erection had not wilted. It was a hardy root-vegetable, surviving against all the odds. The discovery perked him up. Strength lay in the ability to adapt to changing circumstances.

'Where's...' He found he had to struggle to recall his wife's name. 'Where's Valerie?'

'Still asleep,' the young man replied without bothering to turn around. 'I don't think she'll be waking up very soon, either. We were up rather late.'

'Went out, did you?'

'No. We stayed in.' Beckett could hear the mockery in the young man's voice. 'I'll tell her you asked after her, though.'

'Thank you so much.'

Now Philip had heard something in Beckett's voice, something that disturbed him, and he kept glancing around from stirring his eggs in the pan. Whenever he looked around, Beckett smiled at him.

'I don't suppose you could fix me some of that, could you?' Beckett asked.

172

Philip looked back over his shoulder for a longer time, studying him, wondering what his game was. After a while, he shrugged and reached for more eggs. Behind the young man's back, Beckett's pleasant smile turned into a savage grin.

11

After almost eleven hours sleep, Sam came instantly awake. He felt incredible. Every cell in his body felt new, every muscle relaxed but toned; no aches, no pains, no mild throbbing in the head, no nasty taste in the mouth. Horny, too, incredibly horny.

He shrugged off his wrinkled clothes as he walked into the en-suite bathroom, then showered, dried, and dressed, all in a matter of minutes. His sense of well-being was lighter than air, as though his veins contained helium instead of blood. He couldn't remember the last time he'd felt this good. He wanted a huge breakfast, he wanted to make love to Jo, he wanted to run in the sunshine, to shout and scream, to see waves crashing against a rocky shore, and he wanted it all immediately. He laughed. It was rare moments like this one which reminded you that you were alive. He'd *never* felt this good.

The only thing that even came close, he thought, was the satisfaction of having completed a really good day's work, one of those days when the words were like quicksilver on his fingertips and they filled up page after page after…

Sam had been opening the bedroom door as this thought occurred to him, and even before he passed through the doorway he was aware that his good feelings had abruptly vanished. Thinking about

173

writing had broken his dream, the only one from last night that he actually remembered.

In the dream, he was typing away at his computer, not even thinking about his story, just watching the shapes his hands made as they passed over the keyboard in little insectile darts and rushes. He had the impression that he had been working for a long time, but when he looked up at the monitor there were no paragraphs, sentences or words. Not even a solitary letter. Just a legion of tiny scarlet daubs and scratches, like Chinese ideograms written in blood.

Even as he recoiled from the sight, his fingers went on with their work, busily tap-tap-tapping until the whole screen was gradually filled. The bloodstains expanded and mingled together, and when the last of the white had entirely disappeared, the screen itself began to bleed. Blood formed on the glass like condensation and dripped down onto his hands, which never once paused in their mysterious work.

Sam shook himself like a dog.

The corridor outside his bedroom was full of sunlight, but the light seemed trapped, like a butterfly in a killing jar. All Sam's hungers and desires had dissolved, day-dreams succumbing to the acid of reality. His light-headed euphoria became nausea. There was a sound like the murmuring of many voices, but Sam didn't suspect intruders, not this time.

The murmuring was inside his own head.

His last thought before falling asleep last night came back to him in a rush; his computer, recognising that he was home, turning itself on, connecting itself to the part of his brain that had been annexed by Eldritch. He knew now that this had been more than just an idle fantasy.

If he tried, he could lean backwards into his subconscious and hear the murmuring become a roar that made him feel sick to his stomach. If he closed his eyes and concentrated, he could see split-second images that grabbed at him like a powerful wind. He pushed himself away from them, away from his own mind. He did not want to see, he did not want to hear.

But he had to do *something*.

Sam made himself walk down the corridor towards the stairs leading up to his attic office. He looked up and saw the steps ascend into utter darkness, as those to Lionel Hepplewhite's halfway-house had descended into utter darkness.

He wondered what had happened to the windows up there. Were they now offering a view of Eldritch by night?

This close to his office, the sounds in the back of his mind found a new form. The irregular pecking rhythm of a two finger typist, but one who never paused for thought, never broke for lunch, and for whom sleep didn't exist.

Sam's own subconscious.

Eldritch's hold on him had reached a new and critical stage, and he remembered his thoughts just before he had begun *Comeback*, in the vacuum created by Jo's absence. No plan, no synopsis, no outline, no real idea of anything beyond the premise and where and how it began, but none of that mattered, because…

…because the story would write itself.

175

Sometimes, he thought, you can be too damn right for your own good.

Sam wondered what he might see if he went up into his office and turned on the lights. The keys on his keyboard jumping up and down like the ivories on a haunted piano, perhaps. Or some great dark figure hunched in his captain's chair before the computer, not even vaguely human, formed from all the separate elements of the city, a being to complement the soup of odours that made up Eldritch's powerful atmosphere.

Or would he see himself, he wondered. A dark twin, connected to the womb of the book by a rotting umbilicus, flourishing as he declined, until only it lived to survive the book's birth.

Sam took the first three steps up to his office, the only steps to have light on them. As he placed his foot into the darkness of the fourth, the sound of typing abruptly stopped. The low murmuring stopped.

The silence regarded him, the darkness above studied him, gauging his intentions, and the threat he might pose.

Sam withdrew his foot. It tingled as though he had dipped it in icy water. The instant it re-joined its partner on the third step, in the light, the soft tattoo of typing began again. Whatever was up there, it knew he was too afraid to intrude, that his nerve had gone, and it had dismissed him.

Feeling hollow and bone-weary, Sam turned away and went back down the corridor, and all the way he was followed by a scornful chuckle that made his cheeks burn.

When his doorbell rang, Sam numbly went to answer it. In the few moments it took him to get to the front door, the bell rang a further six times. He glanced through the door viewer and saw that his caller was DI Hyams, accompanied by a man Sam assumed to be another plainclothes officer. They stood together at the gate, muttering to each other. Hyams was the one repeatedly pushing the bell.

Sam buzzed them through the gate, not bothering to speak to them through the intercom. He was not at all curious about the reason for Hyams's return, and he wasn't concerned. He wouldn't have been surprised to find that the second policeman was another Eldritch fan Hyams had brought over to get his autograph.

Sam thought he was beyond surprise.

He opened the door, and Hyams and the second policeman walked into the hallway without any polite preliminaries, and without smiles, he noticed. The second thing that struck Sam was that neither of them appeared to have slept. They looked as though they had worked through the night, and had had a hard time of it.

Hyams looked particularly dishevelled, although that might have been the contrast between how he had looked yesterday and how he looked now. Yet the more Sam studied him, the less it appeared that a mere twenty-four hours could account for the enormous change. His face was as red as a beet, and the smell of vodka was no longer a hallucination on Sam's part.

He realised that Hyams had spoken.

'Um, sorry, I didn't catch that.'

'This is DS Morley,' Hyams repeated, none too patiently. 'And I said, it's a bit early, isn't it?'

'What do you mean?' Sam followed Hyams's eyes to his own hand. He was holding a tumbler half-full of whisky. 'Oh. Yes. Bad day.'

'Bad habit,' Hyams said, and plucked the glass from Sam's hand before walking through, uninvited, to the sitting room.

Sam, left speechless by this turn of events, followed Hyams, and Morley followed him.

'Take a seat, Mr Parker,' Hyams said.

Sam, still woolly, selected a chair. Both policemen remained standing. Hyams had set Sam's glass on the mantelpiece, but it was now empty. Sam noticed that Morley spent more of his time watching his DI than he did looking at him. The DS looked distinctly nervous.

'What can I do for you?' he asked Hyams. 'I already told you all I can about Sly Jack Road.'

As much as I'm prepared to, anyway, he thought.

'Don't worry about that,' Hyams replied. 'That line of inquiry is well in hand.'

Sam saw the flicker of astonishment that crossed Morley's face before he hid it.

'We're here to ask you about your relationship with one Jo Branagh,' Hyams said.

Sam discovered that he was not beyond surprise, after all.

'Jo? She's a friend of mine. A girlfriend.'

'A lover?'

Sam glanced from Hyams to Morley. Morley was looking at him now, daring him not to answer.

'Yes, if that's any of your business,' he told Hyams. 'We've been seeing each other for about eight months, something like that.'

'I see. What can you tell us about her?'

'What do you want to know?' Sam shrugged. 'She's twenty-six. She's a mature mathematics student at Middlesex Uni'. Her father's dead, her mother lives in Sussex somewhere…'

A horrible thought occurred to him then. The phone in Jo's bedsit that rang and rang and could not be ignored but was never answered. The black mood she must have left his house in after he failed to return to bed, when he had preferred to sleep on a couch rather than with her.

'Has something happened to her? Is she all right?'

'When did you last see her?' Hyams asked.

'Last night. No,' Sam corrected himself. 'It was the night before. She stayed here with me. Look−'

'Any witnesses?'

'Witnesses?'

'To say that she left here safely.'

Sam took a deep breath. 'No, and I didn't see her leave myself. I was still asleep.'

'What was her frame of mind at that time?'

'She was depressed, I suppose. We'd had an argument the night before.'

'What about?'

'I don't know. Something, nothing. She had her period, and she was upset. We made it up before we went to sleep.'

Hyams moved closer, until he stood over Sam. 'Are you sure this argument wasn't over a precise *something*?' he asked. 'Something you'd recently discovered about her?'

Sam was mystified. 'Like what?'

'That she lived a double life, for instance.'

Sam couldn't think of anything to say. Morley had come closer, too, standing just behind Hyams, and he looked more nervous than ever. There was some other emotion mixed in his eyes, Sam thought. At this moment, he couldn't tell if it was just excitement, or out-and-out hero-worship.

'When did you find out?' Hyams asked. 'Who told you?'

'I don't know what you're talking about.'

Hyams glanced over his shoulder at his DS, repeating Sam's sentence in a ridiculous mocking voice. When he turned back, his red eyes were full of anger.

'She was twenty-one years old, not twenty-six, and she wasn't a mature student of mathematics, or anything else for that matter,' he said. 'There's no dead father and no mother in Sussex. She was an orphan. Left on a doorstep as a baby, and in and out of foster homes and institutions her whole life. She was abused as a child and drifted into prostitution in her early teens. Jo Branagh was an alias she sometimes used. Her real name was Josephine Garrison. Her street-name was a corruption of her Christian name. She called herself—'

'Fee,' Sam whispered.

Hyams and Morley glanced at each other.

'How did you know that?' Hyams said.

'I don't know. Maybe she called herself that once or twice,' he lied. 'I can't remember.' He put his hands over his face. 'She's dead, isn't she? You wouldn't be talking to me like this if she wasn't.'

'Yes, Mr Parker, she's *extremely* dead,' Hyams said.

He backed away and sat down opposite Sam, staring at him intently.

'Do you want to hear the details – or are you already familiar them?'

Hyams questioned Sam ruthlessly about his relationship with Jo, whom he insisted upon calling Fee, and about his movements during the three days immediately preceding the discovery of her body. The Kings Cross pathologist had confirmed that in his opinion she'd been dead for about three days.

There were no witnesses to say that Sam wasn't lying about Jo being at his house, but to Hyams's chagrin he had an alibi for the previous two days and nights. The night before the convention, Sam had had dinner with Nathaniel Longman and three other people. The day and the night before that he had spent at his agent's house in Sevenoaks Weald. DS Morley wrote everything down as though his life depended on it.

At the mention of Sam's agent, Hyams grinned.

'Mr Horace Jepson. It seems to me I've heard that name before.'

'I just told you, he's my agent,' Sam said. 'And if you're an Eldritch Obsess... an Eldritch *fan*, you'd probably have seen–'

'Not in connection to *you*, Mr Parker. In connection to Fee Garrison.'

'To Jo?'

Sam's mind worked frantically. He'd tried his best to keep all knowledge of Jo as far from Horace as possible. Horace was a busybody when it came to Sam's relationships, and could never be trusted to keep his nose out. Sam could hear Horace's voice now. This one's a gold-digger, that one's a flake…

'I seem to remember that a Horace Jepson paid the deposit on Fee Garrison's bedsit. And paid her rent and utility bills for, how long, Morley, ten months?'

'Ten months, sir.'

'About the same amount of time she'd been out of the Kings Cross scene, in other words. And didn't he also pay her a salary?'

'Two thousand a month, sir.'

'That's right. A 'researcher', I think her contract said. What exactly do you think she might have been researching for your agent, Mr Parker? Was it the length of your cock?'

Drunk or not, Hyams was still sharp enough to recognise how upset Sam had been to learn that his girlfriend was not only a prostitute, but also a dead prostitute. Murdered. The author didn't seem shocked or even particularly surprised, he noted, but definitely upset. On the other hand, shocked and surprised exactly described Sam's reaction to the news that his girlfriend had been in the pay of his own agent. It was, Hyams thought, all very jolly.

Sam shook his head. 'I can't explain it. It doesn't make any sense.'

Hyams paused for a moment. His eyes seemed to be spinning. 'You said that your relationship with Fee

182

was based on her having no interest in Eldritch. Did you ever visit her bedsit?'

'Once or twice, a long time ago, when we first started seeing each other. We prefer… preferred to spend our time together here.'

Hyams looked around the comfortable, airy sitting room and nodded.

'Know what we found when we searched her place?'

Sam had a pretty good idea, but he wasn't going to let Hyams know that.

'We found all the Eldritch novels, all of them read to pieces. And about a dozen sketchbooks filled with her illustrations of some of the key scenes. There were other drawings pinned on the walls. Characters, buildings, some maps she'd made… That girl knew Eldritch like a native.'

Hyams stood up.

'We're going to check up on those alibis of yours. If you'll accept a piece of advice, Mr Parker, I'd recommend that you stay right here. Don't go wandering off where it'd be difficult to find you, because I promise you, there's nowhere I won't find you if I have to. And if I have to find you, I'll be *angry*.'

Sam watched Morley trail Hyams across the room. He thought that Morley mostly looked relieved to be going, or getting Hyams out of the house, anyway, like a dog that couldn't be trusted not to bite.

At the doorway, Hyams turned back for a moment, his eyes just red slits.

183

'There's something wrong with you,' he told Sam, ignoring Morley's hand on his arm, urging him away. 'You don't look right.'

'If you want to see something that's *really* wrong,' Sam quietly replied, 'just look in a mirror.'

'*What* did you say?' Hyams said. Morley got both arms around his waist and yanked him towards the door. 'What did you say?'

The front door slammed, and Sam was left alone.

In his mind, he could hear the sound of typing.

12

...Oh well, the Listmaker thought as he levered the knife loose from the young man's back, everybody makes mistakes. The trick is, don't be fazed by it, try to turn it to your advantage.

He knelt above the body for some time, absently jabbing the tip of the knife under a flap of skin he had raised in one of the twenty post mortem stab wounds. And then the idea came to him.

Oh, that's good, he thought, she'll just love that! Something out of nothing, that was his great strength, he decided, as he went back to work with the knife.

Of course, it was all a bit hard on the young man. But there again, he thought, he really shouldn't have been fucking my wife...

The door of Valerie Beckett's bedroom opened with a small snap. It wasn't loud, but it was enough to make her eyelids flicker half-open. As the door closed again

184

she rolled over to the cool side of the mattress, and found her lover's figure in gloom as he placed a tray on the dressing table. Enough light forced its way through the thick curtains to pick out the flower pattern on her white robe as it floated, ghostlike, across the room.

Smiling, Valerie closed her eyes again and she stretched full length on the bed, opening her legs.

'Silly thing, why are you wearing that? Take it off immediately.'

She thought of the night before, a total sensory recall that had her wet in a second. Philip's firm young body moving over hers, his stamina, his strength, the thick hardness of him in her hand and other places, and then his complete abandonment to her experience as she took control. Back and forth, they'd gone, back and forth. He was a boy, he was a man, he was a boy, he was a man. Damn it, he was good. Damn it, so am I, she thought.

She opened her eyes again just as the robe fell to the floor.

What?

Even half-asleep, even in the half-light, it was all wrong.

The naked figure was shorter than it should have been, and bulkier. And yet, there was the mop of dark hair, the diamond of matching hair on the chest. But the face was misshapen and sagging in places, stretched and bulging in others, and the chest, entirely without muscle-tone, hung like a curtain. Below this the body was flabby, pot-bellied, the legs thin and white and marbled with varicose veins, not tanned and heavily muscled from years of tennis. Dark maroon streaks ran down from a frayed line just below the sternum like the hem of a cut-off T-shirt.

And there, pointing out from the fork of the legs, an ugly, massively-veined penis that she recognised instantly, although she had not seen it in its erect state for six, maybe seven years.

'Oh my God!' she hissed through her teeth. She was fully awake now, and everything was cruelly clear.

'I thought you might like me more like this,' Beckett lied, a tuft of his beard, saturated with blood, poking out of Philip's lips. 'I thought it might make it easier on you. No? Well, never mind.'

Beckett pulled Philip's skin off like a hooded sweater, turning it inside out, and tossed it wetly to the floor. The whole of his upper torso, his shoulders, neck and head were a solid red with blood, his beard slicked into a point on his chin, his thinning hair twisted into horns. He looked like a demon.

'Wait a moment, my dear,' he said.

He went back to the dressing table, and then showed his wife what he had brought for her on the breakfast tray. It was a marble rolling pin from the kitchen. Valerie looked from this to her husband's eyes, and then tried to run.

She leapt from the bed to the draped windows, trying to punch through to the glass beyond, and Beckett, racing around the bed, heard one of the panes crack. As she screamed into the fresh aperture, he brought the rolling pin around in a wide arc and swatted his wife to the ground before she could make any more alarming noises.

Valerie hit the ground hard, but was back up on her feet even before Beckett had recovered from the momentum of his swing. She ran across the bedroom in sheer panic and crashed into the wall. Beckett caught her on the rebound with a meaty strike that caved in the crown of her skull. She hit the wall again, breaking her nose, and then surprised Beckett by spinning around and running straight at him, knocking him to the floor. He was too late getting up to stop her reaching the bedroom door, but he saw that it didn't matter.

Whether through terror or brain damage, opening the door was beyond Valerie now, and she simply batted at it with her body, like a fly at the window.

Beckett made sure this time, easing up behind her and waiting for just the right moment, aiming for just the right place. He struck hard and she was dead before she hit the floor.

He dropped the rolling pin, and had to lean forwards with his hands on his knees while he got his breath back. His whole body was sticky with blood and sweat, and his shoulders were stiff with tension. He gagged a few times, but did not vomit.

When he'd recovered, Beckett dragged Valerie's corpse over to the bed and hauled her up onto it. He turned on the bedside lamp and saw with satisfaction that his wife had indeed lost control of her bladder. The smell of it acted like a narcotic upon him. Everything was happening as he had originally foreseen. Everything was back on track.

He crawled onto the bed, roughly thrusting his wife's cooling thighs apart.

Unaware that he was speaking at all, he began to whisper into Valerie's ear, 'She was only The Undertaker's daughter, but anyone cadaver…'

13

Sam hadn't even had to think twice about ignoring DI Hyams's order for him to stay at home, and left his house only minutes after the policemen had. He'd made two quick phone calls first. One to Horace's office and one to his home, where even an answerphone didn't reply. According to his secretary, Horace still hadn't been into his office this week, hadn't phoned, and had missed several important meetings. Rosie had been unable to contact him by phone or email and was getting worried about him. She was thinking heart attacks and strokes.

Sam blithely told her not to be worried, he was sure Horace was fine – and would remain so until he got hold of him. Rosie had laughed, and Sam had forced himself to join her. But a part of him had been deadly serious.

If what Hyams had said were true, if his agent really had hired Jo to spy on him, a part of Sam would have been quite happy to beat Horace to death.

He'd walked straight to the local Hertz office to hire a car, wishing that he'd never given a damn about the environmental damage they caused and the depth of his carbon footprint and had bought his own vehicle, and then set off immediately for Sevenoaks Weald, driving ten miles per hour over the limit whatever the posted speed restrictions. He suspected that Horace was holed up, hiding from him, and Sam knew that he had to see him face to face. The sooner the better.

Like everything else that was happening to him, Sam thought that this new situation was also like a novel. A suspense or a whodunit, where the clues to the criminal's identity seemed impenetrable until all was finally revealed in the climactic moments. Then you said to yourself, Ah, so *that's* what it was all about…

If it really was true that Horace had set Sam up with Jo, engineering their relationship as a means of keeping tabs on what he was writing, maybe even *influencing* what he was writing, there had to have been clues. Sam had just been blind to them. How could he have known that he was living in a novel?

He thought of Horace, meddling in his personal affairs as though they were a part of an agent's duties. If Sam had been in a relationship, Horace had always been digging about it. What's her name, her age, where does she live, what does she do, where is she from, when can I meet her… Once he'd even had a girl he thought unsuitable investigated by a private detective. Once that Sam knew about, that is.

If Sam hadn't been in a relationship, Horace had constantly enquired whether someone was on the horizon, and had been forever trying to push girls onto him. All that nonsense had stopped nine or ten months ago, Sam now realised. Since then, Horace had been the soul of discretion. It was easy, with hindsight, to see why. Horace had been getting regular reports from his researcher. His EO spy.

If it was true.

And if it was, why hadn't Sam seen through the charade? He should have done so almost immediately. Even if people hated the books, even if they'd never read a single genre novel in their lives, everyone had at least *heard* of Eldritch. This wasn't a boast, it was a simple fact. The books, the movies, the graphic novels, the hundreds of dedicated websites, the Xbox and PlayStation games, the reviews, the fan-clubs, the albums of 'music inspired by…'

It had even been announced that the word eldritch would have another definition in the Oxford English dictionary come the next edition: [said of something spooky, strange, uncanny or grotesque. 'Wow, is that *Eldritch*, or what?' From the novels of Sam Parker, 1973−]

Jo had been more or less in the demographic centre of Sam's audience. Whether she was twenty-one as Hyams had claimed or almost twenty-seven as Sam had believed, it would have been almost impossible for her to be ignorant of who he was. Almost. But as soon as he openly told her that he was the author the Eldritch books, the awareness should have darkened her eyes instantly. It was completely impossible that she hadn't heard of his city.

There was only one reason Sam wouldn't have twigged to her deception, and Horace's, and he knew that he had to accept it. A very large part of him hadn't wanted to.

Sam turned off the A21 and a few minutes later drove into the village of Sevenoaks Weald. Horace's home was a large renovated cottage that looked like a postcard. Olde Worlde charm purchased by the square metre. It stood alone in the middle of its plot of land, surrounded by flowers and lawns and embarrassingly fey topiary. The lawns needed mowing, Sam noticed. All the curtains in the cottage were drawn, as though there had been a death.

When he got to the front door, he found it ajar. This was wrong. Horace commuted to and from his bucolic retreat, but he was still a townie. He would keep his door locked, whether he was in or out. If he had any choice in the matter, that was. Sam's smouldering anger diminished slightly, muted by apprehension.

He pushed the door fully open, and the smell hit him.

It was Eldritch all over again, the same symphony of odours he had recognised on his way to meet Lionel Hepplewhite, the exact same atmosphere. He could sense invisible wreaths of it drifting out of the door like smoke.

He was sure now that he wasn't going to find Horace Jepson alive. He no longer had any doubt that Horace was involved in the complex plot Sam found himself living in. He knew. It was like reading the work that he had completed during his sleep, except this was real. Every writer was a microcosmic god, building their tiny universes with words. But Sam's words really were becoming flesh.

Somewhere in the cottage, Horace was dead. Who had killed him?

Probably the Golem, Sam thought. He did Jo first, then he did Horace. Soon, when Hyams had failed to contact Horace by phone to confirm Sam's alibi for the first murder, the policeman would come to the cottage, and he would find what he would find – the second.

Sam could see the order of events like dominoes falling. Like a plot-list that had already been written.

Hertz would have a record of Sam renting the car. He hadn't seen anyone in the village, but he knew that he would have been seen, his description noted. That was the way villages were. Someone would remember the car, and him. They'd know who he was, because he'd been here many times before. Horace's secretary, Rosie, would remember him calling and telling her that the agent would be safe until Sam got his hands on him. She'd tell the police that at the time she'd assumed it was a joke, but now, well…

Sam remembered thinking that a part of him had wanted to beat Horace to death, and he swallowed a mouthful of bile. He very much suspected that a part of him had done just that.

He turned around on the step and looked back towards his car. It wasn't too late to leave, just back out and drive away. Go home, pretend he was never here. Better yet, he could collect his passport and drive to the nearest airport. He had heard that extradition was difficult from certain South American countries. He might be grateful of that in the future.

Come on, run now, he told himself, but he couldn't. He didn't even try.

Comeback was writing itself. The plot was pre-ordained. Sam was living in the novel he was writing. Everything in a novel is of significance. There was a *reason* he was here. He hadn't come all this way to just turn around and run. There was something here for him to do, or learn. Characters in novels who do nothing are eventually edited out. They are unmade. Unknown. Forgotten.

Nobody edits me out of my own book, Sam thought, and stepped into the cottage.

14

DS Morley listened to the incredulous voice coming out of his mobile phone. Sometimes in response he breathed phrases like, *right, okay*, and *yes, I see*, although he was very far from seeing, and clearly nothing was either right or okay. In fact, everything was completely fucked, and had been since the night Honest Bob Allison had been arrested with a dead girl in the back of his car.

After leaving Sam Parker's house, DI Hyams had directed Morley to drive a little way out of town, then ordered him to cruise the country lanes until, finally, he said stop. They sat in the cooling car for fifteen minutes, unspeaking, while Hyams morosely drained Morley's hip flask. Then Hyams had declared his intention to take a piss and disappeared into the trees. Five or six minutes later, Morley's phone had rung, and he'd found himself speaking to a very confused and upset pathologist. When he'd eventually rung off, Hyams was still nowhere to be seen.

The DS waited for a further five minutes, then got out of the car. Hyams had changed a great deal in a very short space of time, and now he was almost a different man altogether. Morley didn't like to leave him alone too long, in case he no longer recognised him.

The woodland where they had stopped must have been largely undisturbed for well over a hundred years, in spite of the B road that snaked through it. The trees were huge, and the undergrowth clung to Morley's trousers as though it wanted to keep them. Pulling free of thorns, he stumbled out into an unexpected clearing and immediately saw Hyams's back.

The DI stood looking down at the ground. A dirt road created by trespassing cars led into the clearing from the north, and the small clearing had been used as a parking place, probably by courting couples or doggers. Condom Central. Blow-Job Junction. Morley couldn't imagine anyone else wanting to come out here, unless…

Unless…

Morley walked up beside Hyams. The DI was staring at the tyre treads of what must have been the last vehicle to park here. Morley could see the signs of a hapless six-point turn pressed into the mulch underfoot. He had a pretty powerful camera on his phone and an even better digital camera back in his boot, so photos weren't a problem, but if Hyams wanted a cast made, they'd have to call out the CSIs.

'You think we'd get a match with Bob's Honda?' he asked.

Hyams nodded, preoccupied.

Morley glanced around the clearing. Heavy foliage made it a very private place. It looked like wilderness, but in reality they were only forty or fifty yards from the road. If he tried very hard, he could see Allison turning off the engine and reaching for Rebecca Walton's throat. He stopped trying so hard.

'How did you know to look out here, Guv?'

'I read it in a book,' Hyams muttered.

Morley let *that* one go over his head. He didn't even try to reach for it.

'Guv, Kings Cross's pathologist has just been on the phone. He's freaked out, big time.'

'Fee?'

'Yeah. He says when he first got her back to the morgue last night, he thought he'd made a mistake. Because when he unbagged her, it looked like she'd been dead longer than his original guess. A *lot* longer. Three to five *days* longer.'

'That's a lot more alibis Parker's got to come up with.'

In spite of his eagerness to pass on the pathologist's curious findings, Morley paused. It was obvious that Hyams was completely hung up on Sam Parker. Obsessed. Morley didn't know why, or why they weren't checking up on the alibis the writer had *already* given them, which seemed a simple enough task. Hyams seemed to have some theory that tied Parker not only to the prostitute's murder but also to Bob Allison's activities and apparent suicide. Increasingly, it was looking more and more to the DS as though his DI didn't want that theory pulled apart by something as trivial as the facts. It was an astonishing about-face in an officer who had always played by the rules.

'But, Guv, listen to this. When the pathologist went back to the body this morning to begin the post mortem proper, it had changed *again*. Now he says it looks like she's been dead for a month, maybe more. He's sitting with the body now with a video camera.

He says she's decomposing so quickly you can nearly see it happening in real time.'

Morley tried to read Hyams's face, and couldn't.

'He says it's like she's melting, even the bones. Melting, and... *evaporating* somehow. She's disappearing right in front of him. He said he'd started to think it might be something called necrotising fassiwhatsit, some kind of rare virus that eats flesh. But then he looked at some tissue samples under a microscope, and he says he didn't know what he was looking at. He's not even sure it's flesh and blood anymore, Guv. He said it best resembles *wood pulp*. How can that be?'

Hyams had wandered away while his DS spoke, and now stood at the far side of the tyre-carved turning circle. If he thought that what Morley was telling him was strange, he wasn't showing it.

'Guv?'

'Come and look at this.'

Morley carefully walked around the perimeter of the tyre tracks, and rejoined Hyams. Now the DI was looking at a number of footprints that led out of the uneven circle of mulch and disappeared into the undergrowth. If you looked carefully, it was possible to see where someone had broken through the undergrowth further on. It was a trail.

'About Bob's size, same kind of sole,' Hyams said of the footprints. 'They're deep though, and the ground isn't that soft.'

'Bob wasn't a heavyweight.'

'No. But if he was carrying the girl's body…'

They followed the trail through the undergrowth, Hyams five feet to its left and Morley five feet to its right, scanning the ground between them. Apart from the trail itself, they saw nothing. Late at night, in almost absolute darkness and carrying Rebecca Walton's dead weight, Allison might have been expected to waver, to avoid the thicker clumps of bracken when they impeded him, skirt the thornier patches of undergrowth when they became too fierce. To lose his way, at least a little. But the trail was as straight as an arrow.

The woodland stopped at a field of wild heather. Bob Allison's trail continued through it, all the way to the other side, on a direct line to the ruins of a burnt-out circular stone-built structure. Once it had been a windmill.

Morley glanced at Hyams, who was breathing more heavily than their hike could account for.

'You think he brought her here to do it?'

'To do *something*,' Hyams replied. 'Of course he did. Come on.'

What remained of the windmill's walls were uneven, like a line of broken teeth, and barely rose above their heads. When they stepped in through the small, low doorway, they saw that a single charred beam had survived the inferno which had destroyed the rest of the structure. It looked like the crossbeam of a gallows. Below it, some of the fallen blocks of smoke-blackened stone had been neatly stacked to form a raised surface, like an altar. On top of it was a full collection of Sam Parker's Eldritch novels. On top of the books, like an offering to a malign god, were Rebecca Walton's lacy black knickers. Neither man would touch anything on the altar, and not just because they would later need to be dusted for fingerprints by the CSI team.

Morley looked at the books, and the work that had gone into arranging the blocks of stone. He instantly waved bye-bye to his preferred explanation of Allison's crime, which was that the girl's death had been mostly an accident, and that what Allison had subsequently done to her body had been the actions of a severely shocked and guilt-ridden man, driven temporarily insane.

'This wasn't a crime of passion,' he said. 'It was premeditated. Planned.'

'Yes,' Hyams replied. 'But by who?'

15

Horace *was* dead, Sam discovered. He *had* been beaten to death. He had been beaten *beyond* death. Sam sat on the sofa in the ruins of the cottage's living room-dining room-study hybrid, amidst the books torn from the shelves, the broken furniture, and the sticky patches and gelatinous heaps which were all that was left of Horace Jepson.

In his hands, Sam held five battered hardbacks he had salvaged from the wreckage. *A Private Place, The Family Man, The Quick of the Night, Double Trouble,* and *Sweet Dream of Death.* These were Lionel Hepplewhite's published Trinity novels, which closely corresponded to Sam's first five Eldritch books: *Sly Jack Road, Imaginary Families, An Hour of Darkness, Underlined Twice*, and *Death in a Dream.*

Sam imagined that Horace must have hidden his secret collection away whenever he visited, and then

198

brought them out again after he was gone. Set them on the same shelf with Sam's Eldritch books. Matching sets. Different times, different generations, same nightmares.

Sam couldn't bring himself to look at Horace's remains again. Once was more than enough. He was sad far beyond his own expectation.

When all he had seen of Horace for fifteen years had been a man cashing his percentage of Sam's substantial royalty cheques and indulging his appetites for food and young women, it had been easy to forget just how important a figure he had been in Sam's life. Back when Sam had only two published but unsuccessful novels and the clothes he stood up in to his name, Horace had been Sam's saviour. Taking a chance on a writer whose work no one else wanted, on a writer who seemed to have stepped so far out of the mainstream he was invisible.

Now, seeing that Horace had owned Hepplewhite's books, Sam realised that the agent had had his own agenda from the start, long before lining him up with Jo. There was a long, long back-story to this tale. But Sam couldn't really blame Horace for what was happening now. He knew that he would have gone on writing about Eldritch whether he was published or not, just as Hepplewhite had, a fiction-junkie addicted to his own city. Horace's involvement had enabled him to pursue his addiction in comfort instead of poverty, that was all.

Of course, it also meant that Eldritch had dug deep into the public consciousness, thereby feeding the dead crime boss's power – according to Hepplewhite, at any rate, but there was no telling how true that might be. If it was, maybe Horace had even *saved* Sam from sharing Hepplewhite's miserable life and his even worse fate, trapped in a halfway house between worlds after the big plan failed to come together.

But it was like selling your soul to the devil, he thought. You might live in comfort, in luxury even, as Sam had, but when the time comes to pay the piper, you find that the cost is too high.

Having become acclimatized to the cottage's mingled odours, half-Eldritch, half-abattoir, Sam was roused from his thoughts as the atmosphere of Eldritch suddenly intensified. He felt a chill puff of air ruffle his jacket collar and a slight pressure build in his ears. The hair at the back of his neck stood up as he felt a presence gathering behind him.

Hepplewhite's books slipped out of his hands and tumbled over the stained carpet. One of them fell open at an illustration, some God-awful pug-ugly in an overcoat and hat which Sam knew was supposed to be Hepplewhite's Golem, his own Karl Wizeman. Sam's own interior image was much more fearsome.

Is that who was behind him now? Is that what was meant to happen here?

Is it time for my character to die, he wondered.

Sam looked around.

'*You.*'

Standing behind the sofa was the girl from Eldritch.

'Yes.' She smiled at him. A sad smile. 'I tried to warn you.'

Sam nodded. 'I know.'

He stood up, uncomfortable to have her standing over him. She wore the same fur coat as the other night, buttoned up, with no trace of any other clothing beneath it. Although he couldn't see her feet, he knew they were still bare, the toenails short but a little ragged, like a city dog's. He was drawn to her, attracted in spite of himself and his fear, and so stood very still, giving nothing.

'Tell me who you are,' he said. 'Tell me your name.'

'I don't have a name, never had one,' the girl said. 'You know why. Think hard, you'll know why.'

Because I didn't give you one, Sam thought, but then realised this wasn't exactly what the girl meant. What she did mean made goose-pimples spring up all over his body.

She saw the idea growing in his eyes, and she nodded solemnly.

'Yes,' she said, 'in that one respect, I take after my father.'

'I've waited a lifetime for this moment,' the girl said into Sam's terrified silence. 'A lifetime, and more.'

Sam swallowed. Unconsciously, he had taken several steps back, and had come perilously close to stepping in a part of Horace.

'You've waited all that time to see your father come back,' he said.

'No. To make sure that he won't. Not *ever*.' She smiled at Sam again, her head at a slight angle. 'You thought you'd set a trap for yourself, didn't you?'

Sam nodded mutely. He still wasn't sure that he hadn't, and she saw it.

201

'You can trust me, I'm on your side,' she said. 'I warned you about your lover, didn't I? I sent you to Lionel Hepplewhite, to bring you closer to the truth. Why do you think I'm here now?'

Sam shrugged.

'I'm here because you brought me here. You *wrote* me. You wrote me here to help you, if I can.'

'I don't understand.'

The girl came around the sofa and sat on it, in exactly the same place Sam had been. The fur of her coat seemed to caress the outside of her thighs as they were revealed. Sam imagined himself kneeling before her, feeling her silken skin closing around him. He closed his eyes.

'My father is using your talent,' the girl said. 'He's using your powers of creation to write him back to life, back into the flesh. And then, eventually, into your *world*. Your agent, your lover, and Wizeman, they are *his* characters, working for *his* ends. I'm one of *your* characters, one intended to stop him and save you.'

'I thought you were Wizeman's grand-daughter,' Sam said. 'You visited him, took him gifts…'

'Yes, I've kept my eye on him over the years, posing as his grand-daughter. He wasn't aware enough to know any different until recently. I knew that my father's first step would be to use him. The Golem always served him well.'

'Why did he kill Jo? Fee, I mean, or whatever her real name was. Why did he kill Horace?'

The girl calmly looked at the agent's battered, dismembered corpse. A native Eldritchian, she would have seen worse on an almost daily basis.

'He would have talked, your agent, once you'd found him. Sung like a bird. You would have made him explain his part in the plot as a collaborator. He'd served his purpose, and he had to die. Fee was a sleeper, drafted into this world the day you began to write *Sly Jack Road*, and my father knew that you were the one. Finally, the one. He left Fee to her own devices. He knew she would find a way into your life. The light of Eldritch drew her like a moth.

'And like your agent, once she had served her purpose and her cover was compromised, she was a waste of energy. Better to get the Golem to send her back to Eldritch, to add to The Light of Souls. That's my father's main source of nourishment. Death feeds him.'

Sam shook his head. 'I don't understand. I don't know what you are. I don't know what *any* of you are.'

'We're the Shaped,' the girl said. 'Whatever is written, we are. The stronger the writing, the more energy and concentration devoted to it by its readers, the more vividly we are drawn. Other cities exist, other sets of characters not shaped by you. Some of them are even pleasant. But everything, everyone, is the Shaped. We are fiction. My father doesn't want to be.'

'And his daughter wants to stop him,' Sam said. 'Why?'

'Because he is evil. The things he would do in your world, the power he would seek... It is unthinkable.'

203

'But if his spirit is so strong, why doesn't he just write himself alive? He's writing the book on his own as it is.'

'That's not true, because the created cannot create. I told you, he has to work *through* you to achieve his aims, using your mind, your ability, and he hides from you what he can. He's been working for fifteen years to bring you here, now. To the cusp of atrocity.'

Sam thought about this for a while, then asked, 'What will happen to me if he succeeds?'

'He'll become you. Or you'll become *him*.' She studied Sam. 'You know that it's happening already, don't you?'

She nodded at his shock.

'Tell me, who is the author of all the evil in Eldritch?'

She was knowingly paraphrasing an expression Lionel Hepplewhite had used to describe the dead crime boss's spirit. It was as if she had been there.

'He is, your father.'

'Yes. In Eldritch.' She leaned forwards and pointed at Sam. 'And in the real world, this world, *you* are.'

Sam put his hands to his head. There was a terrible pressure in there he had to contain. It was a feeling like fingers flexing in his brain.

'Okay, okay. If you're here to help me, tell me what to do. How can I stop him?'

For the first time, the girl seemed uncomfortable. 'You've already started. You've hidden me from him in just the same way as he's hidden his characters from you. But I can only help you so much. To stop

204

him completely, to finish it forever… For that you have to go where he is.'

Sam stared at her. 'I have to go *into* Eldritch?'

'Yes.'

'To Sly Jack Road?'

She nodded, and Sam sighed.

'To the mill house.'

'That's where his spirit is, it's the place that he haunts.'

Sam shook his head. 'I can't do that. I can't.'

The girl stood up and approached him, almost glided towards him until they were bare inches apart. He could smell her body scent, he could smell the dead animal of her fur coat. It was so Eldritch, he thought. The beguiling, side by side with the repulsive.

'Of course you can do it,' she said. 'You're the author, Sam, you can do anything you like. You can do anything you *want*. Just go to the place where the barrier between reality and fiction is weakest, and force yourself in.'

Her voice and her words, intentionally or not, seemed loaded with double-meaning.

'Let me help you. *Make* me help you.'

He grabbed her by the shoulders, his roughness spurred by anger and fear, and he shook her so hard her head snapped back and forth on her elegant neck. The collar of her coat opened a little more, revealing her cleavage.

'Maybe I can do it, maybe I can't,' he told her. 'But I won't do it. I *won't*.'

Touching the girl made Sam feel dizzy and queasy, as it had the first time back at his house. But the sheer feel of her in his hands, even though it was anger, terror and frustration, was intensely satisfying. Maybe *especially* because that's the way it was. And he could see that she liked it, too. Her eyes were shining with a deeper lustre, the pupils suddenly amazingly large. He could feel himself getting hard.

'You can go there on his terms or yours,' she told him.

Her eyes were locked to his. Sam wanted to fall into them. He wanted to find the place where the barrier was weakest, and force his way in.

'Your terms,' she breathed, 'would be better.'

She started to leave him then, to lose her solidity. He could feel her becoming less substantial in his hands, just like before. Her time with him was up. A chapter was coming to an end.

'Write me again,' she said. 'Soon. Before it's too late.'

He thought he would see her begin to slowly fade, but in the end she just went, and he was left with his outstretched hands curled around nothing but air.

They were shaking.

16

The bathroom was swathed in steam as Charles Beckett climbed out of the shower, pink as a shrimp and unable to leave his erect penis alone even while he was towelling himself dry. As far as he was concerned, the day was a roller-coaster ride that had just begun.

He'd had a busy, busy morning, and the afternoon, he thought, would be even busier. If he could ever drag himself away from his wife, that is.

He wanted to ring up the tabloids and tell the world that he had discovered a miracle cure for impotence. Forget Viagra, hormone injections and therapy – murder made you as hard as a rock. And it didn't matter *who* you murdered, either.

He'd already been out to collect his gun. It was a clandestine meeting that had taken place in a room above a closed-down antique shop on Hampstead High Street. The gun was a disappointment, a shabby old sawn-off about a foot and a half long that had come with a box of corroded shells. He had been quick to inform his supplier of his disappointment, and when the man had threatened to remove his merchandise from the market, Beckett, now prepared for life's little ups and downs – and armed from his own kitchen – had smartly planted a meat cleaver into the other man's head.

The man had time for one final word before oblivion took him. It hadn't been one for posterity. It'd sounded like 'noodles'.

Then, bam, the old trouser snake had instantly gone into attack mode again and it was all Beckett could do to make it to his car before slapping off to reduce the pressure. By the time he'd got home, he was ready again and had to visit his wife once more.

Now he wiped the bathroom mirror free of moisture and considered himself. The beard he had cultivated so carefully for so many years no longer fitted with his self-image, and he began to take it off with a twin-blade razor he'd found among Philip's toiletries. The man who emerged from the foam looked like a man of action, a man of the world. A potent man.

207

Beckett could feel himself being drawn back to the master bedroom and his supremely compliant wife, but he was made of sterner stuff now. His time, his true time, was drawing near. He had a job to do, one that would give him full control over the rest of his life.

He raised an invisible shotgun and aimed it at the mirror.

'Parker, I'm coming for you.'

17

Driving out of Horace's village at speed, Sam felt a chill as someone walked over his grave. He shook it off uneasily and found his way back onto the A21, his mind racing, trying to sort everything into a form he might be able to understand. Something he could work with, and act on.

What are my options, he wondered?

Go into Eldritch, that was one. Yeah, right, sure, he thought. Even if it were possible, even if he could do it, which he doubted, would he actually dare to go into his city, the world he had shaped? One simple fact had been repeated so often that it had almost ceased to have meaning, but Sam thought it would be worthwhile to say it one last time. Eldritch was not a *good* place. Look at its citizens. He reckoned he'd last about ten minutes before he ended up in the gutter with his throat cut and his pockets turned out.

Next option? Destroy all that exists of *Comeback*. That idea sounded a lot better. A lot safer.

Obviously, based on his experience the night before, he couldn't simply do it through deleting the files. The computer wouldn't let him. Solution?

Destroy the computer itself. Smash in the screen, stamp all his flash drives to pieces, rip out the hard drive and pulverise the bastard thing with his Inflexible Friend.

Oh yes. That sounded good.

But what if he failed?

Sam's optimistic side told him that it would probably be better not to think about that. But he had to. He had to consider everything. He intended to fight for his life, fight against the dead crime boss coming back and coming into this world. But he knew that he needed a back-up plan. Something to get him out of jail if he fought and lost. He didn't want to end up like Hepplewhite.

A car horn blasted him from his thoughts. He had been drifting into the oncoming lane of traffic. Got to be more careful, he thought.

He didn't want to kill himself, as Hepplewhite had recommended. But if he failed to destroy *Comeback*, he might not even get the chance to try. What he needed was an ally, someone who could do it for him at the crucial moment, if that was what he wanted.

I could do that, he thought suddenly.

If he had created the Eldritch girl to help him, he could also create or manipulate another character to kill him if he got in too deep and couldn't do it himself. He could write his own quick, relatively painless death, and save himself from something far worse.

The idea was very powerful, striking a resonance within Sam which convinced his writer's instinct that he'd made the right choice.

209

He looked at the section of road ahead. It was straight, and almost completely clear. He closed his eyes, and began to follow the sound of tap-tap-tapping all the way to the back of his mind. He intended to interrupt the flow of the story, if he could, despite the terrible nausea being so close to it induced. He intended to insert a necessary piece of business to introduce a character who would be prepared to kill him without hesitation.

But then, on his internal computer screen, reading, instantly knowing, he realised that he'd already done it. The character was already in existence, it was up and running. And when he saw who it was, Sam pulled back away from the story, from the sickness, opened his eyes and began to laugh. Eighty miles an hour, screaming his head off with laughter, almost crying. It really was very funny.

If he wasn't careful, and very lucky, he was going to make the Listmaker the happiest man in either world.

18

'I told that bastard to stay home,' Hyams said. 'Where the fuck has he gone?'

Morley shifted uncomfortably in the driver's seat. They had been ringing Sam Parker's bell on and off for the last quarter of an hour. The door was never answered, and neither was his phone. They had reluctantly concluded that he really had gone out, and Hyams was furious.

'He was under no legal obligation to stay,' Morley ventured.

Hyams spat out the car window. 'Legal obligation, my sweet arsehole.'

'What are we going to do?'

'Wait until he comes back, then arrest him, of course.'

Morley frowned. 'Arrest him on what charge, Guv?'

'I'll think of something later. The important thing is to get him.'

'Guv, you just can't do that.'

'Watch me.'

Morley took a deep breath, and said what he had to say.

'It isn't like the old days anymore, Guv. You know that, you more than anyone. If we arrest Parker on some trumped-up charge, it'll work against us even if he does turn out to be guilty. You know how it works now. It won't matter if we find a dozen bodies in his house, they'll throw out a murder charge if we've arrested him for picking his nose.'

Hyams, his face sour, was making the fingers of his right hand yap-yap-yap as Morley spoke.

'I'm not interested in the law anymore,' he told Morley. 'I'm interested in justice.'

'I think it's comments like that which worry me the most.'

Hyams patted his DS's shoulder none too gently. 'Let me do the worrying. In the meantime, did you see that little corner shop back there? Why don't you take a walk and come back with a little refreshment?'

'Guv, I−'

'Vodka,' Hyams insisted. 'Absolut, if they have it. I feel in an Absolut kind of mood.'

211

Morley thought about arguing, also about asking for some money, but in the end did neither. 'Absolut?' he asked, reaching for the door.

'Yeah − no, wait!'

Morley turned back. Through the windscreen he saw a car approaching Parker's house at high speed. Tyres squealing, it slewed to a halt in front of his gates, directly opposite the policemen's car, and Sam Parker jumped out before the engine had died. He left the driver's door open, sticking out into the road, then unlocked his gate and rushed into his house. The car slowly rolled down the camber of the road until its tyres bounced off the curb. He'd left the handbrake off.

Hyams turned to Morley. 'How about a charge of dangerous driving and suspicious behaviour?'

The DS nodded uncertainly. 'Better than nothing.' He peered across the road through the abandoned car's open door. 'I think he's even left the keys in it.'

Hyams stared at Parker's house, thinking. Morley had turned out to be a good man, after all, but he didn't appreciate the situation they were faced with. Hyams didn't really *understand* it, but he appreciated it to hell and back. Sam Parker was involved in these murders, in them up to his neck, and it had something to do with his books. There wasn't a shred of real evidence to support Hyams's suspicions, but he had one of those feelings.

Parker, his books, they were *doing* something together. Changing things. They had certainly changed Hyams, he realised that, but he was reluctant to acknowledge just how much.

Hyams put his hand on the car door, quickly scanning the street. Then he took his hand off the door again.

'Ready, Guv?'

Hyams shook his head. 'Not yet. Look.'

Morley did. Two men were crossing the road, heading for Parker's house. One was short, scrawny, white and rumpled, the other tall, black, handsome and immaculate. Hyams had noticed them climbing out of a parked Mercedes sports car with tinted windows.

'Who do you suppose *they* are,' Morley asked. 'The Odd Couple?'

'Nathaniel Longman and Nigel Cassidy,' Hyams said. 'Parker's little friends, come for a sleep-over. Well, well, well, the plot thickens.' He sounded pleased with himself. 'These guys are writers, too. They've each had one of Parker's Eldritch books dedicated to them. Cassidy, the runty one, Parker called him *The Luddite*. He called Longman *The Survivor*. They were at the convention with him. Thick as thieves, the three of them.'

Cassidy pushed the bell on Parker's gate, and after a short while Longman spoke into the intercom.

'You think they're involved, too?' Morley asked.

'Of course. They're Parker's accomplices. It's easy to establish an alibi if you have other people doing the dirty work for you.' Hyams rubbed the palms of his hands together rapidly, as though attempting to start a fire. 'Now we're getting to it…'

Morley became more worried as he listened to his DI build his castle in the air. Parker's two callers had added a new turret to the structure. Morley wondered how long the foundations would hold, built as they were on nothing at all. It wasn't that he hadn't seen this prophetic side to policemen before, just never to this apocalyptic degree.

'The question is,' Hyams said, 'how *long* have they been parked there. Did they see *us* at Parker's gate?'

Morley shrugged. He didn't have a clue what to say.

Hyams thought for a moment, then said, 'We'll wait and find out.'

19

Sam opened the door. Cassidy and Longman stood on the steps, smiling at him, just as though the world hadn't gone mad. Then he noticed that even though Longman's smile was quite convincing, it didn't quite cover the apprehension in his large eyes. Cassidy's smile was more of a painful grimace, as though his toenails were being pulled. When he stepped back they came into the hallway, and Sam closed the door again.

Cassidy found Longman's eyes and nodded at the baseball bat Sam held down by his leg.

'Expecting someone else?' Longman asked.

'I wasn't expecting anyone at all. Least of all you two.'

'What about the men in the car across the street?'

Longman described the men he and Cassidy had watched at Sam's gate, and Sam had no difficulty in recognising them as Hyams and Morley. He didn't like the fact that they were watching his house now, but he made no attempt to explain his concerns to his friends. He wouldn't know where to begin.

The three men stood looking at each other like strangers in a lift. Sam was very conscious of the weight of the bat in his hand, the way he was pressing it against his leg, as though to hide it. He had been halfway up the stairs to the first floor when the doorbell had rung. Mounting fear had made him glad of the delay. Now he wasn't so sure.

Why were they here. What were the two of them up to? He could see that something was wrong with them. Cassidy always had something wrong with him, of course, but he had never seen Nathaniel Longman look as uneasy. Even his handsome smile was failing him now.

They're afraid of me, Sam suddenly realised. I'm scaring them, and it has nothing to do with the baseball bat.

A flare went off inside his head, and he knew. Had he written his friends into it, too? Christ, some friend he was.

'Sam, we've got to talk to you,' Longman said.

'So it seems. You want to talk about Eldritch, don't you?'

Cassidy and Longman glanced at one another uneasily.

'We've been doing a lot of thinking,' Longman began. 'Both separately and together, and we−'

'Listen,' Sam interrupted. 'I can guess what you've been thinking about, and I'm sure it was hard for you to come here. I'm sorry, I don't have time to dance around the subject. I'm in a hurry.'

'Eldritch is real,' Cassidy blurted out, suddenly finding his voice.

'What Nigel means,' Longman said, 'is that there have been some strange—'

'Nigel's right. You're both right. Just tell me what you're here for.'

Again the two men exchanged a glance, then seemed to tense themselves, as though preparing to fight.

'You have to stop writing, Sam,' Cassidy said, squaring his narrow shoulders. 'If you won't, we're prepared to make you stop.'

He stuck out his chin in a pugilistic display that made Sam want to laugh. Cassidy was two weights below fly, and might have come off second best against a determined ten-year-old. Longman, who would have made a more serious opponent, nodded in agreement.

Sam smiled. 'Thanks for the thought,' he said, 'but it's gone a little further than you probably suspect. The good news is, I've *already* stopped writing. The bad news is, the book's going great. It's writing itself.'

Cassidy frowned. 'What—'

'Don't bother asking questions, because there are no rational answers. I don't know how it came to this, and I don't know how it could be possible. All I really know is that it's happening, and I've got to try to stop it.'

Sam couldn't tell whether they understood or not, and he didn't care. Suddenly, his sense of time passing was incredibly acute. He raised the bat between them, showed it to them, and Cassidy and Longman moved back a little.

'Now,' he said. 'If you'll excuse me, I was just on my way to take out my computer.'

'We'll come with you,' Longman said.

20

Charles Beckett had winded himself badly climbing over the eight foot wall that enclosed Parker's well-manicured acre and a half. He'd caught his trouser cuff on a loose strand of the barbed wire he'd just snipped and fallen all the way to the ground. He was damned lucky that the shotgun, suspended by a piece of string around his neck and hidden under his jacket, wasn't loaded at the time. The way he was carrying it, it might not have killed him immediately if it had gone off, but it would probably have vaporised his erection. The sound of the shot would have alerted Parker and he'd have run, leaving Beckett to bleed to death.

He couldn't think of anything worse than being on the brink of achieving his goal, only to fall at the last hurdle. Unthinkable.

After he recovered his breath, he headed for a line of large conifer trees that divided the long garden, acting as a screen, and settled down to wait. It wouldn't be long before his chance came, he was eerily sure of that. Everything was going his way.

Only one thing still bothered him.

On his way here he'd had the impression that he wasn't entirely alone. It had felt like he was being followed, although he had tried as hard as possible to make sure that wasn't happening, driving in circles, through one-way systems, darting through red lights.

But the feeling had persisted, of being watched. Spied upon.

Just in case this was true, he had abruptly decided to change his plan. Strength lay in the ability to adapt to changing circumstances. If someone was watching him, it was probably with a view to stopping him killing Sam Parker. Who that someone might be, he didn't know. It didn't really matter. Originally, he had intended to maim Parker with the shotgun, then have some fun torturing the man to death − just as Parker had tortured him creatively for so many years. Now he had decided he was just going to blow the fucker away.

So okay, he wouldn't suffer the way he deserved to, but he'd still be dead. That was good enough for Beckett.

He hunkered down behind the conifers, slotted two cartridges into the shotgun barrels, and then snapped the weapon shut. He shuffled slightly to his left, to give himself a clearer view of the French windows at the back of Parker's large conservatory.

It would be soon.

21

They were almost halfway along the first-floor corridor when Sam heard the typing in his head stop. He halted so abruptly that Cassidy and Longman both walked into his back.

'Did you hear that?' he asked, knowing it was a foolish question. How could they have heard. 'It's stopped.'

'What's stopped?'

'The typing, the book. It knows we're here. *He* knows.'

Longman put his hand on Sam's shoulder. 'Who knows?'

'The crime boss. The dead crime boss.'

He looked at their puzzled faces, and remembered that they didn't know the first thing about the plot of *Comeback*. They didn't even know its title. Their suspicions and fears came from whatever had happened in the past, leaks Sam had been blind to, or *blinded* to. The hidden back-story.

'It doesn't matter,' he said. 'There isn't time to explain.'

'But if it's stopped, that's good, isn't it?'

'I don't know what it means,' Sam admitted. 'But I think it's unlikely to be good.'

Sam jogged the rest of the way along the corridor, Cassidy and Longman at his heels. When he reached the bottom of the steps leading up into the attic, he stopped again. He could feel waves of crushing pressure pouring down out of the darkness of his office, and when he looked at his two friends he could tell that they felt it, too. Their faces were twisted like dishrags against the mingled odours.

'That's what Eldritch smells like,' he told them, surprised when the words came out sounding like a boast.

He put a foot on the first step, grateful beyond words that they both shuffled forward without hesitation, clearly intending to accompany him. But tempting though it was to go up there mob-handed, he knew he couldn't let them. It would amount to

219

murder, and he already had too much blood on his hands.

'This is where you stay,' he told them quietly. 'Wait for me here.'

They shook their heads.

'We're coming with you,' Longman said.

'Nigel, Nat — you don't understand,' Sam said. 'I can imagine something terrible waiting for you up there.'

'We're coming with you, Sam,' Cassidy said. 'We'll take our chances.'

'No, listen to me, please,' Sam insisted. 'I'm not guessing. I tell you, I can *imagine* something terrible waiting for you up there. I *am* imagining it right now, whether I want to or not. Believe me, it's really there, waiting. It'll kill you both.'

'What is it?' Longman asked.

Sam shrugged. 'I'll only know that when it appears.'

His eyes pleaded with each of them in turn.

'Please don't make me responsible for your deaths.'

Longman sighed. 'Okay, Sam, we'll wait.'

'Hang on a minute!' Cassidy said. 'I don't think we should—'

'We'll wait,' Longman repeated, silencing Cassidy with a raised hand. 'As long as we hear the sound of a computer being smashed up, we'll wait. But if we hear anything else, Sam — anything — we're coming up.'

He looked at Cassidy. 'Agreed?'

After a moment, Cassidy begrudgingly nodded.

'Okay,' Sam said. 'Agreed. But both of you, if it comes to it, be very, very careful. It may just be something as simple as a madman with a knife, but it may not. You think you know Eldritch, but you don't. The books have only scratched the surface. Underneath what I uncovered, there are worse horrors.'

The stairs between the first floor and Sam's office were darker than ever, and the absence of light embraced him. He felt as though he were being moved through it, rather than moving of his own volition. It was like being a morsel of food in the intestine of a colossal animal. He stopped when he sensed that he had reached the top of the stairs. He could see nothing, his office was pitch black, and silent.

He reached out to his left, to where the light-switch was, but before he found it the darkness fled. His office instantly became bright, lit not by electric light but by daylight coming in through the two long windows. He had to narrow his eyes against the sudden glare.

His office appeared to be unchanged from the last time he had seen it. As far as he could see, nothing had been disturbed. No monsters lurked in the shadows, because there were no shadows. There was no dark twin, possessively clasping the computer keyboard. The computer wasn't even turned on.

He glanced back into the stairwell. There the darkness remained solid, sealing the office off from the rest of the house like a cork. Maintaining the integrity of the office's atmosphere. Something was definitely going to happen. He had to act before it did.

Desperately trying not to think, to speculate, to imagine anything whatsoever, Sam started across the long room towards his computer. When he was half a dozen paces away, he raised his Inflexible Friend high above his head, tightening his fingers around the handgrip. A deep breath now.

Smash it!

This he *did* allow himself to imagine. The bat cutting through the screen like a blade, the whump of the thing exploding, a shower of sparks. Then on to the tower and the hard-drive.

He arched his back, and brought the bat down from his full height with as much force as he could bring to bear. His eyes reflexively closed as he struck, and the impact shuddered up through his arms and shoulders and shook his whole body. But he heard no smash, only a loud, dull thud.

When Sam opened his eyes, he saw that he had put a major dent in the surface of his desk where the computer monitor had been. The monitor itself had gone, and so had all the other elements of his computer. All that remained was the tangle of power cables, and they were going too, disappearing like fuses burning all the way to the wall sockets. He watched in amazement until the plugs almost audibly popped away, and then he turned back to his desk.

The ceramic dish in which he kept his jumble of flash drives had gone now. And, as he watched, his captain's chair followed.

All around his office, things were beginning to disappear, their images briefly shuddering as though they were passing behind a prism.

Books vanished from shelves, followed by the shelves themselves, his filing cabinets, the galley proofs for *Deep Water*, then the coffee table they had rested on. Even the carpet was beginning to go, as though it were being eaten by a swarm of invisible moths. Soon there would be nothing left. His office would be an empty shell, all his possessions, all his work, transported to another location.

Sam knew where they were bound. Maybe he and Lionel Hepplewhite would be roommates. Maybe he would be somewhere else, somewhere without even a view. The book hadn't stopped writing itself at all. It had simply been moved to a place where he couldn't reach it.

He realised that he had missed his last chance to stop it going too far, and unless he wanted to be trapped for all eternity in a halfway house between worlds, he had to act now.

When his dented desk went shuddering through the prism, Sam turned and ran for the stairs. He vaulted over his leather sofa just before it too began to shimmer.

Cassidy and Longman had heard not one sound since Sam had left them. They were debating in whispers over how much time they should allow to elapse before they followed him, when Sam came racing down out of the darkness, slipping on the final few steps.

The darkness seemed to cling to him in tendrils, and when they pulled him away it snapped back like elastic. They mistook the terror in his eyes for revulsion at the way the darkness had wanted to keep him.

Longman leant over and pulled Sam to his feet, and Sam used the momentum to shove him back into Cassidy. The two became entangled, stumbled and fell, and then Sam was tearing along the corridor away from them.

He heard them calling his name.

'Stay away from me,' he shouted back. 'Don't follow me.'

He went down the stairs to the ground floor as fast as he dared. If he slipped and broke his ankle it would all be over. He made it to the bottom just as Cassidy and Longman reached the top.

'Don't be a fool,' Cassidy shouted. 'We can help you!'

Without answering, Sam bolted across the hall into the sitting room. He slammed the double doors shut and locked them. There were other routes around the house that would take his friends to the garden at the back of the house, but they took longer. Even if they remembered their way around, they would be too late to save him. Or, he thought, to curse him, depending on your point of view.

Sam ran through the house, through the sitting room and the kitchen, into the conservatory and past the plunge pool. He knew he was saying goodbye to it all. He didn't bother to unlock the doors to the garden, just booted them open. He stumbled out onto the patio area, fragments of glass still falling, and stopped. Breathing hard, he put his arms out to his sides, as though he were being crucified.

'Now!' he shouted. 'Do it now!'

A man stepped out from behind the trees that divided his gardens. At first Sam didn't recognise him, but then he mentally added a silver-grey beard, and knew that he'd worked everything just right. He saw his assassin open his jacket, and thought that the shotgun he'd brought should do the trick. But it had to be now.

'Come on, Beckett! Don't think, just do it!'

Beckett, extremely puzzled by Sam's behaviour but quite willing to oblige him this one time, raised his shotgun. Sam closed his eyes. It had to happen, it was for the best, but he didn't want to see it coming.

Make it a head-shot, he thought. Dead centre head-shot. Blow this nightmare away.

He heard two sounds simultaneously. The shotgun blast, and a scream. A split second later, there was a loud, glassy explosion that made him flinch. He opened his eyes and looked behind him. Three conservatory windows to his left had been completely shattered. Beckett had missed.

He looked back towards the trees and saw a dark, bent figure in an overcoat and hat wrestling the shotgun away from Charles Beckett, who was screaming in rage and terror. The gun was tossed aside and Beckett caught around the throat in a vicious, one-handed grip that silenced his screams instantly. The figure turned its head, and Sam saw the Golem's face, a bat-like mockery of a human face, all strange angles and curious flaps and ridges.

Sam was vaguely aware of footsteps racing up behind him, and of Cassidy and Longman's hands on him, pulling, their voices urging him to move, move, move. He was numb.

The Golem threw Beckett to the ground. Beckett heard something in his arm snap but was too terrified to feel pain.

'It has been a long time,' the Golem said heavily, but with evident satisfaction. 'I've waited a long time, *Listmaker*. You should never have betrayed the boss. You should have stayed hidden.'

He glanced across at the empty patio. Through the shattered windows he could see Parker being dragged away.

'It is a pity this must be over so soon. I had hoped for more time with you.'

Beckett began to scramble backwards. Denials surged into his mind, but there they stayed. He wanted to say that he was not the Listmaker, but this monster's words echoed around inside his psyche and a million memories spontaneously exploded there. Scenes, happenings, moments, none of which had ever appeared in any of Parker's novels.

He saw the city the Listmaker had fled to in order to escape the brutal retribution the Golem had inflicted on the three men who had assassinated the crime boss. He remembered his brief time there, and the face of the girl he had pretended to love. He remembered his return to Eldritch after the Golem had been struck down by his disease and become merely Wizeman. He saw his life reinterpreted through the Listmaker's, a series of vignettes, none of which were happy.

'I was young then, inexperienced,' Beckett heard himself say. 'They tricked me. I didn't know that the information they gave me was false.'

'I understand, but it doesn't matter. You helped them.'

'I didn't know!' Beckett screamed as the Golem reached for him.

22

Fearing a long wait, Hyams had sent Morley to the corner shop, after all, and while he'd waited impatiently for his refreshment to arrive, he'd got out of the car to stretch his legs. Then he'd heard glass breaking, and a man, Parker, he presumed, shouting. He'd heard the name Beckett. The shotgun blast had brought him running to the high wall at the side of Parker's property, which he was unable to scale because of the barbed wire. He could hear two men's voices, but he couldn't make out what they were saying, except for certain words.

…betrayal…the boss…

He recoiled, his innards freezing, as one of the men began to scream in agony.

Suddenly, Morley was at his side, breathless, the bottle of vodka swinging about inside a plastic carrier bag. The screaming had stopped. There was no moaning.

'Guv, look!'

Hyams followed Morley's pointing finger. About a hundred yards from where they stood, Sam Parker was being hustled out of his house by his two accomplices. They pulled him away from the car he had abandoned earlier, racing him across the road towards Longman's Mercedes.

'Come on!'

Hyams and Morley ran for their own car. As they reached it, they saw another man come out of Parker's front door. His face as he emerged into the light was astounding ugly, and his dark overcoat was spattered with a glistening substance they both immediately identified as blood.

The Mercedes' engine roared into life and it surged away from the curb, tyres squealing, and then shot in front of the house. Longman wasn't quite in control, and as the Mercedes passed Sam's hire car it caught the open door and ripped it off its hinges. The door spun in the road like a top.

The Golem seemed to see the hire car for the first time. He grinned, revealing two lines of grey teeth that looked serrated, then ran down the steps and jumped into the car. The policemen saw him fumbling around with the dashboard controls and kicking at the pedals. Seconds later, the engine started and the car pulled out, jerkily at first, then smoothing out as it sped away. The car was still in first gear and the engine was screaming.

Hyams and Morley looked after the two vehicles in astonishment.

'Guv, who the fuck was *that*?' Morley asked.

'I don't know – just follow him.'

23

Longman was driving as fast as he dared. He could see that the hire car was following them, and, from the silhouette of the hat, who was driving it. Cassidy, in the back seat, was looking through the window. At the moment he was too pumped-up to realise how fast they were moving.

'Who is it, Sam?' he asked. 'I don't recognise the character.'

'He's new. He's old but he's new.'

Sam quickly explained who the Golem was, and what had happened in his office, but it didn't really help clarify the matter. It spawned a dozen more questions, all of which were difficult to answer in a fast-moving car while you were being chased through London. He told them about Jo, about Horace, and about Charles Beckett. He told them about the crime boss who was dead and didn't want to be, and about his ambition to be more than fiction.

To be the Shaper, not the Shaped.

Cassidy was particularly inquisitive about the crime boss.

'Why doesn't he have a name?'

'I don't know.'

'It's your story, isn't it? *Why* don't you know?'

'For Christ's sake, Nigel, if I knew that I'd know, full stop.'

'But why−'

'There's another car following us,' Longman said.

Sam turned around in his seat to see. He caught glimpses of it around the hire car.

'I think it's the one that was opposite your house when we arrived.'

'Shit,' Sam swore quietly. 'Drunk Dave, that's all we need.'

229

'Drunk Dave Hawkins?' Cassidy asked, startled.

'How many Drunk Dave's are there? Yes, it's Dave. His real name, his name in our world, is Hyams. He's a DI with the Met'. Came to see me about a friend of his who murdered a young girl.'

'I saw that story in the papers,' Longman said. 'Is that what happens in your new book?'

'In the first few pages.'

Cassidy shook his head. 'It's incredible...'

Longman, concentrating on driving, was learning something useful. The Golem wasn't a very good driver. Maybe it was his age, or his deformities, or maybe his reflexes were partially shot because of the Alzheimer's. Maybe it was because the car was so modern, his experience so limited. Whatever the reason, he lost a little ground with every necessary change of gears, and because it was following the hire car, the policemen's car was dropping back, too. Once Longman realised this, he began turning corners at random and seeking out roundabouts.

The hire car dropped further behind, and the policemen's car disappeared from the rear-view mirror altogether.

'Sam, where are we going?' Longman asked.

Sam thought about the Eldritch girl, telling him to go where the barrier was weakest and force his way through. He saw two blue doors, joined by a stairway of darkness. He saw Lionel Hepplewhite's apartment, and his tall, wide window looking out over the River Leeth.

Windows could be broken.

'Camden,' he said. 'Sheridan Row, north of the tube station.'

230

'Do you want the good news or the bad news?' Cassidy asked, turning back from the rear window.

'The good,' Longman said immediately.

'We've completely lost the Golem.'

'What's the bad?' Sam asked.

'I think Drunk Dave's found us again.'

DS Morley had found Longman's Mercedes by inspired guesswork. It had been obvious that the man in Sam Parker's mutilated hire car was unfamiliar with driving. It is hard to effectively follow a car when it is driven poorly. In addition, he'd had Hyams bending his ear continually.

The man in the hire car was secondary, his DI kept telling him. *Parker* was the real target.

Despite his new-found devotion to his DI, Morley was having a hard time understanding the logic in this. In any of it. Castles in the air were one thing, but he had heard the screams coming from Parker's garden, too, and Parker wasn't the one whose clothes had looked like a butcher's apron.

Nevertheless, as the hire car had turned into what Morley knew to be a dead-end street, he had driven on. An experienced driver, he had noted the Mercedes' tactics in trying to lose the hire car, and he applied them himself as though he were being followed. He took the trickiest turns, doubled back on himself, and once performed an illegal U-turn that had Hyams cursing his name. But suddenly, there the Mercedes was, right in front of them, and Hyams had given him a congratulatory punch on the shoulder that rattled his teeth.

Through the tinted glass of the Merc's rear window, he thought he saw a pale face regarding them. 'They know we're here,' he said.

Hyams shrugged. 'Doesn't matter. Let them worry about it.' He twisted the cap off the Absolut and tilted the bottle against his lips. He swallowed four times before lowering it. Morley counted.

'We should radio in about that freak driving Parker's car, Guv. He can't handle it properly, he could kill someone.' Then he remembered the gunshot, and the blood on the old overcoat the freak had been wearing. 'He's probably killed already, and not with a car. We need to report this.'

'No.'

'But Guv−'

'I said no!' Hyams bellowed. 'This is *our* call, Muggins. No one else should be here.'

No one else would go along with him is what he really means, Morley thought. And *our* call means *his* call. And shortly after that, he wondered, who the hell is *Muggins*?

'Sir…you know this is crazy, don't you?'

'I don't know what crazy is. I know what's right and what's wrong. I don't see crazy. I see Rebecca Walton and Fee Garrison, and I see Honest Bob Allison's blood on my shoes, and I know that somehow Sam Parker put it there.'

Hyams drank more vodka. Morley watched him out of the corner of his eye.

The Mercedes was about five minutes away from Camden. The policemen's car was staying back, content merely to follow it seemed. Sam and

Nathaniel Longman were silent and tense, and the calmest person in the car, surprisingly, was Nigel Cassidy. He was always calmer when his mind had a problem to focus on rather than obsessing on his neuroses.

'Sam?' he asked. 'This Golem. He stopped Beckett from blowing you away, right?'

'Right.'

'Even though you *meant* for him to kill you?'

'Yes.'

'So why is the Golem chasing you? It's obvious his boss wants you alive, so it can't be to harm you.'

'I'm not sure. I can think of one reason, though. He probably wants to kill you two just because you're helping me.'

Cassidy thought for a while, then asked Longman, 'Nat, was the Golem chasing us to catch Sam, or was he just chasing us to chase us?'

Longman, his face oily with sweat, tersely replied, 'I'm not sure anyone but you could tell the difference, Nigel. What's your point?'

'I don't know if I have one. It's just a feeling, that he wasn't trying to catch us, just… to drive us on, get us moving. But if that were the case, then we haven't really lost him at all, because−'

All three men heard a screech of tyres behind them. Longman peered into his rear-view mirror as the other two turned about in their seats. Far back, they could see the policemen's car slewed at an angle, just beginning to straighten up and roll forwards again. A car had cut out from a side street, almost causing a collision. It was Sam's hire car.

The Golem's blood-stained overcoat flapped about like a dirty wing where the driver's door had been. His hat was still in place.

'—because he already knows where we're going,' Cassidy finished.

Sam's face lost all its colour. He wondered who had tipped the Golem off, but then thought, *I* did, of course. I'm like a human homing beacon.

He turned to Longman. 'There's not far to go now, Nat. We need to give ourselves a chance. We've got to get there ahead of him.'

Longman nodded, and floored the accelerator.

24

Sheridan Row was relatively quiet. People were shopping, strolling, waiting for buses. There was light traffic. Elbows showed on the frames of drivers' windows, and faces with shades watched the pedestrian show. The proprietor of the cheap-shop was selling inflatables instead of umbrellas. The pub on the corner and the Eager Beaver Cafe had set plastic tables and chairs out on the pavement. Tourists sat there and tried to ignore the exhaust fumes. A children's party was in progress in McDonalds, running the staff ragged. A hazy London afternoon in the summer.

People heard the racing engines long before the first of the cars appeared.

Longman's Mercedes came fast around the corner and people stopped moving, except for their heads which snapped around, drawn to the screaming tyres. Considering its speed, the Merc' did extremely well to keep all four wheels on the road. Longman did even better to rein it in before he sideswiped the oncoming cars on the opposite side of the road, and to brake to an abrupt, shrieking halt before he struck the rear of a transit van that was crawling away from the curb.

Sam climbed out of the car, gesturing desperately to Longman and Cassidy to follow him. Once out of the Merc', Cassidy finally, violently, vomited his guts out, and Longman began to pull him along before he had time to recover. Everybody was watching in amazement as the three men deserted their car in the middle of the road.

Sam squinted into the distance at the blank section of wall between the McDonalds and the Eager Beaver, and saw all the children in cardboard hats gaping at him through plate glass as though he were the Hamburglar on parole.

Heads turned again, Sam's included, as the hire car turned into Sheridan Row, following the same line as Longman. The Golem couldn't handle the car at the speed he had been forced into, and the car, lacking the Merc's superior road-holding, couldn't handle the corner.

The street seemed to become caught in a vacuum of silence as the hire car's off-side wheels left the road and continued to rise like the undercarriage of an aircraft. It travelled eight, ten yards on two wheels, like a stunt car, then lifted one inch too far, abruptly capsized, and then rolled and rolled. Pedestrians caught in the vacuum turned to run, but the twisting, jumping car steamrollered through them, knocking some through windows, crushing others, and overturning two parked cars before spinning to a stop

235

on its roof. Oncoming traffic had braked to an unsteady halt, nose to tail, nose to tail, and there were a hundred yards of minor collisions, shards of red and amber plastic all over the road like precious stones. The vacuum collapsed into chaos.

Car alarms and screaming people. Gaping men and women, who couldn't believe what they had just seen. A voice from a window shouted, 'Was it a bomb, was it a bomb?' Sam turned away from it all, stared at the blank wall and tried to summon up a burst of internal lightning.

Cassidy had gone into a crouch to look into the upside down hire car. He saw the Golem slumped on the interior roof, blood everywhere, petrol and steaming water and brake fluid leaking down onto him through the chassis. He had finally lost his hat, and a terrible wound spanned the diameter of his bald malformed head. He probably had no idea what a safety belt was, and blood was pulsing out of his clothes where the steering wheel had broken his ribcage, as though the ribs had punctured vital organs.

He's finished, Cassidy thought, trying not to puke again.

But then he saw the Golem begin to move, and Cassidy stood up again in a hurry. He blinked against a flash of blue light and he thought that someone had taken his photograph. He envied that person's composure.

Sam grabbed Cassidy's hand and Longman's hand and pulled them out of the road and along the pavement, where people dodged aside to let them through. He knew that he was taking his friends into danger, but it seemed a better option than certain death. He didn't need to see the Golem climbing out of the wreckage to know that.

'Whatever you do,' he told them, 'don't let go of me.'

The blue door loomed before them.

Morley threw his car into Sheridan Row, leaning into the turn like a skier, and then immediately stood on the brakes. His car stopped gently after a gliding skid that brought the back wheels level with the front wheels and left two beautiful arcs of rubber on the road.

The people who were not dead or injured were watching the policemen's car as though they had been waiting for it to arrive. It wasn't precognition, it was shock, and Morley wasn't immune to it. The scale of what they had driven into shook him like a series of blows. The bodies, the dazed and bloody survivors, the hire car on its roof, the smashed cars and windows, all the staring faces. It closed him down for a moment.

Hyams saw only what was important to him. He spotted Parker, Cassidy and Longman easily enough, because they were the only living people who were showing the street their backs. They were moving quickly, running towards something that shone blue in the sunlight.

'Morley, move! Move!'

Without thinking, the DS accelerated forwards, swinging the car around. He did not see the Golem launch himself from the hire car's ruins and begin to race across the road after Sam Parker and his two companions. Only the impact as the policemen's car struck him made the Golem visible. His overcoat billowed like a cape as he was thrown through the air. Morley managed to stop the car again before he ran him over a second time.

He turned the key in the ignition with shaking hands, and the engine beneath the crumpled bonnet died. He couldn't move, couldn't speak. He couldn't go any further. Hyams could bluster and shout and intimidate as much as he wanted, but Morley couldn't follow him anymore. He'd just killed a man.

Then the Golem slowly stood up, his head rising into view above the bonnet. His claw-like hands left bloody prints as he used the car for support. He gave Morley a second-long glance of sheer malice that would stay with the DS for the rest of his life, then spun away and ran down the street, hobbling badly. He left a trail of blood behind him so bright it looked like poster paint.

Morley's paralysis broke as Hyams threw open the car door and climbed out, obviously intending to set off in pursuit. His first impulse was not to follow his DI but to restrain him. Hyams tore his jacket sleeve out of Morley's hands. On the point of following the Golem, he turned back.

'Don't try to follow me…Ken,' Hyams said after a moment where he was sure his DS's forename name was Keith. 'It's over for you.'

Morley clambered over the passenger seat and into the road to see the DI running after the Golem at full pelt.

'Guv! Hyams!'

Then he saw the strangest sight of his life. Miraculous and terrible, he would see it in his dreams, but would never be able to explain it, not even to himself.

Morley saw his DI run into a patch of blue light that hung on a wall like a stained-glass window and disappear forever.

Hyams had gone, and the blue light had gone, nipped off behind his back. Morley heard sirens and looked away from the blank wall. Every face was turned to him in a street that looked like a war-zone.

25

Heedless of the dark, Sam rushed down steps that felt as though he were creating them as he went. Both Cassidy and Longman were behind him, each swearing, each conscious of not being in control of their descent, but Sam kept a tight hold of their hands. He didn't know what would happen if he let go. He might lose them, narrow as the stairwell was. They might fall out of his imagination and find themselves buried in the earth, in the tight, airless places between sewer pipes and electrical conduits, earth and aggregate.

The light from the small corridor at the bottom of the steps appeared more quickly than he remembered. To begin with Sam thought this was because the first time he came here he'd been alone, and alone is a place where the taste of joy has a bitter edge, and the bad things seem to last forever. But even before they reached the corridor, Sam knew that he was wrong. The light from the corridor was *stronger* now, and as he turned the corner into its short length, he saw why.

Hepplewhite's door was open, the light from his apartment spilling out.

Sam moved them all a little closer and then paused, staring into the small sliver of room he could see beyond the flaking doorframe. He saw that the Chinese screen which had hidden Hepplewhite's desk had been knocked over, a hole the size of a man's head punched through it. It lay at an angle against the old desk. Sam could see the keys of the typewriter framed through the hole. They looked like grinning teeth.

He felt a sting of pain in the palm of his right hand as Cassidy's nails bit into his skin. The pressure increased on his other hand, too, as Longman also became agitated. Then Sam heard what they had already noticed, heavy, dragging footsteps clopping down the steps after them, loud breaths that were as harsh on the way out as they were on the way in, and had a horrid, bubbling undercurrent.

Even injured as he was, the Golem was still coming.

Sam pulled his friends to the threshold, all his senses on high alert. No sounds came from within. Sam saw that the rest of the room had been comprehensively trashed, just like Horace Jepson's cottage, and Lionel Hepplewhite lay sprawled in one of his armchairs, dead. His face had been pulped, and his chest was soaked with the blood that had come from it. He looked like the victim of a murderous dentist. One of his artificial hands was missing, and inside his gaping sleeve his arm in cross-section looked like the end of a rolled-up newspaper.

Sam was not at all surprised that Hepplewhite was dead. At this point of the story, it was what he would have done.

He finally pulled Cassidy and Longman all the way into the apartment and risked letting go of their hands. They didn't disappear, but they did look lost and afraid, like tired children about to be abandoned in a fairytale forest. They did not understand where they were or how they had got here, and they were staring at Hepplewhite's body in horror. Both had written any number of deaths in their fiction, but neither of them, before this moment, had really seen it up close. Sam wasn't inured to violent death by any means, but he had found that he could look at it and still function, still think. He saw this as a failing in himself. When had he become so hardened?

Cassidy turned away from the body, reacting to the sound of approaching footsteps. 'He's coming!'

'Close that door,' Sam said quietly. 'Drag the other armchair across and block it.'

Cassidy slammed the door and leant against it until Longman brought the armchair, which they both held in place. Almost immediately, they heard the Golem's footsteps drag up behind the door. They could hear his tortured breathing.

'If you've got a plan,' Longman whispered to Sam, 'now would be a good time to set it in motion.'

The first blow on the door knocked the armchair back a few inches, and Longman and Cassidy scrambled to slam it back.

'Hurry!' Cassidy yelled.

Sam went to Hepplewhite's window and tore down the rotting curtains. Cassidy, glancing back over his shoulder, saw Eldritch glowing in the darkness, and made some awful noise in his throat. It was night again, but this time there was a full moon, just emerging from behind a cloud. Sam saw the frozen Leeth by moonlight. It looked like the trail of a monstrous snail.

'Holy Christ!'

Longman had looked at the window, too, and the shock of it almost drew him away from the chair. Another blow on the door wrenched his attention back, and he leaned on the chair again as hard as he could, his entire body rigid between his feet and his hands.

'Sam, do it!'

Sam went over to the broken Chinese screen and threw it aside. He snatched the ancient typewriter from the desk and ran back across the room, trailing clouds of dust. He launched it at the window, eyes half-closed against the glass that would fly.

Open!

But the typewriter, heavy as it was, simply bounced off the window as though it were a solid wall, and fell with a clang to the floor, splintering the floorboards. Without hesitation, Sam unceremoniously turfed Hepplewhite's body out of his armchair, then began to lift it above his head as he turned to the window again.

'That won't work, Sam.'

He dropped the chair in surprise. The Eldritch girl had materialised at his side. Behind him he heard Longman and Cassidy struggling to keep the Golem out, and fighting their curiosity of the new voice.

'What *will* work?'

'You know.'

Yes, Sam did. He looked at the typewriter. It was broken, but that didn't matter. He didn't need it to write. He glanced once at Cassidy and Longman, once at the girl, and then his eyes focussed on something that no one but he could see, the eternal blank page in his mind. And then he began to write.

Nigel Cassidy heard the jagged grating first. His head turned as he followed the sound to the large window, where the glass was beginning to spider-web with long cracks. Pressure inside the panes snapped some of them into a frosty translucence. Sam stared at nothing, his face showing intense concentration. The girl in the fur coat hovered by him, as though her presence would urge him on.

A particularly heavy blow split the door down its centre and knocked the armchair out of Cassidy and Longman's hands, and a second broke the door completely, sending the chair flying to the other side of the room. The two men backed away as the Golem staggered in. He grinned at them with his grey and bloody teeth.

Without warning, he reached out and caught Cassidy's arm, pulling the little man towards him like a child. Longman threw his fist at the Golem's head, and felt it rebound from skin that felt like leather over solid rock. The Golem shook his head as though irritated by a fly, and his hands found their way around Cassidy's neck.

The window behind them gave a great shudder, and for a second Longman thought that the grinding sounds were the bones in Cassidy's neck. He leapt on the Golem and was batted away, blood running from his brow where the Golem's knuckles had opened a long cut. Dazed, he could only look up as the Golem, now holding Cassidy's throat in one hand, stepped over to him. Nigel's eyes were up in his head somewhere.

Longman's hands tore at the Golem's foot as it was lowered onto his chest, but he couldn't shift it. Suddenly, he couldn't breathe.

In the place where he was, Sam mumbled, 'Jesus, this is difficult.'

'You're trying too hard,' the Eldritch girl replied.

Duncan Hyams stumbled into the doorway behind the struggling men. He sized up the situation with the speed of a born fighter, then stepped forwards and brought his foot up in a vicious arc that ended between the Golem's legs.

The Golem shrieked like an animal, dropping Cassidy and falling to his knees, clutching himself. Longman scrambled up and dragged Cassidy's semi-conscious body away, closer to Sam.

Hyams waited until the two men were clear, then aimed a roundhouse kick at the Golem's head. It connected solidly with his temple, and the Golem went down.

Hyams immediately turned to Sam.

'Sam Parker,' he said. 'You are under–'

Sam came back to himself with a jolt, and the large window vaporised.

A howling vortex of chilling air poured into the apartment. It caught them all, Sam, the girl, Cassidy, Longman and Hyams, and it dragged them out through the hole in reality. Furniture and fittings, all the books and pages of manuscript, and even Hepplewhite's body were gathered up, torn away as if by a tornado.

244

The Golem's hand twitched, found a gap in the floorboards and gripped hard. His body was lifted from the ground and twisted around and around until his shoulder dislocated, while the room was emptied. He endured the storm for a full minute, and then it ended.

No slackening, no easing, just a full stop.

The Golem's body slammed to the floor, and he lay there, shaking, fighting for his breath. A moment or two later, he rolled over in a pool of his own blood and stared at the reformed window, the healed barrier, and at the dark sanctity of Eldritch.

And he smiled.

Part III
THE END

1
Excerpt from Okra:

...DI Dave Hawkins, uncomfortable in the hospital bed with his right leg in plaster from ankle to hip, blandly regarded the young reporter from The Eldritch Clarion. Normally just the sight of a journalist was enough to send him into a rage, never mind an intrusion of this magnitude. But Hawkins was currently doped-out on a combination of booze and the painkillers he'd been given prior to having the multiple fractures in his leg set, and possibly this combination had impaired his judgement.

He'd allowed the reporter to speak, and then it had been too late.

The reporter seemed uninterested in Drunk Dave's personal problems. He did not wish to discuss the rumours that the DI's badly broken leg had been sustained falling down the stone steps of the Breakers Wheel Station after a colossal forty-eight-hour drunken binge. He did not even wish to discuss Okra, the serial killer who was currently terrorising the City of Eldritch.

He wanted to talk about the derelict northern docklands.

'I think there's a story there,' the reporter said. 'A big one.'

'Big.' Dave's head felt pretty big, roughly the size of a hot air balloon. 'What makes you think that?'

The reporter started to hold up fingers, unaware that Hawkins would be seeing them in triplicate, and began to list his reasons. When he'd finished, the reporter gleamed at Hawkins, as though he had impressed the DI, and knew it.

'There's a story there,' he said again, more strongly, 'and I'm going to write it. I think you can help me.'

Hawkins couldn't remember the last time he had agreed with a member of the press. The last time the media had called for the return of hanging, most likely. But he agreed with this reporter now. There was a story in the docklands, more than one. Hundreds, perhaps. But no one would ever write them, least of all this upstart with his young, fresh, earnest face. Hawkins had long ago lost faith in earnest young men. They were just boys playing grown up, and it hurt too much when you had to watch them die.

Eldritch had always been a place where the skin of reality routinely erupted in rashes and boils, disfiguring the city's face. But the evils that briefly flared up and plagued Eldritch's citizens in the thirteen districts had another, more

247

permanent existence in the docklands. The docklands were, as Hawkins knew only too well, the city's open, gangrenous wound, which never healed. There were creatures in the docklands which had forgotten that they had once been human. There were people there that had never been human at all. The docklands were the place where God kept his nightmares.

'Stay away from the docklands,' Hawkins warned the reporter.

It was all he could say. It was all he ever said.

Why did no one ever listen?

2

Sam and the others were somewhere between worlds, and it was like being carried along, tumbling and spinning, in the jet-stream of an aircraft. Complete disorientation was inevitable, and, in a strange way, not entirely unwelcome. To some degree, confusion dulled their expectations of how their journey might end, to the consequences of entering another world.

The roaring cacophony had them all covering their ears, although they had to fight the tearing wind to keep their hands in place. They kept their eyes tightly closed, not just against the wind but against the flotsam and jetsam of Lionel Hepplewhite's apartment, which was with them in the twisting heart of the storm. This included Hepplewhite's ancient bathtub, revolving massively in the air turbulence and narrowly bypassing their bodies like an asteroid ploughing through the solar system, miraculously avoiding collision.

As it was, the smaller items were causing enough damage on their own, cutting and bruising their exposed skin, and tearing at their clothes. Nigel Cassidy's hands and face were striped with paper cuts caused by the loose pages of Hepplewhite's incomplete manuscript for *The Homecoming*. Twice, one or other of the armchairs had bounced off Nathaniel Longman's back and brought cries of pain that no one heard, not even Longman himself. And once, two bodies met in a sly collision that was not an accident.

Curled up into a protective ball, Sam was suffering a bombardment of a different sort. The chaos that surrounded him was also inside him, and images and thoughts whipped through his mind in a bewildering flurry.

He saw himself naked, on his knees on a bed, Jo on all fours facing him, her long hair caressing his thighs; the Eldritch girl knelt behind him, her breasts pressed against his shoulder blades, one forearm locked around his throat, the other arm snaking around his waist to feed his penis into Jo's mouth. He saw himself being carried by dark figures through woodland; a thorn opened a seven-inch long wound on his face, and the figures laughed when he screamed. He saw a man in a concrete cell calmly emasculating himself with a knife, and saying, 'Thank you, thank you,' to someone Sam could not see. He saw Horace Jepson's head broken open, and Jo in a dingy hotel room, some of her on the bed, some of her on the floor, some of her in the hand basin in the corner. He saw two young men dead in the street, looking as though they'd been picked apart by powerful machinery. He saw Charles Beckett's head, twisted so far around that the skin of his wattled neck had split...

Oh God, make them stop! Sam thought. I'll go mad if they don't stop!

Then he remembered that *he* was God.

The images stopped immediately. Banished. The relief was stupendous, like the moment when a painkiller kicks in, but a thousand times stronger.

Sam wasn't finished being shocked, but his mind was steadily recovering and already wondering what he could do to turn off the tornado that was carrying them along so violently. It was only a moment before the answer came, and it was very simple. It was the same solution as the unwelcome images.

I'll write that it stops, he thought. I'll simply write that it—

It didn't end as it began, tentatively, like the first flexing of a muscle. There was no build up, no preliminary struggle for Sam this time. He just did it. As though a switch had been turned, the tornado simply stopped, and Sam began to fall through the dark and silent night.

He cried out, and somewhere in the vastness of space, he heard someone scream in reply.

Even as he felt the earth pulling at him, he had time to think that the scream had sounded like Nigel Cassidy, who, amongst all his other phobias, feared heights. Nigel sounded a long way away.

250

Sam kept his arms wrapped around his head, but he hit the ground hard, and all the air was driven out of him. His next intake of breath made his whole bruised ribcage ache. With his second, slightly less painful breath, he realised that although he had landed, he was still moving. He was sliding, in fact, and at some speed. It took another moment or two to feel the intense chill through his clothes, and to realise that he had landed on the frozen River Leeth itself.

Still sliding, he sat up on the ice and opened his eyes.

He was struck speechless. He was in Eldritch and it was incredible. Beyond words, beyond expression. He had thought the view from Hepplewhite's window amazing, but now in his mind it was reduced to the size of the picture postcard a relative had once sent him from Colorado when he was a child, a view of the Grand Canyon. The grandeur of the photograph had impressed him, and as an adult he had made the trip himself. He had stood in the exact spot where the photograph had been taken, and in that moment, when he had the powerful sense of a circle closing, he had learned something. It was one thing to look at a photograph of the Grand Canyon, and quite another to stand on the rim yourself.

It was the same with Eldritch.

Sam eventually spun to a stop, revolving on his bottom like an ice skater at the climax of a comic routine. He stared captivated at the Eldritch skyline, towering above the darkness of the docklands, and he could not move. The Eldritch moon was low and huge, surrounded by a raft of drifting clouds that

251

continually covered and revealed its face like a sequence of masks. The moonlight faded in and out, a strobe effect in slow motion, bathing Sam's upturned face one moment and plunging him into utter darkness the next. His own masks.

Captivated, was he? More like bewitched.

His mind seemed to unfold like a dark flower. New ideas, new realisations came to him, sure knowledge of his city's life and history, details he had never conjured.

He knew that upstream of the docklands, men still fished in the Leeth, while downstream they did not. As the river passed through the docklands, the water and everything in it became tainted. The fish were sometimes mutated, sometimes their flesh simply turned to poison.

He knew that in 1868 a woman from the Blackpill district, which lay downstream of the docklands, had been convicted of murdering her husband by feeding him a trout she'd found floating on the Leeth. A mob of citizens, with the full backing of the magistrate, had carried out her sentence, tying her to a makeshift raft and setting her adrift on the river to float through the docklands. Then they had raced in horse-drawn carriages to the western edge of the docklands to see what had become of the woman, and when the raft emerged and the woman was gone, her bonds chewed through, they all agreed that she had met a hideous end and that the punishment had fitted the crime.

But Sam knew that the woman had not died. She had been taken, but not killed. Like a cursed character in a fairy story, she had survived and had been transformed, and she lived still over one hundred and fifty years later, although she could never again come out of the water for more than a few moments. Sam could see her in his imagination now, pallid and bloated and gilled, hibernating in the frigid waters under the ice, waiting for the thaw.

Sam saw. Sam knew. Sam could read the reality of this strange world in chapters written in blood.

Finally, he was shaken from his daze by a loud crash which, had he bothered to think about it, he would have known was the sound of Hepplewhite's bathtub smashing into the ice a quarter of a mile downstream. He didn't think about it because there was too much else to occupy his mind. Chief among which was a rising nausea he could feel moving from his stomach to his chest like a restless parasite.

Sam tried to counter this feeling of sickness by taking a huge gulp of the frigid air, only to realise that the air was the very reason for it. Overcome, he lurched to his side and vomited, choking and gagging, then recovering, only to draw in another whooping breath and for the nausea to spike again. Even as he struggled to regain control of himself, a hand pressed to the pain in his chest and tears forcing themselves out through his eyelashes, he knew what was happening to him.

It was like the view from Hepplewhite's window. The view wasn't the real thing, and the odour that Sam had recognised as Eldritch in the past was only the smell of it. This was the actual *atmosphere*, an invisible claw that felt as though it was trying to pull him inside out. Through the pain he could sense it infiltrating him, adapting him, as the murderous wife had somehow been adapted to breathe in the water.

At last the convulsions slowed and then stopped. Sam felt weaker than he had ever been in his life, but the pain was fading from his chest, and although his throat felt raw and inflamed, he could no longer smell Eldritch. It was a part of him now, and he a part of it. He was living fiction.

He leaned back on his heels and wiped the last of the tears from his eyes, the drool from his lips and chin. The moon had emerged from behind a cloud, and its light made the ice luminous. Against the wide field of brightness, he could see many patches of darkness, unidentifiable shapes, most of which, he assumed, were debris from Lionel Hepplewhite's apartment. Then the moon was hidden again, and with its disappearance, Sam finally felt the intensity of the cold for the first time. It was savage.

Instantly, he began to shiver, and to worry about his friends. At least he had a fairly thick jacket on his back. Cassidy and Longman were dressed much more lightly. If their fall had not been as kind as his, and they were somewhere on the river unconscious, it wouldn't be long before they were beyond help.

Sam climbed to his feet carefully. Not only were his legs still weak, but the ice was like polished glass, and it was starting to snow. The drifting clouds boiled over the moon, allowing it to show a quarter of its face, and by this meagre light he saw a clump of darkness he had originally assumed to be debris begin to move.

His heart jumped with gladness. At least one of them is safe, he thought, at least one.

But then he remembered where he was. He was on the Leeth running through Eldritch's derelict northern docklands, and the dark shape he could see rising to its feet less than twenty-five or thirty yards away could have been anything.

Anything.

Sam was rooted to the spot by sudden fear and the knowledge that he would not be able to run over the ice without slipping and falling. He tried not to give in to his fear, and told himself to wait and see. He didn't dare call out a who-goes-there, because he was afraid that the reply might not come from a human being.

The shape stopped moving abruptly, became rigidly still, and Sam knew that it had seen him. He could feel the heat of its gaze.

Then the moon went in again.

3

During the long and dispiriting period of time popularly known as 'overnight', before he became successful and something of a celebrity, Nathaniel Longman had several times been beaten up because he was black. He had also been beaten up because he was gay. Furthermore, he had been beaten up because he was black *and* gay. It had been after learning of these vicious attacks for the first time that Sam had dedicated one of his novels to Longman. Now, as he lay facedown on the frozen river and struggled to pull himself out of the fog of semi-consciousness, Longman felt that he had been beaten up simply because he was *real*.

It might have made for a nice change, he thought, if it didn't hurt so much.

He pushed himself up from the ice, where blood from the gash the Golem had opened on his brow had already frozen into a little maroon coin. It felt as though he'd left a couple of layers of skin from his cheek down there, too. His back was the source of two massive sites of pain where heavy objects had hit him in the tornado that had snatched them all up. The fall to the ice had done something unpleasant to his left shoulder, and he couldn't move that arm without feeling a sharp current of pain. A sudden coughing fit made him feel that his body was close to falling apart.

He did not vomit, however. He had already done that the instant the tornado had stopped and he had caught his first breath of the toxic gas that passed for air here. He'd tumbled to the ice, blindly spraying his half-digested breakfast as he fell. Anything else that had been forced out of him had made its exit while he'd been unconscious, and he'd been spared the experience. A plate-sized patch of vomit lay close by to where his head had been, frozen like his blood.

Blood, he thought as his head continued to clear. Then, the Golem!

Longman shot to his feet in panic. Pain sang in his arm, shoulder and neck, and his head throbbed as it might after a three-day drunk. His mind was in complete uproar.

Can't be in Eldritch, he kept telling himself, can't be, can't be, can't be.

But, of course, he knew that he was. There was the city skyline. Huge and undeniable, it seemed to lean towards him, threatening to fall, and in the legions of lighted windows he saw the level of the city's horror and its inhabitants' knowledge of it. He wondered why on earth he had ever liked to read about the damn place.

Longman shuddered as he felt the snow building on his shoulders and head. Each individual snowflake felt like a tapping finger, and the wind in his ears was like a voice.

Hey you, it whispered. Hey you, *hey you…*

4

Sam could see none of the moon now, not even a sliver, because whatever the clouds left, the thickening snow took away. But he could hear the footsteps that were approaching him; rapid, almost fleshy thuds, like an animal's paws, that never faltered in their course. He felt his feet stepping backwards, and was unable to stop them. He held his arms out, and made his hands into fists that he knew would be useless against a docklands predator.

Or maybe whatever it was had nothing to do with the docklands at all. Maybe it was the Golem. What a comforting thought.

Suddenly, the darkness seemed to pulse before his eyes, and then it hit him hard.

It broke through the feeble defence of his arms, and caught him around the body. His feet slipped and he crashed to the ice with his mouth full of foul-smelling fur. The weight that landed on top of him was lithe with muscle. He tried to push it off, but it clung to him too tightly, and his thrashing legs met nothing it all. It had wrapped its own legs around his waist as tightly as its arms were locked around his

257

neck. Teeth were pressed against his throat, and lips that moved over his skin as though tasting him.

Sam struggled harder, cursing and whipping his head from side to side in attempt to dodge the bite when it came, and he was so frantic that at first the voice he heard did not penetrate.

'Sam!' the voice said. 'Sam! Sam!'

He dared to stop struggling, strained to listen through the enormous sounds of his own panting breath and his thunderous heartbeats.

'Sam, you did it, you're here!'

All his muscles relaxed in relief and his head hit the ice. It was the girl. The Eldritch girl. Her fur coat. The mouth on his throat kissing, not tasting. He found her face with his hands and pulled it towards his own, and he kissed her on the lips. The kiss was mostly for himself, but she took it as though it were all hers. She responded voraciously, and when he finally broke it off, gasping for air, he felt her tongue flicking at his lips while the snow swirled around them.

'Have you ever seen *Dr Zhivago*?' he said.

'No, who's he?' the girl asked.

Sam laughed out loud. He heard his own laughter quite distinctly, as though it were someone else's. He wondered how long it had been since anyone had laughed in the docklands without its cause being another creature's suffering.

'It's just a film,' he told her. 'Help me up.'

The Eldritch girl took Sam's hand and hauled him to his feet with a strength that amazed him. The ice must have been tough on her bare feet, but if she was in discomfort she didn't admit to it. Immediately, she began to pull Sam toward the Leeth's northern embankment.

'Wait,' he said. 'We have to find Nat and Nigel.'

The girl frowned, and although Sam really couldn't see her expression, he felt it.

'Why?' she asked.

'Because they're my friends, and I can't leave them alone out here.'

'You have to.'

'I can't do that.'

'You *have* to,' she insisted. 'You know where we are, Sam. You know what kind of dangers we're tempting every minute we stand here arguing.'

'I'm not arguing,' Sam said. 'They're my friends, and I'm not leaving here without them!'

He turned, intending to stalk away, but after a few steps realised that he had no idea which way to start looking, even if the conspiracy of clouds and moon allowed him to see where he was going. He was angry at the girl's attitude, but at the same time he couldn't blame her. How could she know how important friends were when she'd never had one? It was a miracle she'd turned out as well as she had with the life Sam had allowed her, and the father he'd cursed her with.

'Look,' he tried to explain, 'I care about them, they're important to me.'

He expected her to argue again, but suddenly the girl was behind him, the full length of her body pressed against his back. He hadn't heard her move. She had unfastened her fur coat and now she gathered the thick garment around him so that they were both inside it. Even through his clothes the heat of her naked body against him was almost feverish, and Sam could feel his body responding to the intimacy. Before he knew what he was doing, he'd reached back and his hands were on her hips, on her tight backside, pulling her into him. He felt her grinding against his buttocks, and her scent was very strong.

'If they're important to you, they're important to me,' she breathed into his ear. 'But we need to be practical, Sam. Very soon we're going to have to cut our losses. If either of your friends are injured, or dead, they're going to attract a lot of attention. Even if they don't draw predators, there are always the scavengers. Sometimes they're *worse*.'

Sam hung his head, thinking.

He'd made many allusions to the docklands in his novels. In some it was a place where people went to die, and in others merely the bogeyland with which parents threatened their unruly children. Only once had he actually sent a character in here and followed him, at the climax of *Okra*, when the serial killer had been pursued to his lair by an idealistic young reporter. Both had died terrible deaths in the docklands. The reporter's, ironically, was far worse than the killer's.

He had many ideas of what was loose out here, some of them sharp and clear, others just vague impressions he had no wish to develop in detail. Harsh as it seemed, the girl was right. If they didn't find Cassidy and Longman soon, they would have to leave without them if they wanted to survive themselves.

Sam stared up at the night sky, letting the snow find his face, and only when the moon began to come out of hiding again did he finally speak.

'Fifteen minutes,' he proposed.

'Ten.'

Sam hesitated. 'Okay.'

He stepped out of the girl's embrace and turned to face her. She hadn't refastened her coat yet, and her body was on show to him. It was the same colour as the emerging moon, silvery and iridescent, but with the slightest of rose tints. Her nipples were as dark as dried berries, and her groin entirely shaved of hair. Sam swallowed a couple of times, then closed her coat for her.

'You don't want to get cold,' he said.

'I'm never cold, Sam,' the girl replied, and she made it sound like a promise.

5

Longman had been struggling over the ice for a while. He was becoming caked in snow and he felt brittle to his bones. He had set off in search of Sam and Nigel, hoping that he wouldn't run into the Golem, or the mad-looking policeman who may or may not have been the living embodiment of Drunk Dave Hawkins, or even the strange girl who had appeared from nowhere to help Sam. Beautiful as the girl was, he had disliked her on sight. He had meant to start shouting Sam's name, but when it came to it, he hadn't dared. He knew that it could all too easily attract the wrong sort of attention.

Sam's novel, *Okra*, had been very explicit about what kind of horrors he could expect from the

261

docklands. The young reporter's death stood out in his memory as the embodiment of the way he would least like to die. Only moments ago, he'd thought he'd heard the sounds of a distant struggle, and then, just before the wind took them away, there had been a peal of loony laughter that had made him tremble more than the wind chill factor did. He'd lost no time in hurrying in the opposite direction.

What he *hoped* was the opposite direction.

He stopped as the moon made another brief appearance, its light much diminished by the falling snow. Over to his left, a dark shape had been revealed, lying on the ice. He saw it for only a second before the darkness returned, and he didn't know what it was.

Very carefully, Longman began to shuffle in that direction, wishing with all his heart that the moon would come out again and stay for longer. He didn't like this now-you-see-it-now-you-don't business. It was like a parlour game in hell.

A minute or so later, Longman felt the toes of his shoes strike something hard and he stumbled to his knees. Certain memorable paragraphs from *Okra* suddenly seemed illuminated in his mind, and he held his breath, waiting for an unmentionable creature to leap at him. When nothing did, he slowly reached out with one hand, the other held back and ready to strike if the need arose.

His fingers touched something cold and hard, and then instantly recoiled. When he forced them back, they found something smooth, shaped like a tapering cylinder. Curious, Longman put his other hand to work, and quickly discovered that what he held was in fact a forearm made of marble. More fumbling revealed the rest of a statue, almost certainly that of a man, sunk into the ice up to its waist, the torso bowed backwards like a bridge. Longman wondered what a statue was doing in the middle of the frozen Leeth.

His hands were on the face now, and even though his fingers were numb from the cold, he could tell that the workmanship was incredible, superbly detailed. Little carved teeth in the open mouth, a little carved tongue…

With an almost sentient grasp of malicious timing, the moon emerged from hiding once more, and Longman saw what he'd been exploring with such appreciation.

It was *not* a statue.

6

Sam and the Eldritch girl were shuffling carefully over the ice, hand in hand. The girl was leading. Her night vision apparently being somewhat better than Sam's, she was checking the ice ahead for obstacles while Sam peered left and right into the darkness. Sam was desperately willing the moon to come back out. The minutes were ticking away, and they hadn't found either of his friends.

Christ, he thought. We could have passed them by and never noticed.

He thought they'd found one of them a little while back, but it had turned out to be Hepplewhite's corpse instead. Sam had to turn the body onto its back to be sure of its identity, and had grimaced at the way the body felt under his fingers. It had an unpleasant sponginess to it Sam could only describe as 'pulpy'.

Abruptly, the moon reappeared, and Sam was overjoyed. There, directly in front of them was a large collection of debris from Hepplewhite's apartment. He was convinced that somewhere among the shadows he would find at least one of his friends. Then, as the moon stayed, the sight of one of the pieces erased some of Sam's joy. It was Hepplewhite's heavily ornate desk, reduced to a pile of kindling in the fall. What if Cassidy or Longman were underneath it?

They had no more than begun to investigate when a scream found its way through the falling snow. It came from a long way behind them, and Sam instantly knew that it was Longman. He didn't know how he could be so sure, but he was.

He set off immediately, moving as fast as he dare, slipping and sliding, his arms out to his sides as he tried to stay on his feet. The Eldritch girl kept pace with him easily, her bare feet finding more purchase than his shoes. The scream had been awful, full of hysteria and revulsion. Sam tried not to think about what Longman might have discovered. If he thought about it, he might actually manage to make it worse.

'No more time limits,' he told the girl.

7

Longman couldn't take his eyes off the frozen body. Its clothes had been torn off, and the side of the chest Longman had not touched had a black gaping wound where the heart should have been. The ragged edges of broken ribs showed where something had ripped it out. Two other bodies flanked the first, and although they were even more submerged, Longman could see that their hearts had also been removed.

But it was the first body that continued to mesmerise him. He could see trails in its fine covering of snow that his hands had made, one so close to the heart cavity that it made his pulse hammer. Looking at the face made him feel worse.

I had my fingers in its mouth, Longman thought. In its *mouth*.

Desperate not to have to look at it anymore, Longman turned away for relief − and immediately saw yet another body. He groaned in dismay. This one lay on top of the ice, but looked just as dead. Its face was white as the snow in the moonlight, and its wet cap of red hair gave its head a scalped appearance. It had lost its glasses.

Longman tried, but he couldn't make himself go check Cassidy for a pulse.

Then, through his shock, he heard sounds behind him. Someone was coming.

'Nat? Nat?'

Longman couldn't even react when Sam put his arms around his shoulders. He heard Sam gasp as he saw the tableau of frozen bodies, before realising what else he had found.

'Oh no!'

Sam rushed forward to do what Longman hadn't dared. He went down on his knees by Cassidy's side and began to feel for the pulse in his neck. Longman studied Cassidy's face in the moonlight. The paper cuts on his face looked absurdly deep. The rest of his face was paler than pale, and his eyelids and lips were almost blue.

When Sam eventually turned around, Longman saw blood on his hands, and immediately turned away and retched dryly. He'd seen what had happened to Hepplewhite back in the apartment, and there had been lots of blood there, more than enough. The difference was that he'd never known Hepplewhite, but Nigel was his friend.

'Oh Christ…' Longman muttered when he was able. 'Is he…?'

'No, he's alive,' Sam said. 'He's got a gash on the top of his head you wouldn't believe. He must have hit something as he fell.' He glanced at the frozen bodies. 'Maybe one of those.'

'What does it matter how it happened,' the girl said. 'The important thing is to get out of here.'

Sam nodded.

'His glasses,' Longman said. 'If we can find what he hit we might be able to find his glasses. Without them he'll be helpless.'

'Sam,' the girl said, 'we have no more *time*. We need to go now, and if he can't see and slows us down, we'll just have to leave him behind to take his−'

'Who the fuck are you?' Longman suddenly exploded. 'I mean, who the fuck are you, really?'

The girl considered him coldly. Her lips twitched once, as though she had bitten back a reply.

'Nat,' she's the one person who might be able to get us out of this alive,' Sam said.

'What makes her think she has the right to−'

'Nat, she's *right*. I'd never leave Nigel behind, you know that, but she is right. We don't have time to look for his glasses. This is the fucking docklands, for

266

God's sake. Think about the books.' He pointed at the frozen bodies. 'Think about *them*, and about what happened to them. If there's one place in Eldritch we don't need to spend a lot of time, this is it, right?'

Reluctantly, Longman nodded. His eyes were drawn back to the frozen bodies suspended in the ice.

'Okay, now help me get Nigel up, we've got to get him off the river.'

'I had my hands in its mouth,' Longman said. 'All the way inside…'

'It doesn't matter, it's frozen solid.'

'But how did they get here?'

Sam glanced at the girl, and she nodded at him, as though she knew what was in his mind and was confirming it. 'Those bodies are in something's idea of a deep freeze,' he said. 'When it gets peckish, it comes along and defrosts one.'

Longman goggled at him, then at the frozen bodies. He was wiping his hands obsessively with a handkerchief.

'What kind of something?' he asked.

'Something with a hearty appetite.' Sam seemed to shock himself by laughing out loud at this awful pun, then he shook his head impatiently. 'Come on, Nat. Let's get Nigel up and get out of here, while we still have the moon.'

Longman moved faster than Sam had ever seen him, almost scrambling. Like his verbal dexterity and impeccable manners, Longman's elegant poise was mostly gone. Eldritch had that power, to pile on the pressure, to strip away all pretension until all that was left was the true character. Blood was still drooling from the wound on Longman's forehead and the entire right side of his face looked swollen, most of it covered with a stubble of ice. Frightened and traumatised though Longman was, Sam was pleased to note that his true character was – as Sam had always suspected – that of a survivor. This confirmation gave Sam an unaccountable sense of satisfaction.

Together the two men lifted Cassidy's arms over their shoulders. The girl began to lead the way, north once more, but after a few steps Longman abruptly stopped. Sam slipped, nearly sending Nigel tumbling to the ice again.

'What's wrong?'

Longman looked at him. 'What about the cop?'

'The–?'

'Hyams, is that his name?'

Sam's mouth opened in surprise. His memory of the last few minutes in Hepplewhite's apartment was confused, to say the least.

'Hyams came through with us?'

'I'm almost sure he did.'

8

In a narrow alleyway between two tall warehouse buildings, nested snugly in a deep drift of snow that had gathered against one of the walls, Hyams slowly began to regain consciousness. Immediately, he felt so many strange sensations crowding in around him that he could feel his mind trying to retreat. Back into a dark and silent sleep, where nothing could touch him.

He didn't let it happen.

It was hard to say exactly what he became aware of first. The sight of the clouds scudding over the face of a huge moon, the terrible cold, or the foul miasma of odours that seemed to hover around him like a tiny atmosphere.

One part of the miasma he recognised almost instantly. It was vomit, his own. His shirt and jacket were soaked through with it, and he could taste the remnants in his mouth. Another part of the stench, the part that seemed to rise from beneath him, was something that his addled brain insisted upon identifying with seething maggots, and it was this, more than anything else, that finally made him cast off his inertia. He was moving before he was consciously aware of what he wanted to get away from.

His attempt to rise to his feet told him that his body was shot through with a network of minor pains, and at least one major injury. When he tried to stand, iron bands of pain seemed to close around his left leg. He fell backwards again and his hands sank into something wet and warm, slickly giving.

'What the−'

The texture and the odour combined in his mind then, and for a moment none of his pains existed. He all but hurled himself to his feet and set his back to the wall. He was fully conscious now, and adrenaline was racing through his bloodstream.

In the snow drift where he'd lain, there were two fresh corpses. A man and a woman, side by side, hand in hand. The clothes and skin on their torsos, as well as their faces, looked as though they had been eaten away by an acid. Most of their ribs had gone, too, and

269

it was their internal organs Hyams had touched when he'd fallen backwards.

He glanced at his hands, black in the moonlight with blood, and he realised that his back was wet with blood, not from the snow. He had been on top of the bodies. He had almost been *inside* them.

It took a while, but he got past the impulse to vomit. Somehow he did. Perhaps what helped was the realisation that the condition of the bodies was less than natural. Whatever had killed them, and he didn't rule out simple exposure, the disfigurement, the somehow chemical eating away of their skin and bone had been *done* to them. He therefore deduced that he might also be in danger.

He began to glance around the alleyway in search of a handy weapon, a piece of wood, an iron bar, anything. The alleyway was seemingly endless, prescribing a gentle curve that allowed him about a hundred yards of sight either side of where he had landed. The brick walls, unbroken by doors or windows, were only eight feet apart but seemed at least a hundred feet high. The pocked face of the moon looked down through the narrow gap between roofs like a voyeur.

How he had come to be here was, at best, vague in his mind. It had all happened too quickly and it was all too unbelievable. Flying, falling, blacking out somewhere along the way. He'd probably been knocked unconscious, maybe when an object had hit him before the fall, when the world had been nothing but an evil-smelling wind, and then he'd dropped into this alleyway, bruising himself and injuring his leg. It

270

would have been much worse if he hadn't landed on the bodies, and the bodies hadn't been in a snow drift. He'd been lucky.

But Hyams suddenly had a feeling that it wasn't luck at all.

The walls of the alleyway were approximately a hundred feet high, and he must have fallen a long way before reaching them. The alleyway was about eight feet wide, he was slightly over six feet tall himself, and he hadn't clipped the walls as he'd passed down between them. The snow and the corpses had cushioned his fall. None of this seemed like good fortune. What it felt like was contrivance.

It felt like a fictional device.

'Oh my God…'

At the very moment he realised where he was, the moon hid itself, and the alleyway fell into complete darkness. Instinctively, Hyams pressed his back more firmly against the wall, the soles of his shoes slipping in bloody slush until he crabbed away.

Get out of here, he thought. Get away from the bodies.

He had moved no more than five or six feet before he began to hear a humming noise. Humming or buzzing, he couldn't decide which. He realised that he had closed his eyes, exchanging one darkness for another, just as he had when he'd been afraid as a child, and made himself reopen them.

Out of the corner of his eye, he saw a red glow pulsing from the area around the two bodies. The humming or buzzing waxed and waned with the red glow. He slowly turned his head, and saw something hunched over the bodies.

It looked like the shrivelled, slewed-off skin of an alien insect as big as a man. The red pulse was like its heartbeat, and when it faded the body was reduced to a thin grey shade, and hardly seemed to be there at all. Hyams's legs stopped working properly, and he almost fell again.

The creature's mouth was a long flexible tube, siphoning over the two corpses and undulating as though it were sucking levels of tissue from them. Its eyes, if that's what they were, circled the mouth, three black vulval slits that quivered as it ate. A single limb, thin as an antennae and multi-jointed, twitched over the bodies, seeming to puncture organs as it went, the mouth following to suck up whatever juices flowed out.

The moon came out again, and the creature disappeared. Hyams knew that it was still there, it just couldn't be seen in the light. It must have been there when he landed, and when he was lying there unconscious.

He wondered how it had liked having its dinner interrupted, or if it had regarded his arrival as an actual interruption and not just the early delivery of breakfast. He wondered…

Don't think, he told himself. Just move. Think later.

He began to shamble down the alleyway, away from the creature, trying to look ahead and behind at the same time. His leg didn't hurt at all now, but he still moved with a limp, and he was sweating like a pig in spite of the cold.

This is Parker's fault, he thought. I had him, and then he slipped through my fingers. Got to find him.

He's responsible for this shit, and only he can put it right.

At the end of the alleyway, he found himself facing a wide road choked with snow. Now that he'd seen the front of the buildings he had been behind, and recognised them for what they were, he knew exactly where he was. Not just in Eldritch, but in the docklands. The very word drove another icicle of fear into his mind.

He had a choice of direction, left or right, and he discovered that this was a very difficult decision to make for a man as badly in need of a drink as he was.

Maybe it was just nerves, but he thought there were noises coming from the depth of the alleyway behind him, like something moving, skittering towards him, and he stepped out into the road. He breathed deeply of the icy air. He hadn't realised how rancid the alleyway had smelled until this moment.

Once again he glanced about for something he might use as a weapon and was again defeated by the snow. But then he had a brainstorm.

The knife. The knife with the infinity-shaped handle Bob Allison had killed himself with. It was still in his pocket, snug in its plastic evidence bag. His hand went to his jacket pocket, which had become slightly ripped, and then stopped. If he removed the knife, it would no longer be any use as evidence.

Fuck it, he thought. What evidence did he need anyway? He knew who was ultimately responsible for Bob Allison's death.

He reached into his torn pocket, and discovered that the knife had gone.

9

Sam and Nathaniel Longman were finding carrying Cassidy hard work, and were each privately coming to the same ungenerous opinion: that for such a little man, Cassidy was a heavy bastard. Sam looked up from watching his feet sliding over the ice and saw the dock about twenty paces in front of them. The Eldritch girl was already there, one foot resting on the rung of an iron ladder bolted to the dock wall. Over the edge of the dock he could see the warren of abandoned warehouse buildings that dominated this side of the river.

'Come on!' the girl urged them.

Neither man noticeably responded to her encouragement. Longman plainly didn't trust the girl, and Sam was still annoyed at her. He hadn't wanted to argue with her in front of Nat, but it was hard to bite back on the argument, because she had told him she was wrong about one of his major characters.

Once Nat had mentioned DI Hyams, Sam had wanted to try to find him, too. The girl had first argued that it would be too dangerous, and then gone on to claim that Hyams, like Jo and Horace before him, was actually on her father's team.

Sam had instantly bristled, very much aware of Longman's attention but completely unable to stop himself. Hyams was like Drunk Dave Hawkins, he'd told her. Sometimes misguided, yes, but a completely incorruptible cop. Saying that Hyams was bent was like saying that Hawkins was bent, and that just couldn't be.

The girl had laughed at him. 'Cops can't exist without criminals,' she'd said. 'And vice versa.

They're part of the same machinery. Graft greases the wheels. The system wouldn't work otherwise.'

Sam told her she was wrong, that he knew his characters. 'Graft doesn't grease every wheel in the machine. Not Drunk Dave,' he'd said. 'Not Hyams.'

The girl had come close to Sam, ignoring Longman's suspicious eyes. She'd held Sam tightly, her body moving under her coat as though the fur were her own skin. She had her own way of greasing the wheels.

'Okay, maybe it isn't money or favours,' she'd said. 'Maybe they don't even *know* they're working for my father, but they are. In law, Hyams had no reason to follow you, did he? The reason he wanted to catch you, whether he knew it or not, was to stop you coming into Eldritch. Just like the Golem tried, once he realised what you meant to do. Their persistence is a good thing, though,' she added.

'Why?'

'Because it means my father is afraid of you going to his resting place. It means he thinks we can win.'

Sam had slowed to a halt, even as the girl again encouraged them to hurry. He looked from the girl to the dark warehouses above her head, wondering what had begun to alarm him. Then he had it.

'Why are we going this way?' he asked.

The girl was leading them north, further into the heart of the docklands. He looked back the way they had come, to the south bank. He couldn't see Hepplewhite's window, and didn't know if the apartment even existed anymore, but he did know that if you followed the Old Dock Road far enough, the streetlights eventually began. The way the girl was taking them, there would be no light for a long, long time. If they took a wrong turn, there might *never* be a light.

Longman, mentally and physically exhausted from the constant cold, gradually began to understand the point Sam had made. 'She's taking us into the worst of it,' he said.

The girl gave him a thin smile that was several degrees colder than the ice beneath their feet. 'By all means, feel free to go back,' she said. 'But if the Golem comes after us, he'll come from that direction. Do you want to go walking into his arms? I know he'd be pleased to see you.'

Longman was silent. No, he didn't want to meet the Golem again.

'Besides,' she added, 'going around the docklands that way would take too long, and time is just as important to us as getting out of the docklands is. Perhaps more so.'

'Why?' Sam asked.

'Because of you. You're in Eldritch now. The atmosphere is working on you, turning you into fiction.'

Sam shrugged. He already knew that. Had guessed it, anyway.

'Don't you remember what I told you?' the girl asked. 'If you're fiction, you're the *Shaped*. And the Shaped cannot create. Right now, all your powers of creation are draining out of you. It won't be long before you have none at all.'

She nodded at the realisation she could see on Sam's face.

'And if you can't create the link between worlds, how are you ever going to get back to your own?'

Any further conversation on the subject was forestalled by a loud cracking sound behind them. The ice was breaking. Or being broken. Sam, who had more of an idea of what might be lurking below the frozen surface, made up his mind instantly.

'Climb up ahead of us,' he told the girl. 'Get ready to pull Nigel up.'

Longman was looking behind them fearfully. 'What is it, Sam?'

'You really want to know?'

After a second's consideration, Longman shook his head. At this stage, he thought, the less he knew the better.

The girl was already standing on the dock, having gone up the ladder like a monkey. The two men struggled to lift Cassidy high enough for the girl to snag him under the arms, and the cords stood out in Longman's neck as he fought against his own pain. Finally, the girl hauled Cassidy's unconscious body up and over the dock's lip and let him drop into the snow.

Sam followed Longman up the ladder, giving him a none too gentle push on the behind when the sound of cracking ice was repeated.

'Hurry, Sam,' the girl said. 'Hurry!'

Once they were on the dock, Sam quickly looked back across the frozen river, and for a few seconds he saw an albino-white face glaring back at him from a jagged hole that it − she − had smashed through the ice.

277

The few locks of hair the murderous wife still possessed were tangled with dark weed, and they twined down around abnormally developed shoulders and clung to her pendulous, translucent breasts. A century and a half in the Leeth had changed the geometry of her face radically, and her mouth was almost the full width of her head and full of needle-like teeth. Her eyes seemed to glimmer like black diamonds as she slipped back under the ice.

Whether Sam actually saw any of this or just imagined it, he didn't know, and he wasn't sure if there was a difference any more. But if he had seen it, what did it mean? Had she woken from hibernation out of simple hunger, or had she been awoken for a specific *purpose*, after which she had been free to return to the river bed? And if it were the latter, what had she achieved?

She got us moving again, Sam thought, she finally got us off the ice.

But whose purpose did that really serve?

Sam glanced at the girl. For the first time, he sensed fear in her. Or if not outright fear, certainly apprehension. She kept looking back over her shoulder, as if she thought something was about to leap out at her. He wasn't sure why, but he found himself sharing some of her anxiety. Longman obviously felt nothing, and was trying to lift Cassidy up by himself. When he realised that Sam hadn't come to join him, he looked up.

'If–' he began, but was instantly silenced by a shriek so loud and piercing that he dropped Cassidy's arms and put his hands over his ears.

The shriek was definitely animal, not human, although what kind of animal could produce such a noise it was difficult to imagine. It had the high pitch of a birdcall, but also the volume and depth of a large cat. It came three more times over the next handful of seconds, and each time it came it seemed to be closer. It was coming to them from the direction of the warehouses.

'Sam?' Longman said. 'Sam, is it the same thing that was breaking the ice?' He found the idea that something could break the ice behind them one moment and be ahead of them the next very worrying.

Sam appeared not to have heard him. The concentration on his face was matched by the Eldritch girl's, and for a moment they looked eerily alike.

'Sam, is it the same fucking thing?' Longman hissed, and wondered why he persisted in asking questions to which he didn't wish to know the answers.

'No,' Sam calmly replied after a moment. 'It's some other fucking thing.'

'What?'

Amazingly, Sam smiled. It wasn't a good smile, Longman thought, more of a defence mechanism. 'I think we're about to find out. Listen.'

Longman did, and heard footsteps approaching them. Racing footsteps, crunching their way through the snow. Another animal screech split the frigid air and the three of them saw a young man come careering out through one of the narrow gaps between warehouse buildings, barely staying on his feet as he desperately changed direction. He was running towards them now as though the devil were after him.

279

Sam glanced at the girl, who was staring at the young man, unblinking. At first he thought that she was pointing at him, but then he realised that the finger he'd seen sticking out of her fist wasn't a finger at all. It was a knife. When she nervously passed it from hand to hand, he saw the infinity-shaped handle and felt something in his mind turn over.

Man in a concrete room, accepting a knife, 'thank you, thank you', and then blood, blood, and more blood…

'Sam?' Longman said, already backing away. 'What's–'

Above them, a cloud abruptly obscured the moon. In the darkness, they heard the young man's footsteps coming closer and closer, and his exhausted breathing which sounded like a labouring saw. When the moon reappeared seconds later, he was almost upon them, and they stepped back to allow him to pass, even the Eldritch girl.

The man was short, only a little over five feet, and would have been a young-looking thirty-something if terror had not etched his face with age. His clothes were filthy and torn. From the grime on his face, bright blue eyes shone out in the madness of his flight, and Sam realised that he recognised him.

An involuntary grunt of surprise forced its way out of his lips.

The man's eyes flicked towards him as he passed, and seemed to become locked. He tripped over Cassidy's body and went sprawling in the snow. He was back up on his knees within a second, but even though another screech tore the night in two, he stayed to stare at Sam. He looked astonished and horrified in equal measure.

Sam took a small step towards him and the man immediately threw himself to his feet and ran away. He didn't stop again, but every so often he glanced around, never slowing his pace.

'Sam,' Longman said. 'He knew you. He recognised you.'

Sam nodded. 'That was Johnnie Ronnie Sudds. Small time thief. Some woman at the convention asked about him, remember? He was in−'

'I know what books he was in, Sam, but how could he know you?'

'I don't know.'

Sam turned to the girl, but she was still staring at the gap between warehouse buildings Sudds had emerged from. Suddenly, Sam caught something from her, a mental image, and the idea blossomed in his own mind.

'Oh no…'

Then he saw them, and what little warmth remained in his body leaked away like piss down his leg. He heard Longman beside him swear, and he wished that such a simple escape valve would work for him.

It wasn't the devil Sudds was running from, it was the Guardians of Justice.

They emerged from between the buildings like two juggernauts and pounded through the snow following Sudds's trail, their black flanks glossy and steaming, golden beaks glinting, and their eyes like cauldrons of sulphur.

The first Guardian passed between them, leaping over Cassidy's inert body, the air from its passage buffeting them. The second also passed through, but then slewed to a stop in a great tearing of claws, and turned to face them.

It sniffed at the air, scenting, then turned its head from side to side, regarding them all with each of its baleful eyes.

Sam was holding his breath, and when the Guardian looked directly at him, he felt as though his heart had stopped. The creature looked at Nat Longman, who was unable to restrain a low moan. Then it looked at the Eldritch girl for a long, long time, before it sniffed at Cassidy. Sam saw that the girl's arm had fallen to her side, the knife having disappeared back into her coat somewhere. This time there was no doubt that she was afraid. Terror had done something to her face Sam would have believed impossible. It had made her look plain.

He wanted to speak then. He wanted to say that they were all safe, because the Guardians were there to punish the guilty, and not one of them had anything to be guilty of. But then he thought of all the other things he'd got wrong about the city he thought he'd known as well as the back of his hand, and he decided that silence would probably be the best policy.

The Guardian snorted out Cassidy's odour as though in disgust, included them all in one last comprehensive sweep of its burning eyes, and then it turned away, all its muscles bunching under its pelt. It bounded off after its partner, and while they were still staring after it, they heard the first of Sudds's screams as he was finally brought to ground. The screams were terrible, but they didn't last for long.

Johnnie Ronnie Sudds must have graduated to the big time since he'd last seen him, Sam thought. At least if he ever went to another horror convention and a blue-haired old lady asked him whatever happened to her favourite small time crook, Sam would know what to tell her.

Johnnie got in too deep, lady, and the Guardians ripped him apart.

Another unpleasant interlude.

This time, a delay.

Whose purpose had it served?

10

Hyams was finding the going hard as he limped down a long, wide road made anonymous by the snow, which had coated the tall warehouse buildings as effectively as paint. The snow he walked through was at least eight inches deep, its surface crusted into ice. Mostly it bore his weight, but if his supporting leg slipped on the fresh snow settling on top, it broke and his foot would shoot through to the cobblestones below. He had already fallen three times so far, twisting his ankle in the process, and he was wet from head to foot. Snow had found its way into his clothes and they were in the process of freezing even as he lurched along. He wasn't sure how much more he could take.

When he heard the first of the distant screeches, he tried to stop walking immediately, and he fell again. This time he felt the cobblestones with the whole of his aching, trembling body. Then he simply lay there listening, for the moment unable to rise.

The screeches were high-pitched and seemed to have a metallic quality to them he found completely unnerving. Although they seemed to be far away, distance did little to diminish their menace. They were like the cries of living machine that had been taught to kill, and he thought that they were the worst sounds he had ever heard – until he heard the screams which followed. Hyams felt smothered by the pain they articulated.

The instinct of self-preservation told him he had to get up, had to get out of the docklands, find shelter, warmth and food. Fatigue, fear, and the seductive mattress of the soft snow told him to stay where he was. Here was peace, finally, and the cold didn't feel so very cold once you had submitted to its embrace. His treacherous mind began to assemble a sequence of comforting tableaux like the bait in a trap.

He saw a reconciliation with his ex-fiancé. He saw a wedding. His parents were waiting for him in a green field. Blue skies. Golden figures, shimmering, radiant…

Hyams may have given up right there if he hadn't begun to hear another harrowing sound, this one far closer. It stripped away his false comforts layer by layer, until he was raw and quivering once more. He may still have given up, and died of exposure, if the sound hadn't been exactly what it was. But it was so instantly recognisable, so mournful, that he found it impossible not to respond. It brought out not only the policeman in him, but also the human being, the genetic coding that ensured that the sound simply could not be ignored.

It was the sound of a child sobbing.

Hyams limped as quietly as he could down an alleyway just like the one he had landed in. For a moment he was afraid that he had wandered in a circle and was now walking back into the arms of the carrion creature he had run from. But then he saw windows iced into cataracts set high into the walls, and found that this alleyway was both shorter and straighter, ending in a wide courtyard.

He cautiously entered the courtyard in the near blackness of the buildings' moon-shadows, and for a moment it was all he could do to stand and stare. At the centre of the courtyard, bathed in moonlight, a naked child sat doubled over on a snow-covered hillock, its head buried in its arms as it sobbed. The courtyard amplified the child's cries until the sound of heartbreak was unbearable. Hyams's mind flashed back to the two bodies he'd landed on, a man and a woman.

A mother and father?

'Don't cry,' he said quietly, and the child's head instantly came up, turned about until its eyes found him.

He saw that it was a girl, probably around eleven or twelve years old, and she was the most beautiful child he had ever seen. Her eyes were a dark, dusty blue and her blonde hair, although wet and plastered to her delicate head, was still blonde. She was pale apart from patches of red on her cheeks, and her lips, which were full and ruddy. Her breasts were just beginning to bud, and her small nipples were as red as her lips. Already the lovely young woman she would become could be seen, but Hyams saw most clearly the child who had endured more than any child should have to.

'It's all right,' he said very gently. 'I'm a friend. I'm not going to hurt you. I want to help you.'

It pained him to see the suspicion appear on that perfect face, and he knew then just how many times men had said those same or similar words to her in the past, and how many times she had been betrayed. He stepped forward very slowly, watching her face all the time. When he cleared the buildings' shadows, he stopped and showed the girl his open palms.

'I promise you, I won't hurt you. My name is Duncan Hyams. I'm a policeman. I can help you.'

Maybe it was his words that did the trick, or perhaps it was just that he had stepped out of the shadows, that he was prepared to let her see him. Either way, her suspicion was slowly overtaken by a tentative smile, and eyes that filled with tears and hope in equal measure.

'Please be kind to me,' she whispered. 'Don't…don't…'

'I promise I'll be kind.'

The girl's teary smile grew a little wider, and she became even more beautiful to him. Already he would have done everything to protect her. He would have fought to his last drop of blood.

Her shoulders quivered violently. 'I'm so cold,' she said. 'So cold. Can't you make me warm?'

Hyams looked down at his own soaked and frost-stiffened clothes in dismay. 'I'll try.'

He started across the courtyard towards the girl, who was now holding out her arms to him, but he had gone no more than three or four paces when a loud voice stopped him.

'I wouldn't do that if I were you.'

Hyams spun around, his stiff left leg nearly spilling him to the ground again. The voice had come from the same shadows he had moved through only a minute ago. A man's voice, it had had the rasp of command. He could see nothing in the darkness, even though the girl had apparently seen him easily enough.

'Oh please help me!' the girl said. She was begging him. 'Don't leave me here! Don't let him hurt me.'

'Don't fall for it,' the unseen man said.

'Who are you?' Hyams asked, willing his own voice to match the other's strength. Surprisingly, he found that it did. 'Come out into the light.'

There was a silent pause, and then Hyams heard uneven footsteps crunching through the snow, one foot dragging slightly behind the other. An outstretched hand came forward out of the shadow. In it was a large black revolver.

The rest of the arm followed, and then the man himself. He was at least six feet tall, dressed in a dark overcoat and his face shadowed by the brim of a shabby grey fedora. He limped out into the light, favouring his right leg, and then stopped.

Although he couldn't see the face, Hyams felt recognition swarming all over him. It was the coat and the hat, the commanding rasp of a voice, and the limp left over from the severely broken leg that had prevented the man from hunting the serial killer, Okra.

…if I were you…if I were you…

'You're Dave Hawkins,' Hyams whispered in amazement.

'Yes, and you're Duncan Hyams.' Hawkins pronounced Hyams's name with emphasis on the capitals, and there was bemusement in his voice. 'And that thing behind you is no more a little girl than I am. As a matter of fact, it's rather *less* of a little girl than I am.'

'You're full of fucking shit, Hawkins!'

Hyams turned and stared at the young girl again, this time in astonishment. Her voice was nothing like it had been. It was as though some larger being was speaking through her.

'And *you're* not going to be full of anything tonight,' Hawkins calmly replied. He nodded at Hyams. 'This is one snack you're going to miss.'

'Bastard!' the girl spat. 'Fucking cocksucking bastard! Why do you keep coming back here, ruining it for everyone?'

With his free hand, Hawkins gestured for Hyams to come away from the girl, but Hyams couldn't move.

'You know what I think, Hawkins?' the girl asked. 'You're no hero. I think you're like the rest of the pathetic morsels who come down here. You come to die, but you haven't the guts to go all the way.'

'Hyams, get over here,' Hawkins said.

Moving slowly, from shock as much as from his stiff leg, Hyams went to stand by Drunk Dave Hawkins. Close up, he could see the Eldritch

288

detective's solemn face, his nose swollen by booze and the dark pits of his eyes.

'How long have you wanted to die, Hawkins?' the girl hissed venomously. 'Since the ex-wife, since the brother, since the sister, since the partner? How long have you wanted to die? Why not come to me now, and I'll end it all for you.' She smacked her lips and laughed. 'Yum yum yum!'

Hawkins shot the girl in the forehead.

Hyams fell down in surprise and shock, and felt the sound of the gunshot reverberate in his chest. Then he saw the black bullet hole in the girl's pallid forehead begin to ooze a green substance that looked like washing up liquid, and her angelic face seemed to split open with rage. Then he saw that she really *was* splitting open.

With a convulsive twitch that made Hyams's ears pop, the girl's whole body turned itself inside out. Large brightly coloured organs that looked like the internal flesh of exotic fruit and behaved like tentacles lashed out across the courtyard, digging deep furrows in the snow only a yard short of Hyams's feet. Wicked, barbed thorns came unsheathed at their ends and raked up cobblestones as they retreated. Wide-eyed, he saw that the snow-covered hillock the girl had appeared to be sitting on was just another extension of the creature's body, and it was rooted into the ground beneath.

Hyams frantically scrambled backwards and clambered to his feet. Hawkins hadn't moved back so much as an inch, and stood regarding the creature's impotent rage with a cold smile as the air before him clouded with beaten snow.

'Finished yet, sweetheart?' he asked.

The creature's lethal appendages paused and seemed to waver indecisively in the air for a few seconds. Then, more quickly than Hyams could follow, they all folded back together and the outer shell closed neatly about them, like petals around a flower. Four or five limbs at its base swiftly covered themselves with snow, and the illusion was again complete. The beautiful naked girl stared back at them, no longer sorrowful, just sulky, like a grounded teenager.

Hawkins put his revolver away in a shoulder holster beneath his overcoat, then turned and extended a hand to Hyams. Once he was on his feet, he realised that Hawkins was examining him very closely, frowning as though trying to identify a forgotten but hauntingly familiar tune.

'Duncan Hyams?' he asked.

'That's right.'

Hawkins took a deep breath and nodded. 'I think we could both do with a drink, don't you?'

He turned and left the courtyard without another word. Hyams turned for one last look at the creature that had nearly snared him. Once again, it was the sweetly seductive girl, vulnerable and forlorn. Her smile was innocence itself, but her beautiful blue eyes spoke of murder.

Hyams hurried along the alleyway to catch up with Hawkins, and the two detectives fell into step together, Hyams limping on his left leg, Hawkins limping on his right. Every second step, their shoulders met, and for an instant they looked like conjoined twins.

11

How he and Longman managed to haul Cassidy up and over one of the barricades that cut off the docklands from the rest of the city, Sam would never know. Fear had certainly played its part. Their long journey through the maze of dark alleyways and deep shadows had unnerved them all, and when they were struggling to lift Cassidy above their heads, Sam was sure that he'd heard a gunshot somewhere behind them.

The effort, however, was worth it. Even a foot or so from the barricade, Sam could feel the docklands' peculiar atmosphere losing some of its potency, and it was with a measure of relief that they began to follow the Eldritch girl through the deserted night-time streets of the city. She said they had to find a car so that they could continue their journey, but obviously the docklands' influence extended beyond its own boundaries to some extent. All the cars they had so far discovered were burnt-out wrecks.

The streets themselves were black and ugly, as though at some point in the past, they had burned, too. The snow only served to cover drifts of mouldering garbage, and most of the buildings had their windows and doors sealed with sheet steel. Some of the steel sheets had been peeled back like the lids of sardine cans, and Sam was afraid to look inside.

The Eldritch girl was about five yards ahead of them now. She was walking too fast, and Sam and Nat Longman were both breathing hard, but neither of them complained. Time, she kept warning Sam, time, but she needn't have bothered. The thought of being trapped in Eldritch for good was more than enough encouragement to hurry.

'Sam?'

He glanced across Cassidy's dangling head at Longman. 'What?'

'I think Nigel's dead.'

Sam stopped walking.

'I'm holding his wrist,' Longman explained. 'I can't feel a pulse anymore.'

They laid Cassidy down on the pavement and Sam grabbed his wrist. No pulse. Cassidy's eyelids and lips were now so blue they looked as though they were painted, and his scalp wound had stopped bleeding. Scalp wounds seemed to bleed forever, Sam thought, unless the blood itself ceased to flow, unless the heart had stopped. Sam transferred his hands to Cassidy's neck. Very faintly, he felt a pulse, but it was slow and irregular.

'We've got to get him warm,' he said. 'We need shelter for a while, maybe some brandy, food…'

The girl had come back to stand over them, her shadow erasing Cassidy's face. 'Sam−'

'Don't say it!' he warned.

Longman, his face grey with fatigue and concern, glowered at her.

Sam stood up and took her arm and held it. 'Is there somewhere we can take him? Somewhere on our way. Somewhere close.'

The girl stared deep into his eyes, searching for something and not finding it. Eventually she dropped her eyes.

'Yes,' she said.

'What is it?' Sam asked. 'Some kind of squat?'

The heavily scarred door and its filthy doorway looked as decrepit and unoccupied as the rest of the other buildings close to the docklands. There was no number, no lights, no sign, no nothing, and all the windows were boarded up.

'No, it's a bar.'

Sam looked at the place doubtfully. He could hear no sounds coming from it, no voices or music. He was sure the girl was right, but this was yet another example of something he hadn't written, couldn't even remember creating in his imagination, and so he was disturbed by its unfamiliarity.

'Sam,' Longman whispered. 'Nigel!'

Sam nodded. 'Okay.'

The girl stepped forward and pushed open the door. She led the way into a dark, narrow corridor about twenty feet long, which ended in another featureless door. But now they could hear the muffled bass and drums of a music system, and the low rumble of many voices. Their feet stuck to the filthy carpet as they walked. When the girl opened the second door, the full force of the music hit them in a wave, and fog-like cigarette smoke crept out through the doorway.

'Oh Jesus,' Longman said.

The bar was like a vast, low-ceilinged cavern chamber. There were booths against the walls that faded into invisibility through clouds of smoke that smothered the few lamps. There were lots of tables around which scores of men huddled to drink and play cards. The men looked like they actually belonged in caves, and the only women to be seen who weren't obviously prostitutes were waitresses, shuffling from table to table, half naked.

At the other side of the room, an open staircase led to a second floor, and a trickle of Toms and their tricks were climbing up and down the stairs. The couples on their way up had their arms around each other. On the way down, the men were tucking wallets away and the women were not tactile.

Sam looked at the Eldritch girl. 'You've been here before?'

'When I had to. When I had no other choice. Do you understand?'

'Yes,' Sam nodded slowly. 'I understand too well.'

'Sam?'

He turned to Longman, then realised what had made him speak. The rock music was still pounding out of the speakers, but the buzz of conversation had gone. The bar's customers were completely silent, and as one they were staring at the new arrivals. Sam felt sure that everyone was looking at him, and it reminded him strongly of the Q&A session at the convention.

Soon they'll start asking questions, he thought, and I won't have a clue how to answer them.

'There's a free booth,' the Eldritch girl said. As she led them towards it, the song abruptly ended and another began. Heads turned back to their drinks and games, and a hundred mumbled conversations resumed. Somewhere in the large room, a woman was slapped hard enough to be heard above the music and her cries were met by harsh laughter.

Sam and Longman settled Cassidy into the booth, where he slipped down onto the upholstered bench.

'We need–'

'I'll take care of it,' the girl told Sam.

She left them immediately and went to the bar itself, the only truly bright part of the entire place. Sam watched her speak to the bartender, who glanced over in their direction while he listened. Sam saw him nod a couple of times.

'Nigel? Nigel?'

Sam turned back to see that Longman had sat Cassidy up and was lightly tapping his face even as he began to slide bonelessly back down.

'How is he?'

Longman shook his head. 'Bad. He's breathing, but his chest sounds terrible. His pulse comes and goes.' He looked up. 'Sam, I don't think he's going to make it.'

'Here.'

The girl was back. In her arms she held a bundle of bar towels and a rough blanket. At her side was the barman, who carried a tray upon which were a bottle of brandy, glasses, and a plate piled with curling sandwiches. He was a brutal looking man, heavily muscled, with piss-hole eyes that had seen everything twice and didn't think well of any of it. But after an initial furtive glance, he would not look at Sam.

Longman took the towels and began to dry Cassidy off as best he could, rubbing vigorously in an attempt to improve his friend's circulation. Sam watched as the barman placed the tray on their table. He reached into his jacket for his wallet, hoping that his money would work here.

295

'How much do I owe you?'

'No charge,' the man replied, still refusing to look at him. 'It's on the house.'

The barman quickly stalked away again, as though he was afraid that if he stayed any longer, Sam might draw him into some exchange that would involve eye-contact. Sam watched him shamble away back to his well-lighted bar, looking as though he would rather have run.

'What was that about?' he asked the girl.

'It's obvious,' Longman said interrupted. 'He recognised you, just like J.R. Sudds did back in the docklands.' He plucked the blanket away from the girl and began to tuck it around Cassidy's body. 'They know who you are. They *all* know.'

Sam looked at the girl as she sat down beside him. 'Is that true?'

She shrugged. 'Who knows what's true?'

12

Hyams sat in the passenger seat of Drunk Dave's car. He saw little of the city as they sped away from the docklands, and did not react to the string of near collisions that Dave's poor driving led to. He did not ask why the already thoroughly intoxicated detective was driving himself tonight, instead of allowing DS Keith Muggins to chauffeur him. Hyams already knew.

Hawkins did not want his dogsbody to know that he routinely spent time in the docklands. If he did, Muggins might try to follow in his DI's meandering footsteps, as many others had done before him, and Drunk Dave did not want to be responsible for another death. He had seen far too many devoted colleagues crash and burn on the hellish corners he himself swerved around with insolent ease.

In *Underlined Twice*, the novel in which the detective had made his blistering, shit-faced debut, Sam Parker had introduced Hawkins as "a man born on a bed of four-leafed clover – with an excellent view of the slaughterhouse." Although he had long since felt that he knew Hawkins back to front, only now did Hyams fully appreciate the accuracy of that description. It was just too bad that its author was a criminal.

Halfway through their journey, Hawkins retrieved a mostly empty bottle of Monte Cristo sherry from the glove compartment, and unscrewed the cap with both hands off the steering wheel as he powered the car through a busy intersection. He drank deeply, ignoring the protesting horns of other drivers, then passed the old, dusty bottle to Hyams without a word. Hyams didn't hesitate. He just tilted the bottle and swallowed until it was empty, then dropped it into the rear foot-well.

Hawkins belched. Hyams belched. Then he simply sat and stared at Drunk Dave's profile fading in and out of darkness as they passed a succession of jaundiced streetlights. He noticed that their breathing was in synchronisation, that he blinked when Hawkins did.

They only spoke once during the whole journey, when Hyams cleared his throat and said, 'You know you're fiction, don't you?'

Hawkins smiled bleakly, and replied, 'Everybody's fiction.'

13

Sam took another sip of his brandy, relishing the rough afterburn if not the taste. Like the sandwiches he and Longman had tried, the brandy seemed to have almost no flavour at all, but at least it was warming. They had poured a little of it between Cassidy's blue lips, and even as deeply unconscious as he was it had given him a choking fit. Some of the colour had come back into his face, but the flesh around his eyes was still dark and bruise-like. His pulse continued to waver in strength and consistency, and Longman was more worried about him than ever. He was also angrier with the Eldritch girl than he had been earlier. She was tapping her fingers tunelessly on the table, impatiently waiting for it to be over.

Sam looked up at her suddenly, as an idea came to him.

'I can change things,' he said. 'I can make things happen here, can't I? You're worried about time, why don't I *stop* time? You're worried about getting to Sly Jack Road as quickly as possible, why don't I transport us there, in just one sentence?'

The girl began to shake her head.

'Me, I'm worried about Nigel,' Sam continued. 'Why don't I just make him well again? Put him right over the course of a paragraph, heal his wounds, give him back the blood he's lost?'

'Sam, I don't doubt that you could do any one of those things,' the girl replied. 'But it would be only *one* of them. You don't have the creative power to do more. Stop time and you won't be able to set it going again. Take us immediately to Sly Jack Road, and even if you succeed in completely destroying my father, you'll no longer have the power to get out of Eldritch again. Heal Nigel now and you'll only condemn him to a slower death. He isn't strong enough to survive here, he's weak. You know it's true.'

Sam looked over at Longman, who was holding Cassidy, lending him his body heat. 'Nat?'

Longman glanced around the bar, studying its clientele and wondering how many of the city's other citizens were as brutish and menacing, or even worse. Then he looked at Cassidy's face for the longest time, the white blur, almost unidentifiable without its glasses, and he thought how right his friend had been to fear Eldritch.

'She's right,' he said at last, reluctantly. 'If we can't get out of here, we'll all be dead in a matter of days.' He looked up at the Eldritch girl angrily. 'And it isn't because Nigel's *weak*. It's because he doesn't belong here. No one does. Nobody normal.'

Suddenly it was all too much for Sam. No man should have this kind of choice to make. But he'd already made it, hadn't he? He didn't need Longman's reluctant agreement, just as he hadn't needed the girl's arguments to clarify the bind they were in. To his shame, he had already known he was prepared to let Nigel die. The fact that he still had Longman, The Survivor, seemed to soften the blow. He sickened himself.

Dizzily, Sam rose to his feet. He could hear Longman asking him where he was going, what was wrong, but nausea prevented him from replying. The current music track ended, and, bizarrely, the next song on the jukebox was Tom Jones singing *The Green, Green Grass of Home*. Sam clapped his hand over his mouth and bolted across the bar towards two doors upon which crude matchstick figures had been drawn, one with a hole at its crotch, the other with an erect line jutting from the fork of its legs.

He slammed into the men's toilet, his feet splashing in puddles of yellow urine that had flooded out of the blocked porcelain trough. He stumbled into the single stall and leaned over the toilet bowl, retching up brandy and the two small bites of sandwich he'd taken.

He felt as though he was dying.

The first moment he realised he was not alone was when the girl began to stroke his hair. He was sitting on the toilet, feeling completely hollow. He was cold, yet he was sweating badly and giving off a nauseating odour he had never noticed on himself before.

Sam looked up at the girl, and drew a small measure of comfort from the compassion in her face, and the heat she seemed to radiate. He pulled her to him, and suddenly her coat was open and his lips were pressed to the gentle swell of her smooth belly.

He wanted to say, this is not the time or place, but he didn't. He wanted to say, my friend may be dying – we can't do this. But he didn't. He didn't say anything. The girl's hands clasped around the back of his head, his teeth nipped at the skin of her navel, and the moan she made drove him on.

He lifted her right leg and planted her bare foot on his thigh, then clutched her buttocks with both hands and began to nuzzle at her hairless groin. She rocked and swayed with his bobbing head, and the sounds of pleasure she made were like no other sounds he had ever heard. They filled his mind with a suffocating, velvety darkness that thickened even as he tore at it.

Then she was in his lap and his trousers were open and she was guiding him inside her and she was slick and tight and his mouth was full of her breasts and her hands were tearing at his hair.

And a moment or two later, when someone walked into the toilet, Sam did not hear himself growl, 'Get out, or I'll kill you.' If he had, he would hardly have recognised his own voice.

Longman poured a little more brandy into a glass and carefully lifted it to Cassidy's mouth. As the lip of the glass passed under his nostrils, Cassidy's face twisted and he pulled his head out of Longman's supporting hand.

'Don't give me any more of that shit,' he said, his voice no more than a croak. 'What is it, battery acid?'

'Nigel!' Overjoyed, Longman embraced Cassidy, then quickly released him again when he groaned in pain. 'Sorry, sorry.'

'Doesn't matter. I'm dying, anyway. Cop a feel if you have to...'

'No, you're not going to die.' Longman clasped Cassidy's hands in his own 'You'll be okay. You just need to rest, and then we'll get you to a hospital.'

'A hospital in Eldritch?' Cassidy laughed weakly. 'I'd be better off in the docklands.'

'Nigel−'

'I'm dying, Nat, and we both know it.'

Cassidy opened his eyes finally. The right eye looked okay, but the pupil in the left was the size of a pin-hole, the white full of blood. Longman saw this, and realised that he could forget the optimistic approach. As though sensing his discomfort, Cassidy gave his hands a small squeeze.

'It's okay, Nat, it was just a stupid accident.'

Longman hung his head. 'Jesus, Nigel…'

'But we're not *here* by accident.'

Longman's head came up. 'What do you mean?'

Cassidy tried to turn to face him, but seemed to be looking off to one side, and Longman realised that he was blind.

'Sam drew us into this,' he said. 'He made us part of his plot, as surely as he made the Golem. He brought both of us, just in case something like this happened.' His hand flapped at himself. 'He needed back-up, so that at least one of us would be around if he needed us.'

'Needed us for what?'

Cassidy rolled his head from side to side. 'Don't know, don't know. I'm not sure *he* does, yet. But he will know when the time comes, and if he has to, he'll use you.'

Longman's flesh was crawling. He didn't like, or even understand, anything Cassidy had said, but he felt that everything he said was true.

'Where's Sam, with that girl?'

'Yes.'

'She's…not right. She's false. She's like Jo.'

Longman nodded. Cassidy had just put his finger on the similarity that had been eluding Longman since he'd first set eyes on her. Like Jo, the Eldritch girl was there totally for Sam. No one else mattered. The difference between the two women was that when separated from Sam, Jo had turned into a mannequin. Longman had a feeling that the Eldritch girl might turn into a ravening wolf.

Cassidy was silent and still for a long time, and just as Longman reached out to him in concern, his whole body jerked violently, once, twice, three times.

His blind eyes fixed on the filthy ceiling, he said, 'I wish… I wish... I WISH...'

Longman waited, then asked, 'What do you wish?'

Cassidy didn't reply.

'Nigel, what do you wish? What do you wish?' Frantically he tried to shake Cassidy back to life. '*What do you wish*?'

Longman was still shaking him when a greasy, foul-smelling vapour began to seep through the gaps in Cassidy's clothes like steam.

14

Hawkins had brought Hyams to a coppers' bar which revelled in the name of The Bobby's Helmet. It seemed to Hyams not dissimilar to The Truncheon where Ken Morley had informed him of the discovery of Fee's body, except that it also seemed simultaneously larger and more claustrophobic.

Upon entering, Hawkins had merely waved at the barman and a moment later two glasses and a chilled bottle of Smirnoff Blue had arrived at a table that had been cleared for them. All the policemen, some still in uniform, looked like hard-bitten, hard-drinking men, and Hyams had a sense of the suppressed violence they carried concealed beneath the thinnest of shells. He did not feel at all out of place among them.

He had watched Hawkins fill their glasses to the top, then they clinked them together, and began to drink. By the time the second bottle of vodka arrived, Hyams had told Hawkins most of what he had seen and done, what he knew and what he suspected. He watched Hawkins mulling it all through, hoping that between them they could intuit some kind of plan of action. Both of them knew something very bad was going on, and it hardly mattered that they didn't know exactly what it was. They just wanted to stop it.

Eventually, Hawkins grunted. 'So, this writer bloke…'

'Parker. Sam Parker.'

'Yeah. He told you *what* about his new novel?'

'He said it was about the return of the most evil man who ever walked the streets of Eldritch. Something like that, anyway.'

Hawkins grunted again. 'Well, that's a problem from our point of view,' he said. 'Because the man who was supposed to be Eldritch's epitome of evil is long since dead. Some powerful crime boss who met a very nasty end, long before my time. In fact, that story's so old it's almost a legend. No one really knows how much truth there is to it, if any.'

Hyams slapped the table in frustration, but Hawkins just grinned.

'There's even an old deserted house out in the Heathers district that some people claim was supposed to belong to him. Big rambling place in its own grounds.'

'Who owns it now?' Hyams asked.

'As far as I know the deeds aren't in anyone's name, and that fact in itself seems to add fuel to the legend, because this crime boss was supposed to have no name.'

'What sort of things did he do?'

'The legend says he was behind everything. Every crime, every murder, every perversion, every form of terror in Eldritch. They say he orchestrated it all for his own amusement.'

'Just like Sam Parker,' Hyams muttered.

'If you say so.'

Hyams thought for a moment. In Eldritch, the Heathers district was mostly where the rich people lived. He tossed back another slug of vodka, and said, 'So this big house, in a very nice suburban neighbourhood, is just standing empty. And you're telling me that no one has tried to buy it?'

Hawkins shrugged. 'It's sort of in the same category of real estate as the docklands, if you see what I mean. Even the druggies and the dossers stay well clear. The kids haven't even tried to break the windows.'

Hyams filled their glasses again and noticed that his hand was shaking, although he thought that was probably just the booze.

'Is it haunted?' he asked.

'This is the City of Eldritch, my friend,' Hawkins replied. 'All the fucking houses are haunted.'

Suddenly they became aware that someone was standing beside their table, hovering, but not daring to break into their conversation. Hyams and Hawkins looked up at the same time and saw the confused face of DS Keith Muggins looking down at them. Hyams recognised him instantly from his description in the books. Apart from a few minor differences, he was virtually Ken Morley's doppelganger.

The young DS was glancing from one detective to the other, his mouth hanging open. The two men were of different physiques, their faces were entirely different, and yet Muggins had never seen two men who resembled each other so closely. It was in every gesture, every expression, and it was deep, deep in their eyes.

'Watch out, Muggins, there's a bus coming,' Hyams said, and Muggins's mouth shut like a trap.

'You looking for me?' Hawkins asked, as if poor Muggins ever did anything else whenever he wasn't actually waiting on his DI hand and foot.

'Guv, yes. Come to tell you we're organising a hunt for the Listmaker. Got him as prime suspect in a murder case. A women was found in his digs a few hours ago, battered to death and sexually assaulted.' Muggins, with his hot piece of gossip, paused dramatically. 'Turns out the woman was his *wife*.'

Hawkins was generous to his DS, and managed to look surprised for almost a quarter of a second. 'Well, well, who'd have thought the Listmaker had a wife, eh?' he said, taking another mammoth drink.

'That's what *I* said, Guv. Anyway, we reckon the Listmaker's done a runner out of town, either that or gone to ground somewhere.'

While Hawkins and Muggins discussed where the Listmaker might have flown to, Hyams's mind was doing a little flying of its own.

He thought back to the last time he had seen Parker's house, and about the voices he had heard from behind the high garden walls before and after the shotgun blast. One of them, probably Parker himself, had shouted out a name. The name was Beckett, and after all the trouble at the horror convention, both during the Q&A and afterwards in the lobby, Hyams had no problem deciding that it had been Charles Beckett that Parker had been shouting at. He also remembered the screams of agony coming from behind the garden wall, and the blood all over the overcoat worn by that strange human gargoyle who had gone on to pursue Sam Parker.

If Parker's house were somehow to be transferred to Eldritch, Hyams thought that it would probably appear in the Heathers district. And of course, being an avid Eldritch fan, he was well acquainted with the rumours that Beckett was supposed to have been the inspiration behind the character of the−

'I think we should go to that house you mentioned,' he said abruptly. 'The crime boss's house.'

'Why?'

'Because I think that's where you'll find the Listmaker's corpse.'

Hawkins saw at once that Hyams was deadly serious. In unison, the two DIs stood up, each wobbling in opposite drunken directions, like a man watching himself dance before a mirror. Hyams

307

realised that between them they had demolished two bottles of vodka. And he was still thirsty.

'Looks like you're driving, Muggins,' Hawkins said.

'Yes, Guv, but…' he inclined his head at Hyams questioningly.

'Ah...' Hawkins belated introduced Hyams, describing him as a visiting DI from another city. Muggins pumped Hyams's hand as though he'd found a second idol to worship.

'I can't get over how alike you are,' he marvelled. 'I thought you must be related.'

'Let me try and get this straight, Muggins,' Hawkins growled. 'Which one of us are you trying to insult?'

15

Sam and the Eldritch girl came out of the men's room with their arms around each other, and then froze in the doorway. The bar was completely silent, even the jukebox had quit.

Nathaniel Longman stood halfway between their booth and the doors to the toilets. It was as though he had started to come after Sam and then changed his mind, and now didn't know what to do.

He stood with his arms wrapped around himself, and at first Sam thought he was trying to keep himself warm. But then he realised how afraid and upset his friend was. His face was contorted with an ugly mixture of grief and disgust, and his eyes when they met Sam's were huge and lost. Longman was hugging himself in part out of a subconscious urge to shield himself from harm, in part as a device to comfort himself, and in part as an attempt to stop himself shaking so badly. It was clear that none of these objectives had been achieved.

Sam looked away from Nat's sick-looking face, and he saw that every one of the bar's patrons were staring at their booth with the same intensity that they had stared at Sam when they had all come in off the street. He left the girl and walked over to Longman, and over Nat's shoulder, he saw the spectacle that had attracted so much attention.

Nigel's body lay back against the bench, his eyes open and glassy. His face was yellow, with darker patches that were exactly the same colour as Dijon mustard. A thin steam was rising and curling away from his face, and Sam could actually see his features being steadily eroded away. More steam was sneaking out through the collar and cuffs of his shirt, and like the steam from his face it spiralled up a foot or so and then appeared to either dissipate or simply disappear.

'He died,' Longman whispered into the silence. 'He died, and then… that started to happen… What is it, Sam?'

'That's how they go back,' the Eldritch girl said, coming to join them. 'The visitors, when they die, that's how they leave.'

'*If* they die,' Sam said.

The girl shrugged. 'If, when, it's all the same.'

The majority of Cassidy's face had gone by now, and the surface of his eyes were pulsing, as though the fluid inside them was beginning to boil. The irises had lost most of their colour, and his differently sized pupils stood out in hideous clarity.

'Oh Nigel,' Sam sighed, his voice catching. 'This is terrible.'

He noticed that Nat had turned away, unable to watch Cassidy's disintegration any more. He tried to put his arm around Nat's shoulder, but Longman quickly stepped away out of his reach.

'What is it, Nat? What's wrong?'

Longman looked at them together, Sam and the Eldritch girl, at the bond that now joined them. 'What the hell do you *think* is wrong?' he asked.

'I know,' Sam said. 'It shouldn't have happened. None of it should have happened.'

'No, it shouldn't.'

Sam wiped at his eyes with his fingers, as though he were clearing away tears, although Longman had seen no evidence of them. 'Thank God I still have you, Nat,' he said

His words sent a cold tremor through Longman's body. It was too close to what Nigel had said before he died.

'Did he regain consciousness?' the Eldritch girl asked, frowning. 'Did he say anything?'

Longman could feel her eyes probing into his.

'No,' he said. 'No, I was holding his wrist when I saw him open his eyes. I felt his pulse stop, and he just died.'

He could still feel the girl staring at him. Sam, along with the rest of the bar, was watching Cassidy being stripped down to his bones, then the bones themselves beginning to go. To get away from the girl's eyes, he stepped towards Sam.

'Sam, he's dead, Nigel's dead.'

He allowed Sam to embrace him, but although he was held tightly, with a strength that seemed to mirror the depth of grief he was feeling himself, Longman thought that there seemed to be no warmth to Sam's body, none at all. He was like ice.

The silence which still held in the rest of the bar was abruptly broken by a flurry of screams from upstairs, where the private rooms were. It sounded like a woman was being beaten to death. No one in the bar reacted.

'Come on,' Sam said. 'Let's get out of this place.'

16

Hyams, Hawkins, and DS Muggins stood together in the chill shadow thrown by the huge, decrepit house. The rising sun was still weak, its outline barely visible through a thick grey wash of cloud and smog that ran along the horizon. Their footsteps had made a neat trail in the snow around the side of the house, as they'd carefully walked in each other's tracks to avoid disturbing the scene. There was only one other set of prints, and they approached the rear of the house from the opposite side of the grounds.

'Looks like he came in over the rear wall and tried to break in,' Muggins said, nodding at the French doors where the pane of glass closest to the lock had been knocked through.

'That's the way it looks,' Hawkins agreed.

The Listmaker lay in the snow a body's length from the house, frozen and dead. Both Eldritch policemen had already commented on the fact that the Listmaker had tried to change his appearance by shaving off his beard, and agreed that as awful as the beard had been, it was better than the naked face they were now confronted by.

'Of course,' Hawkins had said, 'in all fairness, it may have looked better when he was alive.'

The hand he must have used to shatter the window glass had a small fresh cut on it, the open flesh frozen almost black. There was no other visible sign of injury, and nothing substantial to indicate the cause of death, but his face was radically contorted, his lips drawn back over yellow horse-like teeth.

'Heart attack?' Muggins speculated.

Hawkins glanced up at the dark house's rear elevation, and involuntarily shivered. 'Who knows, maybe this time it's just like it looks. Maybe he really did die of fright.'

'Wonder why he decided to hole up here?' Muggins said.

'This place must have meant something to him,' Hawkins replied, then said to himself, 'There are too many coincidences here, even for Eldritch.'

'What happened to this crime boss?' Hyams asked, watching Hawkins think.

'Like I told you, he's dead, killed they say by three of his contemp–'

'No, that's not right, Guv.'

Muggins looked mortified that had dared to interrupt his hero, but Hawkins just looked at him for a moment and then nodded.

'Yes, that's right. That's another part of the legend, isn't it? Not dead, *destroyed*.'

'You can't kill what was never really alive,' Muggins intoned as though quoting from the Bible.

'Although, if your theory holds any water,' Hawkins told Hyams, 'then he can't have been destroyed completely. There would have to be something of him left.'

'That's right.'

'*If* your theory holds water.'

Hyams stared at him. 'Tell me the truth, is what I've suggested any more unlikely than what's down there in the docklands?'

'The docklands?' Muggins asked in alarm. 'Guv, you haven't−'

'Hip-flask!' Hawkins loudly commanded, holding out his hand.

Muggins, who knew when he'd been told to shut up, immediately reached into his coat and passed the flask over. He watched Hawkins unscrew the lid and take a large drink. The DI swallowed, grimaced with distaste, and turned an enquiring eye on his DS.

'Sorry,' Muggins apologised. 'It was on offer.'

'Evidently.' Despite the whisky's poor quality, Hawkins took another enormous draft of it. He swished it around in his mouth while staring back at Hyams, then swallowed.

'Where was he supposed to have been destroyed?' Hyams asked.

'Up near Sly Jack Road, in an old watermill. I've seen it, it's a complete wreck.'

Sly Jack Road. It really wasn't much of a surprise. Hyams thought of the ruined windmill which he and DS Morley had discovered, and the stone altar they had found inside. Where the girl had been sacrificed by DS Allison. All the Eldritch novels displayed on top, like the paraphernalia of a religious ceremony.

Hawkins had been glancing between the hip-flask and Muggins as though the two had deliberately conspired to spoil his breakfast. He took one final, grudging sip before passing the flask on to Hyams.

Hyams sniffed first, then tasted the whisky, and shrugged noncommittally.

'Is Sly Jack Road far from here?' he asked.

'Not far at all. Muggins?'

'Guv?'

'Tell me, what do you hear when you close your eyes?'

Muggins frowned slightly at the change of the conversation's direction, but obligingly closed his eyes anyway, cocking his head to listen to whatever it was his DI had picked up on. Hawkins immediately felled him with a right-handed upper-cut that lifted him off his feet. He went down on the snow a yard from the Listmaker's body and didn't move.

'The whisky isn't that bad,' Hyams said.

'By the time he wakes up, whatever is going to happen will already have happened, and it'll be over,' Hawkins said. 'I'm not going to see him die.'

'He wouldn't have stayed behind if you'd ordered him to?'

'Not this one,' Hawkins said, giving Muggins's shoulder a sharp poke with the toe of his shoe, a gesture that was almost affectionate. 'All heart and no brain.'

17

Sam didn't know where the girl got the car, and nor did he even think of asking once they began to cross the City of Eldritch in the cold, thin light of its reluctant dawn. The sight of his creation, illuminated not by moonlight or the disorienting yellow of sodium streetlights, left him deaf to his companions. His thoughts turned inwards upon themselves. He saw Eldritch afresh with a level of detachment he had been unable to achieve while in the midst of writing his stories, and he realised for the first time what a truly dangerous game creation could be.

It wasn't the monsters which frightened him now. Nor was it the ancient curses, or the psychopaths. It was the gaps he had left undocumented; in society, in the infrastructure, in ecology and the environment, simply everywhere. Even in his characters. No matter how well he thought he had drawn them at the time, they were only sketches, incomplete, unfinished, they were not whole. Inadvertently, he had created an entire population, a city, a microcosm of a whole world, which was horribly dysfunctional in every respect.

It wasn't difficult to see how it had happened. As a writer of popular fiction, he didn't have the chance to dot all the *i*s and cross all the *t*s. No writer did, genre or mainstream. Readers didn't need or want to know every character's back-story, how their lives functioned outside of the current storyline, or how an incidentally mentioned one-way traffic system might really function in a winter rush-hour. And so all these details remained unrecorded, and uncreated. The result was disorder and chaos, a city which looked as though it was being seen through a smashed funhouse mirror, incomplete and distorted. Almost everyone was insane.

Of course, there were some places Sam saw that hung together better than others. Those places in the books where he had spent a lot of time creating detail, or where the separate storylines of his novels had crossed like ley-lines. But these locations were small islands in a vast and tumultuous ocean, and there remained a general sense of wrongness that shocked him, and made him ashamed of his own callous irresponsibility.

It was the school that hurt him the most. A large junior school he'd created on a whim for *Bad Blue*, when a news helicopter passed over the city and the children in the school yard waved at the pilot and the pilot waved back. It had been a nothing scene. Just a short paragraph, no more. Completely unimportant, just colour. A whim.

That was why he found the aftermath so chilling.

All the children were still there, permanently on their lunch break, condemned to hopscotch and football, to tease and be bullied for the rest of eternity. The children had no names, no homes, no parents, and no chance of escape.

Sam had to close his eyes as they drove past the closed and locked gates. A number of pupils stood with their heads between the railings as though watching the car pass. But they couldn't watch, not really, because they had no faces. The helicopter had been too high to see such tiny details.

In the darkness behind his eyelids, Sam remembered thinking of himself earlier as God. But

God was perfect, and it showed in the natural order of His world, where everything flowed together so smoothly that the human race simply accepted it, and for the most part never thought of giving thanks to its Author.

Sam may have been some kind of god to Eldritch and its citizens, but he was an imperfect god, whose experiments in creation had resulted in a mutated freak of a world, a nightmare place of unrelenting pain and anguish.

But there is a name for that sort of place, and there is a word for that kind of god, and Sam knew it.

He was the devil.

The Eldritch girl swung the car off Sly Jack Road, along a rutted track, and cut the engine in a small clearing. It whispered to a stop, the tyres slicing through the snow to the frozen mulch below.

'Sam, we're here.'

Cautiously, he opened his eyes.

The bare trees looked black against all the snow, as though they had been charred by a forest fire and now stood surrounded by layers of white ash. The low sun lancing through the windscreen pierced his eyes, and Sam thought how very Eldritch this whole scene was. That they should be moving towards the novel's climax in broad daylight, when in any normal, self-respecting work of genre fiction it would surely have been set in the dark of night, in the middle of a deafening thunderstorm with lightning crackling through the air. Atmosphere, it was called. But this place didn't need atmosphere. Sly Jack Road had its own.

'I feel sick,' Sam said, his voice shaking. He pressed the palm of his hand against his forehead and it came away shining with sweat. 'I've got a fever, I'm burning up.'

'We're very close to the end now,' the girl said. 'We must hurry. No more delays.'

She got out of the car and began to walk around it.

'Nat?' There was no reply from the back of the car. 'Nat?'

Sam turned around, and saw Longman staring coldly back. He didn't understand the antagonism in the other man's face.

'Nat, what's the—'

'Why do you need me, Sam? Exactly why do you want me with you, when it seems that only you can do what has to be done?'

Sam shook his head in confusion. He was feverish. Droplets of his sweat were flung onto the car's cracked leather upholstery. 'What do you mean? I need your help. You're my friend, you understand me.'

The Eldritch girl opened Sam's door and held out her hand to him. 'Let him stay here, we don't need him.'

'*I need him*,' Sam shouted, and was surprised to see the girl step back from the unaccustomed heat of his anger, that trace of the stranger in his voice. But she nodded her acceptance quickly enough, and then came forward again, a little more tentatively, as though she thought he might take a bite out of her. A strange half-smile on her face told him that she wouldn't altogether mind if he did.

318

Sam looked back over his shoulder at Longman.
'Nat, please.'
Longman turned his head away.
'Please. Nat, I'm begging you…'

18

Hawkins only pulled the handbrake on when the bumpers of the two cars were touching. The way the first car had been left, this meant that it was now effectively trapped in the clearing. There was no way it could drive away through the forest, the trees were set too close together and the ground too uneven.

'No one's leaving unless we want them to,' Hawkins said, climbing out of Muggins's car, tossing his fedora back onto the driver's seat.

Hawkins limped around the abandoned car and looked inside while Hyams got out and stretched. Then he went around to the front and placed his hand flat on the scratched and dented bonnet.

'Still warm. In these temperatures that means they can't have been gone for long.' He went back towards Hyams. 'It's been hot-wired. Your man know how to do that?'

'I don't know. I think he may be capable of anything.'

Hyams stood looking around the clearing. Even allowing for the seasonal discrepancy between worlds, it was very familiar. The trees seemed much older and had grown more wildly than in the real-world clearing he had visited with Ken Morley, but it was the same place, all right. He even knew in which direction Parker's trail would lead them.

Hawkins was examining the disturbed snow. 'There are three of them,' he said.

'Parker and his two accomplices. Longman and Cassidy.'

'One of them is barefoot,' Hawkins said, eyebrows raised.

Hyams shrugged. He didn't know which one of them that was. 'Come on, we can catch them before they reach the watermill.'

'Wait a minute,' Hawkins said, and waited for Hyams to turn. 'I've been thinking. Maybe it would be better if you stayed here. This could be dangerous, and I'm the only real policeman here. The only one with any authority.'

Hyams stared at him. 'You said you didn't want to see Muggins die, so you already knew it was going to be dangerous. Now you're worried about me?'

He laughed at Hawkins' dead-pan expression.

'That overgrown Venus Flytrap in the docklands was right, wasn't it? You *do* want to die, and you think that if no one else gets killed today it may finally be your turn. The curse will be broken.'

Hawkins stared back, saying nothing, giving no sign that he even understood what Hyams was saying.

'Good try, Dave, but I know you too well, you see. And you know me too well to think that I'd ever let you go on alone. Whatever happens to you also happens to me. Perhaps you were right, and everybody is fiction, and it's only how we cope with it that makes a difference, that makes us what we are.'

Hawkins considered for a moment, and then asked, 'Does everybody in your world talk too much?'

19

Sam was on his last legs. His face was a bright red, his breath coming in hot little gusts that hurt his lungs, and every part of him ached. The Eldritch girl had started off merely helping him, now she was all but carrying him, ploughing through the snow almost at jogging speed on an unerringly straight line.

Longman was trotting behind them, knowing that time was running out for him. Not only for him, but for Sam, too. He *was* Sam's friend, and he knew that his friend had to be woken from the Eldritch girl's influence, made to realise that she was not quite what she seemed.

For God's sake, he thought, *say* something.

'Why couldn't Sam have just finished off the crime boss from the comfort of his own office? Why didn't he just write it?'

The girl didn't answer.

'Think about it, Sam. You know where she's taking us, but what are we going to find there? What are you supposed to do? If she won't tell me, she at least ought to tell you, don't you think?'

'He'll know,' the girl said, never breaking her stride. 'He'll know, don't you worry.'

'But I do worry, I worry for both of us.'

Longman moved alongside them and tried to get Sam to look at him by grabbing his shoulder, but he pulled his hand away almost instantly. Even through his clothes, Sam's skin really did feel as though it were burning.

'Sam, I don't know how and I don't know why, but you're being used just as much as any other character. Can't you see that?'

'Nat... Nat, I—'

Then Sam tripped over something buried in the snow. He was torn from the girl's supporting arms and he went down heavily, rolling to a stop face down. Longman and the girl reached him at the same time, and while Longman tried to lift him, the girl actually tried to drag him forward. As he came up, a terrible scream erupted from Sam's throat, and Longman saw that his right cheek had been sliced open by something concealed beneath the snow, a rock or a thorn maybe.

'Let him go!' Longman shouted, but the girl had no intention of obeying him. He hung onto Sam desperately, but the girl was so strong she was pulling him along, too, his feet sliding through the snow.

Sam, caught between them, was suddenly filled with terror. There was snow in his eyes, and he was blind. He was in pain. He was being dragged through the forest, carried to fate more terrible than he could ever have imagined. Hadn't this happened to him before?

He began to scream again, thrashing his arms and legs in attempt to break free. Then he was sitting on the snow, still screaming inarticulately as though his tongue had been removed. A pair of cool hands settled on his burning face, one of them sliding in his blood, and a calm voice came to sooth him.

'It's okay, you're safe – it's not *then*, it's *now*.'

His panic gradually left him. Sam cleared his eyes and saw Longman on the ground a few feet away, holding one hand to his ribs where one of Sam's kicks must have connected. Longman was not looking back at him, but at something over his shoulder.

'Nearly there, Sam. Not long now,' the girl whispered.

He turned to see what Longman was staring at. Behind him the enormous trees seemed to form an arched tunnel, and at its end he saw a field of snow that in summer would be wild with heather. Beyond was a frozen pond, and beside it the smoke-blackened remains of the mill house.

Sam found himself bundled to his feet again, his arm thrown around the Eldritch girl's shoulders. Longman appeared at his side, still clutching his broken ribs.

'Don't leave me, Nat,' Sam said. 'Promise me you'll stay. I need you.'

The girl began to move again before the indecision left Longman's face, but Sam could hear his footsteps following and he smiled thankfully.

They had gone no more than a dozen paces when a figure stepped out from behind one of the trees and placed himself directly in their path. He was covered in blood from his injuries, his body even more bent, and his head trauma so severe that he should long ago have died.

It was the Golem.

'Don't worry,' the Eldritch girl said, walking Sam forward without hesitation. 'He won't hurt us, I promise.'

20

Hyams came to the top of an incline just ahead of Dave Hawkins and saw, less than two hundred yards ahead, his quarry, Sam Parker. He stood in a cluster of other people, and looked like he needed the support of the woman who held his arm around her shoulders. Longman was also there, and seemed to be edging around the others. As for the last member of the group, it was hard to tell if it was Cassidy or not because he was bent over, and seemed, of all things, to be kissing Sam Parker's right hand.

Hawkins came up beside Hyams, and took in the distant scene.

'So that's His Unholiness,' he said.

Without conferring, the two detectives began walking towards the group, hurrying their limps along but not attempting to run.

Longman could hardly believe what he was seeing, that monster kissing Sam's hand as though he were the Pope, murmuring away in some foreign language while the girl held Sam still. She had said the Golem wouldn't hurt them, but Nat didn't know if her promise applied to him, too, so he was being very cautious. He had almost made it around to the back of the group, when the Golem looked up like an animal scenting danger, and his eyes seemed to glow.

They all turned, and Longman saw the two men moving toward them.

He recognised the policeman, Hyams, instantly, and in the next moment realised who was with him. Once his mind had made the connection, it was as though he were seeing double.

'Okay, Parker, it's over,' Hyams called across the ground that separated them.

Out of the corner of his eye, Longman saw the Eldritch girl press something into the Golem's hands. Whatever it was, the Golem tucked it away in his overcoat pocket before Longman could see it properly. Then the girl immediately began to lead Sam through the tunnel of trees and on towards the field.

Longman heard Sam call for him, but he couldn't move. He stood and watched as the Golem went to intercept the two detectives.

Hyams reacted first as he saw Sam slipping away, skipping into a limping run that was supposed to take him well wide of the Golem. The Golem didn't even seem to see him, and was apparently fixated on Hawkins, who was ambling forward with a gentle smile on his face. But then, just as Hyams began to pass him by three or four yards to his right, the Golem somehow lashed out across that distance and sent the policeman tumbling through the air and into the trunk of a tree, where he fell to the ground, stunned.

Incredibly, Longman saw that the Golem seemed not to have moved at all. He still blocked the track through the trees and was beckoning Hawkins on with both hands. 'Come,' he said, his voice barely understandable. 'Come on, policeman, come to me.'

He cackled when Hawkins stopped moving.

'Are you afraid, policeman?'

'Absolutely petrified,' Hawkins said, then reached into his coat and brought out his revolver.

The Golem gave a shriek of anger and hurled himself forward. In one fluid, casual movement, Hawkins raised the pistol, aimed and shot twice. The first bullet took the Golem high on the shoulder, spinning him around, the second tore out his throat and he fell down in the snow, his whole body spasming.

A spray of blood had speckled Longman's face, and he began to back away, until the detective's revolver settled on him.

'Stay right where you are and you won't get hurt. I want you to − *shit*!'

The Golem was suddenly on his feet again, clasping the startled Hawkins in a bear-hug. Blood was pulsing out of the Golem's ruined throat, and he was trying to get at Hawkins's neck with his grey and yellow teeth.

Longman watched them wrestle, their feet slipping in the snow, the detective trying to wedge his revolver in between them. The Golem's head darted forward like a snake's and tore a strip of flesh from the side of Hawkins's neck. In retaliation, another shot went off and Longman saw a lump of muscle the size of a grapefruit blown out of the Golem's thigh. A formless cry erupted from the monster's wreck of a throat and echoed around the trees, but he only tightened his grip on the detective, who was now almost blue from lack of oxygen.

Longman heard Sam's voice calling him from the distance, and when he turned he saw that the Eldritch girl had managed to get Sam halfway across the snow-covered field, the ruins of the mill house looming over them like a haunted castle.

No, he thought. You're not going to have him.

He began to edge away from the desperate fight going on behind him. Sam shouted his name again, and he began to run, then to sprint. He knew what he had to do now. Hyams and Hawkins were the good guys, Sam had said so, and even argued with the girl when she had tried to set him against them. The Golem was in the process of killing the good guys, and the girl obviously had some kind of control over him. Which meant that if anyone was working for the crime boss, it was his daughter.

He had already guessed it, of course. Cassidy, in his last few moments of life, had known.

The time for talking was done. He had to act.

Sam was having hallucinations as the girl half-pulled, half-carried him towards the mill house. Sometimes the snow beneath his feet blinded him, and at other times it disappeared to be replaced by a lush carpet of heather he could actually smell and feel brushing his legs. Sometimes when he glanced up the mill house looked no more menacing than a huge rotten tooth, yet at others it was surrounded by a halo of evil flames that he could feel scorching his face.

'Sam! Sam!'

Longman came running up, breathing hard with his hand against his ribs. He stepped in front of them and blocked the way.

'Sam, she's betrayed you. She's on *his* side. She isn't taking you to destroy him, she's *delivering* you. This isn't your plot, Sam. He wants you there!'

The girl brushed him aside, and Longman kicked her feet out from under her. Sam and the girl went sprawling. Longman grabbed Sam under the arms and tried to pull him away. He hadn't got more than a few steps before the girl was on her feet again, stalking towards him, her hands hooked into claws.

In a curiously emotionless voice that completely terrified Longman, he heard Sam say to the girl, 'Just don't kill him.'

21

Hyams opened his eyes and rolled over. He could see the field beyond the trees, and he could see its three occupants. Still stunned from his collision with the tree, he saw the girl in the long fur coat strike Longman so hard that he flew through the air almost as far as Hyams himself had. Then the girl pulled Sam up from the ground, as easily as she might lift a doll.

Two more gunshots hammered at the forest's silence. Hyams groggily turned his head and saw the Golem slipping to his knees, his arms still clinging to Hawkins. A seemingly unending flood of deep crimson blood fell from his chest and stomach, and the detective's clothes were soaked.

Hyams climbed to his feet and started toward them, but Hawkins breathlessly ordered him to go after the others. 'Don't worry about me,' he said. 'This bastard's almost finished.'

Wearily he rested the muzzle of his revolver on the Golem's forehead.

'Go on, I said!'

Hyams nodded and began to limp down the track, picking up speed as he went. He had almost reached the field when a terrible pain in his chest brought him to a sudden halt. At the same time, he heard a scream of agony from behind him.

He turned and saw that the Golem had somehow got back on his feet, and that he and Hawkins appeared to be slow-dancing around and around in the bloody snow. Drunk Dave's revolver was knocked from his hand and fell to the ground, a small black angle almost lost in all the white, and the Golem was viciously twisting a knife into his chest.

'No,' Hyams said. 'No!'

The Golem stepped back, leaving the knife embedded in Hawkins's chest, and watched the detective collapse. Drunk Dave had finally found the death he had sought for so long. Eldritch, of course, had arranged that it had come at precisely the wrong moment.

Hyams saw that the knife jutting from Dave's body had a bone handle in the shape of the infinity symbol, and he knew that this was fate.

He began to run back, screaming obscenities at the Golem who slowly turned to face him.

Only half-conscious, Longman was tumbled onto a stone floor that smelled like an old bonfire. Cold, ancient ash tickled his nose when he breathed.

'See,' he heard the Eldritch girl say, 'I brought him, and he's alive, just like you wanted. Now do it, do it while there's still time.'

Longman waited for Sam to reach for him, to drag him to an altar and offer him as some kind of blood sacrifice to an evil deity, but that didn't happen. He heard footsteps moving towards his head, but they simply passed him by. When he tried to get up he only got as far as his knees, and then he fell down again. The pain in his ribs and his shoulder were bad enough, but now his face where the girl had hit him made those pains feel insignificant. Every movement he made sent waves of nausea rolling through his head. His tongue seemed swollen, and when he carefully used it to explore his mouth, he found that several of his teeth were missing or broken.

'Yes, that's right — there,' the girl said.

Longman forced himself to look up, wincing even at the feeble rays of daylight coming in from an open doorway off to his right. In the centre of the burnt-out mill house, Sam stood ankle deep in a pile of dark ashes beside the millstones, smoke-blackened and cracked. Slowly he sank to his knees. He looked drugged and out of control as he began to feel around in the ashes.

'Don't do it, Sam,' Longman said, spitting out blood.

'I can't stop,' Sam replied without turning his head. 'I can't!'

Hyams found himself dancing the last waltz with the Golem, just as Hawkins had before him. He had managed to snatch the revolver from the snow, but the Golem held his wrist in an unbreakable grip and he was unable to bring the weapon to bear. The Golem's other hand was around Hyams's throat, choking him. Around and around they danced, the light going out of Hyams's world as he began to lose consciousness.

He felt his legs begin to give out, and out of the corner of his eye he saw Drunk Dave's body transfixed by the Golem's knife. The sight of it made Hyams's own chest ache in empathy. The Eldritch detective's face showed no pain, just relief, and yet Hyams was galvanised with anger.

As they came within a step of the detective's body, he twisted in the Golem's grip, kicking as hard as he could at the monster's injured leg, and suddenly the Golem was on his knees. Hyams found his gun-hand suddenly free as the Golem tried to steady himself. This was his chance. Even as the pain in his chest seemed to expand, he swung the pistol at the Golem's face and savagely jammed the barrel inside his mouth. He pulled the trigger twice, and the Golem's head came apart.

He fell back a few steps, his ears ringing. He watched the Golem topple backwards, but the only victory cry he could manage sounded like a whimper. The pain in his chest had become unbearable, and when he looked down he realised why. The handle of the Golem's knife jutted out from his ribcage, rising and falling with his every breath.

Whatever happens to you, Hawkins, also happens to me, he thought.

He had believed that he'd overpowered the Golem, but he'd been wrong. The monster had only released Hyams's gun-hand and gone to his knees in order to retrieve his own weapon from Drunk Dave's chest. The blade felt like a sliver of ice that reached all the way to Hyams's spine. In shock, he pulled the knife out of his chest, and moaned as blood poured out of him.

He could feel himself dying, and he found that he wanted to lie down beside Drunk Dave Hawkins.

Together at the last. But then, through the waves of grey despair that were settling on him like snow, he saw the distant mill house. He knew that Sam Parker was inside, and now he silently promised himself – and Dave Hawkins – that he would stop Parker before he died.

Calling on his last reserves of strength, but in truth driven on by nothing but will, Hyams began to trudge forward.

22

Longman realised that something was happening. He heard it first, a noise which when it began sounded like a church choir, and then, when it grew louder, sounded like a choir in hell. Hundreds, no thousands of voices, raised in screams of unbearable anguish. Then he began to see it, the air in the mill house achieving a thin opaqueness, a visible texture shaping itself, bending the light.

With his hands over his ears, Longman watched as the air became filled with half-formed faces, their mouths open wide to scream. Their breath was the atmosphere of Eldritch at its worst, a rank and fetid stench that had Longman gagging. He saw Sam look around him in bewilderment, his hands coming up from the ashes as he too covered his ears. The Eldritch girl swiped at the apparitions as though they were gnats, her fingers splitting the cheeks and foreheads like knives, only for them to instantly reform.

Victims. Longman suddenly knew that they were the crime boss's victims, their spirits raised in protest.

'Ignore them!' the girl shouted at Sam. 'They're only the dead, they can't hurt you! You own them!'

Sam closed his eyes and lowered his hands. He clasped them before his chest, and looked as though he were praying. One by one the faces began to melt away, their terrible cries fading. But once they had gone, Longman realised that they had done something to the air, somehow charging it. It now seemed primed, poised on the brink of an unspeakable drop.

Longman could feel another power in here with them, something huge and lithe and cunning. And ready. Sam's hands dropped, dangling against his thighs, and then he opened his eyes.

Longman prayed for something to happen, some miracle.

'*Come back*,' the girl whispered. It sounded like her very own prayer.

Hyams ground to a stop when he was only ten more paces from the mill house, now finding the effort of breathing an even greater challenge than walking. He tried to gather himself, because the world was becoming alarmingly colourless as he lost more and more blood. He had been holding his free hand against his chest wound in an attempt to staunch the flow of blood, but without a great deal of success. He had kept his other hand well away from his body, so that blood wouldn't make the revolver slip in his hand when he fired. If he even got a chance to fire.

I will, he told himself. I will.

He managed to take two more faltering steps before he became aware of the noises behind him, the sound of footsteps plodding through snow, and he

333

stopped again. He didn't dare look around while he was on the move, because he was likely to trip over his own feet. He knew that if that happened, he'd never get up again.

Fighting for his breath, he turned.

Hyams wasn't sure whether he was surprised or not by the sight of the Golem lurching across the field towards him. In the end, he decided that he wasn't, although in any sane world the Golem would be dead three times over by now. If he'd had the energy, he might have laughed aloud at this thought. In any *sane* world, the fucking monster wouldn't exist in the first place.

His head no more than a few bloody fragments of shell dangling from a twitching stalk of vertebra, the Golem trudged doggedly onward, closing the gap between them, his large hands convulsively snatching at the air. Despite losing four out of his five senses, he seemed to be following the trail of blood Hyams had left across the field almost perfectly, as though they were trains on the same track.

Hyams started moving again, concentrating hard on the mill house's single doorway. He had to reach it before the Golem reached him.

Longman gasped as Sam once more buried his hands into the pile of ash. A matching gasp, this one of pleasure, came from the girl, as though Sam's hands had invaded her.

'Please, Sam,' Longman said. 'Fight it, please–'

'Shut up!' the girl spat.

She edged closer to Sam, and looked as though she wanted to push him face-first into the ash, but didn't quite dare touch him.

Despite the warning, Longman opened his mouth to speak again, but then shut it as the light from the doorway to his right was suddenly diminished. He saw Hyams's battered body fill the frame, and thought that his prayers had been answered.

The detective leant heavily against the blackened wall, one hand lost in the centre of his bloody chest, the other dangling at his side, holding Drunk Dave's revolver tightly. His face had no colour to it at all as he paused to let his eyes adjust to the dimness inside the mill house. With her back to the doorway and all her attention centred on Sam, the girl hadn't seen or heard him arrive.

Hyams unsteadily focussed on the back of Sam's head and raised the revolver, his whole arm shaking. Longman felt a bizarre impulse to shout out a warning to Sam, but he knew there was no other way to stop it now. Maybe there never had been another way.

Bracing his shoulder against the stone wall, Hyams carefully sighted on Sam's head. He pulled on the trigger, squeezing as though it were taking all his remaining strength. He was smiling. The hammer lifted, and lifted, paused for a heart-stopping fraction of a second — and then fell with a dry click on an empty chamber.

The Golem had taken all Hawkins's bullets.

The girl whirled around in time to see Hyams lifting the gun up to his eyes and frowning at it. Then he was thrown forward, his head landing next to

Longman's with a terrible crack. Longman saw immediately that the policeman was dead. The horrible greasy vapour which had erased Nigel Cassidy from Eldritch was already beginning to rise from the backs of his hands and his scalp.

So much for prayers, Longman thought hopelessly.

The doorway was now filled with another body, but it was one the girl dismissed immediately. The Golem was nothing more than a walking piece of raw meat, only his twitching nerves truly alive. But he had done his duty to the very last.

The girl moved forward again to stand over Sam.

Ignoring all his pains, knowing that he had to at least *try* to stop this, Longman slowly heaved himself to his feet. He began to stumble toward Sam, but the Eldritch girl turned and grabbed him by the throat. Effortlessly, she walked him backwards and held him against one of the walls, and no matter how hard he struggled, he could not move. Longman knew that if it wasn't for Sam, she would have snapped his neck like a twig.

'Come back!' she called to Sam. 'Now!'

23

Sam took a deep breath, and with it the remainder of his reluctance seemed to vanish. He dug his fingers even deeper into the pile of cold ash, and they touched something that felt hot. The shape of it was unmistakable, and he lifted it out and held it before him like a trophy.

It was a skull, blackened by fire, streaked with the lines of old fractures that had never had the chance to heal. The relic had a weight to it that had nothing to do with its size or the bone it was made of, as though inside it there was another deeper, darker universe where the gravity was crushing.

Sam thought he heard a voice say, *I've been waiting for you...*

He stared into the empty sockets, and they seemed to stare back at him. Sam knew now why the crime boss's ruined face in his dream of the prologue had seemed so disturbingly familiar. It was his own. As he held the skull he could feel the pressure of fingertips on his own jaw, against his own temples.

He's me, I'm him, he thought. I am me.

Sam brought the skull even closer to his body, and then began to squeeze it with all his might. His fingers broke through the brittle cranium and he felt fingers enter his own head. He brought the heels of his hands together and he felt his own temples compressing.

Abruptly the skull collapsed in his hands, and a gust of ancient corruption rose from the fragments. It enveloped him, and his mind seemed to expand like the blast-front of an explosion. Gasping, his face raised as though to the heavens, he let the powdery remnants of the skull to tumble back into the ashes.

Everything became very clear.

The girl let Longman go and he dropped to the ground beside the Golem, who had begun to sag, dark blood pooling around his feet. Longman watched the girl run eagerly to Sam, extending her hands to help him up, but Sam knocked them away and rose to his feet under his own power. Then the girl was all over him, her hands caressing every part of him she could reach.

'Flesh, flesh,' she kept repeating. 'Back in the flesh.'

When the object of her adoration turned to face him, Longman groaned in dismay. He looked like Sam, but not quite enough to *be* Sam. Nothing physical had happened to his face, but the difference was there and it was unmistakable. It was as obvious as the contrast between Eldritch and the real world.

'The way back!' the girl said. 'Do you still have the power, can you create it?'

The man who had been Sam Parker closed his eyes. Concentration corrugated his brow and his hands clenched into tight fists, but nothing seemed to happen.

'Try, try harder!' the girl urged.

Without even bothering to open his eyes, the man struck the girl across the face for her insolence and one of her lips split open. But after she straightened up again, drooling blood, Longman saw that her face was lit with a sick pleasure.

Suddenly, Longman heard a crackling sound begin at the other side of the mill house, and when he looked in that direction he saw a tiny silver worm of light suspended in the air, blurring the air around it like a heat haze. As he continued to watch, the light slowly lengthened and expanded until it was two feet wide and over three feet high. It made a sound like tearing linen, and the mill house suddenly smelled of ozone. The light then seemed to burn itself out, leaving behind a jagged rip that spanned dimensions.

A cold wind twisted through it, making the edges ripple.

Compared to the tornado Sam had been able to conjure up to bring them to Eldritch, this tiny rip was nothing. Nevertheless, it *was* there, and through it Longman could see the moonlit interior of an old building, ruined in exactly the same way as the mill house had been ruined, by fire. The one wall he could see was curved. It was a windmill. A pile of dark stones formed a kind of low table, and a row of books had been carefully arranged on top.

He could even see the title of one of them. It was *Sly Jack Road*.

'You've done it!' the girl said.

Impulsively, she rushed toward the opening, but the man grabbed her by her coat and hauled her back just in time as the rip seemed to shudder, flicker partially close, then snap open again. A series of vertical lines began to strobe across it, like the edges of the pages in a flicker-book, and what sounded like a series of small explosions made the whole thing waver.

'No,' the girl whispered. 'Please, no…'

Without a word, the man reached down and found a piece of rubble among the ashes and he launched it at the rip. It hit one of the fine strobing lines, and was sliced in two as though by a laser, one half passing through to the other side, the other dropping to the ground in the mill house, where it lay smoking.

The girl screamed in frustration. She turned away and began striking out at the walls, kicking, punching and scratching, shrieking and sobbing. She was like a cornered wild animal, stripped of all natural reason.

And then her wild, streaming eyes found Longman.

'*You* held us back,' she said.

She rushed at him and dragged him up from the ground and ran him into the wall, sending a starburst of negative lights whirling through his head. Longman felt one of her hands at his throat and the other on his face, her fingers seeking his eyes as he twisted his head from side to side.

It was his turn now, he knew. Death was coming. Longman could feel it slowly approaching him, taking its time. He felt the girl's nails beginning to gouge at his tightly-closed eyelids, drawing blood. Her other hand was crushing his throat. Death was here now. It was reaching out for him…

But then Longman found himself snatched from the girl's grip by a much stronger force, and a darkly powerful voice said, 'He is *mine*.'

The man who had been Sam Parker held Nathaniel Longman off the ground by two great fistfuls of his jacket and shirt, and brought him closer, their faces only an inch or two apart.

'Open your eyes,' the man whispered.

Longman didn't dare. His daughter was bad enough. What would this man do to him, just for being here when his plan failed?

'Nat, open your eyes.'

Reluctantly, Longman did as he was told, and to his astonishment he saw that there was still a little of Sam left in the man's face. Perhaps it was the little bit of Sam which remained in his voice that had given Longman the courage to open his eyes in the first place.

'I'm going to try to save you, Nat,' Sam whispered.

Longman blinked in surprise. 'How—'

'I'm going to *try*. It may kill you, but what other choice do we have left? You couldn't survive here, anyway. But I can. I'll have to.'

His small smile, and the sadness in his eyes, broke Longman's heart.

'If it doesn't work,' Sam said, 'at least it will be quicker than her way.'

He glanced to his right where the ragged hole in time and space hung waiting, but now seemed even more dangerously unstable. Hardly a second or two went by now without a new series of whickering lines of power moving through the rip like interference on a television set. It was smaller than it had been a moment ago, its edges feathering as they tried to draw together. The image of the ruined windmill on the other side seemed fainter, less there.

Longman followed Sam's eye-line. He realised what Sam meant to do, and his face froze in terror.

'Goodbye, Nat,' Sam said. 'Please believe me when I say that I am still your friend.'

Then he threw Longman at the rip, and the mill house was suddenly blown full of thick blood vapour, as though Longman had exploded.

24

Longman screamed in agony, screamed until he thought his lungs would burst, until the tender flesh of his larynx seemed to hang in tatters.

The pain was far beyond his own experience, beyond anything that he could ever have imagined. The whole right side of his upper body, from scalp to waist, felt as though it was being eaten away by burning chemicals. He writhed about helplessly on the dirt floor, unable to think, unable even to hear his own screams because of the immense roar of the closing rip.

Finally, when he could scream no more and lay with his tear-streaked face pressed into the dirt, he used his left arm to examine his injuries. His hand passed carefully over his raw right arm and shoulder, and up to his burning head, where his fingers met a shocking slick smoothness that he recognised a moment later as his own skull. Perhaps because he was in shock, he was unable to resist exploring further, and he discovered that he had lost an ear and a large section of his scalp.

Longman forced himself to his knees. He was at the other side of the makeshift stone altar, and he realised that he must have first landed on top of it and then slid off. The books that had been so carefully placed on the altar were now scattered all around him, mostly saturated with his blood. He quickly checked the rest of his body, and was relieved to find that he wasn't missing any limbs.

It could have been worse, he told himself. It could have been *much* worse. The rip could easily have torn him in two.

And then it hit him.

It had *worked*. He'd made it through, he was back in the real world, and he was alive. Sam had saved him. The realisation of that simple fact seemed to block out the worst of the pain, and—

Sam. Longman was safe, but Sam wasn't. Sam was still trapped.

Stricken with a terrible sense of guilt, Longman hauled himself to his feet using the stone altar as a ladder. The rip was still there, but it was now only inches wide. Its edges were visibly drawing closer together, and the mill house beyond had taken on a misty faintness. But then, as Longman watched, a figure stepped forward, almost touching the rip itself, daring to stand close to the immense power that had stripped the flesh from Longman's head.

A three-inch-wide section of Sam's face smiled at Longman as he raised a hand in farewell, and Longman could only watch in horror as the rip closed another inch. Another series of power lines flicked through the rip as it tightened – and Longman suddenly had an inspiration, an idea so vast that he was staggering around the altar before it had fully formed in his mind.

He stopped a few steps away from the rip and waved his good arm, making sure that Sam could see him. He pointed at himself, and then he pointed at Sam. He shouted words that he knew Sam would never hear, because he could not hear them himself. But he shouted the same words over and over again. He pointed to himself, and he pointed to Sam. To himself, to Sam.

He saw Sam frown.

Longman turned around in desperation, and retrieved one of Sam's novels from the windmill's dirt floor. By a happy coincidence, it was *Bad Blue*, the book Sam had dedicated to Longman, The Survivor, so many years ago. He whirled back to the rip, now less than an inch wide, its edges beginning to melt together. He waved the book and held it up so Sam could see it. He pointed at himself, he pointed at the book. He pointed at Sam, then at the book. He screamed his inaudible words.

Himself, the book, Sam, the book, himself, Sam.

The rip was now only as wide as Sam's iris, but it was enough for Longman to realise that Sam was shaking his head. He didn't understand, he didn't get it.

In sheer frustration, Longman threw the book at the disappearing rip, and as though it was the signal it had been waiting for, the rip imploded.

The force of it shredded the book into a blizzard of confetti, and pulled Longman towards its epicentre, as though it would like to do the same to him. Before he was able to brace his legs, he found himself standing precisely in the place the rip had been, his eyes tightly closed, every muscle tensed, as he waited for the pain to arrive.

But the last vestige of its power had gone.

It was over.

In the sudden, shocking silence, Longman fell to his knees as ripped pages fell around him and stuck to his body and his bloody clothes, and he began to sob. He cried for Sam, trapped in Eldritch, and he cried for Nigel Cassidy, who had died a miserable, pointless death in that terrible city, with only an unfinished sentence as an epitaph. Despite the pain he was in, Longman did not cry for himself.

Sam had been right all along. He was The Survivor.

A short while later, when Longman began to struggle to his feet, his hand closed on a single page of the destroyed book. Like himself, it had survived with only a certain amount of damage, and the three words, the only words on the entire page, were perfectly legible in the moonlight.

Seeing them now, Longman wished that he'd had the presence of mind to open the book to this page and hold it up to the rip. If Sam could have read these three words, he might have understood, for they encapsulated everything Longman had been trying to tell him.

The three words were:

Stories Never End

That's right, Longman thought. They don't.

THE EPILOGUE

He opens his eyes. The high ceiling is cracked, and rain patters at the uncovered windows. The girl shares his bed, naked beside him, but she is asleep. He has been in Eldritch for almost two months now. This is no time at all. It seems like forever.

At the window he looks out at the dark grounds. The rain is driving the snow away as winter loses its grip. Behind him, the girl begins to whimper in her sleep and reaches out over the mattress for him, as she does several times each night. He ignores her. She is his daughter, and she calls him Daddy when they fuck, but he does not love her. It is hard to feel love, he has found, when his chest no longer shudders to the twin tremors of a heartbeat, when his flesh is cold as the flesh of a fish.

But none of this matters to him at all.

Everything has been tidied away with ridiculous ease, all the bodies buried in shallow graves in the woodland around Sly Jack Road, in ground that will suck them deeper for its own satisfaction. The Golem hadn't quite been dead when they buried him, but that detail had seemed insignificant.

Over the weeks, his mind has constantly gone back to the last moments in the mill house, both in his dreams and in his waking hours. Slowly, his thoughts have focussed more and more clearly on Longman's mouth and the shapes it had made.

For a time, he had thought Longman was shouting, 'I'll write to you,' which, clearly, was nonsense. But now he has watched Longman's lips so many times in his memory that he can read them. And the message was not nonsense at all.

It wasn't, 'I'll write to you.'

Longman, pointing to himself, to the book, to the man he thought was Sam Parker.

It was, 'I'll write *for* you.'

For the first time he truly understands the instinctive strategy that made him draw two of Parker's closest friends into the plot of *Comeback*. He understands why he kept one of them, the one best able to survive, to the very end. And he understands exactly why they had to be writers.

He can *feel* it beginning. As surely as he feels his daughter squirming beneath his weight every night, he feels it.

Even now, probably in some private hospital bed recovering from his injuries, Nathaniel Longman is writing the next Eldritch novel. He will claim that he is writing it in tribute to the author Sam Parker, his good friend, who has vanished from the face of the earth, and Parker's greedy publishers will have given him permission to do so in a heartbeat. But in reality, Longman will be writing in the belief that Sam Parker had saved his life and is stranded in his own evil city.

In the mistaken belief that his friend can still be saved.

A part of his mind, deadened by the atmosphere of the Shaped, is tingling as it begins to return to life, and at this point he probably knows more about the new novel than Longman himself. He even has an image of the finished book in his mind, a whole display of them in the window of a large bookshop.

He can see the cover, a perfect Eldritch cover, just a sea of absolute blackness, over which hangs a single, desolate star. The star is his, and it is rising again.

Below this, he can see the title Longman has given it, a bitter-sweet memento from his visit to Eldritch.

It seems that the book will be called, *I Wish...*

Other Works

Crime
(writing as PJ Shann)
The Queen of Hearts
Perfect Day
Perfect Peace
The Hunted Man 1: Old Dog New Trick
The Hunted Man 2: Identity Crisis
The Crime Short Story Collection

Horror
(writing as Jim Mullaney)
The 1st Horror Short Story Collection
The 2nd Horror Short Story Collection

Please visit me at:
storiesneverend1.wordpress.com
or my **Amazon Authors Page**
or contact me at:
crimemysterysuspense@gmail.com

Thanks for Reading

37529638R00201

Printed in Poland
by Amazon Fulfillment
Poland Sp. z o.o., Wrocław